Caerwin & M.
A Historical Romance

By Lizzie Ashworth

Caerwin & Marcellus
by Lizzie Ashworth

Copyright 2016 Lizzie Ashworth

All rights reserved. This book is copyright material and must not be copied, translated, reproduced, transferred, distributed, leased, licensed or publicly performed or used in any form without prior written permission of the author, as allowed under the terms and conditions under which it was purchased or as strictly permitted by applicable copyright law. Any unauthorized distribution, circulation or use of this text may be a direct infringement of the author's rights, and those responsible may be liable in law accordingly.

Certain events and persons in this story are factual and based on historical accounts. For more information, please see the section entitled "Author's Notes."

This image of the Roman Forum postdates our story by nearly 300 years, but it beautifully portrays the layout of the Forum and surrounding buildings. In the foreground to the extreme right is the Tabularium. Beyond, also on the far right, is the Basilica Julia. The Temple of Saturn is hidden between these two large buildings. Some structures shown here didn't exist at the time of our story in 50 AD such as the Arch of Septimius Severus, center foreground, which blocks our view of the heart of the Forum.

Jen Ebbeler, professor of Classics at the University of Texas, Austin, posted this image to her blog http://teachingwithoutpants.blogspot.com/2015/05/the-ruin-of-rome-or-something-happened.html Repeated efforts to contact her for permission to use this image have gone unanswered. I've used it as background for my cover because more than any other image found, this shows the vitality of Roman life in the Eternal City.

Si vis amari ama.

If you want to be loved, love.

Seneca the Younger
65 AD

Table of Contents

Chapter One 7

Chapter Two 25

Chapter Three...60

Chapter Four...84

Chapter Five 107

Chapter Six...133

Chapter Seven 158

Chapter Eight 188

Chapter Nine 210

Chapter Ten..238

Chapter Eleven...261

Chapter Twelve 298

Chapter Thirteen...318

Author's Notes 343

A Glossary of Foreign Terms...347

Quotes 356

Please note that foreign terms are defined in the Glossary at the end of the book.

Chapter One

The red and gold standards of Legio Fourteen Gemina hung limp in late afternoon heat as Caerwin passed through the fortress gates. Two legionaries still stinking of battle gripped her arms as they dragged her from the wagon she shared with dead men. They had treated her harshly all the way from the battleground as though she personally had been the reason so many of their companions had died. Shoved inside with the door slammed behind her, she slid to the floor of the tiny room and let the tears come.

"Nooo," she wailed quietly, shaking her head from side to side, denying the reality of once again being trapped inside the Roman compound. Sobs heaved her chest. All her effort, a plan months in the making, the terrifying wagon ride and the salt man's assault, all of it wasted. The sound of the bolt sliding shut transformed inside her chest as if the ribs sheltering her heart locked together.

Her hunger and thirst hardly registered, nor did the filth and blood coating her skin. After a time, she had no tears left. She glanced around the room—the familiar bed, the small table, the trunk for her things. Sitting as if they waited for her return. At the barred window, she looked out at the dusty procession of weary men as they returned to their barracks. They moved past like the coursing River Severn, like wind sweeping through the forest. Not part of her, nor was she part of them.

Under the hot summer sun, the Via Principia seethed with activity—orderly ranks of soldiers casting sharp shadows, wagons carrying the injured to the hospital, tribunes and centurions with the horsehair-crests of their helmets swaying in the force of their movement as they strode along with their men. Her stomach knotted in on itself, long empty and lined with nauseating bile. Blood still stained her hands, Seisyll's blood.

The image of his lifeless body crumpled on the ground followed her like a companion even though his death was two days past. She could still hear his voice as it had come to her that first day of her escape. She could see his unruly white hair flying in the wind. That stubborn old man had been more of a friend than she realized, there for her when she hadn't known how much she needed one. Now he'd truly become a ghost and forever would be unless she could send someone back to that blood-soaked hillside to give him a proper burial. She turned away from the window.

Sounds mingled—distant shouts of command, wagons, men's groans. Doors closing. The clatter of pans in the kitchen. Tutonius would be driving his workers hard to bring food to the table on such short notice. Or maybe they'd known all along how quickly Caradoc and the assembled native forces would be vanquished. How easily they would die on the Roman sword.

Her renewed residence in this place brought forth all the teachings Antius and Senna had instilled in her. Latin words she'd tried to forget. Daily routines in the fortress. Memories of her brief time in the Ordovices camp already became indistinct, jumbled into her memories of the Cornovii hillfort at the Wrekin. She could almost see the hand of wind and time sweeping across those hilltops, burying an entire people. She sat on the side of the bed, motionless, willing her thoughts to stop.

A sharp knock rattled the door then immediately the bolt slid and the door opened.

Marcellus. Against her will, her gaze traveled up his body. He still wore the undergarments of his battle gear, the *braccae* and short tunic molded against his form. His black hair lay damp against his skull. A glance at his eyes caught the fury of his mood and she quickly looked away.

His silence swelled in her ears. She could think of nothing to say. She had thought she loved him at the battlefield, but now she only felt confusion.

"Much as I am pleased with your good health, I cannot curb my anger for what you did," he said in a low voice. "You risked your life and for what? That you would once again watch your warriors fight and die?"

"I wished again that I could die with them," she said quietly, examining the blood stains on her hands. The death of Seisyll flashed in her mind, his white hair fluttering in the wind as he fell.

"I gave you my trust, allowed you the freedoms you asked for. In return, you betrayed me."

"You would have done the same," she said.

"Much harm could have come to you," he said in a harsh voice, "if not from the Thracians or the camp followers, then from the wild men roaming this countryside."

She slammed her fist to the bed and stood up to face him. "Much harm did come to me," she said, her words hissing through her teeth. "Your cunning lover Silverus charged the salt man with my rape. I was to be fully dishonored then sold to slavers. For a moment, the gods smiled on me. I killed him with his own knife."

His face lost color as he heard her. "Who is this salt man?"

"A merchant from the marketplace. I hired him to take me out. He agreed to a sum for his trouble. I should have known there was more to it. I was fooled."

His stance changed. "How did Silverus learn of it? How can you know these things?"

"After he slavered over me and delivered his filthy seed, the salt man gloated. He would have my valuables and the wealth Silverus had bestowed on him as well. I don't know if Antius watched me, or if Silverus had spies. Somehow he knew I planned to leave."

Marcellus seized her hands. "I'm sorry. If Antius was party to this, I'll have him flogged. I wish Silverus were still alive so that I might kill him myself. I'm sorry for every terrible moment you must have suffered. But if you hadn't left my protection here, none of those things would have happened."

"Really?" She jerked her hands away. "It was here under your protection that your esteemed commander beat me with his fists, was it not? He cut my most tender flesh, remember, so that I would bleed like a virgin when he forced himself on me."

Hot tears streaked down her face and she turned away. "He never asked if I remained a maid. He ruined me. I had thought you…with me…" Words choked in her throat.

"Caerwin." Marcellus' arms came around her as he pulled her against his chest. "The gods! That knowledge burns in my chest like a knife. I swear I will never allow…"

"You can't swear anything, Marcellus. You belong to Rome. Whatever Rome demands."

"That ends in a few weeks when my service is over. We'll travel to Rome as citizens."

"You the citizen, me the slave." She twisted, trying to get out of his arms.

"Stop. Don't do this." He gripped tighter. "I thought you understood what I faced here."

His masculine scent filled her nose and sent gooseflesh down her arms. Her body still betrayed her. She wanted to scream and claw his face. Rip her clothes and cover herself with ashes.

He nestled his face against her hair. "When I saw you on the battlefield, I couldn't believe my eyes. I grieved for you."

"You grieved that I escaped your control," she said stiffly. She couldn't weaken, couldn't fall into this trap again. "Silverus and Antius, they did not grieve."

She could hear his heart beating against her cheek through the thin fabric covering his chest. He was everything she might want in a man—if only he wasn't a Roman.

"I forbade them to speak of you," he said. "No one knew my heart better than you. You knew that. You cared so little that you risked everything to escape me. Do you know how that harms me?"

"You are harmed?" Caerwin forced a laugh. "I feel little sympathy."

"Yes, I'm still part of the Fourteenth Legion. But that ends the next cycle of the moon. After that, I'm just a man. Now or then,

I won't allow you to suffer more harm." He stepped back and frowned. "You force me to keep you locked up."

She met his eyes. "I expect no less. Please, keep reminding me I'm your slave and prisoner. I am relieved of any questioning."

His eyes glinted, dark and dangerous. "Don't test me."

~~~

"I didn't believe them when they said you were here," the older woman said, brushing back a loose strand of coppery hair. "So many harms could have befallen you. Foolish girl." She clucked and shook her head.

"Senna," Caerwin said. The sight of Senna pleased her. Then her pleasure turned to despair. "I wish I were not here. I wish I had died alongside my friend like the rest of my people. Instead I am tortured again in Roman camp."

Senna lifted an eyebrow. "And no wiser for the experience, evidently."

"Wiser?" Caerwin snorted in disgust. How could she forget that Senna worked for Marcellus? "Why are you here?"

"The commander says you're to be tended and fed." Senna turned to the side table and poured water into a basin. "I shall wash you first."

"I won't be washed," Caerwin said, folding her arms across her chest. She wore a thigh-length tunic of dingy woven wool, a cast-off from one of the tribesmen she'd helped feed at the Ordovices hillfort. A length of blue and yellow plaid fabric draped from her shoulders, held by a simple bronze pin. She pulled it tighter around her arms as if to double her resolve.

Senna's gaze fastened on the smears of blood that spread from Caerwin's hands to her forearms. "You wish to eat the blood?"

"I don't wish to eat. I won't live like this again."

"You'll provoke Marcellus? Do you know what suffering you caused in him, how he paced through sleepless nights? He blamed himself that you escaped. He thought terrible things would happen to you out there alone. He refused to send me away, hoping he'd find you."

Marcellus. Caerwin gulped, reminded how he looked when she first saw him. She had been overjoyed at the sight, not just because he stayed the sword poised to pierce her chest but because he stood like a god on the battlefield, his red-crested helmet glinting in the sun, his shoulders wide in his armor. For one long moment as he held her against his chest, nothing else in the world mattered—not that her adopted tribe had suffered the same slaughter as the Cornovii a year and a half before, not that her dear friend Seisyll lay dead at her feet for exacting vengeance on that snake Silverus, not that she would surely now be brought back to slavery in Roman camp. Only Marcellus mattered.

She took a deep ragged breath. Those feelings had disappeared in the miserable two-day trek back to the fortress, in the realization of her renewed slavery. She could never forgive herself for the way she felt about Marcellus. If she loved him, her feelings came from sorcery.

"Terrible things did happen. But they were no more terrible than what happened to me here." She bit her lip at her lie. The salt man's rape had been far more disgusting than anything Marcellus had done. But at least she hadn't suffered the kind of abuse she'd experienced at the hands of Scapula, a man Marcellus honored in every act.

"I don't care what Marcellus thinks," she said. "Let him be provoked. What will he do, whip me? Subject me to his abuse?" Her laugh died in her throat. "I'm accustomed to his punishment."

A tremor rippled through her at the memory of Marcellus standing over her, lash in hand. Slow heat spread through her nether regions as remembered him plying her body. Her nipples tightened.

"The gods!" she exclaimed. "Is there no end to this torment?"

"I think you want him in ways you don't understand, child," Senna said quietly. "But I can do nothing with a stubborn mule who can't see her way to greener pastures." She leaned close to Caerwin. "Even when those green pastures are right in front of her face."

Senna grasped the door latch, waved in a kitchen worker, and directed him to set a tray of food beside the water pitcher. She followed him out the doorway, thrusting her head back in the opening for a last word. "It makes me happy to see you, dear girl. I thought you might be dead."

Caerwin sat on the bed, her hands gripped tightly over the edge of the mattress. That moment on the battlefield when Marcellus had stopped her certain slaughter at the hands of Silverus' men seemed now like a dream, his sudden arrival the same electrifying shock as her first sight of him in the clearing at the Wrekin. Both of them frozen as if cast in a spell. He'd been terrifying, stern, and overwhelming on that tall horse. Yet his dark eyes conveyed a thousand messages she understood in ways she did not want to understand.

How could one man be so many things?

More urgently, why did she care? He wanted her as a plaything, then and now. It had become a contest of wills. He had held her against her will. She had escaped. Now he held her again. Surely he saw this as a triumph. At the least, he was redeemed in the eyes of his men, again the victor.

She sighed and looked around the room. Her room. Months had passed here. Every corner held memories of those times. Outside the room, she could picture the praetorium's corridors, the courtyard and its altar to household gods, the kitchen with Tutonius bustling about, the dining hall. On the other side of that wall stood the bedchamber of Marcellus, its furnishings and shape likewise etched in her memory. Further down the corridor was the room where Antius stayed. No doubt that miserable little man waited there now, smirking at her renewed captivity.

One fact thrilled her. Silverus was dead. She wished to stand over him on the battlefield and slash off his head with his own sword. She wished that crows pecked his eyes and worms burrowed into his flesh. Instead, he and the rest of the Roman dead would be carefully brought back for proper rites. The Romans missed nothing.

Her time away had been short but living with her own kind had filled her with happiness. Smells and sounds of the tribe resonated as the heartbeat within her chest, so long known and so prized after her time away from it. She couldn't reconcile the two conflicting worlds, both of them fully formed in her mind's eye. She felt stretched between them like a thread pulled so tight the fibers gave up their strength.

A cursory glance at the food tray revealed a portion of bread, a generous wedge of cheese, a pear, and olives, a disgusting reminder of Rome. Oddly, her mouth watered for the olives more than the other food. But she would take none of it. She returned to stand at the window, her filthy hands gripping the bars as she stared out. Evening mist rose from the river to hang in the dusky air above the fortress walls. Shadows deepened across the Via Principia as stragglers hurried from the gates and more wagons creaked to a stop at the hospital.

Despite her wish not to think of Marcellus, she could think of little else. He lived like Rome, taking what he wanted, invincible. Sooner or later, he would make his demands. She would fight him like she always did and then yield to his mastery. Her stomach roiled and she turned only moments before retching into the waste pail.

~~~

Murmurs rose and fell outside the door. Footsteps approached and passed by. The night sky cleared to reveal its starry display. She felt as though she had never slept and had forgotten how.

A glorious summer had passed in the Ordovices camp, the dusty hot scent of crushed grasses and the regular stamp of men's feet punctuating her days. Now the season neared its end. Soon frost would color the hillsides with red and gold and heavy rains would flood the valley. She would see none of the frost covered heather with its magical icy spider webs. As she languished locked away in this Roman fortress, the great festivals of Lunastal and later Samhainn would pass without her.

She spent the night in fitful sleep, waking at intervals not knowing where she was, remembering then trying to forget. The morning trumpet startled her awake. Sometime in the night she had pulled the covers over her, but she still wore her grimy clothing. Blood coating her hands had cracked into tiny lines. She examined the dark brown rims of her nails as if they belonged to someone else.

A knock sounded. Caerwin said nothing as Tutonius stepped into the room with a platter. His gaze conveyed concern and curiosity, but he said nothing as he took away the untouched food from yesterday. She looked away and waited until he closed the door and his footsteps died off. Judging by the smell, roasted fowl lay on the platter. She didn't bother to get up.

The fabric of the bed covering occupied her full attention. The loosely woven linen had been hemmed, doubtless the work of some slave. The corner between her fingers held twenty stitches in the length of her thumb joint. Careful short stitches. The weave of the fabric also garnered her close examination. She counted how many throws of the shuttle, how many threads in the weft. Her thumbnail moved each thin thread slightly as she counted. Again.

Hours passed as outside sounds invaded her room. Wagon wheels. Footsteps. Changing of the guard. They wafted over her like the river's current. More than once, her door opened and closed. She didn't turn.

"Caerwin!"

The door slammed at the same time Marcellus spoke her name, startling her awake. Or had she slept? In the hours that passed, she didn't know if she slept or if time simply washed past.

His hand grasped her shoulder. She let him turn her. Her body rolled over, tangling her legs in the bed covering and twisting her in the tunic.

"No more," he said fiercely. He took her hands and pulled her to a sitting position with her bare feet off the side of the bed. "You'll be washed. You'll wear clean clothes. Then you'll eat. Obey or I'll whip you."

"Whip me then," she said. Her voice sounded strange to her ears. "I don't care."

~~~

She stood shivering in the evening chill as Senna scrubbed her naked body. Marcellus held her while Senna cleaned her hands then tied her wrists above her head, the rope fastened to a hook on the wall. Senna clucked and sighed as she lathered the soap cloth and rinsed Caerwin clean.

"You're your own worst enemy," she said, drying her feet. The woman wrapped a shawl around Caerwin's torso and tucked the corner tight between her breasts to hold the fabric in place.

"I don't care," Caerwin said. "This is all a dream."

"You'll eat now," Senna said, holding a portion of cold chicken to Caerwin's mouth.

Caerwin turned her body away and closed her eyes. She heard Senna's sigh. The door closed.

Silence pressed against her ears. Waiting in bondage satisfied her in strange ways. Any choice had been removed. Her mind need not trouble with decisions or plans. Her life narrowed down to the moment, the silence. The oddly clean feeling of extended hunger pleased her, too, an emptiness of her body to match the emptiness of her mind.

Waiting for what? It didn't matter. Her hands and arms had lost blood flow. Cold prickled her palms. If she waited long enough, perhaps all her blood would settle in her feet and she would fly to the forests of Ande-Dubnos and see the blackened face of Gwyn ap Nudd. She strained to hear the baying of Gwyn's hounds, messengers of death.

Instead the jangle of harness and creak of wagon wheels passed her ears. Shouts of men speaking their foreign tongue. Slowly it all faded away.

～～～

She sensed Marcellus before she heard him. His hands sent shock waves down her sides, smoothing up her clammy arms then down to her hips. Her body responded instantly as it had since the first time he touched her. Against her will, he had made her his toy.

"Will you eat?" His voice seemed hoarse.

Her eyes opened to see the flicker of an oil lamp's flame. Framed against that light, Marcellus' dark form loomed. He wore only his tunic. His fierce stare pierced the shadows.

She considered whether to speak. What would it matter if she said 'yes' or 'no'? She closed her eyes.

She heard the whistle of the lash before it burned her skin. The leather tendrils warmed her buttocks and then her thighs. She trembled from the anger that radiated from him. Slowly, the blows of the lash heated her back and shoulders, her thighs and calves until she couldn't stop the tears rolling down her face.

The cleansing tears emptied more of her. Whatever she was, now she was less. She imagined shrinking to nothing.

"Damn you," he cursed. The lash renewed its stinging path down her back. "Why do you harm yourself this way? Why, my queen?" His words broke off into a sob. "My beautiful wild queen."

The lash fell from his hand as he caressed her buttocks. He pulled her against him so that the heat of his body penetrated her back. His breath fanned her neck and his lips brushed her shoulders.

"Hurt me more," she said. Her words came through clenched teeth, not because of the pain. She cared nothing about the lashing. "Make me feel nothing, I beg you."

"I can't bear this," he said.

She felt him shaking against her and knew he wept. Slowly, he turned her to face him, kissed her, and released her wrists.

She sank to the floor. He gathered her in his arms and placed her on her narrow bed. He stroked her wet cheeks, raining light kisses on her forehead, chin, and shoulders.

"There is no pleasure in this," he whispered.

The blows barely registered as the lash stung her arms and shoulders, but the flogger's tendrils brought fresh tears as he reached her breasts. More tears burned down her cheeks as the lash striped her stomach and thighs. She kept her eyes tightly closed, not willing to see his face or his exertion.

"Will you let me feed you?"

"I want to die," she said.

"The gods!" The leather licked between her legs. "I put the whip where my mouth and hands long to go. Will you yield now?"

"No."

His chest heaved as he scourged her. Screams ripped from her throat. She passed into another frame of mind, limp in his hands as his touch switched from the lash to his tongue. Her pain changed to need so extreme she could not keep from crying his name. He brought her quickly to orgasm with his mouth.

"Hurt me," she said. "Please, Marcellus."

He ripped off his clothing before shoving her legs apart. His rock-hard shaft drove to her center. She arched off the bed to meet him, blind to everything but the force of his taking, his grunts, his hands tight on her shoulders holding her fast against his thrusts. Each lunge drove her higher until she thought she might explode into a thousand pieces. White light glazed her vision. She didn't know if she lived or died.

She only knew Marcellus over her, holding her, in her.

~~~

"Open," he said.

She opened her mouth. His fingers brushed her lips as he placed meat on her tongue.

"Do you like the taste?"

The tangy rich flavor provoked her saliva. She chewed with more pleasure than she expected. Another bite, this time of tender cabbage flavored with salt and garlic.

He shifted his legs, bringing her bottom more squarely over his thighs so that his left arm wrapped around her back and his hand rested on her hip. With his right hand, he brought another piece of bread to her lips. As she chewed, his lips grazed her cheek and temple. His breath teased the hair that lay loose against her ear.

"Why, Marcellus? Why do you insist?"

"Shh. No questions, no discussions."

"But..."

"No," he said firmly. "First you will eat. When you've regained your right mind, we'll talk more."

~~~

"I burn," she said. Her fingers twisted in the fabric of his tunic. "I need you."

She heard his fingers dip again in the jar of honey-berry balm but she couldn't look. If she opened her eyes, she would see the smooth white walls of a square room, the familiar furnishings of his bedchamber. She would see the dark hair curled at his temples and the indescribable expression on his face. She couldn't bear to see any of it.

The cool mixture touched her swollen flesh like a welcome breeze. Much as she anticipated the touch, she still jumped when his tongue licked at her overheated flesh. Long strokes of his tongue, little sucking motions—her hands sought anything to grip.

"This is worse than the lashing," she groaned.

He nibbled and licked her tormented flesh. His fingers penetrated her openings and stroked until her body jumped in response. Wave after wave of excruciating need rose and crashed.

A sea of sensation flooded her, each time building higher until she screamed a low continuous cry.

She didn't know when he turned her, or whether his hands slapped her. She didn't know whether his *mentula* penetrated or if her body only remembered the times before. She didn't know if this was the day he brought her to his lap to eat meat or the day he fed her fish.

His hands comforted her. He muttered words of love and despair. She begged for more pain, more punishment that would blur her thoughts and keep her focused only on this moment. She hated him for forcing her to live.

~~~

"You're killing him."

Caerwin heard Senna's words from a distance, the same distance from which she watched and heard everything. Just beyond that distance, behind a careful wall she struggled each day to build up, sprawled the dead body of Seisyll. His worn staff lay under him, his ragged clothes pooled in fluid heaps. She knelt on the rocky ground, holding his gaping wounds as if she could restore him to life. His blood had congealed like black pudding.

Sometimes in her dreams she asked him if he still felt pain. He smiled and said he did not. He stood straight in those dreams. His eyes carried the fire she'd seen in his blue eyes. And happiness.

Beyond Seisyll on that steep hillside, she saw hundreds of men contorted in positions of death, some of them Roman, most of them native. Roman legionaries walked among them, occasionally thrusting a sword into the chests of those who groaned. Sounds of fighting had died away in the distance.

The scene changed to the Wrekin, the death cries and clash of battle. Virico begging her to direct the sword to his heart. Her mother's face as the parade of slaves passed by.

All was lost.

Nausea came up in a hot rush and she bent to the side of her chair. The heave produced nothing. Clammy shivers raced up her chest. She trembled as she gripped the chair.

Senna placed a cool cloth on Caerwin's forehead. "If I didn't know better, I'd think you were with child," she said quietly.

Caerwin managed a short laugh. "What a fine mother I would be."

"You would be a fine mother. You're a gentle loving person. Do I think for a moment that anyone could live through what you've lived through and not be affected? No, of course not. Sit up, now, let me finish this braid."

"Doesn't he care about my hair anymore? He used to demand curls and fancy arrangements. He didn't want it worn in my custom."

"He's a desperate man, dear girl. He'll try anything."

Senna's hands tugged at the long strands, restraining the last of the hair from the sides of Caerwin's face. Caerwin turned, looking at Senna as if she'd seen her for the first time. The older woman's forehead wrinkled in a frown and her lips had set in a thin line.

"I'm sorry," Caerwin whispered. Tears brimmed her eyes.

"There, now, don't start again. Let's just finish the hair and then we'll walk outside. The sky is clear today."

They stood at the courtyard entry facing the Principia. She hardly wondered that she stood outside. Everything passed like a continuing dream. A wagon master called to the dock hands as they rolled a large amphora onto the dock. The clang of hammer on metal echoed from the forge. Men hurried from place to place. Ants.

Like ants. Her young cousin Eppeno's words echoed in her ears. *They'll be squashed beneath our feet.* Silverus' sword flashed. Eppeno's head fell sideways off his neck, an odd angle for a head. His life blood pulsed slowly onto the ground. So long ago, and yet the memory burned as if it all happened yesterday.

"See?" Senna lifted her hand, directing Caerwin's gaze to the deep blue arc of sky above them. "Can you remember such a beautiful sky? I can't think of a time when it seemed so clear."

Caerwin stared upward. As far as she'd been able to throw rocks as a child, she'd never pierced the canopy. Clouds, the sun and moon, all of them moved in their own path across the great expanse. Birds flew so high she could hardly see them but still they didn't disappear above the sky. Did the sky go on forever?

"Nothing changes," she said. Words felt thick on her tongue. "The days repeat themselves. Am I to live forever in a day that keeps repeating?"

"But it is changing," Senna argued. "The days already grow shorter. Marcellus will soon be relieved of his duty and we'll travel to Rome. You'll find a whole new world."

Caerwin stiffened at the words. Of all the times she heard that Marcellus neared the end of his command, none of them had struck her as harshly as now. He faced a mountain of difficulties— the tangle of his father's estate, the angry woman who was not his mother. They had talked about it, back in the winter and spring before her escape. Back in a time when they'd been friends.

None of that mattered now. Marcellus could find his own way. She had nothing to offer him. "He can't take me from my home," she said.

"Is this your home?" Senna took her hand, keeping her from turning back to the room. "Where is your home, Caerwin?"

"This land is my home. This river, these hills. The graves of my ancestors."

"But not this fortress?" Senna asked.

"No, of course not." Caerwin pulled her hand away. "I'm tired. I'm sick of what my life has become. But I'm not out of my mind. This fortress will someday be gone. All the marks of Rome will be washed away. I'll live here then."

"None of us will live that long, I fear," Senna said. "Rome won't fade so easily. Remember your lessons? Rome has already ruled the world for three hundred years and only grows stronger."

"They feed off the lives of others."

"As the eagle takes his prey. You cannot change the flight of the eagle."

"I won't be snatched in its claws," she said. "I'll reach up and tear out its heart."

Senna sighed. "Why must you always fight? Can't you make a home with Marcellus? Can't he be your refuge?"

"He's my captor," Caerwin said. "He says he loves me but he keeps me from the things I cherish most."

"The things you cherish most? What is left of that, dear girl? Think about it! Don't you realize your family is gone, your home, your village? The land belongs to Rome."

"Don't tell me that!" she shouted, jerking her hands away. "This land will always belong to us. They may kill us all and tread on our bones, but this land will never belong to Rome."

"Don't think of Rome, then," Senna said. She lowered her voice. "Think only of Marcellus. Remember the rumors—he may be only half Roman. Remember his kindness."

"I feel no comfort with Marcellus," Caerwin turned, gripping Senna's plump hands. She pushed away her certain knowledge of Marcellus' twisted parentage. He had embraced his father's traditions. That's all that mattered. "I care about nothing. Marcellus makes me feel with the lash. Can I live that way? Is that comfort?"

"You've seen too much. These things take time. You'll recover, I'm sure of it."

"I know you believe that. Marcellus says the same. He talks to me now, tells everything to me, of his life, of the army, of Rome. He speaks of the battle and what he thought when he saw me at the tip of that legionary's sword. He speaks of the justice done to Silverus, as if he wishes to relieve me of any guilt. I feel no guilt that Silverus died. I only wish that I had driven the knife to his heart by my own hand. At least then Seisyll would have been spared.

"I did that for my brother," she continued. "Did you know? I held my brother's hands—they were cold. I pressed them around the hilt of his sword and drove the tip to his heart. I watched his life slip away into his death dream." She reached up to touch the tears streaming down her face. She hadn't realized she was crying.

"Silverus didn't deserve to die so quickly," she said fiercely. "He should have been tortured for all he did. A thousand cuts. Crows pecking his eyes while he lay helpless on the ground with his skin peeled off. And Seisyll—he didn't deserve to die at all. He had lost so much."

"You gave him reason to die, don't you see that?" Senna said. "Didn't you say he thought of himself as a ghost?"

"Yes." Caerwin remembered the sparkle in his eyes when they had first agreed to join forces. "He was a ghost."

"He waited for you. The spirits sent him to be your protector, and he fulfilled his purpose. You gave him that."

"No." Caerwin turned away, fighting back tears. "I gave him death."

She hurried back to her room, Senna at her heels. She threw herself onto the bed and curled up sideways, tugging the familiar sheet to her chin where the counted threads occupied her full attention. She refused to answer Senna's questions or respond to her pleas. Finally the door closed and she drifted again.

Chapter Two

Early morning drizzle veiled the Principia building across the roadway. More distant structures like the warehouses appeared as gray shapes. Near Caerwin's bedchamber window, a long box-like wagon sat mounted on oversized wheels. A team of four large mules were hitched to it. Through openings in its side, she could see the movements of Antius as he positioned articles handed to him by Senna and one of the other slaves. She pressed her head against her window bars, trying to gain a better vantage.

A second wagon with low sides waited behind it, this one more familiar in size and shape. Another team of mules jostled their harnesses as two legionaries loaded crates and trunks into the wagon bed. She recognized Antius' trunk and his desk, Senna's trunk. Oiled leather sheeting quickly covered the furniture against the damp as the men fastened ties on either side.

She spun away from the window, clenching her hands together. Her breath came fast and shallow. So this would be the day. No one had warned her.

The bolt slid on her door and Senna appeared. Antius stood behind her, his face an inscrutable mask in the shadow of his cloak hood. His dark eyes examined her briefly as they entered her room.

"The trunk," Senna said, motioning.

Droplets of moisture beaded on Senna's hair, which she wore fastened back in a bun. Her forehead wrinkled in a frown as she directed the two men. Caerwin caught their curious glance, but they quickly looked away as if to view her carried some tremendous risk. Antius gazed around the room and addressed Senna as if Caerwin wasn't there.

"What more of her things are to go?" he said.

"I'll pack her *loculus*," Senna said. "It will ride with her in the *carpentum*, not the baggage wagon."

Caerwin stood with her fists on her hips as the men carried her truck through the doorway. Antius disappeared behind them.

Senna moved briskly, gathering the comb, hair pins and clasps, Caerwin's sleeping tunic, the hooded cloak that hung by the door, and the small copper box that held the jewelry Marcellus had given her. Her golden torque lay on the side table. Senna looked at her questioningly.

"You can't wear this on the journey," she said.

"It can stay here with me," Caerwin said.

Senna's frown deepened. "Why must you make your life so difficult? You will not stay here."

"I've told Marcellus as much," Caerwin said.

"Yes, we've heard those conversations on the other side of the house. He hasn't changed his mind. You'll go one way or the other."

Caerwin snatched up the torque and twisted it around her neck. The metal weighed on her collarbones, oddly reassuring.

"I'm Cornovii," she said, crossing her arms across her chest. "I am of this land and only this land."

"Yes, just as I was of the Atrebates tribe. Now I'm here. Life moves on. The gods, when will you stop acting like a child?"

"Leave me," Caerwin said, her lips narrowed to a thin line. "The *loculus* stays with me."

Senna stood motionless for a few moments, her fingers tight on the leather satchel. With a last angry glance, she dropped the bag on the small table and stalked out of the room.

Caerwin slammed the door behind her then heaved on her heavy bed frame until the head board braced against the door. After another moment's thought, she dragged her chair and then the table to reinforce the bed's weight. Water sloshed in the flagon and one of the drinking cups fell to the floor.

She surveyed her work, confident that no one could open the door. Once Marcellus saw that he couldn't force her out, he would commence on his journey. Perhaps he would make good his longstanding threat to give her to the troops, make her a barracks whore. Or worse, throw her to the camp followers to use as they wished. None of that mattered. She would not be taken from her home land and carried away to some foreign place she already hated.

She climbed to the middle of her bed and sat with her back against the door. The last days had stretched her nerves to breaking. Unfamiliar voices and footsteps passed along the corridors. The replacement legate for Marcellus had arrived with his retinue, taking over many of the Praetorium rooms and bringing strange smells to the courtyard altar of Vesta. The new incense, whatever its name or source, defiled her sense of the altar. For so long she had seen it not as the place of the Roman goddess of the hearth, but as a shrine to her people's river goddess Sabrina.

She hadn't seen Marcellus but once since the last half moon. His face had become unfamiliar, his cheeks creased with tension as he gave his commands. He'd not taken up the flogger or held her on his lap to eat. She had suffered the indignity of feeling hunger and accepting food for its own sake. He had successfully broken her resolve not to eat. She no longer felt empty or clean.

Fury had replaced the emptiness, a long slow fire of rage that kindled fresh each morning when she woke and grew as the day's hours passed. Everything fed it—the voice of Antius, the Latin words shouted near and far, the scene outside as legionaries marched past in their shining armor, this army of ants with their flashing red cloaks and shields painted with lightning bolts. Her skin itched with the heat of her anger. The scroll showing the map of Britannia had been ripped and chewed until she had reduced it to tiny ragged pieces, an event that provoked Marcellus to remove every item of value from her room including her supply of wine.

Voices neared her door. The door bolt threw. The door jammed against the bed frame with a loud thump.

"Caerwin."

Marcellus. She bit her lip, yielding to her sudden urge to smile. He would not win this battle.

The door pushed in a renewed attempt to open.

"Open the door."

"Go without me," she said. "I won't leave my country."

"Open it now," he said, shoving hard against the bedframe. The bed moved slightly.

She pressed her back against the door. "Go away."

"Caerwin—don't you remember all we talked about? There's so much I want to show you, so much for you to see and enjoy. There's nothing here for you. Open the door."

"No. I care nothing for Rome. Leave me."

She heard his muttered curses then relaxed as she heard his footsteps move away. She only had to prove her resolve. Once he rode out and the wagons followed, she would throw herself on the mercy of Tutonius or even the new legate. With a less vigilant master, she could once again slip away.

Once free, she wouldn't stop until she reached the western mountains. Seisyll had been right—they should have continued far past the Ordovices camp, even to the fabled lands beyond the western sea. Surely somewhere she would be safe from the Romans. She would live out her days without taking a mate, without children. Perhaps she would live in a cave where she would tend her fire and store her food. She'd craft clothes from skins and keep dogs as her companions. Perhaps a horse…

A heavy thump jarred her. The door shoved open slightly. She gripped the mattress with both hands, pressing backwards.

Men's voices—at least two men. And Marcellus. The hair stood up on her neck.

Another strong shove. The bed's legs screeched as they scooted on the tiled floor. The flagon of water teetered and fell. No amount of pressing backwards slowed the movement. In moments, the door had pushed her, the bed, and the assembled furniture far into the small room's center. Marcellus stood in the doorway with two burly legionaries behind him.

"No!" She whirled around on the bed, crouching as if with her teeth and claws she would defend herself from their invasion.

"Hold her," Marcellus instructed the men, taking a coil of rope from Antius who stood just beyond the men.

Her breath caught as the full realization of her circumstance settled in her mind. With a surge of red-hot fury, she threw herself at Marcellus, striking his chest with her fists and thrashing her legs against the men who sought to grip her ankles.

"No! Don't touch me!" she screamed. "I won't go!"

"You'll only injure yourself," Marcellus said, grappling with her fists as she delivered more blows to his chest.

"No, Marcellus, please!" Her cries became ragged as his big hands held her wrists. She tugged and fought, trying to bite him. The men held her ankles together, but she could still kick with both feet as they finished the knot. One of them held her legs tight against his side as the other made his last loop.

In the end, she lay trussed on her bed like a goat ready for slaughter, her wrists bound and tied off by rope length to the fastening around her ankles. She couldn't kick or hit. Her screams continued, curses she summoned from the ancient gods.

"May the gods fall on you with their anger," she ranted, twisting away as Marcellus scooped his arms under her. "May you…"

"Quiet!" he thundered. "You wake the dead."

In one quick movement, he lifted her to his shoulder so that from her midsection up, she faced down his backside. She bucked against his iron grip, but he simply pulled her more tightly under his forearm.

Her breath jarred from her body as he ducked through the doorway and strode along the corridor. The bright light of day illuminated the soggy morning air, causing her to blink. In moments, he had delivered her to the box-like wagon, lifted her in through the small doorway, and eased her to the floor boards.

"Dear me," Senna muttered.

Caerwin glanced up at the older woman sitting in the far corner, infuriated afresh that her struggles made her a spectacle to the entire legion. Marcellus climbed in behind her, stepped over her trussed form, and then lifted her again to a bench seat located across the back of the carriage. Once he sat her there, he busied himself fastening another rope from her waist to a railing above her head.

"I won't go," she said. "I'll die before I leave my land."

"You won't do anything," he said, frowning down on her. He adjusted her position on the padded bench seat then re-checked the knots. "You'll go along just as I promised. Try not to embarrass yourself further."

"Embarrass you, you mean," she said, snarling. "I'm not some piece of furniture you can pack away when you please."

He shot her a dark glance and backed out of the carriage, leaving her to tug against the restraints. The rope chafed her wrists and ankles, but the men had done their work well. There was no give in the knots and she couldn't lift her wrists from the restraining length down to her ankles. The rope around her waist fastened behind her up to the carriage railing leaving her no room to shift sideways or move away from the seat.

She refused to look at Senna or Antius where they sat facing her. The bench Caerwin occupied left room for two additional persons. Would Marcellus ride beside her? The thought temporarily calmed her. If he would, perhaps she could convince him to release her. She would make her most earnest plea.

Not that she hadn't tried before. All her words fell on deaf ears. He spoke of the journey, described the lands they would pass through, the length of their travel, what awaited in Rome. The challenges he faced both legal and political. She refused to hear it, at one point covering her ears with her hands to demonstrate her refusal to accept his plans for her.

Time slipped by as the cool wet air chilled her temper. She sat helpless as shouts and harness noise continued outside. Several tribunes and centurions gathered. A quick rap on the door and the carriage door yanked open. Tutonius stood there, behind him a few of the *praetorium* kitchen help and others who had become familiar faces during her months here.

"We brought you something," Tutonius said, holding out a small pot like the ones filled with kitchen herbs and spices. A concerned expression creased his wide face. "It's dirt. We thought you could take a bit of your homeland with you."

Senna took the jar, lifted the lid, and showed it to Caerwin. Dirt. Caerwin's jaw dropped as she looked at Tutonius and the smiling faces behind him. Hot tears filled her eyes.

"Thank you," she said as sobs rolled up. "What kindness."

They bid her farewell and a good journey. Antius closed the carriage door and Senna secured the small crock in her satchel. A man on horseback appeared outside the carriage window, and Caerwin realized it was Marcellus. Dressed in full armor with his red cloak draped behind him, this warrior had been a curse on her existence since the fateful battle at the Wrekin.

The knot of men shouted well wishes and Marcellus called them by name. Then he leaned to the window beside her. "Good journey, Caerwin. We'll rest at midday."

With that, he kicked the horse forward and she watched his proud bearing as his horse trotted ahead. Why did the mere shape of his torso cause gooseflesh to erupt along her arms? The curve of his neck into his shoulder—she had just been thrown over that shoulder like a bag of grain, yet the view now felt like an embrace. Her nostrils flared in disgust.

The wagon master shouted and snapped his whip and the wagon lurched. The big wheels thumped as they rolled over the rock-paved surface of the Via Principia. More men's voices called from the distance, wishing him well.

He had carried his duty well, had led these men into battle more times than she could count and each time managed to bring them victory. Perversely, she felt proud of his ability to lead. Her brother Virico had been a man like that.

They rolled through the gates and turned northeast onto an unfamiliar roadway. The iron-rimmed wheels clacked over the paving stones. In the turning, she saw the wagon behind with its stacks of baggage. A group of armored men rode behind, at least ten she counted before the wagon straightened onto the roadway and she lost sight.

~~~

Still bound in low clouds, the day brightened as they traveled. The team trotted at a fair pace, creating a rocking motion that both lulled her and chafed at her bonds. Increasingly grateful for the window view, Caerwin studied the landscape. If she escaped—no, *when* she escaped, she would need to recognize her way across the countryside. She wouldn't need a small pot of this land. She would have all of it.

As they traveled further from the fortress, the surrounding lands shifted from cleared fields to dense forest as far as she could see. They crossed a river and she prayed to the river goddess. She was shocked to recognize the Wrekin looming in the distance, its long rugged profile framed against the misty sky. Scenes of her life there filled her mind, her mother's cheese making, the quiet hours of early morning, the joyful shouts of men back from hunting, the songs everyone sang together at the festival fires. Hot tears slid down her cheeks and sobs heaved her chest.

Gone. They were all gone.

Never before had she so fully felt the pain of her loss. Never before had she realized how much her life had changed, how she floated now like a leaf on a river, fully at the mercy of the currents and wind. Marcellus held total control over her life, but he could do nothing to fill the chasm her family and tribe had occupied. They had been a community of kinsmen, joined by tradition and blood.

At the Wrekin, she knew the patterns of the seasons, what berries would ripen and the best thickets for finding them. She knew the sounds of the wind in the trees, the call of the birds, the insect songs that sang her to sleep at night. There had been the crackle of fire and the scent of its smoke joining the aroma of lamb stew, of hearth bread and the fat sizzle of meat. There had been the hypnotic rhythm of the loom, the whooshing shuttle throw and the clack of the reed slammed down against the fell. Dogs barked in the distance, sometimes in company of bleating sheep, but always the soft murmur of other voices and laughter.

Her throat ached as the landscape passed in a blur. The carriage traveled faster than she'd ever imagined. The farther they journeyed, the greater her grief. What if she couldn't escape? What if this was to be the last time her eyes surveyed this land?

Her sobs broke into wails as the north end of the Wrekin vanished from view. She fought with her bonds, trying desperately to pull loose the knots at her wrists. With her knees bent, she worked at the rope around her ankles until her fingertips became raw. Her cry rose in pitch.

"The gods!" Senna lurched from the opposing bench and sat beside Caerwin, wrapping her arms around her shoulders and pulling her close. "Try to calm yourself," she said, smoothing back the loose hair that stuck to Caerwin's wet neck.

Caerwin shook her head. "Nooo," she wailed.

"Think on good things, of what an exciting journey lies ahead, the discoveries you'll make."

"There is nothing good. I hurt inside."

"You can't change what has happened," Senna said. "The only hope lies ahead."

"You don't know how this feels," Caerwin sobbed.

"Yes, I really do, dear," Senna insisted. She opened the strap on her *loculus* and searched inside until she found a worn cloth. With water from her canteen, she wet the cloth and wiped Caerwin's face.

"You'll make yourself sick with this weeping," Senna said. "Listen now. I was but a small child when the Romans came to our lands. We resisted the same as your tribe. The fighting men died. The legion sold the rest of us as slaves. I was too young to really understand the meaning of everything, but I was terrified by what I saw happening around me—our houses burned, our things taken. Worst was the lamentation of my mother and aunts. My older sisters took up their cry. I thought the world had come to an end."

She shrugged, soothing Caerwin in slow caresses along her arm and shoulder. "Of course, our world *had* come to an end. But another world awaited us. After a time—I don't know how long—my mother was bought by a country family who needed another household servant. It could have been much worse. But they saw how strong she was, and they allowed her to keep me. Every day she worked hard and every night she cried, stuffing her face into the bedclothes so her cries wouldn't be heard.

"I cried too, little quiet cries in sympathy for what she suffered even though I didn't understand it. I think she tried to calm herself for my sake. But here's the thing: I hardly remember those days now. I've learned much and found many pleasures in my life. I've loved and been loved. I've been fortunate to recognize early in life that your days are what you make of them. You must learn that."

The wagon jostled and Caerwin swayed more snugly into Senna's warm hold. The crying had exhausted her but tears still filled her eyes. She risked a glance toward Antius, who fortunately kept his gaze riveted on the passing scenery. Her emotion was too intense to share with that smug Greek.

Senna's story continued. Nothing she could say would relieve the crushing pain in Caerwin's chest. But her words distracted Caerwin.

"The family had children and I played with them. There were many advantages in that villa—water ran in a fountain, which astonished me. They had beautiful furniture, finer than any I'd ever seen. The floors were smooth white marble, cool under my bare feet in the summer and heated to warm our feet in the winter. I loved it better than our round house in the village where it was always dim and smoky.

"The family brought me along with their own children when the tutors came, and I learned the magic of written words. My mother watched these things and took great comfort in it. She was a clever woman—she saw that Rome would rule all lands and wanted me to have advantage. She regretted that I was to be a slave, but she believed that if I knew words, I would find a good position. She taught me useful skills too, about grooming, fashion in clothing and hair arrangements, the use of perfumes and cosmetics, talents she learned watching the lady of the house.

"She was right, of course. Very wise. I've enjoyed good positions. Each year in the celebration of the Vestals, I make offerings to my mother. She became my mother goddess more than Juno."

Caerwin resisted Senna's words. There could be no advantage in slavery no matter what skills a person might learn. Skills to serve oneself or one's tribe held great value, but to use one's energy and days in service to a hated master…she could never accept that kind of life. Senna's gentle voice filled her head like a comforting wind. Gradually her tears stopped. Fatigue overcame her. The motion of the wagon rocked her but Senna held her tight. The words became more difficult to track and she fell asleep.

Stillness. Caerwin blinked. She was alone in the carriage. Her gaze quickly surveyed the scene outside the window. They sat quietly in a cleared area beside the roadway. Men stood guard in small groups. Ahead, she could see a stream crossing and horses drinking there.

The carriage door yanked open and Marcellus climbed inside. An expression of concern creased his face as he examined her.

"I'll release you long enough to relieve yourself," he said, tugging at the rope. "Senna will assist you."

"I'm endlessly grateful," she said. "Shall I have a crumb for my breakfast?"

"You'll have food. And drink."

"Oh generous master."

His dark stare unsettled her. "Just stop it, Caerwin. I have enough concern without your obstruction. And don't get any ideas. I'll have your rope in my hands while you're out."

Her stiff legs cramped as she stood. The carriage interior allowed her full height but not quite the height of Marcellus. He released the knot from the roof railing and let it trail across the carriage floor. Senna retrieved a waste pail from under the bench, a disgusting reminder of her entrapment. At least she wasn't forced to relieve herself in front of Antius. Release came immediately then Senna helped her through the doorway where Marcellus waited.

The ground seemed to move in her first steps, but she quickly regained her balance. Her surroundings were nothing but forest as far as she could see, that and the Roman road stretching straight and wide into the distance. She counted six men at the stream crossing, holding the horses as they drank and grazed. Four other men stood on either side of the caravan, their hands on their weapons as they kept their attention focused on their surroundings.

Evidently the mighty Roman army still had much to fear from her countrymen. The idea gave small comfort. No one would come for her—no one knew her. She guessed they had reached the territories of the Coritani, a loose confederation of tribes sometimes mentioned by her brother regarding his dealings in trade.

As for Marcellus—he glowered at her from the other end of her rope a mere arm's length away. He marched along, forcing her steps faster to some imaginary point where he stopped, turned then tugged her back along the same path.

"Why delay?" she taunted. "Can you not ride but a short time before you must rest?"

"I stop for you," he growled. "And for the beasts. We have many miles to travel before nightfall."

"By all means, keep me as you would keep your horse," she said. She cut her eyes toward him. "Will you ride me tonight?"

He seized her arm and pulled her against his chest. "I would ride you now, but it would be a disservice to the men. Brigands patrol this road and we carry valuables. Not the least," he said, pressing the torque against her throat, "your precious neck piece."

Her fingers traced the ornate braided band of polished metal and lingered on the circled terminals with their delicate engraved features. Her brother's torque. And before him, her father, and her father's father and so back into the glorious Cornovii past. Marcellus' fingers brushed over hers and his face hovered so close she could see streaks of amber in his dark eyes.

He touched her cheek. "Senna tells me you exhausted yourself with crying. Your eyes bear the marks."

She caught her breath, resisting her yielding to his forceful presence.

"Don't look on me," she said, turning her face away. "At least give me the dignity of my grief."

"I regret your grief, but you've got more to think of than your past."

The heat of his body radiated through her chest. Despite his armor, she could feel his desire rising against her belly. Fury warred with need, the inexplicable craving he aroused in her even with the torturous lash. She fought against his grasp.

"The gods! Do you know the desire you provoke in me?" he whispered. "I am surely bewitched and you are the goddess Venus made flesh."

"I am Caerwin of the Cornovii," she replied hotly. "A woman captured by your army and made a plaything by its commander."

"Sent by Jove himself to torment me," he said. "When I have steered you through this journey and hold you safely in the bedchamber of my *domus*, there will be no more word play. The only words on your lips will be my name and your cries to the gods."

He shoved her away. A red flush colored his cheeks and his nostrils flared. But for the bonds around her wrists, she would have flown at him with her fists and claws. He teased her with his power over her, his constant reminding that she belonged to him. Her pulse throbbed in her neck, drumming against the gold band.

"I despise the ground you walk on. I despise everything about you."

His jaw pulsed in anger and his flush darkened. "Keep your taunts handy. I'll give you plenty of time to exhaust them while you're tied to my bed and I bring you repeatedly to the brink of satisfaction." He leaned in and brushed her lips with his. His big hand buried between her legs and lifted her. "I'll tighten your nipples between my teeth and cause your clitoris to throb. Then I will leave you to cry for me."

She spat at him, her only weapon with her hands held low by the tie connected to her ankles. He stiffened, wiped the spittle from his jaw then pushed her forward at such a pace that she had to run in tiny steps allowed by the rope. At the carriage, Senna and Antius exchanged glances as Marcellus lifted her to the interior then followed her to the seat where he once again fastened her waist tie to the railing. Without saying anything further, he slammed the carriage door and called to the men.

~~~

The entourage continued its hot, jostling journey. Senna fed her from the baskets stowed under their seats: cold meat, bread, cheese, olives. Caerwin longed for wine but didn't ask. They traveled in the same configuration with Marcellus and two other men in the lead followed by the carriage, then the baggage wagon and the rest of the horsemen at the back.

She learned from conversation between Senna and Antius that like Marcellus, these men had finished their military service and would escort them all the way to Rome, engaged to such service by a generous payment from Marcellus. Having recently traveled this route, Senna knew something about their overnight stays, first in a place called Manduessedum where they slept in a stone building with multiple sleeping rooms and a central hall. The next night passed in a similar structure at a village named Magiovinium. At each stop they gained fresh horses or mules.

As they journeyed southeast, the landscape changed from mostly dense woodlands to cleared fields. More traffic populated the roadway which continued its remarkable size wide enough to accommodate two carriages side by side. Caerwin watched out the window, passing from moods of agitation and fury to extended periods of curious observation. The land fell continuously giving ease to the horses. Streams gave way to marshes. Birds flew up from the woodlands and fields, and occasional wildlife stared back as they passed.

More than once a contingent of Roman forces met them along the roadway, no doubt on their way to quench some hopeful uprising or to molest innocent villagers. Each morning she renewed her resolve against Marcellus. But in the nights, he held her next to him in the sleeping room. Each night she extended her rope as far as she could to escape his touch, but he chuckled and pulled her next to his warm body. Halfway through the night, she would wake disoriented then curl deeper into his arms.

She hated herself for every concession. Her weary bumpy hours passed with the certain knowledge that in every mile further from her home, the difficulty of her escape and return westward became more extreme. She ignored Senna's periodic attempts to engage her in conversation. The woman served as the mouthpiece for Marcellus' persuasion.

~~~

Midday of the third day, they arrived at a substantial settlement named Verulamium. In outlying fields, herds of grazing sheep and cattle alternated with healthy crops. Houses, stables, barns, and commercial structures sprawled over low hills that dropped down to a river with wide marshes. Structures of various shapes and sizes filled her view, all of them built mostly of wood in the peculiar rectangular style of the Romans. They stopped finally at the center of the settlement amid heavy traffic of wagons and pedestrians and in front of a large timber and stone house of pleasing proportions. A man in a white toga met Marcellus at the gate, calling his name and slapping his back as if they had been long acquainted.

Once introductory remarks had concluded and attendants took charge of the baggage wagons, Marcellus came to the carriage to relieve her bonds.

"Do not embarrass me before my old friend Gaius," he said in a low voice. "Can you agree to that?"

"What torment would he bestow on me?" she said, rubbing her wrists.

A heavy sigh escaped Marcellus. "He's nothing like Ostorius Scapula, if that's what you mean. He's an educated man with an enlightened view of the world. If you behave well, you may learn something in his presence."

"I'm curious how a man with enlightened view accepts the Roman invasion of another people's country," she said, moving her now-freed legs.

His eyes narrowed. "Can you not simply attend our company, enjoy the food and conversation, and learn how civilized people behave?"

"I've seen enough of your 'civilized' people," she said with a snort. "You flatter yourselves."

Gaius led the way, accompanied by a servant. Senna and Antius walked ahead with Marcellus gripping Caerwin's arm tightly as he escorted her through the home's long atrium. Clear water glistened in a rectangular pool surrounded by flowering plants and short cropped grass. A statue of Vesta stood at the far end and, on the right side, a larger statue of Jupiter. As they progressed along the covered walkway, Caerwin caught glimpses of spacious rooms and beautiful furniture.

Delivered to a secured chamber in the recesses of the house, Caerwin listened in annoyance as Senna gave her advice on proper behavior. It seemed Marcellus planned to bring her to the dinner table. The thought captured her imagination.

Outside the room's window, slaves labored in gardens where young shrubs and flowering plants outlined a thriving showplace. A rising chorus of crickets and night-calling birds momentarily transported her to the Wrekin. In the nearest bed of rich soil, thickets of strong smelling thyme, savory, chives, and mint reminded her of the Cornovii herb garden that was tended by her mother and other matrons of the clan. She turned away from the window having no idea what Senna had been saying.

Briefly, she considered attempting escape. If Senna left her side, she could climb out the window and walk through the garden, climb the short wall, and emerge into the streets of the settlement. Perhaps no one would stop her. Perhaps she could elicit interest from a passerby and gain transport on a wagon. Images of the salt man's disgusting grin penetrated her daydream. The world was full of men like that, and the roadway thronged with Roman military forces. It would be a matter of time before Marcellus would regain possession. A very short time.

"You're thinking of escape," Senna said. "Have you learned nothing?"

"I'm not," Caerwin lied. "I'm thinking of the garden my mother used to grow. She stewed lamb with mint."

Senna peered at her askance then answered a short knock at the door. After a brief exchange of words, Senna turned.

"We're to visit the bathhouse," she said. "Surely you'll enjoy this."

They followed a group of women to a large building a short distance away.

"I'm surprised Marcellus trusts you out of his sight," Senna murmured, helping Caerwin remove her tunic. "Keep in mind there are guards at the entries."

"I can hardly escape without clothing," Caerwin said.

Senna's face creased in a smile. "You wouldn't pass without notice."

Women crowded the changing room, a long room with benches and cubicles built to hold an individual's belongings. Caerwin moved slowly, shocked by the ease in which strangers bared themselves to each other. Clutching towels, she and Senna sat in a steam room until sweat poured down their necks. They next entered a room with high ornate walls and fantastic designs on the floors formed by colorful small tiles, a masterful surrounding to a large rectangular pool of glistening water. Stepping gingerly down wide curving steps, Caerwin discovered the water had been warmed.

"Are these all women of the household?" she whispered to Senna as she sank into the water.

"I think so," Senna replied. "I have met only a few, but I know from my journey last year that Gaius' wife Cassia is the woman in the corner." She nodded slightly in that direction. "Beside her, I think these must be the women Marcellus mentioned, the sister of Gaius and her sister-in-law, the younger one."

Caerwin tried not to openly stare. The younger woman's smooth skin had an olive tone and her hair was lustrous black. How did a person gain such color? Beside her, the woman Senna thought Gaius' sister had a body shorter and thicker than the other and her hair not so ebony. Caerwin startled as the woman's gaze locked with hers and she flushed and looked away.

Quiet conversation and water sounds rippled over the pool's surface.

"What of the men?" she asked Senna. This was the first time she'd seen Senna without clothing, and she tried not to let her eyes linger on the older woman's body, voluptuous even though her tummy pooched and her breasts sagged slightly. Her body reminded Caerwin of her mother.

"In Rome, men and women may mingle in the baths. Here, where the accommodations are smaller and Rome's influence not yet settled, the men wait out the women's time."

Caerwin's thought drifted, imagining how it would be to see nude men and women together in the pool. Marcellus' father's intrigues with Silverus and Antius took place in the baths at Rome. She imagined Marcellus as a young man, vulnerable and yet eager to please his father in his sex games. The idea disgusted and excited her at the same time. No matter what sexual indulgence might be involved, what person would not want to spend his time in such sensory pleasure?

The water soothed her in ways she had never known. This was not the River Severn coursing around her with its mud incasing her feet and fish darting between her legs. Nor was it a cold spring pool like the one she had enjoyed near the camp of the Ordovices. This water caressed her, reminded her of Marcellus' tongue between her legs. Her nipples tightened.

Once she had dried, Senna rubbed aromatic oils on her body and that, along with clean soft clothing, eased the irritation from the ropes on her skin. She felt relaxed and bemused at her situation. Oddly, she was able to avoid thinking of her plight, her desire for escape, or any other distress that had plagued her travel thus far. Instead, thoughts of Marcellus and his naked body consumed her.

~~~

As Senna released Caerwin's hand at the entry to the dining room, Caerwin spotted Marcellus. Her cheeks burned under his heated stare. The torpor induced by her warm bath flooded back, weakening her knees. Senna had fastened Caerwin's hair with twisted strands caught up to her crown, a style most pleasing to Marcellus. She wore the gold torque and the silver and gold bracelets. Senna had dressed her in a blue linen *stola* and matching *palla* commissioned by Marcellus upon her return to Roman camp. The faded blue color displeased her, but Marcellus insisted on it and required a darker blue border along the *stola's* neckline and hem. His eyes glittered as he watched her.

She swallowed, incited not only by the languor of her limbs and the scent of the fragrant oils rising from her bosom, but by the mere sight of Marcellus. He wore a white toga. His handsome face and rugged stature exuded strength and vigor, somehow more powerful without his armor. The muscles and veins of his forearms particularly captured her attention, potent reminders of his position over her in lovemaking. And of his firm grip on the lash. His lips quirked as she stared at him, curling into a half smile at one corner and reminding her of the service of his tongue. Heat spread from her cheeks to her neck as she walked toward him.

As instructed by Senna, Caerwin accepted her place at the near end of the second couch. The position placed her at the corner nearest Marcellus, who reclined at the head couch beside Gaius and his wife Cassia. He stood, taking her hand to make introductions.

"My lovely consort, Caerwin," he said, "is the heiress of a recently deposed native kingdom, the Cornovii. Luckily, I was able to extract her from the battleground before she came to any harm. She has made fast progress in learning our language as well as our ways. I'm taking her to Rome."

Caerwin's cheeks burned as eight sets of eyes settled on her. One by one, the others were introduced. To her left were Messalia and her husband Tartius or Tertius, a local merchant specializing in imports of oil, grain, and other Roman foodstuffs. Across from her, the third couch held Gaius' sister Leticia and the olive-skinned woman Junia. She recognized them from the baths. To Junia's right, a man named Otho made a show of his deference to Marcellus.

"Another Briton savage," Junia remarked. "What possible worth is to be gained from these people? You say she's learned the language?"

Caerwin's nostrils flared at the insult. This woman clearly thought highly of herself. Her hair had been curled into a mound on top of her head, her eyes encircled with sooty powder, and her neck draped with a most fantastic ornament hanging with glittering jewels. Small holes punctured her ear lobes from which dangled gold wire strung with the same jewels as her neckpiece. Beside her, Leticia's flowing *stola* of dark red cloth faded into insignificance.

"Yes," Caerwin said, not waiting for Marcellus to reply. She felt very calm as she took a singsong tone to her voice in mockery of the other woman, thankful no one but Marcellus knew the normal timbre of her voice. "Shall I recite for you?"

Marcellus pressed his hand against hers until pain shot up her arm.

"How adorable. She garbles Latin. Why, yes," Junia said. Her dark eyes sparkled. "What will you recite?"

"Will Horace suffice?" Without waiting and despite Marcellus continuing his pressure on her hand, she cleared her throat.

By all the heavenly gods that rule the world,
And command the human race,
What does this hubbub mean, and all these savage
Faces, turned towards me alone?

Marcellus interrupted her. "She has been a most diligent student with my Greek Antius. He remarks that she has quick mind."

"Fire spouts from her mouth as well as her head," Junia said with a thin smile. "Is that your natural hair color?"

"Quick indeed," Gaius said, intervening in the escalating clash with a reproving glance at Junia. "You say she's of the Cornovii—wasn't that the rebellion of spring last year?"

"The one," Marcellus said.

Caerwin's pulse pounded in her ears as she thought of all the ways she could assail this vapid Junia. With his eyes narrowed in a stern glance, Marcellus released her hand. She swallowed a mouthful of wine as servants brought plates of oysters and stuffed eggs. A man played a lute at the far side of the room and incense burned at the altar of their household gods. The nervous knot in her stomach suppressed her appetite, although at the bath house she'd been starving.

"A curious neckpiece," Leticia remarked.

"If I'm allowed to speak…" Caerwin leveled her gaze at Marcellus.

His mouth quirked, obviously restraining laughter. "We all know Horace," he said. "And his lengthy Epode on the witch's incantation is familiar. But please." He waved his hand.

Let him mock her then. She looked at Leticia, a woman with a sharp nose and weak chin. She wore her hair back with a small cluster of curls fastened at the crown, and her only jewelry was a black stone mounted on the pin fastening her *palla*. Butter surely wouldn't melt in her mouth.

"The torque is the only thing I have left, thanks to almighty Rome. My mother and other kin were sold as slaves. My brother and the other men of our tribe were slaughtered. But this." She fingered the gold band. "Generations of ruling Cornovii have passed this down. As you see, I have nothing to rule."

Leticia's face remained emotionless. Caerwin regretted telling her anything.

"I'm sorry you've suffered so much," Cassia said in a sympathetic voice. "Leticia's husband recently fell in battle here leading Legio II Augusta. She sees a different side of your story. Dear, I assure you a better world lays ahead. You'll find Rome has much to offer."

"I can't imagine more of Rome could be better in any way," Caerwin said.

"Nothing like the savagery or deprivation endemic to this place," Leticia said. "In Rome's long glorious history, we've had our troubled moments. Our emperor Claudius has done well to erase much of the terror of Caligula's reign. And before him, the tyrant Tiberius…"

"Strong words, dear sister, considering we still enjoy the rule of the Julio-Claudian house," Gaius reminded.

"Claudius is a far more tolerant Caesar," Leticia replied. "My late husband—Norbanus Quartus," she added, frowning toward Caerwin. "He suffered great losses under the tyrants, as did many of Rome's finest families. His sister and I…" She put her hand on Junia's arm. "I'm hoping to avoid Rome and go straight to our villa at Tivoli."

Junia turned to her with an insincere smile and placed her hand over Leticia's. "One of our losses was the Palatine *domus*. Such a beautiful home and perfectly situated in Rome. Losing it to royal intrigues infuriated my brother." She shook her head and smiled at Marcellus. "I plan to stay in Rome a short time for business reasons—if our host permits."

Caerwin stared at her and then Marcellus. Did she mean…did he? He made no remark as Junia continued.

"Once my business concludes, I'll return to Neopolis and supervise our silk trade," Junia said. "If I gain my uncle's permission. Like my father, he believes women should only serve husbands. But I thrive on the trade. There's nothing innately inferior in the female mind that she can't tend to commerce."

"Or any other business," Gaius said. He patted his wife's arm. "Running a household being, of course, the primary duty."

"And that difficult enough," Cassia said with a smile. "But dear, with Quartus' passing, your uncle gains control of the Norbanus industry."

"My father's brother is even more infirm than my father in his last years." Junia shook her head. "I hated the loom and the prospect of children even as a child. I wandered the warehouses, studied the shipment manifests, and greeted the many merchants who brought wares to our storerooms. I particularly enjoyed studying the differing qualities of the weave. My father never approved."

"I didn't know," Cassia said faintly, glancing at Felicia.

"When I was pledged in marriage, there were no choices. My husband never appreciated my talents. I calculate mathematics without effort and have skill in bargaining, as my father acknowledged even in my youth. He regretted that he educated me." Junia sipped her wine and looked around the table. "The industry excites me. Something new every day. You know the old fables about silk growing on trees have been overturned by new scientific discoveries."

"Oh, I heard something of this," Cassia said. "Is it Pliny who claims the threads are spun by moths?"

"By their worms," Junia said.

"Disgusting," Leticia said with a shiver. "If his theory proves true, I may stop wearing it."

Otho lifted his cup for more wine and turned to Junia. "Unless Parthia invites yet another war, silk shipments along the old routes would come much faster. Don't your shipping schedules work best with the Parthian road?"

"Quartus instructed his managers to solicit those shipments," Junia said. "Personally, I would expand our operation and buy ships. Less than a hundred ships carrying silk ply the shipping lanes from India each year and the supply lags far behind demand. It's a faster route than overland. The only problem is the mixing of goods—who wants a beautiful *stola* reeking of cloves? I can only hope the Parthian king keeps his promise to stay out of Armenia. Then the roads would stay open and merchants from the east would have a stronger bargaining position."

"Vitellius has done a masterful job in Parthian negotiations," Otho replied. "I served in Legio Twelve there ten years ago when the latest crisis erupted."

"The *Fulminatrix*," Marcellus remarked. "An excellent legion with an illustrious past. Julius Caesar in his victory over Pompey—a most glorious rout!"

Gaius chuckled. "Unless of course you sided with the Senate. Were you with the Fourteenth under Germanicus?" Gaius asked Marcellus. "I can only now speak of the despicable treachery in the murder of that fine man. Everyone saw Tiberius' hand in it."

The men took over the discussion with animated commentary about military actions in northern Gaul and conflicts with the Germanic tribes. Caerwin shifted her attention away from the conversation. Much as she disliked Junia, she found the woman's impertinent style and her knowledge of commerce interesting. As for military actions, she wished to know nothing of Roman battles.

None of these names or places were known to her except the unwelcome reminder of the foot stamp of a thousand armed men, their curved red shields, and the gold lightning bolts emblazoned on their fronts. The smell of death rose around her, so great was the hated memory. She nibbled at a stuffed egg.

"What are your plans, Marcellus?" Gaius asked, gesturing to the attendant for another round of wine.

"Yes," Junia said. "Tell us—do you think you'll miss the excitement of battle?"

Marcellus stared at her briefly. "The excitement? It's a dirty business, cutting men open and watching them die."

"I didn't mean to say you enjoyed killing. But to be a warrior, the courage, the success—gaining new lands for the Empire, winning the praise of your commander—and I'm sure there were spoils. I've heard the natives hold a few fine things." Her eyes fell on Caerwin's torque then shifted back to Marcellus. "Did you make a gift of this to your slave?"

"It was hers," Marcellus said. "And she's not my slave."

"Indeed?" Junia said, cocking her eyebrow.

Caerwin's spoonful of soup stopped halfway to her mouth. What?

"The gods, man, what do you intend?" Gaius' voice rasped through the still night air.

Caerwin shrank to the side of her dark bedchamber window and flattened herself against the wall. She had meant only to look at the stars until the men's voices approached. She held her breath.

"I mean to make her my wife," Marcellus said.

"You can't marry a provincial. She's a *peregrinus* and always will be."

"I had thought to declare her a slave and then free her," Marcellus said. "But as much study as I've be able to gain on recent changes in the law, it seems Augustan reforms require that slaves must reach the age of thirty before they can be freed."

"Yes, that's the law enacted twenty years ago, although many ignore it and no great reprisal follows. We know the way of laws—we can skirt them if we dare and hope no one notices. You can't enjoy that deviation, dear friend. You'll be under pressure to live above reproach. I fear to add to your misery, but there are those in Rome who wish to destroy you."

The voices became more distant and Caerwin risked extending her face into the dark night air. Crickets droned. A breeze rustled, bringing the sharp scent of mint to her nose. The men walked further into the distance and she only managed to hear a few words.

"…Petrus…"

"…monetary damages, and his emotions run to the extreme. He's a…"

She exhaled in frustration as she waited in the dark room. Whatever did Gaius mean, a *peregrinus*? How could she not be a slave?

"*Peregrinus?*" Senna set down the oil lamp and turned back the bed covers before starting to undo Caerwin's elaborate hair arrangement. "The term refers to a person native to a territory conquered by Rome. Not a citizen of Rome."

"Can one such person not marry a citizen of Rome?"

"No—citizens marry only other citizens. That's a strict law."

Marcellus did not come to her that night. Now that he knew he couldn't marry, would he cast her aside? He had never asked her to marry. What if she didn't wish to be his bride?

She sighed. For all real purposes, she had already become his bride and had done since that first day when he ripped off her marriage dress and spread her with his hand. Despite the assault of Scapula and later the salt man, she knew Marcellus as the only man to touch her in a caring manner and bring her to the full pleasure of her body. He had spoken of love. She had thought the same in moments when hatred of Rome did not consume her.

She lay in the moonlight thinking of his lips and how they moved when he talked. She couldn't recall a previous time when she had been in his company for such a long time without him touching her and sparking desire in her body—except when he'd been wounded. Her eyes popped open as she realized that even without his touch, she wanted him—his kiss, the force of his hands on her body, the sting of the lash warming her skin until she trembled.

Her legs threshed under the blanket. The gods! He had threatened. Did he now carry out his threat that he would tease her, bring her to the brink, and then leave her to suffer? Did he mean to hold her aside while he slept with other women? Or men? What if Junia had diverted his attention and even now shared her secrets with him in some other part of this house?

She grasped her breasts with both hands, trying to quench the need that brought her nipples to hard points. Curses on that man. Double curses on her for being so weak.

~~~

The next morning a fresh team of six horses pawed the ground waiting to pull the carriage. More luggage added another baggage wagon and as she and Senna exited the front portal of the residence, she saw Leticia and Junia standing beside the carriage in traveling cloaks. She refused to believe it until Marcellus took her aside.

"These women are of noble families," he said. "It's our privilege to travel with them. Be doubly respectful to Leticia. She still mourns the loss of her husband. Have the same respect for Junia, although it hardly seems she mourns her brother. You will hold your tongue and ignore whatever taunts she might send your way. Do you understand?"

Caerwin ripped her hands out of his. "Why can't they find their own transport? Why must they travel with us?"

"Gaius asked my favor and I've long since agreed to this arrangement. He favors me in other ways as well. Why can't you control your tongue?"

"Have you said that to her? She purposefully incites me."

"Only because she sees that she can. You play into her hands." He took her elbow to steer her further from curious onlookers.

"I know her scheme. I've seen women like her before. *Lupa*," she hissed. "She wants you and thinks to disgrace me and insult me, to bring me down in your eyes." She yanked her elbow from his grip. "You seem well flattered by her attention."

Unexpectedly, the expression on Marcellus' face shifted from a gathering storm as he broke out in a roaring laugh. He lowered his face toward her and took her mouth in a ravishment she had not experienced since before the journey began. He gripped her against his body until she could feel his arousal against her stomach. When he had thoroughly kissed her to the point that her mind spun and her knees weakened, he released her.

His dark eyes gleamed. "Never doubt where my affections lie, little wild cat," he said. "I have no intentions with Junia, whether she knows it or not."

Caerwin straightened her clothing and glanced past Marcellus' arm at the two women. They had not failed to notice the embrace. She shot them a triumphant glance. "Perhaps you should make sure they know it," she said. "But then, perhaps you enjoy the flattery. It only adds to your inflated ego."

He laughed again, pulling her close to his side as he walked her to the carriage.

~~~

As the carriage hurtled down the roadway, hardly a mile passed without Junia's incessant chatter. She spoke of theaters and chariot races and other amusements she looked forward to in Rome and how she had suffered greatly in her months of residence in a barbarous wasteland such as Britannia. She especially went on about how much she enjoyed a particular Roman shop or festival and then, with a pointed glance, remarked not everyone could appreciate the finer points of civilization.

Caerwin huffed at Junia's sideways smirks and grew incensed at her treatment of Porcia. When the slave slipped in adjusting Junia's hair, the accident earned her a brisk slap on the face. Junia made insulting remarks and forced her slave to sit on the dirty carriage floor when ample space remained open on the padded bench seat. Caerwin occupied her imagination by thinking of various tortures to inflict on the dusky shrew.

Much to Caerwin's relief, this day she was not shamed by being tied. She could only imagine Junia's remarks if she were. Marcellus relented on his use of ropes to contain her, his confidence bolstered by the long distance they had traveled. Her resistance had changed, too. Her tears had dried. She grew increasingly numb. The constant motion of the carriage lulled her just as the bath's warm water had done. Marcellus' kiss still tingled on her lips.

Caerwin studied the passing landscape and tried to ignore Junia's chatter along with the noise of the grinding wheels, the horses' hoof beats, or the jangle of the harnesses. Other times the incessant drone of her shrill voice pricked her skin like the tip of a needle and she was forced to turn to Senna to contrive one or another topic in hopes of drowning out the patter. As miles passed, Senna talked in low tones of her early womanhood and a tragic love affair, a story which managed to distract Caerwin not only from the two women but also from the questions still echoing in her mind.

In the long lapses in Senna's conversation, Caerwin's thoughts returned to Marcellus' words. If she was not a slave, how could he 'own' her, tie her, keep her captive? If he couldn't have her as a wife, why did he bring her?

They had journeyed a long distance from any landscape she knew. The familiar hills had given way to rolling terrain within the first day. They had crossed more rivers, streams, and bogs than she could count. Roman legionaries in groups from ten to one hundred thronged the roadways morning and night. The steady movement of the carriage lulled her to contemplation.

Aside from the distance and difficult journey complicating any escape plan, Caerwin grudgingly admitted to her renewed tolerance of Marcellus. He had been the central force in her life for a year and a half, aside from the two months she had managed to stay with the Ordovices. He had cared for her when she wanted nothing but death. She still hated what he had done in leading the Roman army against her people, but she understood Senna's insistent point that he had no choice.

Leaving the great river valley of the goddess Sabrina made her sad. Leaving the ground where her family had lived and died would always hurt her in ways she couldn't express. If she let herself dwell on the reality of leaving the lands of her people and venturing to another part of the world, panic gripped her throat.

But in truth, the continuing annoying presence of Leticia and Junia distracted her. The view outside the carriage window engaged her curiosity. Her desire for Marcellus lingered between her legs, and she couldn't summon the strength to keep fighting.

On the fifth day, the landscape shifted to ever more abundant marshlands and vast flocks of strange birds. The air smelled different. The carriage slowed to shouts from the men on horseback. The road dipped and sloped downhill. Finally the horses stopped. Moments later, a legionary appeared at the carriage door and assisted the two noble women as they stepped outside.

Caerwin followed Senna and Antius, afraid of what lay ahead. As she stepped down, her shoes sank in loose pale earth. As far as she could see, a body of water stretched into the distance. The sight of it froze her heart in her chest. Nothing in her life had prepared her for such a view. Even from the heights of the Wrekin where she could survey distant hills, fields and forest, and the river's sparkling course and marshes across the Cornovii lands, she had never seen such distance, such a stark expense of sky and water.

A stiff breeze tore at her clothing and hair. White water rolled and curled onto the beach with a crashing noise. She stood on sandy ground and stared first at the choppy green water and then along the beach that stretched as far as she could see in both directions. Nearby, a broad river emptied into the sea. Birds wheeled and cried overhead.

"It's the end of the earth," Caerwin muttered.

"It takes only a few hours to cross," Senna remarked. "I assure you there is earth on the other side."

"The gods! This is surely not the natural course of human travel. We are not fish!"

"The gods allow us boats," Senna said, squeezing her arm in encouragement. She gestured to a pavilion where Marcellus stood with a few of his men. "See? He makes generous offerings to Neptune and Salacia. The gods will protect our journey."

"Why must I go?" Caerwin said. "This is my place in the world." She motioned toward the sea. "That is Rome's. They should never have come."

Her hands became clammy as she watched the waves crashing toward her then retreating. They had ventured only a short distance from the carriage, but the rest of their party already walked down a paved roadway toward a platform that extended into the water where floating vessels rocked in the waves. Shouts called back and forth as Junia scolded the men unloading the wagons. Their voices whipped away in the wind.

"If I go, I will have no hope for escape," Caerwin said. "I'll never see my home again."

"Why torture yourself with such thoughts?" Senna snapped. "Does your home still exist? Who is there waiting for you?"

Caerwin stared at Senna. "What provokes you?"

"You provoke me," Senna said. "You cling to the past as if you could go back. You can't. There's nothing wrong with your mind, yet you refuse to use it. Where is your curiosity about new places? Where is your sense of adventure for what might lie ahead? Most of all, where is your heart regarding Marcellus? Do you not see how he helps you and gives you so much, how much he needs your support?"

"What does it matter to you?" Caerwin replied hotly. "You will have a job whether for me or another."

"I care about you, for whatever reason I can't explain. Call it a weakness, I suppose." Senna crossed her arms, frowning. Her hair blew across her face and she pushed it back. "Who would you have if not for me?"

"You care for me out of pity?" Caerwin turned away, trying to subdue a wave of unexpected emotion. "I'm not to be pitied."

"I care for you as if you were my own child," Senna said, putting her arm around her. "The daughter I never had. I wish the best for you, even if you spurn me like you spurn Marcellus."

Caerwin kept her face turned from Senna and refused to follow as the men on the dock called for them. She didn't trust herself to speak. Her throat had tightened.

If she ran, she could outdistance the men. She could climb the steep embankment, take one of the horses, and make good on her hope for escape. For a moment, excitement coursed through her at the prospect.

Then reality set in. The long journey. She had no money, no one to turn to. Even if she escaped Marcellus and the Roman army, what would she have even at the Wrekin? Senna was right. She had no home. She swallowed around the big knot in her throat and blinked tears from her eyes.

She had no home.

Marcellus strode toward her. "What are you waiting for?" he said. "We'll miss the tide."

"Have the gods taken your wits?" she said, motioning toward the sea. "We would die out there."

"We won't die. Roman ships ply the seas every day," he said. "It's a sturdy boat, a *liburna*, what we call a long ship. See the oars extended from the openings? Men sit on benches inside to pull those oars. But with the right tides and wind, the sails do most of the work. We'll make good time."

Caerwin stared at the huge pole extending upward from the center of the ship, at the thicket of oars emerging from the ship's sides and the small figures of men moving along the quay and the ship's deck. The ship itself was larger than the Cornovii meeting lodge, at least one hundred feet long and perhaps five rods wide. Men of her tribe had used small craft to ply the River Severn, but those boats held only two or three men.

"We'll fall to an abyss out there," Antius said, coming close behind Marcellus to mutter his inflammatory remark. "Sea monsters will gobble you up at the edge."

"Antius, enough," Marcellus said. "Take yourself to the ship and leave your remarks." He took Caerwin's arm. "Hurry."

Caerwin took long steps beside Marcellus, hardly able to keep up with his stride. The sandy ground shifted under her footsteps, further eroding her equilibrium. In the distance, other boats rocked on the waves, fishermen hauled in nets, a *liburna* like this one moved far offshore with its big square sail billowed. Men carrying goods hurried past them on the wide pier. The boards underfoot creaked with each passage. The ship rocked, tugging the huge ropes that held it fast. The splash of waves against its sides renewed her terror.

Antius stood at the ship's railing shouting at two men lifting a small trunk. Her trunk, she realized, filled with her garments and the few items she owned. Her hands gripped by two sailors, Senna stepped across the gap to the ship's deck. As Senna walked toward the back end of the ship, Caerwin spotted Leticia and Junia amid the group of men onboard who had accompanied the journey thus far.

These people were all going home.

"We'll miss the tide," the *trierarchus* shouted, a burly man in tight *braccae* and a belted tunic. His conical felt hat folded to the side. "Come aboard."

"Now," Marcellus said, taking her elbow. "They won't wait for us."

"Let them leave, then. I'm not going." She jerked her arm away from his grip and whirled back toward the shore. Her shaky legs picked up strength as she ran. She didn't care that the Wrekin would be deserted or that the ghost of Seisyll roamed the far hills. That was where she should be, not here in this scrap of timber set adrift on endless water.

Before her footsteps ever reached dry land, Marcellus caught up with her. Below, waves sloshed against the quay pilings. The fishy smell of her surroundings gathered in the base of her throat and she thought she might be sick. Even as Marcellus grabbed her around the waist and pulled her next to his body, she held her cold hand over her mouth. Her gorge fell back and she swallowed a mouthful of saliva.

"Do you think that after all this I would allow you to escape?" His voice grated on her ear, harsh and angry. "Stop defying me."

She fought, jabbing with her elbows and ripping at his hands to release his grip. "Do you think that after all this I will give up trying to gain my freedom? I'm not a Roman. Last night you said I wasn't your slave. Let me go, Marcellus. I'm part of this land. These are my rivers, my hills. I need this dirt under my feet. I won't leave. If you take me away, I'll die."

"You will not die. You'll find new rivers, new hills. You'll have gardens and a beautiful, secure home, just as I've promised." Cursing, he hustled her down the gangway and onto the ship's deck. She fought him the entire distance but she couldn't break his tight grasp. Breathless, she stood in his iron grip on the tilting shipboard and refused to acknowledge the critical glances from others.

Shouts went up among the crew. The *trierarchus* directing the ship's operation ordered the marines under his command. At his shout, the thick rope lines were cast off. The line of oars dipped into the water and pushed. The ship lunged eastward.

Looking around in a frantic last hope of escape, she spotted their gear tied under a net behind the small roofed area where Marcellus held her. The sensation of watching the shoreline fall away sent her senses reeling. It was the most bizarre feeling, as if she and the rest of the ship had become the only stationary place on earth while the rest of the world had begun to slowly retreat. Crewmen pulled on ropes causing a great sheet of cloth to rise up the tall mast. Below, along the ship's sides, an even line of oars dipped and rose to the beat of a drum, thrusting the ship forward with each stroke. Steady wind swelled the sail and they moved even faster.

Her breath hitched. Marcellus held her against him with one arm while his other hand gripped the railing. Water splashed against the ship's sides as they coursed along. Another cry went up and the distant drum beat stopped as the rowers shipped the oars and sealed up the lower oar ports.

Land became a distant dark line. Stiff wind whipped the water's surface to white froth, causing the boat to rock forward and back. Men shouted from the high rigging. The sail snapped and billowed.

She cleared her throat and turned to Marcellus, but her words stopped short. His short dark hair lay back in the wind and the tanned skin of his face had taken a rosy hue. For a moment, she could only think of his beauty, the curl of his sensual mouth, the strength of his shoulders. A familiar war waged in her chest, one side wanting only to stay forever in his arms and the other side wanting nothing more than to never see him again. Or to know anything of Rome and its cruel depredations.

"Is it to be like this the whole journey?" she said.

A long silence followed, as if he had to bring himself back from far away. "No," he said finally. "It will be worse."

Chapter Three

Wind howled through the rigging. Dark clouds scudded overhead. The *trierarchus* shouted orders, words Caerwin didn't try to understand. Behind her, legionaries muttered about the strain on the mast. Marines scrambled to lower the sail halfway, reducing the speed. The seas were too high to open the lower oar ports, and the ship wallowed in troughs of high waves. Men on the rowing benches seized their oars and the upper bank of oars immediately buried in the frothing water.

Caerwin's meager breakfast soon flew over the railing as Marcellus held her. Even when she had nothing left, her stomach turned in protest. Her hands shook as she gripped the shelter wall, holding a cloth to her mouth. A mist of sea water coated her hot cheeks. Her stomach ached and her hands trembled. As the ship lifted and dropped, she wanted to curl up on the wet planking of the deck and never again move or speak.

She was not alone in the sickness. A line of legionaries shadowed the railing. She gained some small pleasure to see Junia also heaving over the sides with her face looking distinctly green.

Marcellus spoke in low urgent tones to the *trierarchus*. Caerwin couldn't hear what they said, but the *trierarchus* shook his head and motioned to the sky.

"These storms come up," Marcellus said, returning to the tense knot of people clustered in the small aft shelter. "Wind from the west means it won't be a strong storm. They can't keep the sail up in concern for the mast. We're mid crossing where the waters mix and currents are confused. He's an experienced man. We have nothing to fear, but it may take longer until the winds calm."

"We shall surely die," she groaned as another wave of sickness seized her stomach.

"It's worse than death," Senna said. Her face had gone white under her freckles. "It wasn't like this before.

"These waters have a reputation," one of the legionaries said.

"Not the time for gossip," Marcellus scolded. "We'll be fine."

Caerwin felt his advice for patience was a token gesture in the face of nature's wretched intent. Clearly the gods did not mean for men to cross these waters. Only the arrogance of Rome would lead to any other conclusion. The ship rocked and tossed despite its size and heavy burden. Her desperate sickness relieved slightly after a time as the winds calmed a bit and the ship's movement became more familiar.

~~~

They made landfall at a place called Gesoriacum which lay in the inner reaches of a wide cove where a river spilled into the sea. With the sail down, the last stroke of oars brought the ship to bump against the wharf. The anchor splashed down and crewmen threw out thick ropes to men waiting. The port bustled with activity of wagons, carts, horses, and men. Water lapped against the hulls of nearby ships loaded with amphora, bundles of goods, bags of grain, and men headed the way she had just come. Always men in overpowering numbers, these ants of Rome marching out to conquer the world.

Caerwin hardly cared. The stressful journey across the water left her exhausted. After hours of constant motion, stillness came as an enormous relief. Her knees gave way as she stepped onto the wide gangplank. Marcellus kept her steady as they made their way down the long pier toward the curve of hilly land.

With Senna, Antius, and the rest of their party strangling behind, they walked up the sloping roadway into a sprawling settlement surrounding a walled fort. Vendors wandered along hawking apples, bread, and crafted goods. Streets angled up hillsides past taverns, shops, and homes. Marcellus arranged for a night's stay at a local inn which sat at the crest of one of the hills, a tidy stone and timber configuration similar to the *praetorium*.

Once settled in a small room, Caerwin collapsed on the bed, briefly napping until Senna roused her for dinner. Accompanied by

Senna, they walked to the dining room entry. The smoky air stank of oil lamps and fish. At the end of a long table, Marcellus engaged in conversation with Junia. Caerwin watched as Junia placed her hand on his arm. She said something and he threw back his head in laughter.

"I won't eat," Caerwin said, turning to leave. She lifted her *palla* to cover her head.

"You'll give him to her?" Senna asked, arching her eyebrow.

"What?"

"She wants him. It's easy to see. What man wouldn't be flattered?" Senna steered her firmly toward the table. "She plays her game, but his heart is yours. Unless you keep refusing him."

"I don't want his heart," she said. "Home is..."

Senna's dark glance cut off her words. "The gods, child! Think carefully. This is no time for foolishness."

In the dim crowded room, benches surrounded a long table. The innkeeper and a helper served the meal of fish, vegetables, and bread to several strangers along with the company under Marcellus' watch. She and Senna took a place at the far side. Sour wine flowed freely but she couldn't abide the flavor. Raucous conversation rattled her nerves. She barely tasted her food as she cast furtive glances toward Marcellus, Junia, and Leticia. Finally Caerwin lifted her *palla* to overhang her forehead so that she couldn't see them.

After the meal, she hurried to the bedchamber with Senna. Marcellus arrived a short time later, and with her finger raised in caution, Senna departed. Caerwin sat at the foot of the bed, still fully dressed.

"Have you recovered from the crossing?" he said. The single oil lamp cast his features in shadow.

"What does it matter to you?"

He sat on the bed and began removing his boots. His dark gaze raked her. "It matters."

She turned her face away and said nothing further. Neither did he. She twisted her fingers in the folds of her *stola* as the familiar sounds of his undressing progressed. The waist band with its dagger sheath. The armored vest. When he had stripped down to his tunic, he stood up.

"Shall I undress you?" he said.

"Why not?" she said, trying not to gaze on his muscled body. The lamp cast him in dark and light lines. "I'm your slave, in fact if not in word. Here to please you."

She couldn't make out the expression on his face. He stood in silence for a moment, then leaned down and brushed her lips with his. Tremors shivered through her body.

She was tired in ways she'd never known, worn down from the long journey so far and especially by the terror of crossing the sea. Part of her yearned for his embrace. Did he intend to take advantage of her weakened state?

Yes, of course he did. She crossed her arms. "I'm tired."

"As am I." His lips traced the line of her jaw and neck. His hands held her shoulders then brushed down her arms. He released the pin, unwrapped the *palla* and tossed it aside, then loosed the clasps on her stola so that the garment fell to the tie around her waist. Only the thin fabric of her *tunica intima* covered her breasts.

He bent quickly to take a nipple into his mouth, wetting the cloth covering as he teased the stiff peak. Then the other. The flesh between her legs throbbed.

"Marcellus," she began.

"Don't fight me," he said, his voice stern. "I've wanted you for days, since before we began this journey. It may be weeks before I have privacy enough to take you again."

"Don't take me, then," she said, struggling in his continuing torment of her breasts. He had released her waist tie and sent the *stola* to the floor so that now his hands held free rein on her body. The tunic's wet spots kept her nipples pebbled as his hands grasped her buttocks.

"Jupiter's stones, but your flesh is sweet," he groaned, massaging her backside, gripping and kneading. "There's no spot on your body I don't desire."

His breath warmed her neck as his scent rose, that curious smell that she had known from the first day with this man. Musky and sharp, it sent gooseflesh down her arms.

"Don't you also desire Junia?" she said. "Why bother with me when you could have her?"

"Do you wish me to have Junia?" he said.

"No." She shook her head. "Yes. Have her and send me back. I would take the torment of another crossing if I could be forever free of Rome."

He stood back long enough to rip his tunic over his head then pulled hers off as well. Before her, he stood like a god with his *mentula* erect and straining toward her. His eyelids dipped slightly as he looked on her, as his hands cupped her breasts.

"You would have me leave you?" he said softly. "Never touch you again?"

She nodded but could not form words.

"You would give Junia your place?" he said.

"Why not?" she whispered. "She already takes my place. She holds your attention at every turn."

His low rumbling laughter vibrated in her ears. Again he lowered his mouth to her breasts, holding each in turn as he teased the nipples to aching points. The exquisite torment curled her toes, but she refused to reach for him or admit her growing need. It was only when he touched between her legs to lightly stroke her bared mound that she hopped in frustration.

"Junia could not take your place," he said. "She's an accomplished woman and offers entertaining company, and I'm her escort for the duration of this journey. But, gods preserve me, you're the one who fires my loins."

He crouched in front of her, his hands grazing her legs from her buttocks to her ankles, his thumbs teasing her mound. He held her vulva open to gain access to the tiny hot appendage that throbbed even more as his tongue stroked over it. Using his elbows to spread her legs further apart, Marcellus licked again and grinned up at her when she gasped.

"Don't you like this?"

"I...I can't resist the need you provoke," she said. "I wish it weren't so."

He leaned forward again to lick that same spot. "You're like a stubborn mule, my little queen. Only the whip tames you."

His ministrations progressed at a maddeningly slow pace, little flicks and nibbles accompanied by the occasional trust of a single finger into her increasingly wet opening. She burned for him. Her swollen breasts throbbed, connected in a line of fire to the coals smoldering between her thighs. Still he did nothing more than to crouch at her feet, teasing and playing until her body quivered.

"By the gods, I die," she said.

"By the gods, indeed. They have made perfection in you," he murmured, plying again with his finger. "There is no perfume, no honeyed wine, sweeter than your nectar."

She yearned for his penetration. Fever grew inside her, desperate for him to fill her. This tender love play far surpassed the lash in its torture. His fingers danced over her and in her, now stroking in steady rhythm as he took her clitoris between his lips to suck.

A loud knock rattled the door. "Sir! Are you there?"

"May a thousand curses fall on this man," Marcellus muttered. He stood up and grabbed his tunic as he stalked to the door. "What?" he bellowed.

"There's a messenger just arrived, says he must see you."

"*Futuo!*" Marcellus cursed as he jammed his arms through the tunic. "Who sends it?"

"Calidius Vedius."

"Cal..."

Marcellus stood without moving. Caerwin thought he even held his breath. His eyes met hers in a look so distant her heart skipped a beat.

"I'll be right there," he said.

"Whatever it is, let them wait," Caerwin said, clasping her arms tightly around her chest.

"I can't do that." He pulled on his boots, dropped a kiss on her forehead, and rushed out of the room.

~~~

Rain crept around the carriage shutters and dripped onto the floor by Caerwin's feet. Marcellus had not returned to her from his meeting with the messenger and she had spent the night alone in the room. The desire he had kindled remained a knot low in her abdomen.

For two days they had endured drenching rain and everything in the carriage stank of horse dung and wet wood, not to mention the spicy fragrance soaking the two noble women's handkerchiefs which they kept close to their noses. Antius hovered uncomfortably on a stool perched between the two benches so that Marcellus could find space on the bench. Senna sat between Caerwin and Marcellus, an arrangement that annoyed Caerwin.

"This uncle you mention," Marcellus said, directing his words to Junia. "Do you know if he would give testimony on my behalf?"

Their continuing conversation had brought Caerwin's nerves to screaming pitch. With little gestures and flattering smiles, Junia intensified her flirtation with Marcellus. Caerwin harbored the growing suspicion that the messenger who interrupted them that night had been none other than Junia. Otherwise why hadn't he returned to the bedchamber?

He had hardly shared a smile with her since. He brushed off her questions about the message, saying simply that these were matters best kept private. Often when she looked at him, his jaw pulsed and his eyes took a faraway look. When he did talk, he brought up topics of no interest to her and addressed his conversation to the two women.

If he meant what he said that he cared nothing for Junia's attention, why did he give her audience?

"He did most of the traveling for silk purchases. He brought us children trinkets when he came to the port." Junia leaned forward to rest her arms on her knees, arranging the folds of her gold-colored *palla*. "I was his favorite. I think he would do whatever I asked."

"He also traded in slaves at a market near Syria," Leticia said.

"You're thinking of Side," Junia said. "Near Lycia. The slave trade centers there and has done for the last century since the lands came under Roman rule. My uncle brought us several accomplished slaves from there. My tutors were Syrian." Her gaze leveled on Caerwin. "Their people were far more advanced than the tribes of Britannia. By the time of Rome's infancy, they had raised up temples and cities, watched them suffer the ravages of time and war, and built them yet again. They've known writing for a thousand years. The Persians and the Greeks have both made it their vassal state, and now Rome. Unlike your savage lands, Syrians have something to offer Rome besides manual labor."

"Or nothing to offer," Caerwin said in annoyance. "Once they've used up the wealth, what's left to interest them?"

"She makes a point," Antius said. Caerwin stared at him in surprise. "Greece is much the same," he said, stretching one of his legs out in front of him. "Roman coffers find little value in our country these days, now that they've taken all we had. Except the people. As with the Syrians, they value those of us who are educated. Before their exposure to Greece, the Romans lived in bare houses without ornament. They saw our columns, statues, mosaics on the floors, tapestries and paintings on the walls, and copied it all."

"You forget that we grew from the Etruscans, an earlier people of Roman lands who perfected their culture. Yes, we share much with Greece—as it was in its glory," Marcellus said. "But early Greece learned much from Egypt and Babylonia. That's the way of it. Why shouldn't we adopt what other great cultures have learned? Any student of Greece can tell you how much Rome has gained from the Greeks in trade, banking, administration, art, literature, philosophy, even earth science. I appreciate my father's effort to secure a Greek as my tutor."

He nodded toward Antius. "What use would any of this learning serve if it couldn't stand the test of time and the natural course of decay? Greece decayed. It lost its strength just as Egypt before it. You should be proud that what Greece had developed was deemed important enough that Rome took it over."

"Not exactly the facts," Antius countered. His face flushed dark with anger. "Roman armies killed us, raided our temples, and subjugated our people. They've added nothing to what we preserved."

Marcellus eased back and took a drink from his flask of water as the carriage rocked forward. "Odd that in all our years, we've never aired our views on this topic. I can't blame you for allegiance to your ancestry. But surely you'll acknowledge that Rome has done nothing that Greece hadn't done a hundred times before. As far back as Troy, Greeks plundered their neighbors. It was the great Greek general Alexander who brought down the long success of Egypt. Even the Macedonian defeat followed on the heels of earlier Greek victories. The gods favored Rome in that contest. We had only half the men that fought under Perseus."

"What does it matter?" Junia exclaimed. "These old battles took place long ago. The world today is Rome's—whatever we need, we can take. Syrian tabbouleh, Greek art, these live on as part of Rome."

Antius ran his hands through his hair and straightened his cloak. "Especially true of Greece. I repeat the words of your own

Horace—'Greece, though captured, took its wild conqueror captive.'"

Caerwin's gaze lingered on Antius as she pondered his words. Although he had spent many hours teaching her the history of Rome and Greece, those lessons had come amidst her studies of words and language, maps and social habits. She hadn't fully understood the scope. Only at this moment did the expanse of knowledge she had yet to grasp confront her. Her surprise at Antius' defense against Junia ripened into appreciation for what his people had suffered.

What of the Cornovii past or tradition could stand in comparison to these more advanced civilizations? How many other lands had advanced so far past the Cornovii? Maybe Junia had the right to look down on her. The Cornovii had no books, no words that recounted their traditions. There were stories she'd heard since her earliest memory, long complicated accounts of their rulers and battles, marriages that joined tribes, even old legends of early people who raised the standing stones. The task of memory in preserving those tales was not given to the women but to the men. Perhaps the older women who all their lives had heard these long-sung tales could recount at least part of the tradition. But for herself, she could remember only the names of a few kings. The men were gone and with them the stories. Nothing remained.

Perhaps Senna spoke truth that as a captive of Rome, Caerwin would gain much more than she lost. How did one measure the value of family or tribal tradition? Her gaze settled on Porcia and her wretched posture at Junia's feet. No harm fell greater than the simple fact of slavery, humans ripped from their families, homes, and communities and forced to serve masters where before each person had answered to no man.

Everything that had been Cornovii now seemed like water seeping through her fingers.

"What happened to your family, Antius?" she asked.

The older man's eyebrows rose. He seemed momentarily without speech then his posture straightened. "The Kleitos were longtime citizens of Athens. My great grandfathers fought unsuccessfully against Sulla's legions. They all died in the conflict. What Sulla did to our temples, to the entire city of Athens should win him eternal torment in Tartarus. I pray for it."

He ran his hands through his thinning hair. "After a generation in the high country trying to survive as a farmer of goats and olives, my father returned to the city and managed to improve his standing. He worked as a clerk for the Roman storehouses and insisted on education for his children."

"Does he still live?" Caerwin asked.

"He died nine years ago," Antius said. "My mother before that. But they lived as free people despite how many around them fell into slavery. My father never borrowed money."

"You were young when first brought into my household," Marcellus said. He studied Antius. "Did you come willingly?"

Antius looked at him with a grim smile. "Willingly? I had no choice unless to join an auxiliary. I'm not built for battle."

"I also had no choice," Marcellus said. "Even men born to noble Roman families must fight. It's the way of the empire."

"What happens when the empire has conquered every land of the earth and plundered all its riches?" Caerwin said. "What's left?"

"Those days are far off, if they ever come," Leticia remarked. "Just consider the spices and silk my husband traded. Britannia provides a wealth of grain, salt, and meat. And metals like silver and gold. Quartus told me the lands to the east are full of treasure. The gods are pleased by faithful worshippers and Rome honors its gods. We offer generously of what we gain."

"While the people are slaughtered," Caerwin said. "Is that the way of your gods?"

"Many more become useful slaves than die," Junia said. "That's the way of it. There is all of Africa and its dark secrets.

Gold, ivory, grain. The riches of Egypt alone could sustain us for a hundred years."

"Leeches feed off our bodies much the same way," Caerwin said. "Is there no shame in Rome taking what is not Rome's?"

"The gods demand that Rome advance the world," Marcellus said.

"What god said this?" Caerwin said. "Wait, I know the answer. Rome says it, so it must be true."

"It's the way of the world," Antius said in a weary tone. "Just as the wagon rocks along this wretched roadway. Just as rain falls from the sky. These things are the will of the gods."

"A malleable will it seems," Caerwin said. "Call it the will of the gods or Rome's destiny, it's really just armed men taking by force whatever they can."

"Where would you be today, Cornovii princess?" Junia said, "If Rome had not come to your land, would you not still eat lowly foods and sleep on the ground? Would you not wear your wretched homespun cloth and wander the hillsides plucking wild greens? You enjoy the ownership of an important man who is willing to endure your constant harassment." She flashed a smile at Marcellus. "I for one would not have the patience."

Caerwin lunged across the short distance to Junia and grabbed her hair before slamming the woman's head against the carriage wall. Junia's fingernails bit into Caerwin's neck, ripping the flesh. Marcellus tore them apart then clasped a strong arm around Caerwin's middle to throw her back into her seat.

"Enough," he said in a hoarse voice. "Caerwin, for the sake of the gods, have you no respect? Junia, curb your tongue."

Senna's steady grip on Caerwin's arm forced her to stay seated. "The day has been long," Senna said in a low tense voice. "We all feel stifled for air."

"There is nothing to respect in a woman who throws herself at a man," Caerwin said in a trembling voice. "I would gladly spend the rest of my life as a Cornovii than spend one day as one who finds herself so ugly she must paint her face to be satisfied with her appearance."

Porcia gasped and turned to see her mistress's reaction. Junia's expression shifted briefly as her lips formed a thin line. Then she laughed. "Oh, the savage *Brittunculi* fails to find the pity she craves so she attempts witty discourse. How tired you make us." She looked again at Marcellus and smiled. "If we can set aside this bothersome interruption, I should like to ask about your fleet and whether we might find some useful exchange. With my brother Quartus gone and with my uncle's indulgence, I intend to expand the Norbanus enterprise. It would profit our traffic to possess our own means of shipping. If you would be interested in divesting your estate of its vessels, or at least part of that fleet, I'd be quite eager to hear what price you would require."

"It's premature to consider a sale," Marcellus said. "Much weighs on me. The managers assure me in brief letters but until I see the accounts and verify them, I won't take any action. And there are other legal matters…"

His words trailed off. Caerwin turned to see his hands clenched together and his gaze cast down. She grudgingly admitted to the cleverness of Junia's tactics. If Marcellus saw through her ploy, why did he encourage her? Surely nothing in his obligation to Gaius required that he hang on the woman's every word. She folded her arms and leaned into the corner. Outside the shuttered windows and the continuing splash of rain, surely the countryside of Gaul stretched out in miserable sameness.

~~~

Each night found the party at ever more grim lodging—small rooms and few so that the women lodged in one crowded space with the slaves left to sleep on the floor. Senna whispered about fleas and other vermin. Everyone grumbled about the food and especially the pedestrian quality of the wine which no amount of sweetening could improve.

Roadside stations required proof of the emperor's permission to travel the imperial road, which Marcellus could provide, and payment per person, which he also provided. Caerwin knew little of the transactions or the amounts required, but Marcellus grew increasingly short tempered which she assumed had to do with his costs. Whatever favorable mood he might summon benefited the two guests.

Caerwin had long since lost her temper with the women and with Marcellus' concessions to them. Leticia hardly missed a moment to lecture on matters of religious devotion. At each stop, she gave offerings to Adiona and Abeona, goddesses of safe journeys. She frequently launched into discussion of the role of women in producing children, caring for the home, and honoring the gods, words clearly meant for Junia. In private, Senna related information from Porcia that Junia had been divorced the previous year and the husband remarried. This news cheered Caerwin in countless ways.

The weather didn't help. Three days of rain impeded their progress and kept them in hostile closed company within the carriage. Caerwin retreated from the conversation, periodically lapsing into deep melancholy about the growing distance between her and her homeland. At every shift in his position, Marcellus captured her reluctant attention—his familiar hands, the strength of his arms, his legs, the timbre of his voice. Then Junia's shrill voice and caustic remarks reinvigorated Caerwin's anger.

On the fourth night, they stopped at a large settlement named Augusta Suessionum. She stood outside the carriage to stretch. The sky had cleared to a bank of dark clouds in the west and a few early stars emerging overhead. A wide river rolled through the town, spanned by a sturdy bridge where a smaller stream coursed into the larger.

The settlement's homes and shops and some larger official buildings covered two adjacent low hills. Walking felt wonderful and she was disappointed in the short distance to the inn. It consisted of rooms built behind a tavern which enjoyed a healthy trade of locals as well as travelers. Marcellus left the women by the fire pit while he obtained a flagon of wine.

"The fire feels good," Senna said, extending her legs. "The journey already wears on me and we've only just started."

Marcellus set down five cups and poured wine. "Better than the last," he said after taking a drink. "Thank the gods. Now if the food serves well…"

"Please Juno let the beds be free of vermin," Letitica said. "I long for a decent night's sleep."

"We can't be assured of anything," Junia said. "Take a look at the clientele."

Caerwin scanned the room as she sipped her wine, eager to gain some relief from a crushing headache. Oil lamps sat along the walls, sending their flickering illumination down on tables crowded with a confusing assortment of people—mostly unshaven men in rough dress, some staring in their direction. No wonder Marcellus still wore his sword. Nearby, their retinue of armed legionaries took up two tables, a further deterrent to anyone who might think to bother their party. Serving women carried drinks and food back and forth to the tables, and some accompanied men at the tables. Loud conversation and laughter filled the low-ceilinged room.

"I want desperately to walk," she said, motioning to the doorway. "I need exercise. Could we not step out there?"

"Not safe," Marcellus said. "I won't trouble my men to accompany us."

"Might I ride then, tomorrow? If the sky is clear? I can't bear sitting another day."

His brow wrinkled more deeply.

"I must," she insisted. "I would wear *braccae* and a tunic. I would wrap myself in my *palla* if necessary."

His mouth twitched. "A novel idea. But foolish. You'd quickly tire of the horse's back."

"Surely you don't encourage her," Junia said.

"Let me tire then," Caerwin said, glaring at Junia. "Even a few hours out of this unpleasant company would be welcome."

"Definitely a savage," Junia said. "What proper woman would consider such a thing?"

"Who asked you?" Caerwin snapped. "You probably couldn't stay seated on a horse if your life depended on it."

Marcellus sighed. "Can we just have dinner?"

The next day Caerwin made use of a pair of Marcellus' *braccae*, although the size of them required her to fold them around her waist to hold them up. Senna tried to deter her, but she dismissed the older woman's concerns with a flip of her hand. She wore her tunic with its hem lifted to the top of her thighs, long socks wrapped under her shoe laces, and the *palla* covering her head, shoulders, and torso with the last of its length settling across her lap. More than one man surveyed her with a questioning look. She didn't care.

The eastern sky had barely lightened when they set off on the stone-paved road across flat land flush with crops ready for harvest. The morning air smelled sweet. Birds sang. A few white clouds hung in the sky. Marcellus rode to the center of the roadway with her beside him while the two front legionaries rode immediately behind.

She thrilled to the rush of air as she rode. After days of rain, the sunny morning felt wonderful. At first every other concern flew from her thoughts. The horse sat sturdy and reassuring under her and the grip of the reins gave her control. But even though Marcellus had chosen the smallest of the horses, her thighs soon ached. By midmorning, her bottom burned from slamming against the saddle. She couldn't very well rein down to a walk—the entourage moved at a steady trot.

She urged her horse forward to ride beside Marcellus in order to exchange conversation, soliciting his comments on the lay of the land and the progress of their journey. He talked about his march with the Fourteenth to the coast from the Rhine. He described how

Gaul spread far wider than Britannia. If they were lucky, only a half moon would pass before they reached the south shore. Once through Gaul, they faced more distance by boat.

Soon, though, she gave up talking. Her words jumped from her chest as her bottom slammed against the horse's back and Marcellus grinned at her efforts. Even with the *braccae* to protect her legs, the movement chafed and bruised. Occasionally Marcellus would look at her with a questioning expression and she would force a smile.

They stopped for lunch beside a cleared field. She slid off the horse, biting back tears at the pain between her legs. Senna joined her as they retired to some nearby bushes. Walking helped ease the stiffness in her legs and it was a lovely place to look around. Framed against the blue sky and surrounding green forest, gleaming yellow fields marched off to blue hills in the distance. The air smelled faintly of earth and ripe grain.

"Are you ready for the carriage?" Marcellus loomed over her, shading her from the bright sunlight.

She tore off a bite of the dense bread. "I'll adjust."

"You won't be able to walk by the end of the day," he said.

"I won't need to walk. Go," she said, waving her hand. "Tend to the delicate ladies waiting for your next word."

"You have to stop reacting to Junia," he said. "She amuses herself by baiting you. You fall into her trap."

Caerwin paused chewing to give Marcellus a look of disbelief. "The gods! You're the one falling into her trap. Oh, I might buy your ships. Oh, what a strong man you are." She shook her head. "Have you no awareness of how she plays you?"

"I know what I'm doing," he said tersely. "Her connections will prove useful. You don't know all the forces at work. At any rate, there's no quenching her, especially by a Briton."

The bread and cheese Caerwin had eaten so far congealed in a knot halfway to her stomach. "Is this how it will be, then? I'm to be treated as a lesser human because I'm not Roman? How can you bring me to this?"

He tried to put his arm around her, but she whirled away trying not to flinch from the movement.

"It doesn't have to be about you," he said. "I've provided the clothing, the attendance of a trained maidservant, and a tutor, but you must learn for yourself how the women of Rome behave. I have concerns of much greater magnitude than your irritation with Junia. For the gods, Caerwin, do you always think only of yourself?"

Stunned by his harsh reprimand, she raised her fist, wishing she could hit him hard enough to make him understand. Her voice shook as she spoke. "If that witch Junia is the example of how I must behave, I will happily remain a savage."

Caerwin didn't wait for his response, but tucked her remaining cheese and bread into the folds of her wrapped *palla* and stalked back to her horse. The exercise of her stiff legs cost her dearly, but she would not limp.

The beast snuffled as it grazed the thick grasses. She gripped the long mane and rested her forehead against the horse's neck. What Marcellus said cut to her core. He echoed Senna.

Had she overlooked some key point? How could she ever learn to act like a woman of Rome? From birth, these women had been trained in the manners, words, and traditions of Rome. Even the most diligent study could not gain that for her.

Besides, she argued silently, who would want to be like Junia? She was evil in the most cunning way, always watching for a moment to slip in her knife. Having once made her stab, she just as quickly took on the part of the aggrieved party. She was a cheat and liar…Caerwin couldn't think of enough words to describe all the circuitous paths of Junia's depravity.

Gritting her teeth, she threw herself onto the horse, only barely able to avoid crying out.

Was he right? Did she only think of herself?

~~~

The journey resumed at a punishing speed. The pain of her riding brought tears to her eyes. Surely she could endure, but as each mile passed and with each torturous slap of her thighs against the horse, she hardly controlled her need to stop riding. The day would never end.

At first, she didn't make sense of a loud crack that broke the drone of carriage wheels and horses hooves. Marcellus pulled up as they turned to look behind. Then she saw the carriage tilt wildly to its front corner as a wheel spun away from the coach. Cries rose inside the carriage as the axle dropped.

Marcellus wheeled his horse around and kicked its sides, sending it lunging toward the carriage. The wagon master's shouts echoed through the air. She pulled up, holding position at the front along with the legionaries.

The team of horses spooked and the carriage hurtled forward. Her horse cantered sideways as she maneuvered out of the carriage's path. The legionaries tried to block the runaway team, but the horses were wild-eyed. They thundered past dragging the carriage. A distance later as she watched in disbelief, the broken axle end caught on a seam between the paving stones and flipped the conveyance sideways.

Louder screams pierced the air as the carriage slid fully onto its side, dragging behind the horses. The sound of rending boards and groaning of wood against stone slowed as the weight of the carriage pulled on the team. Galloping down the distance, Marcellus and two legionaries grappled with the terrified horses and finally pulled them to a stop.

As if dreaming, Caerwin watched as rough men ran silently from the adjacent woods. Rudely dressed and wielding swords and lances, they immediately attacked Marcellus and the two legionaries. She turned behind to the legionaries with the two baggage wagons. Shouts erupted as more men ran toward them from the trees.

She kicked her horse, clinging to the reins as she detoured off the road and away from the fighting. Then she changed her mind, steering the horse back toward Marcellus as she realized she might fall prey to even more attackers. She kept the horse in motion, crossed then re-crossing the road as she struggled to determine her safest position.

At first the Romans fought from horseback, giving them advantage over the men on the ground. Shouts, grunts, and the clang of weapons reamed the afternoon silence. The bandits seized one of the baggage wagons, disabling the wagon master with a blow to the head and steering the team of mules off the road.

Without shields or the benefit of any organized formation, one then another of the outnumbered legionaries fell or were dragged from their horses. Her horse spun as she wheeled around trying to stay beyond the reach of the brigands.

Dismounted, Marcellus and the one surviving front legionary stood back to back to fight. Behind her, the rear guard legionaries formed a tight knot in the same tactic as Marcellus. As she watched, one after another of the thugs fell back clutching mortal wounds.

Despite her effort to find a safe place, a man ran up to her and seized her horse's bridle. A dense beard covered his lower face. He wore a dark cloak thrown over his shoulder. A knife glinted in his hand.

She plunged her boot into his chest. He grabbed her foot, but she yanked away. She kicked the horse's sides but the man's grip didn't relent.

Another man appeared on the other side of her horse. "Your gold," he yelled in coarse Latin. "Give it."

"Curses on you!" she shouted, trying again to pull her horse free.

The horse circled the man, rearing as she kicked its sides. Its front hooves nicked the man's legs coming down and the man swore as he lost his hold on the bridle. The second man grabbed her clothes as he tried to dislodge her from the horse.

Caerwin leaned forward to urge the horse to run, but the first man grabbed her leg and pulled her down. She fell sideways, hitting the ground hard on her side. For a moment, she couldn't breathe.

He crouched over her with his knife held to her throat.

"We'll take it then," he said.

She felt the knife blade press her skin. Watching him with strange detachment, she noted the stench of his breath and the short scar marking his cheek. Brown hair hung around his face in oily strands. He studied her with dark eyes.

"You're of the tribes, are you not?" he said, fingering her hair. As he spoke, the other man seized the familiar gold band. It yielded to his grasp, twisting off her neck. Visions of the salt man rose in her mind. This time she had no knife.

The second man's hands skimmed her breasts and down past her waist as he searched for more valuables.

"She's got nothing," he said.

"Go on then," the first man said. "I'll bring her along."

The second man ran away with her torque. Sounds of fighting continued. Dimly, she heard men shouting from the woods. Had all the legionaries died? Had Marcellus?

"Are you of the tribes?" the first man repeated.

"Cornovii," she said hoarsely. "Of Britannia."

His eyes flickered. She had thought he would kill her or drag her away, but he stood up, holding the knife loosely as if he hadn't decided what to do. She licked her lips.

He turned at the sound of a horse approaching at full gallop. Before she could speak, before she could comprehend what was happening, a sword flashed through the air and the man's head flew off his body. His torso bent slightly as he fell backwards.

The horse's hooves skidded to a stop, throwing up dirt. In moments Marcellus knelt beside her, his eyes black as night.

"Are you harmed?" he said.

"No," she said, swallowing as she shook her head. "Not by his knife. I came down hard from the horse." Her hand went to her neck. "They took my gold."

He pulled her to a sitting position. "Broken?"

She tested her movement. "No, I think," she said.

With his help, she stood. Pain lanced from her hip down her right leg—she couldn't put full weight on it. She looked up at Marcellus and realized blood dripped down his arm.

She stepped back to examine him more fully. His breath came heavily. Veins protruded along his sweat-glazed neck. A terrible frown darkened his eyes and tightened the lines of his mouth. A gash lay open along his left arm above the elbow. Nicks and cuts marred his hands and forearms. His sword remained tightly gripped in his right hand, blood running to its tip.

"Have they gone?" she said, looking around. One of the baggage wagons remained.

"The ones that can," he said. His attention shifted far ahead where the carriage remained on its side. "Can you ride?"

"I think so."

He motioned and shouted orders to the rear guard. Once mounted, it took only moments for them to reach the carriage. Two legionaries climbed to the top to pull open the door. The wagon master lay on the ground some distance behind, groaning loudly.

She heard Antius voice. "We can't climb out," he shouted.

"Throw me the rope," Marcellus yelled to Antius. "Can you find it?"

The carriage rocked with Antius' movement.

Marcellus shouted to a legionary holding the team. "Duccius, bring the team around."

Long minutes passed while Marcellus and Duccius fastened the rope between the carriage frame and the team's harness. The men gripped the rigging on the lead horses and walked them away from the carriage. Creaking, the battered conveyance eased upward and then slammed to its three remaining wheels with a loud thump. The door immediately flew open and Antius emerged.

"The women," he said hoarsely. "Senna."

Marcellus plunged through the doorway. Caerwin looked inside. Senna lay on the far side of the sloping carriage floor, slumped with her head at a terrible angle and her clothing wrapped around her body. Leticia slumped at the end of the bench holding her arm. Junia and Porcia sat dazed and weeping, struggling to stand.

Caerwin stepped up to enter the carriage.

"No," Marcellus said. "Stay out. Make a place where I can lay her."

Caerwin spread her *palla* on the ground beside the road. Marcellus knelt as he gently lowered Senna. Her eyes stared open.

"Senna!" Caerwin grabbed her hand, chafing it between her own. Her throat closed on the name even as she spoke it.

Marcellus returned to the carriage. Junia's wails sent the hair up on Caerwin's neck. Moments later, Junia emerged followed by Marcellus, who carried the swooning Leticia. He set her nearby on the end of Caerwin's *palla*, where she groaned and wept holding her arm. Blood caked around her mouth and her cheek was swollen.

Caerwin gazed only briefly at Junia who also nursed wounds. But Senna…no breath passed her nostrils. Senna was dead.

Chapter Four

Summoned by the two legionaries Marcellus dispatched on the best horses, help finally arrived from the nearest roadhouse. Darkness had fallen by the time a wagon delivered them to an inn in nearby Durocortorum, a well-established Roman town. Marcellus remained with the carriage until the last of the dead legionaries had been retrieved from the scene and brought to the village.

As soon as they arrived at the inn, Junia and Porcia attended Leticia in one of the inn's rooms. The woman had fainted several times from the pain and her dark eyes hung eerily in a face blanched pasty white. Her forearm bent at an unnatural angle. A *medicus* arrived minutes later, an older man who stooped slightly and had a habit of running a hand over his balding head. Led by Porcia, he hurried to Leticia.

A few other people occupied seats in the tavern, gawking openly at the disheveled newcomers. Antius poured wine in both their cups as they waited for Marcellus.

"She was a good woman," Antius said, clutching his cup. He winced as he lifted it to his mouth. "One of the few I've admired."

Caerwin stared at him blankly, unable to organize her thoughts. Senna. This woman who had become her best friend, who treated her like a beloved daughter. How could she be gone?

Caerwin didn't calculate how much time passed before Marcellus finally joined them. He sat heavily on the bench beside Antius who poured wine and pushed it into Marcellus' hand.

Grim lines creased the sides of Marcellus' mouth. The expression on his face startled Caerwin. He looked like an old man. Blood continued to leak from the gash on his bicep and the thought occurred to her, out of the blankness, that he might die.

"The *medicus* needs to sew you," she said.

He stared at her without speaking as Antius hurried to the innkeeper. Several minutes later, the doctor returned. He rinsed the wound thoroughly before bathing it in honey and sewing it with fine sinew. Somewhat revived by the wine and pinched by the sewing, Marcellus fidgeted and cursed.

"Gaius warned there might be brigands plundering the traffic on this road," he said, grimacing as he tried to stand up. He retrieved coins from his belt pouch and pressed them into the *medicus'* hand. "I failed to observe proper vigilance."

Caerwin exchanged glances with Antius. The exhausted group sat around a fire without much conversation as the innkeeper delivered bread and bowls of hot stew. She had no appetite.

"I've allowed his sister to be gravely injured," Marcellus said after a long silence. "She can't continue the journey." He looked at Caerwin with a stricken expression. "And we've lost Senna."

"A sizeable loss," Antius said.

"I should have checked the wagons!" Marcellus said. "The axle was cut partway. My men…" He dropped his head into his hands. "We survived years in battle together—the worst places, the most dangerous conflicts—Germania, Britannia. To be killed on the public road. It's a travesty. It's a failure of my duty."

"You did not fail in your duty," Antius said. "You've lost four men and Senna but the rest of us survive. Leticia will recover. Surely there are those in this town who know Gaius and would offer hospitality to her." He waited but Marcellus said nothing. "It's a terrible occurrence," Antius continued. "But it's not your fault. There's nothing to be done now."

Their attention shifted as Junia and Porcia returned. Marcellus stood up and Junia took the opportunity to solicit his embrace. He avoided Caerwin's gaze as he put his arm around Junia and offered quiet words of comfort.

"Skin is torn off my back," Junia said. "Porcia suffers a swelling on her head—there's nothing for it. I hurt to breathe but he found no ribs broken." Her eyes were wet. She rested her head against his chest. "I grieve for Leticia. She's in great pain."

Caerwin stiffened at Junia's bold contact with Marcellus but said nothing. Her fingers wandered to her neck. It felt bare without the torque.

The gold piece had been passed down for generations and worn by their leader—her grandfather, father, her brother Virico. How many times had her fingertip wandered to a dent on its side, a scar from one of many battles they had fought and won to protect their hillforts and herds. Its loss shocked her. She felt as if a cold veil had settled over her, a requiem for her tribe whose last marker was now truly wiped from the earth.

Dreams of Seisyll haunted her sleep. He wandered the abandoned battleground where she last saw him, his white hair blowing in the wind. Surely now Senna wandered too.

~~~

A process of attending the dead commenced early the next morning. The disposition of remains consumed Marcellus who stalked around with an ashen face and terrible frown. In the absence of home or family for the dead, he engaged a priest of the Temple of Jupiter to accept the bodies and prepare them for cremation. Senna and the men were laid out in the recesses of the temple. Marcellus spoke words before a handful of priests in attendance, mentioning the names of the dead and what he knew of their lives.

Caerwin stood beside Senna's body and used her comb to smooth the gray-streaked russet hair. Familiar hands folded across the waist of the stiff body, hands that had bathed her, fashioned her hair, held her close. Her eyes had been closed and a coin placed on her mouth, evidently a Roman tradition.

Reluctantly, she had gone through Senna's things. Most of it she gave to the priest for distribution to those in need. It wasn't much—her modest wardrobe, shoes, hair combs and small statues of Juno, Minerva and another goddess. When she came to the pot of earth, she brushed what had spilled back into the pottery container and held it between her hands.

It was all she had left.

Even though she willed tears to release her anguish, she couldn't cry. This pain on top of all her other pain had taken her to a new place. She felt cold and numb. Her body hurt, not just from her fall but in her heart. She wished she knew more of Senna's native Atrebates tribe, where their lands had been located. She might have found someone who knew their traditions. It seemed wrong that Senna would be buried by Roman custom.

Standing at Senna's side, she regretted her hateful resistance to Senna's advice. How could she have made it through all these months at the fortress without Senna's kind words and helping hands, her tender regard? Finally something inside her loosened. Tears began rolling down her cheeks as she thought of all the times Senna had soothed her, complimented her on her beauty, her strength. Until now, she hadn't let herself acknowledge how much Senna comforted her, how much her advice pushed her toward a more mature outlook. What good was it now to realize such things when she couldn't embrace Senna or tell her how much it meant to know she cared?

With her eyes swollen from crying, Caerwin waited outside on the temple steps along with Antius. Marcellus met with the temple priests to provide funds so that when the ceremony of cremation could be arranged, a healthy sow would be offered to Ceres. Once the disposition of the legionaries' and Senna's bodies had been settled, Marcellus dictated a lengthy message addressed to Gaius and sent it by paid messenger. After speaking again with the tribune in charge of the city, he accompanied Leticia to a family willing to host her until she recovered.

The next morning, a contingent of road guards arrived to report their long effort in surrounding countryside in rousting farmers in their search for the bandits. They had followed tracks made by the heavily loaded baggage wagon, but the trail eventually led back to the road nearer Suessionum and disappeared on the stone. The torque had vanished along with the robbers. The expression in Marcellus' eyes when he told her only added to her sense of loss. Nothing of the wagon's contents had been recovered. Trunks belonging to several of the legionaries and Leticia had been lost.

Beyond that brief update, Marcellus related little of his transactions. He left the inn early and didn't return until late, often with Antius limping along several paces behind him. Caerwin welcomed the delay in their journey. Her body ached, especially the hip which hit the ground when she fell from the horse. Junia complained of weakness in her left shoulder and carried herself awkwardly from the bruising on her back. Porcia suffered headaches but kept her characteristic silence. None of them voiced their grievances at any length as it was Leticia who had suffered the worst of it. The pall of death hung over them.

At length, Marcellus announced the continuation of the journey. The new carriage wasn't as finely appointed as the other. Rain had set in again, and he complained that winter approached with many miles yet to travel. He hardly looked at her. They rode in silence, the one small recompense being Junia's chastened mood.

~~~

Caerwin kept no mental record of the places they spent the night, only that the accommodations required the women to share a room. By mutual yet silent agreement, she and Junia didn't speak. The road tracked southeast. After the sixth day, the terrain became hilly and their pace slowed. They crossed another great river at Cabilonnum and then their route switched southward. The hills grew ever more extreme and she wished for Senna's company to discuss the sights. They changed horses every night.

She rode in the carriage, content to let the countryside blur past her vision in a stream of trees, fields, mountains, and sky. If Junia talked, Caerwin didn't hear it. Only Marcellus brought her focus to the painful present, the disastrous loss of Senna, and the length of journey still ahead.

His attention riveted on the passing countryside and the readiness of his men. From Durocortorum, a new group of six hired men rode at the rear while the surviving legionaries rode at the front with Marcellus. Each morning as they loaded into the carriage, he directed a thorough examination of the axles. Southward, the road followed a river valley through higher hills and dense forests. But it was the ninth day that a cloud bank to the east rose ever higher until she realized in astonishment that the clouds were mountains. Snowcapped peaks pierced the sky, one after another in a jagged line marching off to the north and south. The Alps. Antius supplied the word for her. She'd never heard it before.

The town of Lugdunum perched on a curved hill above the confluence of two mighty rivers. In itself, the city and its environs awed Caerwin with orderly streets and buildings crowded side by side within stone-built walls. Magnificent structures housed temples, homes of the wealthy, and government offices, all shining in the late afternoon sun that reflected off the rivers like gemstones. Yet it was the stunning heights that rose to the east, those fearsome peaks capped with snow that set the place apart from anything she had ever imagined. She found herself whispering as they approached their night's accommodation as if in fear of angering the mountain gods.

Marcellus regained some of his humor there, enough that he set aside a full day for them to visit the baths, the markets, and the temple honoring Emperor Claudius in this, the town of his birth. These were lands long held by Romans, well supplied and safe from banditry. Caerwin welcomed the break in their travel but grew increasingly restive with the way Marcellus treated Junia. Her hands gripped into fists when he deferred to Junia's wishes for where they took meals, the place they would visit next, even her choice of a new silk *stola* and matching *palla* with embroidered trim. In the one brief moment Caerwin managed to confront him, he said his duty required it.

Junia seized maximum benefit from her damages. The woman missed no opportunity to cling to Marcellus' arm or monopolize his attention. As they ambled along the streets in bright sunshine, Caerwin fumed as she traipsed along behind with Antius and Porcia.

"What duty? He betrays me," she said, whispering to Antius. "He says one thing and does another."

"He tries to make amends," Antius said. "It has nothing to do with you."

Caerwin withdrew more into herself as the journey continued. Her hand repeatedly went to her bare neck. Memories assailed her, her mother at the fireside, her early years watching her father and brother drive sheep down the hillside, even the children's songs she knew by heart. She could no longer remember their faces except a few features frozen in time—her mother's cheek where the lines of age had begun to crease, her brother Virico's fierce command as he lay dying.

Live for the rest of us.

Invariably her attention came back to Marcellus. Whether she wished it or not, he had become her only positive thought. When rain assaulted the countryside, his presence in the carriage consumed her. When he rode at the front of their entourage, she counted the time until she would see him. At night when he strode around the inn making arrangements, her gaze followed him, admiring, longing. His presence blotted out the immeasurable losses in the rest of her life.

Perversely, thoughts of Marcellus brought her full circle. Mounted on that big white horse, sword in hand, he had led the destruction of her family, her village, her way of life. He had forced her body to know him. When confronted with the simple truth of his role as commander of the Roman army, she hated him. Surely the gods of cruelty laughed at her dilemma.

She distracted herself from thinking of Marcellus by asking Antius to talk about what appeared outside the carriage windows—the mountains, the villages, the expanse of the mighty Rhone River which never veered far from their route. As they passed through Vienne, he remarked on the massive temple under construction, Claudius' monument to Augustus Caesar and his wife Livia. With their overnight stay at Arausio, they walked the upper rim of a great theatre with its semi-circle of tiered stone benches, enough seating for seven thousand.

"The actors take the stage," Antius explained. "The tall wall behind is fitted to suit the story."

Caerwin stared in wonder at the three-story façade embellished with marble mosaics of many different colors. There were columns, friezes, and statuary including an image of Apollo. The sheer size and beauty of the place left her speechless. That it existed solely for purposes of entertainment shocked her even more.

The more she learned of Rome, the more depressed she became. Nothing of these spectacular accomplishments astonished Marcellus or Junia. The nearer she came to the world of Rome, the more foreign everything became. She could never feel at home here. She had thought herself a leaf floating down a river. Now she saw that she was a tiny leaf adrift in an endless sea. She left the better part of her meals on her plate and lay awake as tears ran down her temples.

Four days later they arrived at Arles. The Rhone spread wide here. Ships tied at massive quays rocked against the current. A team of men shifted the baggage to a *liburna* and Caerwin realized with a sinking stomach that they would again sail on dangerous waters.

The evening meal at a well-appointed inn centered on a sumptuous fish platter which Caerwin enjoyed more than she expected. Despite ample accommodation, Marcellus didn't come to her. The next morning, he counted out payment to the hired bodyguards before they returned north. After well wishes and payment, he bid farewell to two of the legionaries headed west toward Hispania where they would rejoin their families.

Caerwin's hands trembled as they boarded the ship. Strong cold winds buffeted the vessel as they hoist anchor and the rowers sank their oars.

"The *mistral*," Marcellus said of the wind, gripping her as the current and oars propelled them down the wide river. "These winds demand extreme respect in the Gulf of Lions."

Wind whistled through the ship's rigging as they entered a wide delta laced with small streams and swampland. As they raced south, the southern flank of the Alps broke into sharp peaks that cascaded down to the water's edge. Finally the swift current and fierce wind brought them to the throat of the river where they confronted a cobalt sea.

Caerwin could see by the body language of Marcellus and the crew that the waters here made them nervous. Ahead, the sea churned in a froth of white-capped waves. The boat rocked and heaved as the *trierarchus* and his assistant braced themselves to hold grip on the steering oars. He shouted orders for the sail, but as the ropes burned through the crew's hands, the wind billowed the sail at one-fourth its height, sending the ship scudding along the rough waters.

With the help of the rowers and all hands on deck, they hewed to the east driven by the *mistrals* and only partly controlled by the mighty efforts of the crew. Isolated black rocks pierced the waves near the shore and Caerwin imagined that the Alps themselves boiled the water in anger for the water's intrusion over its lower ranks. Indeed, the stark mountains gave way stubbornly, dropping precipitously to the shoreline all along their route.

She huddled in the small aft shelter as the ship galloped over choppy waves. At any moment she thought the vessel might roll to its side and send them all to a watery grave. The prow of the ship cleaved the water sending up mist that wet her and everything onboard. Gulls hovered overhead as if waiting to pluck at dead bodies. She didn't ask Antius if this was a bad omen.

Strangely, she didn't become sick. These waters weren't like the crossing from Britannia. There the waves had been larger and higher. Here the boat shuddered in the churning water instead of rocking like a wild horse.

They traveled further east and then south. Gradually the winds relented and the *trierarchus* called for full sail. The journey continued three days, each night anchored at an island on this endless journey to Rome. Finally a coastline followed them along the east as they progressed southward.

"We arrive at Portus," Marcellus said tiredly. "The emperor's prized project nears completion."

She had no words as the harbor came into view. A beehive of industry surrounded the ongoing construction surrounded by boats of all sizes, crowded with men and machines of bizarre configuration. The scale of the site and the skills required to build it exceeded her grasp—two enormous seawalls extended into the sea like curving arms. Inside the arms, another set of walls sheltered a long island with a lighthouse and an enormous statue standing watch over the port.

Caerwin observed their surroundings agog at the density and variety of the ships anchored there—long distance merchant ships, small fishing boats, medium sized vessels engaged in coastal trade. Marcellus pointed and explained as they progressed. Barges moved cargo from ships to the quays while teams of rowers powered smaller boats that pulled ships in and out of the harbor. Still other small boats stood alongside large ships anchored farther out to receive their wares and deliver them to warehouses in the harbor.

The *trierarchus* shouted commands as they negotiated the harbor entry and the inner channels that led to a tranquil body of water contained by five equal sides. She glanced at Marcellus in wonder. These Romans! Even the sea obeyed their control.

Their boat nestled alongside a stone quay as their party disembarked. Marcellus immediately secured two wagons. The remaining legionaries set off in different directions, eager to reach their homes. With the baggage loaded, the remaining party moved to the east end of the harbor complex where they would rest and take a midday meal before traveling the short distance to Rome.

A cluster of taverns and eating places lined the wide roadway. After a delicious meal of fried fishcakes and roasted chickpeas, Caerwin and the other two women waited in the carriage. The baggage wagon had pulled forward so that both conveyances waited in the shade of tall trees.

Outside her window, she watched Marcellus. Antius attended him. He stood fully in her view outside the front of the carriage as he began divesting himself of his weapons. Except in a triumphal parade, no one could enter Rome bearing trappings of war. Antius received each item, making a stack that she guessed would be put away in the trunk: the sword, the red sash around his midsection, the wide leather straps he wore across his chest bearing his medals of commendation. Caerwin shifted uncomfortably as her mind raced ahead to the inevitable conclusion of this process. Surely he wouldn't…

The segmented torso armor clanked as it joined the pile, reminding Caerwin of all the nights she had watched him undress from the comfort of his bed. Or discomfort in the certain knowledge of what would come next. She wriggled on the seat, unable to look away.

Marcellus pulled his tunic over his head. Her mouth went dry. It had been weeks since she'd seen him undressed. He stood in the dappled sunlight in nothing but the cloth that wrapped his loins. The gods! Had there ever been a man of such beauty as this? Muscle bulged over his shoulders and chest. A narrow line of body hair descended briefly down his lean abdomen. The wound on his bicep left a puckered red line. His hands, his forearms, the line of his jaw…

She licked her lips, absorbed fully in this vision of manhood standing just yards away. Everything about him incited her. Her breath came in short light bursts. Her pulse throbbed in her throat—and in less modest places. Moisture crept between her tightly clenched thighs.

Antius unfolded the long white yardage of Marcellus' toga then sorted out the tunic with its two red stripes. Marcellus paused, standing fully facing Caerwin and meeting her riveted gaze. She gasped at the unmistakable knowledge in his dark eyes, the slight smile curling his lips. By the goddess Sabrina! He had intentionally positioned himself to disrobe in her view. He had purposefully captured her attention to display himself.

He turned slightly to an angle so that the front of his loincloth gave full evidence of his pleasure in her attention. Her eyes closed in the sensation of him over her. She could feel him in her. She squirmed. Her nipples hardened. Her hands filmed with sweat. She wanted him in ways she'd never known possible.

"What mystery holds your adoration?" Junia said. Her forehead wrinkled as she gazed at Caerwin. "I must know."

Caerwin's face heated as she tore her gaze away from Marcellus. Just as he had placed himself in her view, he had also made it impossible for Junia or Porcia to see him. Unless Junia came to Caerwin's place in the carriage.

"I…It's…" Caerwin stammered. What could she say? Against her intention, her gaze drew back to Marcellus.

The moment had passed. Marcellus had already shrugged into his tunic and Antius had begun to wrap the toga. "An eagle," she said finally to Junia. "Powerful animal. Quite beautiful."

"Indeed," Junia said suspiciously.

Let her question. Even if Caerwin had tried, she could not keep her eyes from Marcellus. As Antius walked around him slowly covering that magnificent body with yards of white cloth, naked emotion permeated Antius' expression. As his hands touched Marcellus at the shoulder, at the waist, Antius' hands lingered, caressed.

He loved him. She'd known it a long time. But at this moment, that relationship gained new dimension. Of course he loved him. Unexpectedly, she realized her long antipathy for the old Greek had begun to soften.

~~~

As they neared Rome, houses and workshops dotted the countryside alongside tidy farms. Once the city came into view, the houses became taller and more closely built, the roadway more crowded with carts and pedestrians. Fires smoldered in places outside the city walls. They stopped at a stable where wagons and carts lined up at the side of the road.

She paced outside the carriage as they waited for the hour they could enter the city. The air smelled of horse dung, sewage, and unknown exotics. Her body suffered the fatigue and bruising of their long journey. She had longed for its end and now that the end approached, she could hardly believe it. Finally the tenth hour came and the line of wagons began to move.

Nothing anyone had said could have prepared Caerwin for the sight that was Rome. Even before they entered the city's gate and passed the great expanse of its perimeter wall, the city's profile of towering buildings took her breath. The work of human hands swallowed the contours of hills and valleys as if the land itself had erupted into streets, shelters, and more people than she imagined could populate the entire earth.

Hardly anything of the natural world survived. As they progressed through the city, odors of animal dung, cooking fires, and human waste clung to the back of her tongue. People thronged along every shadowed passage, spilled from taverns, lingered at small streetside stalls where food was sold. The narrow streets hardly allowed room for the carriage to pass alongside pedestrians and crowds gathered at the shops.

"I've had the villa opened for us and a meal prepared," Marcellus said. Caerwin looked over at him only to see he spoke to Junia. "We'll have baths and grooming before we eat. Are you hungry?"

Caerwin flinched. All this time, all the struggle to arrive here. Her consuming grief in being torn from her roots. The loss of Senna's life. And now he welcomed Junia here, not her?

Only a short time ago, he had purposefully aroused her. But with the niceties, he turned to Junia. She shouldn't care. Hadn't he made it clear over the weeks of their journey that his attention rested with precious Junia?

Despite her wish not to care, the hurt went deeper than anything she could put into words. Her fists clenched in her lap. In every possible way, he had forced her—taken her captive, overpowered her resistance, invaded her senses. Even after all this time, he could still ply her, make her want him, and at the same time, cultivate a relationship with a different woman.

Amid the traffic of people and carts, one after another shining building rose high into the descending dusk, surpassing even the theater at Arausio. At the temples, tall fluted columns soared upward, resting on ornate pediments and capped with flourishes of carved stone that reflected the late red-gold rays of the sun. Astonishing colorful architecture appeared at every corner, statues that appeared as real life. She swallowed, rubbing her fingertips against her sweating palms.

"What do you think of the city?" he said.

She knew he spoke to her. She refused to look at him. She didn't trust herself not to shout her innermost thoughts. "It's a crowded stinking place," she said finally, keeping her face turned to the window.

"Surely that's not all you see," he said.

She tried to ignore the hurt in his voice. He'd done this to himself. She turned to face him and couldn't keep her voice from trembling. "Don't ask me for my thoughts if you don't want to hear them," she said.

He turned his face and didn't reply, but his jaw pulsed and his lips thinned to a tense line.

Briefly, she viewed his profile as if he were a stranger. His straight nose and firm chin, the thrust of his jaw—it was the face and carriage of a powerful man comfortable in his position of authority. The white folds of his toga fell to the bench beside him, partly covering the stern posture of his shoulders. She thought briefly of the thug who had threatened her life, the man whose head fell to one blow of Marcellus' sword. How many men had he overpowered with his strength and cunning, his skill honed in battle? Her gaze drifted over his big hands, hands that had tormented her, held her, brought her to the greatest pleasure she had ever known. Gooseflesh raced over her at the memory.

He sat stiffly in the carriage's shadowed recesses as if protecting some inner wound, and perhaps he did. By Senna's account, he cared for her and went to great lengths to accommodate her. In her most feeling moments, she wished she could believe it. Dear Senna. How much simpler it would be to look at him in pleasure, to laugh at his comments and exchange words as they had done so many times before. Before…

Her fingers twisted in her lap. Before Junia. Before his seemingly infinite capacity to cater to the woman's every whim. Before his attention riveted on Junia first and Caerwin as an afterthought. If at all. Before he brought her across the sea and a greater expanse of land than she ever knew existed, separating her permanently from her inheritance, her ancestry, and the spirits of her dead kinsmen. Before she'd been forced to give up any hope of freedom. She touched her bare neck.

Nothing left. Tears blurred the view outside the carriage window. The three moons that had passed since the battle with Caradoc had done little to relieve the deep grief framing her waking moments. She mourned Seisyll, the countless native men who had died, the freedom she had briefly seized then lost. Again. In moments like this, when Marcellus exerted silent pressure that she meet his expectations, when she confronted the truth of her station in life, not screaming and ripping her hair required the greatest of effort.

Their conveyance climbed a curving road to the top of a hill overlooking the city's center. Below, the late day's stark orange and shadowed glimpses of the city reflected its stunning magnitude. She simply could not believe it was real. These Romans truly were ants in a hive, all fed by the blood of other people. Stillness grew inside her, distance from Marcellus, from anyone in the carriage, from anything else in the world.

Twilight had fallen by the time they arrived at the red gates of a walled compound. Even here, buildings joined along each side of the roadway as far as she could see. Two servants with torches emerged while a third man secured the horses. An aging doorman in a red tunic and yellow cape hurried forward to bow toward Marcellus.

"Sir, we're so pleased to have you back. Are you well?"

"Thanks Rufus, we are well," Marcellus said. "It's good to be back."

Caerwin's gaze held on Rufus. Weathered creases marked a face that had seen a lot of life. He reminded her of Seisyll with his white hair and easy smile. Her heart twisted at the thought.

She moved stiffly as she stepped out of the carriage, relieved that at least for the moment, in this spot the air didn't reek of crowded humanity. Marcellus moved ahead, escorting Junia through the entry. Caerwin's nostrils flared as she saw his hand touch Junia's back. Surely it would be a matter of hours before he bedded the conniving bitch.

Hanging lamps illuminated their passage into the atrium and cast wavering spots of light that reflected off a sparkling rectangular pool. Above the pool, the high roof supported by rows of ornate columns opened to a darkening sky. Underfoot, brightly colored bits of tile formed fantastic beasts, works of art that begged not to be trod upon and yet each person's feet passed over it as if mere ground. A life-sized statue of Jupiter stood in the near corner, his muscular nude form draped with garlands. Further along the left wall, a beautiful woman stood frozen in stone with a staff and long-tailed bird in her hands. At the far end, a third statue peered into the shadowy atrium, a woman wearing a military helmet and an owl perched on her hand.

Marcellus disappeared through a doorway with Junia, Porcia trailing behind. Antius followed carrying his satchel. Caerwin considered turning around and walking out. This could never be a home to her. The statues watched her with their eerie painted eyes.

Moments later, a woman with dark hair and wearing a white belted tunic approached from the back of the house. She held a tray with a cup of cool water.

"For your refreshment," she said, bowing slightly toward Caerwin. "I'm Varinia. Please follow me."

Caerwin swallowed the refreshing water. She hardly registered on the beauty surrounding her as she followed Varinia toward a doorway in the near left corner. Voices echoed across the atrium, familiar kitchen clatter, the splash of fountains, all of it weighing on her already overwhelmed senses. But her disinterest vanished as Varinia opened the door. As the housekeeper hurried to light more lamps, some shaped like little buildings or ships, others hanging in elaborate brass holders, Caerwin could only stand and gawk.

An enormous bed draped in white bedclothes occupied the far right wall. At each corner of the bed stood a tall carved post of dark wood which supported a canopy of rose and gold silk. Animal skins spread here and there on the marble floor, offering soft respite from the stone's coolness. How would it be to unlace her dusty sandals and rest her tired feet on that soft fur? She wanted to crawl among the heaped pillows and drift away into dreams.

As they took a few steps into the room, she noted a long table against the wall near the bed, its polished surface ornamented with a silver ewer and goblets on a tray, a glass flagon of wine and another of water, and a platter heaped with grapes, pomegranates, and plums. Another tray held cheeses and bread. Her mouth watered.

On her left, two chairs accompanied an ornate table, all of them carved like the bedposts with intricate vines, flowers, and animals. Rose colored fabric covered the chair seats. Underneath the arrangement spread a woven rug of turquoise, green, and gold strands. The wall above featured a mural of distant hills and a red-roofed villa. Herdsmen and their sheep dotted one hillside while distinctive cultivated rows spread over another. It was as if she looked at the scene in real life.

To the far side of the room, doors stood open to a small private garden where yet another pool glittered in the moonlight.

"There must be a mistake," Caerwin said.

Varinia turned to her. "Is something amiss?"

"This room—it's too much. I'm only a slave." Or whatever he wished to call her. She picked up her satchel to leave.

Varinia frowned. "The master said you were to come here."

"This room can't be only for me," Caerwin insisted.

"No," Varinia agreed, scrutinizing her with a curious expression. "It's the master's bedchamber." She looked up as two men arrived at the doorway. "Is this yours?" she said, looking at Caerwin.

Caerwin struggled to speak as she looked blankly at the men. They carried her trunk. "Yes," she said. "But put it only just inside the door. I won't be staying in this room."

Varinia exchanged glances with the men. "Perhaps…"

Caerwin shook her head. "Just leave it."

She crossed her arms as Varinia ushered the men out ahead of her. Caerwin watched the door close, halfway expecting to hear a bolt slide. So he wished to have her waiting in his bedchamber.

Nothing could spell out her place more clearly. The size of the room had changed, the richness of the furnishings, but her status stayed the same. She would be his sex slave just as he had forced her from the first.

Her shoes dropped to the floor with a plop as she pulled them loose. At the moment, she could hardly summon appropriate outrage. She walked toward the bread and cheese and poured a goblet full of wine and gulped half of it before sitting at the table to tear off a portion of bread. Slowly, she unwove her long braid, scrubbed her scalp with her fingertips, and fanned the hair loose over her shoulders.

Wine tingled through her veins as she stretched her hands toward the ceiling. Desire had simmered since that first night in Gaul when the messenger had interrupted their lovemaking. Marcellus had hardly touched her since. That reckless part of her wanted nothing more than to take up where they'd left off with his mouth between her thighs and his hands probing her secrets. The sight of his bared chest this afternoon had brought the memory roaring back to life.

Opposing that, fury nestled in her chest like embers, firing down her limbs and sharpening her tongue. Where was he this very minute but with Junia? The words she wanted to say flared like fire to dead grass then quickly spread to ever more insulting curses. She couldn't think of enough curses to satisfy her outrage.

She gulped a cup of water, poured more wine then wandered around the room, touching the beasts carved in wood, the tiny human figures painted on the wall. What would it be like to enjoy such wealth, such power over the world that the most fantastic dream could be wrought in wood, paint, or stone? The wine flowered through her nose and forehead. She marveled at the creamy cheese and the herbs seasoning the soft bread. Grapes burst on her tongue with acid sweetness. Her head buzzed.

She stood at the garden door looking out into the night. Moonlight glinted off the small pool. Seized with the fatigue of the long journey and the dusty last miles, she tugged off her clothing and stepped in. A wide seat allowed her the luxury of settling breast deep in lukewarm water.

Her resentment against this place and its people caused a momentary pang of regret. These creations were meant to bring pleasure, not this bitterness that overwhelmed the flavor of good wine and left her ill at ease in the midst of a wonderful bath. What did he intend?

More importantly, what did she want?

"The gods!" Marcellus said, startling her. "Cupid sends me mortal wound."

She spun around and stood up. He had walked silently halfway across the room. A wide smile sent his face into dark lines and white teeth.

"Words cannot describe the radiance before me," he said in a husky voice. "You grow more beautiful with each passing day."

"A clever turn of phrase," she said, uncomfortable with her nudity. She shrugged her shoulders so that the wavy strands of her hair covered her breasts. "You're well practiced."

"I see," he said. He paused then motioned toward the mural. "That's our country villa. Where we'll live once I've sorted out my legal problems. If I retain any inheritance," he added in grim voice. He looked at her wine cup and lifted his own. "To better days."

The night air chilled her wet skin and she grabbed her tunic against herself. She didn't want to accept anything from him, even a toast to the future. Still, she brought her cup to his and they drank together.

"Why do you want me here?" she said. "Am I to be used like your bed and left alone when you go about your daily business?"

His dark eyes riveted on her. "How would you have me use you?"

She didn't answer. The wine had muddled her mind. What she wanted to say slipped away like the breeze rustling the leaves outside in the garden. Briefly, she chased her thoughts but couldn't grasp them.

"Perhaps I'm not suitable to be more than a slave." Her words came out without warning. "Junia is more to your liking."

Marcellus stood still for several moments. Then he began to unwrap the long white cloth of his toga. The image hit her like a fist, Marcellus standing beside the carriage in nothing but his loincloth. In a moment of panic, she clutched her tunic more tightly thinking he might turn to the door and usher her out to some small room like he'd done at the fortress. Instead, wearing only his short tunic, he set his wine cup on the table and then took hers from her hands.

"Junia and her family have suffered harm while under my watch. Why can't you understand I have responsibilities?"

"Are you so blind? She wants you."

"I already have someone in my heart," he said, pulling her tunic out of her hands and wrapping her against his warm chest.

His arms came around her and even though she wanted to resist, even more she wanted exactly this. Just the touch of his chest against hers shunted away every objection. She inhaled, reveling in the scent of his skin. Why did he do this to her?

Within that familiar comfort a sharp pain crushed her heart. He would make her his then abandon her just as he had done before. His closeness and tender words hurt more than his neglect. "I never wished to be in your heart."

"I didn't ask it," he whispered. "Do you think I could have known? I took you as a plaything. The gods willed you become much more."

"I don't believe you. You say what's convenient when you want something."

His lips grazed her forehead and cheek. "What will I do with you, my little queen? What sorcery must I cast to make you trust me?"

She wanted to find words to protest. She wanted to walk away. But the muscles of his back shifted under her hands, and she thought of how he looked without clothes, how his body took up the shadows and light of a lamp's flame, how the dappled sunlight earlier that day had cast him as a god. She thought of the countless times he came to her in desire and incited her response, how he satisfied and pleased her. She clung to him, aware of the need that bloomed against the press of his loins. Tears filled her eyes.

"I wish that too, Marcellus. But perhaps that can never be." Her words ended on a stifled sob.

"The gods be cursed!" he said, holding her away from him to examine her face. "Look at me." He held her chin up with his hand. "Finally you see your new home and you stand before me with tears? Why?"

"I don't know," she sobbed. "It's too much."

"You're tired. So am I." He trailed kisses down her neck and dragged her hair away from her breasts. "I had thought we could have a few moments to rest before dinner. There are weighty matters to discuss, but they must wait until tomorrow."

He sighed as his lips surrounded her nipple. Pain and desire flew down her stomach as his teeth grazed the puckered tip. Her chest shuddered in another sob.

"Almighty Jove, you erase all sense from my mind," he said. His lips kissed away her line of tears.

"Marcellus…"

Whatever she meant to say vanished as he ripped off his tunic and bent his face to her breasts. His mouth moved from one to the other, licking, sucking, biting. His groans vibrated her flesh. In moments, his fingers had opened her vulva.

"Wet," he said. "Gods be kind."

She didn't want to be wet. Tears slid down her face as he stroked her wetness and slid a finger inside. Any effort to summon anger failed as his touch rushed past her defenses. Her hands slid over his shoulders and along his neck to tangle in his hair. A joyful cry hovered in her throat.

He crouched, lowering his mouth to join his hands. The room spun in lamp light. He held her open to the lash of his tongue, spreading her legs as he used both hands to pleasure her.

A sudden orgasm curled through her. She stifled her cry, one fist in her mouth and the other gripping his hair as his mouth and hands continued his plunder. Resisting her efforts to pull away, he kept her shaking in the throes of release, his tongue now licking inside her and returning to suck again on the hot bud. Her knees could not hold her.

He lifted her to the bed then crouched over her with his cock in his hand, directing it to her mouth. Still burning with need, she took him eagerly, licking around the distended crown before bringing his length along her tongue. Never before had she enjoyed his taste so much, not only the taste but also the silken hardness.

She grabbed the shaft with her hands and sat up to bring him to her throat. Moaning in pleasure, she scrubbed him between her tongue and the roof of her mouth, grazed him with her teeth, and rocked forward to feel his thickness at the back of her throat.

"I die," he said, seizing her hair. He lunged toward her, burying himself deep in her mouth.

Moments later, he pushed her back and lay between her legs to immediately thrust inside. Cradling her shoulders in his arms, he moved slowly at first.

"My sweet wild queen," he whispered. "I can never get enough of you."

His movement increased in pace and force. Her body shook in the impact. He held her wrists against the bed as he fucked her. She could think of nothing, no wish, no anger, no wonder. Her mind slipped to some distant place of showering stars against mossy dark.

They rose together, flying ever upward, rising, rising. Then, stiffening, Marcellus drove deep to her womb and held there as his seed filled her. She shuddered against him. He cradled her. Her hands grasped his sides. Slowly, as he emptied his last drops, her touch soothed him and came to rest on his back as he relaxed against her.

    Moments passed. Their ragged breathing calmed. Her thought began again, and she wanted him always in her, on her, protecting her from her fears, her wants, her anger. He grunted as he lifted himself off and settled beside her, dragging the soft blankets over their bodies. His arms still surrounded her as she fell into a sound sleep.

Chapter Five

Slabs of red-swirled marble formed a shelf along one side of the dining room. Ornate silver goblets and three silver flagons were displayed there alongside knives with enameled handles, silver spoons, and dark red platters and bowls whose surfaces were emblazoned with intricate raised figures. Caerwin trailed her fingertips along the display, distracted by clatter and loud voices emanating from the nearby kitchen. With Marcellus occupied in his office, she had spent the early morning hours exploring the house. The slight headache from her wine indulgence the night before had finally relented, aided by a sumptuous breakfast of hot bread, sliced roasted fowl, and fruit. Sunlight poured through the *comfluvium* above the atrium pool and reflected off the high ceilings of the surrounding rooms.

She made her way around the eating area. Intense red-orange fabric covered the padded seats of three wide couches which surrounded three sides of a low square table, all framed in the same dark carved wood as the bedroom furniture. Across the head wall, a painted scene of feasting erupted against a red background—women and men costumed in sumptuous folds of gold, yellow, and green cloth rested on wide couches. On the right hand wall, a painted orchard portrayed golden ripe pears glistening among the branches while colorful birds flitted from tree to tree. Under the trees, thickets of blue flowers emerged from grass and shrubbery and behind a blue lake gleamed. The left wall featured ornate platters holding lifelike loaves of bread, whole fish, roasted fowl, and fruit. Intricate geometric patterns rimmed the room's upper and lower borders.

In the room's far corner, a bronze bust of a man occupied a short column. In another corner stood a painted marble of some goddess, bared to the waist with folds of her clothing draped from her hips. An exquisite small bronze figure stood in the center of the table, one arm holding a drinking vessel aloft while the other held forward a platter. It was all simply too much to believe.

"I'd wager nothing this fine can be found in all Britannia," Junia said from the wide arched entry.

Caerwin turned, instantly furious. "Spying suits you," she said.

"You think too highly of yourself." As Junia smiled, her rouged cheeks rounded like plums. "Why would I bother to spy on you? I'm merely admiring the many beautiful features of the Antistius *domus*."

"Planning how you can make it yours, I'm sure," Caerwin said, folding her arms. "Do you ever tire of your games?"

Junia waved her hand. "What games? What troubles you is that I'm a far better match for Marcellus than you. You know nothing of Roman ways. You could never adequately manage such a complicated household. He's an important man who deserves a suitable wife. A merger of our wealth would secure the future for both of us."

"Your arrogance is exceeded only by your craving for what you can't have." Caerwin said. Her face felt hot. Had Marcellus made some arrangement with Junia? Was that what he wanted to talk about? "He cares nothing for you. He only feels obligated because of the accident."

"The flaming mouse tries to roar," Junia said with a laugh. "Clearly you have no understanding of Roman law. He can never marry you. You aren't a citizen."

Antius cleared his throat as he stepped into the room. "You're to join Marcellus in his study," he said, motioning to Caerwin.

Her chin lifted as she breezed past Junia. Let the singed woman burn darker in the flaming rivers of Tartarus. Her mood improved as she silently thanked Antius not only for his timely arrival but also for providing lessons that described the Roman underworld. She imagined Junia ignited in a sea of fire.

"I might wish you to teach me more lessons on all things Roman," she said as she followed him.

He turned and studied her with his dark gaze. "Once we've settled, I might have time."

"I wish to know curses. Can you teach me that?"

He tried and failed to suppress a grin. "Perhaps."

The study where Marcellus waited sat adjacent to the vestibule. He stood at an opening into a front walled garden that paralleled the one off his bedchamber. Except this one had no pool. A line of flowering thorn bushes bordered the compound wall with blossoms of white and shades of red which filled the air with a dusty sweet aroma. Bright sunlight flooded through the open doorway. She resisted the urge to go wrap her arms around him.

Last night he'd made love to her, let her sleep a while, then coaxed her awake to eat dinner. Then he took her again to bed to simply hold her in his arms while they slept. She hardly remembered anything more than his intense attention to her. He had already dressed when she woke this morning, and she wondered if she had dreamed the entire encounter.

The soreness between her legs confirmed the memory, that and the droplets of his seed that periodically leaked into her linen *subligaculum*. She bit her lip, resisting the smile that rose at the sight of him.

"I have only a few moments before I go to the Forum," Marcellus said, dismissing Antius with a wave of the hand. "I've given Antius the task of finding you suitable assistance. It may take a few days, so Varinia will be available if you need someone."

He scrubbed his face with his hands and looked out to the garden. "You are not to leave this house unless you make arrangements with me in advance. I'll assign two men who will always go with you, whether or not you're in the company of a servant of this house. The streets are not safe for a woman alone."

Her good mood vanished. It was as if nothing had happened the night before. Not a 'Good morning,' not a kiss…nothing. The tenderness had been replaced by this stern, worried man she hardly knew. Her temper flared. "Have you issued similar orders for Junia?"

He frowned, perching on his chair and gathering some wax tablets. "Junia has lived in Rome. She knows what to do. Whatever occurs between me and Junia is none of your concern. I thought I made that plain last night."

"All you said last night was that you had things to tell me. Is she to stay here?"

"Is that all you remember of our time together?" he said.

"No, but…"

"Am I clear on the need for safety?"

"Of course. I'm once again confined to a prison."

"For the sake of the gods!" he thundered. He slammed his fist to the desk and stood up. "Am I speaking to a child or a woman? If you wish to be treated as a child, I will make further restrictions," he said, stepping close to her. "Should I say 'Don't put your hand in the fire'?"

His lips had thinned and small red spots appeared on his cheeks. She chewed her lip, tempted to push him further. Why she wanted to provoke him escaped her reasoning. She crossed her arms and refused to meet his glare.

"Is that all?"

"No." He stepped back and adjusted his toga. The white cloth dazzled in the sunlight and reflected against his tan skin. "But the rest of it can wait."

He was like a bull in the meadow, charging one way and then another, stomping the heather and bothering the cows. She stepped aside as he strode out of the room. Immediately she felt loss. She didn't want him to leave. On the other hand, she wanted him out of her sight and out of her thoughts.

A steady commotion brought Caerwin from the bedchamber to the atrium. Junia stood with her fists on her hips lecturing her growing bevy of slaves. They wore specially made tunics, some red, some orange, which Antius said aggrandized her status. Porcia stood beside two other women while Junia spoke to a burly man and his three companions. Four other male slaves stood to the side.

Whatever the complaint, Junia swiftly finished her rebuke and hurried out the door. Caerwin waited beside Rufus as they watched her climb into her elaborate chair which the burly man and his three companions then lifted to their shoulders while Junia scolded them to keep the chair level. As the assembly joined the pedestrian traffic already making its way down the avenue, Rufus looked at Caerwin with a lopsided grin.

"They'll dump her if they get the least excuse," he said. "Hopefully in horse dung."

She laughed. "I'd love to see it."

"Me, too. She's heavy with the whip on all of them."

"I don't like her."

"Good for you!"

Caerwin inhaled the early morning air. Crows called from their hidden perches. A low mist lay in the river valley below, reminding her of the River Severn. She swallowed her melancholy and went back inside.

~~~

Loud voices issued from Marcellus' office. Caerwin recognized his voice but not those of at least two other men. This was different from the early morning sessions that grew with each passing day, men lined up in the vestibule to wait their turn to ask one thing or another from Marcellus.

Those were clients, Antius had explained. As word of Marcellus' return spread, more men joined the morning lineup. As a wealthy patron, he had a duty to provide assistance to freedmen whom he or his family had released from slavery or to businessmen who had earned legal or financial favors from the Antistius family. In return, these men accompanied Marcellus at the Forum giving support to his discussions and protection to his person. Caerwin understood it in terms of the Cornovii ruling men who settled disputes among tribesmen and offered needed support in times of crisis.

It seemed excessive that Romans conducted this business on a daily basis. Even more unsettling was Marcellus' increasing ill humor. Since the first night, he had not touched her. By the end of the day when there might have been opportunity, he moved like a man in shackles, hardly taking the time to remove his outer garments and shoes before falling asleep. Why he insisted on her sleeping in his bedchamber escaped her understanding.

Three days ago, she raised the question. Perhaps she could have a room of her own, she said.

"No," he said in an angry voice.

She could get no more from him, no explanation for his increasingly dark mood, no time for conversation. After his morning *salutatio* with his clients, he rushed out to the Forum in the company of Antius and a handful of those followers. Sometimes he didn't return for the midday meal but ate at the food shops before going to the baths.

The men's voices rose and fell. Overcome by curiosity, Caerwin loitered in the vestibule, shamelessly eavesdropping. A few words here and there failed to reveal any clue to the topic of discussion. Finally the door opened and two men in white togas rushed out, followed by Marcellus whose gaze flittered over her as if she weren't there.

He left the door open but went back inside. She heard him talking quietly with Antius.

"You might as well come in," Marcellus said after a few moments.

She stepped to the door and looked in. They sat, Marcellus at his desk and Antius in a side chair, both with worried expressions. His eyes raked over her simple linen tunic then narrowed in a fierce frown. "You seem unduly concerned with my affairs."

"How could I not?" she said. "The entire household surely heard you."

"At least they know to turn a deaf ear. Unlike someone standing before me. Why aren't you dressed?"

"I'm not deaf, and it concerns me if it concerns you. My fortunes depend on yours, do they not?" She glanced down at her tunic, which—she admitted—failed to disguise her salient features. Why did it matter? They'd both seen her naked. "As for my clothing—am I to create garments out of air? I have no helper to take Senna's place. I don't know how to arrange my hair in the styles you prefer and I have only the blue stola and the old tan one and I'm sick of them both."

Marcellus leaned back and shifted his shoulders. "Yes, yes, Senna. Jove's stones. What's the progress, Antius?"

"I've made inquiries with two respected dealers. They're bringing people on Thursday." He turned to Caerwin. "Your master has more pressing matters to attend than you. You should leave him alone."

"Then why am I criticized about my appearance?" she said, putting her hand on her hip. "Am I to hide?"

"Let no one see you like this," Marcellus said. "I asked Varinia to tend you. Why has she not?"

"She has the household and your army of slaves to keep after. I've lost count of the servants populating this place," Caerwin said. "What would you have her neglect? Water supplies? The waste buckets? The barber or the room servants? Kitchen staff? The hair style alone requires most of a morning."

"The house had been closed except for Rufus," Antius said. "I was lucky that we found Varinia—she knew of the house from her early years. The rest are new."

"Some of questionable quality," Marcellus said. "This head cook Gordianus—I can hear him roar at all hours of the day and night. Does he not know how to manage his staff?"

"He finds them unsuitable," Antius said. "We've replaced half of them and he's no better pleased. He's particularly annoyed with the pastry cook Junia brought in but the woman insists on keeping him. I've asked if he wishes to have no pastry cook and he only threatens me with his knife."

"Junia." Marcellus leaned back and closed his eyes. "Do we know yet if he's a thief?"

"So far it seems he is not."

Marcellus sat up and leveled his gaze on Caerwin. "Then it seems my most pressing problem is your appearance."

Did he make a joke? Her temper flared.

"What? My appearance?" She leaned over the desk to stab the air with her finger. "You hardly set your eyes on me in the few times we're together, and the hair is to be redone after one night's sleep. What's wrong with a braid?"

"It's the appearance of a savage. You're in Rome and must do as Romans do."

His lips twitched as his gaze wandered down the front of her tunic which, she belatedly realized, had gaped to provide a full view of her breasts. She stood up quickly and pressed the fabric flat to her chest.

For a moment, his gaze seared her with shocking intensity. His nostrils flared. She imagined him dragging her over the desk and her pulse quickened.

His forehead creased. "Enough! Antius, redouble your efforts on her behalf," he said finally. "As to the rest of it—why should you hear it?"

She straightened her shoulders. "Whatever affects you affects me."

"So it's yourself that concerns you, not what might happen to me?"

The question took her off guard. "I must look after myself," she said. "I also care what happens to you."

"Do you indeed? For what reason? Am I not your constant oppressor?"

"Marcellus—why must you ask?" The lines around his mouth deepened as she looked at him. What did he expect her to say? She fidgeted with her belt. "You've helped me as well," she said finally.

He sighed. "If I take you into my confidence, whatever you hear in this room goes no further. Can I trust you in that?"

"Can you trust me in anything?" she said. "I'm treated like a child."

"Hear, hear," Marcellus said, clapping his hands lightly. "Why would that be?" He leaned forward to rest his elbows on the polished desk top and gripped his hands together. "These are grave problems that you won't understand. Much of my future—and yours—depends on resolving them. Why should I trust you to hear of it?"

Caerwin shrugged, feigning nonchalance. "I might be of use. Unlike the rest of your household, I'm not born to accept the ways of Rome. I'm not afraid to speak my mind."

Antius coughed into his hand.

Marcellus cocked his eyebrow. "Are you now a jurist? Do you understand the rights of damaged parties? What is the law regarding children born to a female slave and a Roman citizen?"

"The seriousness of your tone says these are difficult questions," she said, lifting her chin. "I would remind you that the three of us heard the same words about your paternity. What is the law, then? I would know."

Marcellus looked at Antius and folded his arms.

"The law is that a child of slave cannot inherit," Antius said. "The child is a bastard."

Caerwin weighed the information. "We're the only ones who know."

Marcellus shook his head. "Tulla knows I'm not her child. I don't know what else she knows or who she may have told. She's never held any fondness for me."

"It would be unwise to ask," Antius said. "She would see her way to your vulnerability."

"What could she possibly gain by harming you?" Caerwin said.

"She could win the entire estate for herself and her daughters," Antius said.

"But surely after all this time…" Caerwin began.

"So I thought," Marcellus said. "Nine years ago when Petrus died, I came to settle these affairs. I consulted Fabianus, the respected jurist Petrus engaged to write his will. He assured me that the laws of *fideicommissum* guaranteed full protection of my interests. By leaving the estate to him with the directive to pass it on to me, my father ensured that I would inherit even if Tulla complained. At least, that's what I understand of it. Fabianus said the laws of inheritance and trusts are complex and that I shouldn't worry. Now he's dead and I don't know what will unfold."

"Why would Manlius raise the issue if there weren't problems?" Antius said. "He and Praetextus both seem to think there's more involved than the Clodius complaint."

Caerwin's head had begun to throb. These must be the men who'd been shouting. She perched on a nearby seat, trying to understand.

"I'm at a disadvantage in many ways," Marcellus said. "I need more clients to stand with me in court but I don't have time to build a following. I need spies but I don't know who to trust. One misplaced word to the wrong person could expose my weakness. I wished not to stir up dust around these matters."

"It seems the dust is stirred," Antius said. "We can send messages asking for meetings with your old acquaintances and your father's freedmen. What do you think Vedius intends?"

"I need stronger footing," Marcellus said. "I need time to think. He insists we meet. I can't keep stalling." He rubbed his forehead. "Call for Gordianus and see if the tyrant has prepared our lunch. I don't care what he serves. I'm famished. Then I'll rejoice in the pleasure of a long bath with no discussion of these issues."

Caerwin trailed behind the two men as they retired to the *peristylium* for the late morning meal. Laughter and loud voices of the servants with their midday meal drifted in from their gathering place under a large tree in the back garden. She envied their association. Even newly brought together in the Antistius household, they enjoyed kinship in their shared status. Half-slave, half-free, she enjoyed none of that.

Even as she chewed the dense bread, green salad, and cold lamb from the night before, she pondered the peculiar and daunting tangles of Roman life. The back half of the *domus* was much larger than she had originally realized. An upper floor accommodated servant sleeping rooms while the lower provided more sleeping cubicles and storage needed for such a large household.

Only, aside from the swarm of slaves, it wasn't a large household. She, Marcellus, and Junia occupied atrium bedchambers, Junia now in the third room after complaining about features of the first two she tried. Her criticisms cast a pall through the house. Had there been laughter and happiness in the house while Marcellus grew up, time when he played with his younger sisters and enjoyed the indulgence of both parents?

Tulla must have hated him, a child not her own put upon her to cover a scandal. Her life had been ruined just as much as Petrus or Marcellus. Had he ever known affection from the woman he believed to be his mother? Or felt any for her?

Caerwin remembered the tone of Marcellus' voice when he spoke of Kensa, how she smelled of cut grass and how her embrace had given him peace and happiness he found nowhere else. Even with that, he hadn't been permitted the joy of knowing she was his grandmother.

So much of life's pleasures had been withheld from him. She wanted to hug his head against her breast and stroke his hair, whisper words of comfort like Kensa had done. Why couldn't she tell him she cared about him?

Petrus and Tulla must have settled into a poisonous stand-off that leaked into the air around them. Antius had entered the picture by the time Marcellus was twelve. By then his father found his pleasure elsewhere, had already taken up with Silverus in his routines of perversion. Tulla must have known about his dalliances. Did memories of life in this house contribute to the ominous mood surrounding Marcellus?

How did people live this way?

What if Junia was right? What if Marcellus planned to marry her—or someone like her, someone a citizen—in order to satisfy the law? Senna had told her of Roman marriages, couples joined not by love or attraction but by the political or financial interests of their families. Would he force her to accept such an arrangement? Would she have any choice?

Her appetite dwindled and she left some of the lamb. Marcellus treated her like a plaything because that's all she was. He wanted her groomed and well-dressed to please himself, to join the collection of amusements and art objects displayed in every corner. He indulged her request to hear his troubles, but even after all his explanations she knew nothing she hadn't known before except names like Praetextus, Manlius, and Vedius, which told her nothing. Maybe he'd given up any hope of marriage and said whatever he thought she wanted to hear in order to pacify her.

Even a savage from Britannia knew there had to be much more he hadn't bothered to say.

~~~

That afternoon a steady splash of rain through the roof opening into the pool below echoed through the empty atrium. Caerwin snugged her worn *palla* around her shoulders and shivered. The onset of the winter season had brought cloudy skies, rain, and cooler temperatures but nothing like the fog, mists, and cold she had known in Britannia. The clever hypocaust system caused heat to radiate up from the tiled floor, offsetting the chill in the air. Less messy than the Cornovii round huts with fires blazing in the central hearth, but also less comforting.

She stopped at the altar of Vesta where a sacred lamp burned day and night. The marble likeness reminded her of Senna. Had her spirit found place here?

Senna had been in her thoughts more than ever. The woman's steady presence in her life over the last year and a half was sorely missed. What words of wisdom would she have offered now? What cautions? And what of her mother? What advice would she have given? Caerwin burned incense at the fire in front of Vesta and sent a silent prayer to the goddess.

A tear escaped down her cheek as she looked around the dim room. Beyond the rows of ornate columns, doors to all the bedchambers hovered in shadow. The room's beauty would cheer her more but for the plaster death masks of Petrus, Labeo, and earlier *paterfamiliases* of the Antistia gens. In a line extending from the *lararium* shrine, they watched from their honored places on the alcove walls. A black cloth draped from the Petrus mask, marking him as the most recent death. Like the others, a bronze plaque below the mask listed his accomplishments and positions. Notably fewer remarks appeared below Petrus than below his father or other predecessors.

She studied his face, curious to know if she could discern any hint of his personality. Who was this man who suffered such a tragic loss of his first love? Had his heart broken over Rhian? Is that what drove him to the arms of male lovers and the corruption of his own son? Marcellus was also Rhian's son—why hadn't Petrus honored that?

Did he know that the girl he loved was also his sister? She glanced at Labeo. His was an older face with a furrowed brow and seams beside his large nose. Fierce. She shuddered. Would he have explained to his son that Rhian was his sister? Would Rhian's mother Kensa have told him?

Upon their arrival in Rome, Marcellus had hired men to search for Kensa and Rhian. So far nothing had been found. Surely Kensa would know the answers. But she would also be old by now, quite possibly dead.

She gazed again at Petrus. It was too much to comprehend that a man could become that unfeeling. His fixed eyes stared blankly into the room's shadows from a not unpleasant face—a strong brow and jaw like Marcellus, a straight nose, a slightly cleft chin. But there was nothing restful about his expression in death. His face strained forward as if resisting death to the last moment.

Another chill grabbed her back. Something of this man seemed to hover in the air. He had died at his own hand. Perhaps his spirit walked this room. She glanced around.

The lips—she resisted the urge to touch them. Thin and unappealing, his mouth held nothing in common with Marcellus whose lips she could picture clearly in her mind, sensually curved and easily yielding to the hint of a smile. Not lately, she corrected her thought. His temper grew shorter along with the days.

She had given up expecting him to come to her. He refused to release her from staying in his bedchamber but he didn't touch her. She had mentally sorted through all the reasons he might avoid her and nothing fit into place. The most reasonable conclusion was that he visited Junia's bed. But if that were true, why would he want Caerwin in his bedchamber?

~~~

"Can you not simply tell me the problems?" Caerwin said. She remained clothed and stood by the table eating grapes. "I have a right to know."

Marcellus sat on the side of the bed. "I spend every day struggling with these matters. I don't wish to think of them each night."

"Just the names," she insisted. "Not any explanation."

He swore. "The names? You know them, do you not? My inheritance is at risk. Damages are claimed by the family of a man my father allegedly degraded. The shipping business begs for my attention. The farms in Tunisia remain ungoverned. I've received sex from men and if word of that is made known, I lose my standing." He turned to her. "You. I can't have you as a wife because you're Briton."

"But you said—I thought…"

"Yes, I said I would ask the emperor for your citizenship. But my jurists tell me Emperor Claudius is sensitive on questions of citizenship and we must tread lightly. Building projects and criminal trials add to the burden of his days and he becomes easily annoyed. At this point, I dare not pursue the pleading I had hoped to make. At any rate, the court hearing arrives and I'm ill prepared."

"I don't understand. Does this mean…"

"It means there is much before me. I have duties to Rome. By law I'm required to marry and produce three children in order to rightfully inherit the estate." He threw himself back onto the pillows and ran his fingers through his hair. "And then there's Gaius and the injuries to Leticia as well as to Junia. He has grounds to sue me for damages."

"Junia?" Caerwin whirled around. "What injuries? Have you seen her body? Is it what I suspected, she has enticed you to her bed?"

His breath hissed out between his teeth. "No, Caerwin, I haven't seen her body. I trust her to tell me the truth. Her back and ribs continue to bother her."

"She lies like the snake she is. She abuses your trust."

"This is exactly what I did not want."

"What is it about her that causes your blindness—her exotic looks? Her clever use of cosmetics? Her wealth?"

"Her family," he said. "Her uncle Norbanus Magnus still commands respect in the Empire's inner circles. Her brother

Quartus is missed in royal company. If she speaks badly of me, my prospects will sink even deeper. And it's not only that. There are financial matters…"

Caerwin sighed. "I'm learning to live without you." A long silence ensued. Had she spoken too boldly? What he said about her citizenship—she couldn't track where that might lead.

"Perhaps that's best," he said finally.

Her jaw slacked in disbelief. She had expected his anger or his touch, anything to dispute her growing resignation. Instead, he had affirmed it!

"Then why do you insist that I stay in this room? Is it a matter of your pride? Must you tame me and show me off to the world as your conquest?"

"It has nothing to do with that. Can't you just end this and go to sleep?"

She tore off her clothing and threw it on the floor. "This, Marcellus. See this?" She pointed at her nipples, which pebbled not from the cool air but from her desire. "And this?" She drew her fingertips through her vulva and held the glistening moisture toward him. "Wretched weakness that it is, I still want you. I still expect you to touch me, to say and do the things you have taught me to expect."

He rose from the bed and stalked toward her, his eyes dark with anger. She shrank back, terrified he would shove her out to the atrium to be shamed.

"You need to learn when to silence your tongue, vixen," he said in a hoarse whisper. "Yes, I want you. I keep you here because I can't bear to be away from you. I keep myself from touching you because I have nothing to offer you. Don't you understand? There is no promise I can make, yet you insist on shoving yourself in front of me, tempting me, teasing me, until my tolerance reaches breaking point."

"You want me here," she said. "But you don't want me? What does that mean?"

He seized her arm, pulling her up against his thin tunic. His hard *mentula* bruised against her. "What if I got you with child? Now that I see the obstacles in my path, I can't risk it. Do you think I could bear seeing my child born as a bastard?"

His mouth descended and even in its ugly snarl, she tilted her face up to meet him. She breathed him in. His lips crushed hers. His tongue rammed inside her mouth, lashing until her jaw gaped open and heat flooded up her chest.

He drew back, shaking. "Get out." He grabbed her tunic and jammed it against her chest. His hand brushed her breast and he jerked as if burned. "Take another bedchamber. Sleep with the slaves. I don't care."

~~~

Varinia watched with a skeptical expression as she carried Caerwin's things out of Marcellus' bedchamber. Caerwin had passed the rest of the night sequestered in the new, smaller bedchamber. It had taken hours for her to gain sleep after his furious dismissal. The morning hours brought no relief. His words kept repeating in her ears.

The smaller room sat across the atrium from the dining room, as far from him as she could get. The room wasn't as large as Marcellus' opulent bedchamber at the front end of the atrium but neither was it as small as her cell at the fortress. The size or quality hardly mattered.

She dismissed Varinia and closed the door. In the nearly two weeks since their arrival, her small trunk had been replaced with a larger ornate chest. She pushed the lid up and retrieved the small pot of dirt. The rough surface of the cheap rust-colored pottery rasped under her thumbs as she caressed the jar. After a time, she opened the lid and inhaled the scent of her home earth.

"Mighty Cernunnos, please hear my prayer. Protect Marcellus. Bring him the peace of all wild nature, each season and creature who knows their way under your care. Protect Tutonius and welcome Senna to her rest. Watch over my mother and kinsmen, wherever they may be. Please guide Seisyll so that he does not forever wander."

She whispered in her native tongue. Such language had not passed her lips in months. Even her thoughts had begun to form in Latin. She crouched and scooted the clay pot under her bed, far to the top so it would rest under her head when she slept.

Her act and prayer lightened her heart. She looked around the room. Beyond the bed, a table and two chairs tucked into the far corner where she could stand to look out the window just as she had at the fortress. Only here the window's view didn't open over the Via Principia with its steady traffic of legionaries and tribunes. A narrow garden occupied a space between the house and the high compound wall, a perimeter filled with shrubbery, flowers, vegetables, and herbs. Now with the onset of winter, only the rosemary and some trimmed bushes endured.

She closed the shutters against the cold and sat on the side of the bed. She refused to cry. She would lock Marcellus and his tempestuous manner from her thoughts. Hadn't her life been absorbed by him long enough? Surely there were other pursuits that could occupy her days. She stood up and went into the atrium.

Sounds from the kitchen and the quiet chatter of household staff wafted through the wide doorway that led to the back part of the house. The murmur of workers reminded her of the roundhouse at the Wrekin, women working the loom or preparing food, men fashioning tools or repairing weapons. The incessant activity of children…

Would it ever be safe for Marcellus to get her with child? She imagined its beauty, the tender touch of its tiny hands. How Marcellus would look at her when she delivered him a son or daughter. She could think of nothing more perfect.

Or more impossible.

Her steps turned to the pool where she watched raindrops fall through the *compluvium* from the gray sky. Perhaps today she could convince Gordianus to allow her in the kitchen. She desperately needed to find something to occupy her time.

The entry door opened. Rushing past the doorman, Antius cursed in Greek as he hurried into the sheltering atrium followed by a group of people she'd never seen. They stood momentarily preoccupied with removing their wet cloaks and shaking water from their shoes.

Antius shouted and two slaves scurried from the back of the house to assist. After straightening his clothing, he spotted Caerwin. Water droplets still wet his seamed face.

"You'll be pleased to learn that I've obtained staff to assist you," he said. He grabbed a towel from one of the slaves and, scowling, dried his face and hands. "Marcellus demanded that you be properly served. I think I've covered every possible need."

He motioned to the others, bringing them forward one by one. "This is Gethia. She'll see to your hair, whatever you require to meet his approval. Otherwise she'll serve Varinia."

Caerwin surveyed the older woman. Her light brown hair, brown eyes, and round face topped a plump body that tugged at the lines of her tunic. The woman looked at her with a tired expression and her gaze lingered on Caerwin's frazzled braid.

"Everyone, this is Caerwin," Antius said hurriedly. "She's from Britannia and favored by the master of this house. You'll serve her as you would any noble woman."

Gethia exchanged glances with the other three women in the group.

"This is Fimbria, your bedchamber servant," Antius continued, bringing another woman forward. "She'll tend your clothing and assist you in dressing. Her duty includes expanding your wardrobe, which needs considerable improvement."

Dark hair fastened in a severe bun on the back of Fimbria's head. A quick once over by her dark eyes brought a friendly smile. "We'll have some fun with this, won't we?" she said. "I have contacts all over Rome, some of the best fabric shops." She looked at Caerwin's worn boots. "Am I also to see to her shoes?"

"Yes, yes, the shoes, of course," Antius said. He motioned to another woman. "Hermia is your groomer. She'll wash you, accompany you to the baths, and tend your other bodily needs."

By now Caerwin had become overwhelmed at the sudden prospect of a herd of slaves following her every step. She'd been appalled at Junia's increasing army with a man or woman designated for every tiny act and every hour of the day. Her eyes met Hermia's and much to her relief, she saw some recognition in the woman's expression that said she understood. It helped that like Senna, the woman's skin was freckled and her hair muddled between brown and red. Unlike Senna, a youthful bounce exuded from the woman even though she must be a few years older than Caerwin.

"Come forward, Domitia," Antius said, motioning to an older woman with a pinched look around her mouth. Caerwin disliked her on sight. "Domitia is to manage your schedule. There are festivals and other events which must be observed. If you aspire to be the proper companion to Marcellus, you must attend these events and understand what your role shall be."

Domitia watched her with dark eyes and shrugged her *palla* more closely around her arms. "It will be my pleasure," Domitia said. Why did Caerwin feel that she meant the opposite of what her words said?

"As for these two…" Antius motioned the men forward. "Pantera is to tutor you in subjects of history, language and rhetoric. Tatian will instruct you on Roman law, customs, and manners. You'll have morning sessions each day. Decide the order of the studies according to your need."

As Caerwin looked at these two men, she realized she would have not a moment to herself. Neither resembled Antius, but they carried themselves with similar arrogance. Pantera's head was bald and his belly strained the belt around his tunic. He nodded as she gazed at him and pursed his lips as if he suspected her incapable of the task set before her. The younger Tatian, on the other hand, smiled easily and laughed as he spoke.

"It will be a pleasure, lady," he said. "I trust you're eager to learn Roman ways."

"Yes, eager," she said. "And somewhat apprehensive." She turned to Antius. "This is a daunting development, to suddenly have so many attending my every moment."

"You'll need more," he said dismissively. "A footman, a secretary, litter bearers. But Marcellus wishes to keep the household to a minimum until he can see his way forward. Command them as you will. Although…" He paused to address the group. "You answer to me as well."

"Thank you," she said. "I think."

"Thank Marcellus," he said. "It's his money."

~~~

The walls of Caerwin's small room closed in around her. Her tutors had provided several scrolls for reading, but she couldn't keep her attention from straying. She'd sent away the women, annoyed with them buzzing around her like insects. She wanted Marcellus. Conversation with him, even embattled, would fill this craving for his company even if she couldn't have his embrace.

She stamped her foot and stood with the shutters open, allowing the brazier's heat to escape into the cold dusk. What if she prayed to be relieved of her affection for Marcellus? Could the gods take him out of her heart?

That he lived in her heart could no longer be denied. The passing hours and days drove that truth through her every thought. He was the only thing she cared about. The realization caught her off guard.

Hadn't she known this before? As early as those first months at the fortress, she had tried to deny her attraction. Senna had cautioned her about avoiding her feelings, warned her not to abuse Marcellus. Had her abuse finally turned him away? Did he hesitate to petition the emperor because his emotions for her had begun to flag?

Suddenly filled with a sense of urgency, Caerwin ripped open her bedroom door and hurried toward his room. She would tell him, clearly, that she loved him. Exactly how, she didn't know. Several declarations began and stopped in the time it took for her steps to cover the distance.

She prepared to knock. But what would she say? As her fist hesitated, the door opened. Marcellus filled her frame of vision. A god draped in his white toga, the sight of him alone weakened her knees. Words failed her.

I love you. She would say it. Those simple words would be enough. He'd hold her in his arms. Nothing else mattered.

She opened her mouth to speak then promptly closed it as Junia stepped into view. Despite her olive complexion, her cheeks bore a red flush and her eyes were overbright. Caerwin's gaze lurched back to Marcellus.

"Did you need something?" he said.

His brusque tone startled her.

"I...no, it's nothing," she stammered.

Junia came up behind him and put her hand on his arm. "We'll be late," she said, smiling up at Marcellus.

Caerwin gaped at him in disbelief. Had they...? She couldn't form the thought. He stepped toward her but then Junia took his arm and he stopped.

Caerwin could make nothing of his expression except the anger. Why should he be angry? She was the one who'd clearly been betrayed. Junia in his bedchamber could mean only one thing.

Her gaze quickly inventoried his black hair, the features of his strong face, his wide shoulders, even the span of his hands. His dark eyes glittered as she looked at him. Her intentions fully escaped her as overwhelming hurt flooded her senses.

I love you, she wanted to shout. *I need you. I want you. Hold me and never let me go.*

A short time in her own bedchamber and he had welcomed Junia with open arms. He asked for trust. She spun around and ran back to her room.

~~~

Caerwin stood in the atrium near the entry as Rufus' red tunic reflected midday light. Fimbria waved in the attendants unloading the entire contents of their packs, armloads of yardage for her review. They stacked the bundles on a nearby table. Expertly separating the colorful cloth by fabric type, Fimbria asked the attendant and his slave to wait outside and turned to Caerwin.

"I love red and orange colors and they're very fashionable these days, but I'm not sure they're best for your complexion." She set aside bright orange, bright red, yellow, and a pinkish orange and picked up a large fold of dark orange cloth to hold at Caerwin's shoulder. She cocked her head to the side as she studied the effect. "Maybe. Or something a bit darker. Let's try this *carbasus lina.*"

The russet cloth felt soft and comforting to Caerwin's touch, but she had no idea about its effect on her coloring. Whoever thought of such things?

"Yes, that's good," Fimbria said. "Now of course any of these would work." She began gathering folded lengths of blue, green, and brown fabric.

Almost all of it felt light and pleasing compared to the rough homespun linen and woolens that Caerwin had grown up wearing. She especially liked the *carbasus lina*, a blend of cotton and linen, but the cotton alone—*carbasus*—exhibited almost the same supple richness. Then Fimbria pressed the exquisite lengths of *serica* into her hands, the Chinese silk Junia had praised. The fabric magically shifted color according to the play of light, one moment favoring blue, the next a bluish green. Gold to red in another piece. Red to purple in another.

"Antius has set a strict budget, so we can have only one silk," Fimbria said. "A pound of it costs an equal weight in gold.

Fortunately, enough for a *stola* and *palla* weigh less than a pound. And it shouldn't be the purple—that's the most expensive of all dyes. Do you want silk?"

Caerwin shook her head. "Do I? How would I know?"

Fimbria laughed. "Yes, well then, of the cotton, we can have three or four, depending on how many heavier garments you'll want for cold days. I think this," she said, picked up a thickly woven length of deep brown wool blended with flax. "The color is good and with a long sleeved *stola* in this, you could use different colored *pallas* to change the appearance."

She dropped the wool and put her hand on her hip. "What do you think?"

"I—don't think anything," Caerwin said. "I don't know this fashion you speak of, whether one color or one fabric is better than another. What is this?" She picked up a sheer fabric in pale pink weave. She could see her hand through the cloth. "Has the weaver done so poorly?"

Fimbria's dark eyes sparkled in amusement. She lifted her eyebrow and leaned close. "It's meant to be sheer—it's called *ralla* and ladies use it for *tunica intima*…for enticing their husbands."

Caerwin flushed. The thought of standing before Marcellus in a tunic made of this…she shook her head. The occasion might never arise. Why give hope where there was none?

Then she thought of Junia and her mouth dried. Senna was right. Why give him to her?

"Yes, I see," she said. "Is there white?"

They rummaged through the stack until Fimbria found a length of white *ralla*. She set it beside the blue silk, the russet *carbasus lina* and another in brilliant deep purple—twice dyed in the best Tyrian juice and affordable in the less expensive cloth— and cotton in intense turquoise and also dark green that reminded Caerwin of the cedars on the Wrekin. The wool blend in dark brown joined the stack, along with another in dark red. Fimbria also pulled out lengths of white cotton for several utilitarian tunics.

"Now this," she said, seizing a woven cloth with small designs embossed in the weave. "This is *polymita damask*, the most celebrated of the goddess Minerva's gifts."

Caerwin grasped the cloth to examine it more closely. Multiple colored threads formed patterns in the luminous, heavy material. Like the silk, colors shifted in changing light. "How do they do this, do you know?"

"The weft is twisted," Fimbria said. "A laborious process performed with multiple leashes on the looms of Egypt. These fabrics all come from Alexandria. They say the weaving there is done by men, not women."

"Men?" Caerwin walked near the pool to see the fabric in the weak daylight. Shades of pink, gold, brown, and white threads formed a flowerlike, raised pattern she could trace with her fingertip. "It's stunning work."

The doorman pushed open the door to admit Junia and her gang of slaves. Dressed in one of her new garments, a *stola* of bright red with a *palla* of the same color trimmed in orange handwork, Junia waved them toward the house's interior as she paused to take in Caerwin and the collection of fabrics.

"At long last," Junia said, fingering the silk. "Perhaps I would dare to invite guests here if you're to be properly attired. Although it would be a shame to waste *serica* on you." She glanced at Fimbria. "You have your work cut out for you."

"I think she'll be lovely in *serica*," Fimbria said. "We've chosen the blue. Probably not a good color on you, though." She smiled. "A pleasant day to you, then."

Junia opened her mouth to reply then closed it, frowned, and turned away.

"How did you do that?" Caerwin said, her gaze following Junia's back. "She usually berates me more thoroughly. I can never defend myself."

"My pleasure," Fimbria said quietly. "I have no affection for her sort, always full of venom. Sadly, Rome seems overfull of them. What do you have that she wants, anyway? That's usually at the heart of such treatment."

"There's probably no limit on what she wants. She thinks I have Marcellus, and she wants him."

"Ah." Fimbria nodded. "But you don't have him?"

Caerwin shrugged. "I don't know."

With several bolts of cloth in their arms, the two women retreated to Caerwin's bedchamber where Fimbria measured her, made her marks on a wax tablet, and discussed which fabrics to sew in which pattern.

After a time, the doorman knocked to announce another visitor.

"Oh, thank you Rufus," Fimbria said. "The shoes."

They met the leather vendor and his attendant in the atrium where soft leathers were chosen for sandals, slippers, and two pairs of short boots. Fimbria cut swatches of fabric to have the leather dyed to match.

The concept, indeed the entire process, caused Caerwin's head to ache. Since the morning, when Hermia had awakened her shortly after Marcellus left, her life had not been her own. Gethia had fastened up her hair in tight curls around her forehead while Tatian embarked on another lesson in Roman social manners. His engaging personality made it easy for her to give her attention fully, but the information overfilled her mind.

In spite of her determined effort not to think of Marcellus, what she wanted most was to understand more about the threats confronting him. To him it hardly mattered whether she understood, but she needed to know. She refused to exist only as an ornament.

Chapter Six

Caerwin followed Antius and Tatian as they hurried down the steep curving roadway from their home neighborhood on the *Collis Quirinalis*. Clouds scudded across the sky, threatening rain. Fimbria followed along with Cotta and Falco, the two men Marcellus had commanded to guard her. Far ahead, already out of sight, were Marcellus and his group of clients. She wore the brown wool *stola* and kept her *palla* over her hair as he had instructed.

He had first refused her demand to attend the preliminary hearing. Then she threatened to slip out unattended. For a moment she thought he would strike her and she closed her eyes. Then his footsteps moved away. Only at the door did he turn and grant her permission. His face remained an angry mask.

Despite the several times she had gone out, the hilly streets of Rome still terrified her, winding narrow corridors lined with tall apartment houses and crowded with people. How could so many people live in one place? They occupied tiny rooms smaller than any Cornovii hut, all crammed side by side, on top of each other, like sheep herded into a slaughtering pen. What could possibly bring them all here where so many had to scrape by on daily grain rations and a diet of gruel?

Shops at street level fronted the multi-storied buildings hosting every imaginable enterprise from taverns and food stalls to shops selling vegetables or wine, butchers offering hanging cuts of raw and cured meat, barbers wielding razors and scissors. Displayed on tables spreading into the edges of the streets and protected at night by shutters, the wares of tanners, weavers, fabric merchants, hat makers, book vendors, and jewelers lined every passageway. As they passed yet another bakery, the scent of freshly baked bread momentarily subdued the more common smells of human waste and the acrid scent of urine collected in huge amphora on street corners for the *fullones* who mixed it with water to use in cleaning clothes.

They passed under an aqueduct's high arches, crossed the center of the Forum, and approached the massive *Basilica Julia*. Rows of pillars outlined its lower level. Successive rows framed a second and third level, each level with statues of Roman nobles positioned between the pillars. Once inside, she staggered backwards peering up at the highest roof lofted above the others so that morning light poured down into the building's interior.

Multiple court hearings occupied various spots in the cavernous building. The group pushed through crowds until they reached the area of the place where Marcellus' case would be presented. Benches on stair-stepped platforms lined either side of the center aisle, all of them filled with spectators. At the front, a man sat on an elevated platform robed in a toga chalked to dazzling white.

Antius stopped as they neared the thicket of men gathered at the table where Marcellus stood alongside the two men Caerwin had seen leaving Marcellus' office that morning. She recognized several of the men standing behind Marcellus, clients and freedmen who frequented the morning *salutationes*.

Tatian leaned toward her. "That's his *advocati* Quintillius Manlius with the gold ring on his forefinger and Marius Praetextus on his right, his *causidici*. I've heard him argue cases before. He's absolutely brilliant."

Opposing them were three men, all in tunics under the folds of their togas with two narrow red stripes down the front like Marcellus and his two men.

"That's Clodius Galarius, the plaintiff," Tatian said, pointing to a man with thin brown hair. "To his right is his *causidici*, Plinius Arrianus." He ducked his head to whisper close to her ear. "He's also highly accomplished in law. This won't be easy going."

Caerwin bit her lip. A red flush marked Marcellus' cheeks. His jaw was closely shaven and his dark hair groomed close to his skull. The man he faced, this Clodius Galarius, was also carefully groomed. He stared angrily at Marcellus and lifted his chin belligerently as if challenging Marcellus to a fist fight.

Behind Galarius and his legal team sat an unruly audience of hangers-on plus a knot of attendants. Whispering crowds filled the rest of the benches on both sides of the space. Further away in the building, voices rose and fell in other court proceedings. The *praetor* governing the hearing, Flavius Maximus, stood and the surrounding crowd grew silent.

"Plaintiff, state your charge."

Plinius Arrianus stood. "Our claim, gentlemen, is that during the formative years of my client's brother's youth, certain illegal activities were perpetuated against his person in spite of his status as a freeborn male and against the laws of our great Empire. These activities were committed by Antistius Petrus, the now-deceased father of this man." He pointed at Marcellus.

"These abuses so broke this young man—the family's beloved Clodius Melonius—that upon gaining a full understanding of his degraded status, he took his own life. We ask you to condemn Antistius Marcellus to a payment of no less than one million sestertii to offset the great suffering of the Clodius family."

At this a wail arose from the crowd behind Clodius. A woman stood, waving her arms and sobbing as she tugged at her hair. Angry shouts emerged around her. Two other women pulled her back into her seat as sounds of sobbing continued.

"His mother, I'm sure," Tatian said, rolling his eyes. "So predictable."

The *praetor* turned to Marcellus and his legal representatives. "What say you?"

Marius Praetextus stood. "Sir, these are absurd charges to bring against a man as noble as my client. Antistius Marcellus has served honorably in Rome's Fourteenth Legion Gemina in its conquest of Britannia and has only in the last few weeks returned from those savage shores. Despite injury and deprivation, he has given the Empire his leadership and bravery. Before, during, and after his military duty, he has in all ways conducted himself honorably.

"Yet, upon returning home after ten years of hard duty, he finds this man lying in wait with a superfluous and usurious civil suit meant to deprive him of his wealth and resources. Such an act is a disgrace to the Empire."

Praetextus gestured angrily toward Galarius. "There is no merit in suing for damages that are more than ten years old. There is no justice in trying to extract satisfaction from a son for whatever sins his father might have committed. But sir, let me say, there is more than lack of merit in this preposterous case. This is avarice in its coldest form."

"As the court may know, there were many abnormal and untoward acts committed during the reign of Tiberius, not the least being his disregard for the honorable traditions which guide our steps. He took many young people to his Capri estate and committed all manner of foul deeds upon their persons. His successor Caligula carried forth this disgusting habit. We put to you, sir, that this one Melonius, the beloved brother mourned by Clodius Galarius and his family, was among those who suffered such infamy."

A ripple rushed through the crowd. Flavius Maximus held up his hand.

Praetuxtus cleared his throat and waved his arm. "At the same time he corrupted youth, these former disgraced emperors of Rome preyed upon the fortunes of many of our finest families. Among those forced to shame was this very same Antistius Petrus, who honorably took his own life upon the accusation of sex crimes. The emperor then took this man's hard won interests in lucrative gold mines in Hispania, an act typical of those last years which all of us regret as a grievous offense against the reputation of our glorious Rome.

"Is it too much to see the way these threads connect? Do we not understand how conveniently the boy became a pawn whereby

Antistius Petrus was disgraced and forced to an early death by a power-mad despot who wanted his wealth? Melonius was among many promising young men Antistius Petrus sponsored in fully innocent and above-board activities appropriate to a man of his standing.

"We bring men who will stand on behalf of our client." He turned, calling out names and pointing as each man in turn stood and lifted his fist in acclamation. "From the house of Gellius. From the house of Nepius. From the house of Oranius. From the house of Calventius. From the house of Norbanus."

Caerwin craned her neck to see this Norbanus, uncle of Junia. The white-haired man stood and lifted his arm.

"For that Marcellus suffers the continued harassment of Junia?" Caerwin said.

"*Shh*. He's well known," Tatian said.

More names were called in the lengthy proof of Marcellus' standing. Finally Praetextus thanked them and turned to the *praetor*.

"These are the matters we present in our defense, sir. We pray you immediately dismiss the charge. We can never know if Antistius Petrus touched this boy. There was no suicide note, no proof of this alleged act. As far as we know, the date or place of the alleged offense hasn't even been stated. If the plaintiff presses his cause, we'll have no choice but to file countercharges against Clodius Galarius for slander."

The crowd murmured. The *praetor* sat in silence a few moments before turning to the Clodius counsel. "What is your response?"

"We too can bring forth a lengthy presentation of men who stand behind the Clodius house. But why should we trouble ourselves today with such a display? The facts in this case are simple. This man..." Plinius Arrianus pointed at Marcellus, "must make amends for the wrongs of his father, according to our laws. It is his duty as a citizen of Rome."

The *praetor* Flavius Maximus raised his hand. "This matter deserves a full hearing of evidence, the testimony of witnesses, and whatever documentation can be presented by either side. I will call in both parties to agree on a judge and we will proceed on the Ides of December."

~~~

It hurt not to be with him. Each day passed in Caerwin's agonizing conflict between avoidance and confrontation. When he caught her looking at him, he turned his head and hurried away. When she could no longer keep her eyes from adoring him, he seemed to feel her gaze and would look up for a moment of raw emotion so great they both reacted as if burned.

Most painful were the dinners when he demanded her presence at the table and then made a show of ignoring her. She became accomplished at flirting with every other man except him. Her senses had become so finely tuned that when she entered the dining room in his presence, her hand trembled and her nipples tightened. She only had to look up to see his face with its stony expression. Then her resolve hardened.

With the trial looming, evenings divided between Marcellus going out on invitation from various important households and equally important gatherings at the Antistius *domus*. He never took her with him when he went out, but he did on occasion take Junia. On those nights when she watched him leave with her, Caerwin paced the length of the atrium muttering and clenching her fists. More than once, she followed the methods Tatian had shown her in preparing curses, pressing the stylus to form careful small letters on a sheet of lead, rolling it, piercing the roll with a long nail and burying it in the garden where the curses would be forever preserved.

"*I curse Norbanus Junia,*" she wrote. "*And her life and mind and memory and liver and lungs mixed up together, and her words, thoughts and memory; thus may she be unable to speak what things are concealed, nor be able to laugh.*"

On another, she used Tatian's suggestion. *Gaia, Hermes, Gods of the Underworld, receive Junia, sister of Quartus.* Just carving the words on the soft metal plate gave her immense satisfaction.

The dinners at home had become an arena for flattering supporters and persuading fence sitters. Exotic dishes. Three musicians instead of one. Dancers. Poets. The best wine, the freshest winter vegetables, and wild game from the nearby forests provoked exclamation and praise. Caerwin became skilled at deflecting questions and inserting clever remarks all while her senses staggered under the weight of tension radiating from Marcellus.

Junia attended as well, dressed in her finery and extravagant jewels. She placed herself between unaccompanied men, frequently darting glances at Marcellus as if to gain approval for her flirtations. The men enjoyed the effort.

Caerwin did not. But she forced herself to learn from it, all the little winks and ducks of her head, the delicate manner in which she took food. The woman performed a clever act meant to show her fascination and absolute dependence on men for her every need. Caerwin sometimes failed to chew as she watched the display.

Men's eyes often rested on Caerwin as well. She tried to exhibit the same behavior as Junia but more than once she caught Marcellus watching her with a furious expression. What did he expect?

Putting himself forth as a bold and courageous warrior, Marcellus bragged of his battles and the difficulties of warfare, much to the amusement and admiration of his guests. Such self-aggrandizement didn't suit him and Caerwin could see that the effort took its toll. He hardly ate. He drank too much. No one but her seemed to notice.

At least, the dinners garnered exuberant praise. Gordianus proved his worth with meals of uncommon extravagance: roasted dormice stuffed with pork and pine nuts, marinated sow udder, succulent cuts of kid or young pig, peacock breast framed in brilliant blue feathers, wild game from rabbit to ibex, oysters and mussels with herbed butter, and elaborate desserts from exotic fruits to pastries layered with soft cheese and honey.

Tatian attended wearing tunics of red or blue or his favorite color turquoise which set off his skin tones in a most flattering way. He stood behind the head table in the corner nearest Marcellus and made certain the wine cups never emptied. Even more obsequious to the guests, he suffered the occasional pinch or pat on the ass by a half drunk man to whom he would giggle appropriately.

The entire ritual of courtship to improve social standing exhausted Caerwin, not so much for herself but for the expense Marcellus surely suffered and for the enormous toll on the staff. Bones, shells, and other inedible bits littered the dining room floor and slaves regularly swept up the mess to keep from slipping as they served. Guests ate until they vomited, as was evidently the habit in Rome, and it was left to the slaves to quickly clean the mess.

"Roman meals disgust me," Caerwin said tiredly. It had been a long dinner lasting well into the night.

Hermia released the shoulder clasps holding the *stola* together and helped Caerwin step out of the garment. The small bedchamber had chilled despite the heated floor and coals glimmering in the brazier had yet to warm the space.

"They say the savages of Britannia eat only cow meat and drink only beer. We would find that equally disgusting," Hermia said as she turned back the bed covers.

"Falsehoods," Caerwin said hotly. She poured wine, trying to ignore the stupid woman's remark. Why did Romans always look down on those unlike themselves? What was wrong with differences? Besides, they had nothing to feel so proud about. She had limited her intake at the meal not only to avoid the excesses on display all around her but because Marcellus had seated Junia at the head table. Her fury wasn't limited to Junia. Tatian, dressed in a lavish green silk tunic so short his lower buttocks showed when he bent over, had hovered by Marcellus. Their interchanges captured her attention.

"Their sexual behavior disgusts me as well."

"Oh? Did they couple on the couches? I've seen that before."

"I shudder to think. No. But Junia practically crawls into his lap and Tatian's always with him. His affection is easy to see—such adoring glances, so eager."

"What does it matter?"

Caerwin sipped the wine and stepped closer to the brazier. "I tell myself it doesn't matter. Tatian is a slave and men of Rome take slaves whenever they wish. There's nothing implied by it. It's sex."

Hermia sat on the side of the bed. "That's true. So why did you ask?"

Caerwin's hand gripped the goblet stem. "Every moment I think he might touch someone, I burn inside. I think of how much they desire and admire him and how flattered Marcellus must be." She sat in the chair and leaned her head back against the wall. "Do men not feel such things?"

"Everyone has feelings," Hermia said. "How could we not? I had feelings for my former mistress Clemenia. I loved the fragrance of her skin. She had generous lips that I loved to kiss. I miss her."

"Is that how it always goes? We love someone and then lose them?" Caerwin's throat tightened. "Why suffer such torment? Why not avoid such feelings?"

"Can you?" Hermia stepped to the table and boldly poured some wine for herself then sat in the other chair. She had never asked and often assumed such privileges, but Caerwin hadn't found the courage to deny her. "Does your heart not long for this man no matter how you try to stop it? The gods have their own plans despite what we wish."

Caerwin nodded. "I think of him with someone else and it hurts as if a knife lodged in my chest."

"Do you think Junia or Tatian will take your place in his affections?"

"He tells me he has no interest in Junia." Caerwin chewed her lip. "I think—he could enjoy Tatian. Perhaps I fool myself. Perhaps I'm no longer in his affections."

The oil lamps dimmed and flickered as if a breeze had passed through the room. As if spirits moved about. The hair on Caerwin's neck went up.

She could hear Senna's voice, all the times she had reminded Caerwin of how much Marcellus cared for her. Hadn't he saved her from the slavers? Hadn't he held her in his arms, made her eat when she only wanted to die?

Hermia wasn't Senna. She hadn't witnessed the months of their relationship. Hermia couldn't know what Senna knew. Tears sprang to Caerwin's eyes.

Loneliness had started to weigh on her.

"I don't know," she said. A sob escaped her. "He said he'd never loved anyone like he loved me. But such feelings can change. I've become a burden. Another problem to solve in a long list of terrible problems. How could he love me?"

Hermia plucked a grape from the tray. "How could you love him? Haven't you said he led his legion against your people and took you captive? Didn't he hold you prisoner? Even here, aren't you his prisoner? Why do you care what he does?"

"I can't help myself," Caerwin said.

"Exactly. It's not our choice," Hermia continued. "The gods will it. But if you must know, you could ask Tatian."

"Do you think he'd tell me?"

"Why not? You have no real power over him, so he has nothing to fear if you know." She smiled and leaned toward

Caerwin. "That Tatian is a busy man. There is much gossip about him—he serves women as well as men. How do you think he became so well educated? It's unheard of for a common slave, yet he circulates freely among the noblemen. They say his *mentula* is enormous." She laughed and poured more wine. "Nothing propels a man, any man, to higher standing than an oversized prick."

Caerwin gasped. She hadn't considered women exchanging embraces. Now this. "People say these things?"

"Why not? Those of us in service are the ones who know all the secrets. Some are more discrete than others, but we live with our masters. We see everything."

"What other secrets do you know? Do you know anything of Junia?" Caerwin downed the rest of her wine, instantly regretful of asking.

"Junia? She's a beautiful woman with great wealth. She'd make him a good wife. I've heard little of her activities. She keeps her mouth closed." Hermia caught a glimpse of Caerwin's face. "What else do you expect me to say? I only repeat what you have said."

"Then something else, anything besides Junia."

"I know that the small service I offer you in the baths causes you to want more."

Caerwin stared at Hermia. Her face heated in the memory of the regular massage and oiling after baths and of the woman's often intimate touch. "The small service…touching me? You think I want more?"

Hermia's eyes narrowed as she smiled. "Do you deny it?"

"Do such acts mean so much?"

Hermia shrugged. "It's not that it holds meaning. It's a normal human activity and the outcome is pleasure. Why can't that be enough?"

Why indeed? Was it possible to simply engage in erotic acts and garner no lingering emotion? Did Tatian meet with Marcellus to engage? She desperately wanted to know more about their relationship. "I…it seems reasonable when you say it like that."

"You're young. You'll learn to know the difference between pleasuring and true emotion. Perhaps this 'love' you feel for Marcellus is really only the result of his pleasuring. Have you thought of that?"

"I haven't said I feel love for Marcellus."

"You drag through your days as only a woman can when she believes herself in love."

Caerwin stood up, suddenly restless and in need of some urgent act. The room spun slightly, reminding her of her cups of wine. "Pleasure me then," she said abruptly. "I must know."

She tugged off her tunic and lay stiffly on her back. The bed dipped as Hermia knelt beside her. The woman's warm hands swept up her sides and brushed over her breasts.

"It will be my pleasure, sweetness. Just relax now, let me take you away from your worries."

Slowly, Caerwin's muscles relaxed as Hermia touched her from her toes to her forehead. The gentle caressing motion soon became the only thought occupying her mind. When Hermia's fingertips circled her nipples, a shiver ran through her. She hadn't known how much she had longed to be touched. Her skin felt alive under Hermia's embrace.

If only it could be Marcellus' embrace. Weeks had passed since their arrival. Only that first night here had he taken her. She needed him. Why couldn't he at least hold her or kiss her?

The magical soothing warmth of Hermia's hands shunted her sad thoughts away. She forced herself to think only of Hermia. Gooseflesh pimpled her arms as Hermia spread Caerwin's legs to expose her clean-plucked vulva.

"You have a beautiful *cunnus*," Hermia murmured. "Such a stiff little crest, too."

Caerwin jumped as Hermia's fingers touched her clitoris. Heat swelled her labia. She whimpered and tossed, uncomfortable and at the same time tantalized.

Hermia played around the edges, only occasionally placing pressure on the spot that craved pressure the most. The fluid leaking from her arousal became an instrument of torture as Hermia spread it up and around the tip, circling and pressing until Caerwin's thighs clenched together.

Hermia pushed Caerwin's knees up and spread her feet further apart. The air smelled of wine and flowers. The oil lamp flickered. With her most vulnerable parts fully exposed, she felt the same submission she felt when Marcellus tied her. She longed to be bound, to feel the ropes on her wrists, to hear the whistle of the lash in those last seconds before the leather tendrils seared her skin. To inhale his scent as his excitement grew…

Marcellus! Her need for him crowded everything else out of her mind. To have him over her, his cock plunging deep…

Hermia pinched the tip of her clitoris and forced it up and back in short jerking motions. Perspiration flushed over Caerwin's skin as her orgasm erupted. Gasping, she sat up and pushed Hermia away.

"This is…I can't. Please, leave me," she said, clasping her hand between her legs. She wanted to erase everything that had just happened.

"I thought you wanted this," Hermia said.

"I didn't know," Caerwin said. She felt nauseous. "Just go."

~~~

"Each day, yes, it matters," Domitia said.

"See, didn't I say?" Fimbria said. Crouching, she adjusted the russet *stola*'s length.

"It's a waste," Caerwin replied. "No one sees me but you and the other servants. Why bother?"

The three women crowded the bedchamber with Domitia seated at the table. Her scowl had become a familiar feature.

Fortunately, the morning had warmed and sunlight flooded through the open window.

"It's for you," Fimbria said. "Don't you feel more assured and beautiful when you're well dressed?" She stood up and stepped back to assess the garment.

"It's also for your master," Domitia said. "He wishes you to be well dressed. You must do his bidding."

"He never sees me. He's gone before I take breakfast."

"Then you must rise earlier," Domitia said. "Each morning you must greet him with a smile and a lovely appearance. You must attend the Forum shops and temples. His reputation will suffer if you don't take part in the proper festivals. We have many upcoming events and you must be ready with proper demeanor."

"Already you've missed the Plebian Games," Domitia continued. "The feast for Jupiter went especially well this year. And two days of games—have you been to the chariot races yet?"

"Marcellus has no time for games," Caerwin said. "Antius mentioned them."

"You've also missed the Kalends for the month with the ceremonies at the temples of Neptune and Pietas. Today is the *Bona Dea*. In a few days, we must join the celebration of Agonalia. Then Saturnalia will be upon us.

"You'll exhaust her," Fimbria said. "Surely you don't think she must attend every festival."

"I have an impossible task," Domitia said in a sharp voice. "How am I to teach her ways of a proper Roman woman if she ignores my advice?"

"I think this *stola* requires nicer pins," Fimbria said. She rummaged in Caerwin's small box of valuables and stood up with her arms folded across her chest, looking at Domitia. "Can we agree that at least she should be properly attired before she begins making social rounds? Surely you can't expect that she learn so much overnight."

"What is this *Bona Dea*?" Caerwin said.

"The Good Goddess protects all women. She also protects Rome and our harvests. Vestals give blood sacrifice to the goddess Juno and offer prayers. It's only for women and everyone drinks strong wine. There are things that happen when the women are overtaken by wine, pleasures not spoken out loud. All proper women attend," Domitia said.

Caerwin thought of Hermia's touch and heat rose to her cheeks.

"Not all," Fimbria said. "The old…"

"Don't bother with that," Domitia said. "It's my responsibility to see that she goes."

"Please, can we be finished for now?" Caerwin said, looking at Domitia. "I'll think on the *Bona Dea* festival."

Domitia stood up. "Very well. I'll come again after lunch."

Fimbria waited until she left. "She's disagreeable enough, isn't she? The *Bona Dea* has a scandalous history. You'd be well served not to attend."

"Why would she urge me to?"

"Clearly she doesn't have your best interests in mind. She bears watching. Antius didn't mention jewelry, but you must have more than this." She motioned to the box. "What do you recommend?"

"I'll ask Antius," Caerwin said. "About more jewelry and about Domitia."

~~~

Caerwin sat with Pantera in the *peristylium.* Sunlight warmed her head, making her restless. Her lessons with him exhausted her patience. He consumed another fish cake then wiped his fingers before turning to her.

"Do you remember the second step we discussed last week?"

"Yes. *Dispositio.*"

"Tell me the steps," he said.

She sighed. In spite of unfamiliar terms and formalized organization, she had quickly seen that the Roman art of rhetoric differed little from the patterns of debate long honored among the Cornovii. Facts in support of a particular viewpoint were developed and arranged then delivered in a persuasive manner. She'd grown up listening to the men of their tribe present arguments in exactly this manner.

"First, the introduction," she said. "Present the case briefly, then expand with a more detailed explanation—*narratio*." She proceeded through the rest of the steps.

"Very good. What's the example for a legal argument?" Pantera said, taking a drink from his wine cup. "Such as might occur in court."

The example he had explained to her before had lodged firmly in her thoughts. This was what Marcellus faced in defending himself and despite the distance between them, her concern had grown on his behalf.

"The prosecutor must first declare the charges against the defendant," she said, "and provide the relevant facts. Then he must present the evidence that proves guilt."

"Ah if only all men practiced such judicious thought," Pantera said, taking another pastry from the nearby platter. "My former master judged me unworthy of manumission on the minor trifle in my use of wine. What man does not enjoy his wine? An entirely specious argument."

"Or woman," she said.

"Yes, yes, women enjoy wine as well. Except my wife who follows the old admonitions against its use by women. She blames me for excesses yet *sestertii* flow through her fingers like water in the fountains."

"I didn't know you had a wife."

"Slaves can't legally marry, but we pledged ourselves many years ago. She belongs to another household," he said. "Along with our children. I suffer such tragedy, a sin for a learned Greek such as myself. The playwrights surely use me as a model for their creations. My father would turn over in his grave."

"You can see her, surely," she said.

"The children as well, when they're not squawking for a coin. She has trained them, you see, to extort money from me. As if they weren't well fed. The little beggars will soon be sold, and then Musia will rip her hair and beat on me for failing to save sufficient funds to buy them myself."

He eyed her as he drained his cup. "Why would I want them? Even if I could afford to buy them, which is completely out of the question, what would I do with them? Only the oldest pleases me and he's already of an age that he should join the auxiliary legions and make a way for himself."

The man's cheeks had flushed. She'd learned in the first week of their lessons that as his wine intake advanced through the morning, his ability to teach fell off. He arranged his pace in a way that guaranteed he would be on hand for the midday meal. His ability to teach paled in comparison to Antius or Tatian, who presented information in a manner she found much more instructive. Perhaps she would speak to Antius and suggest that Marcellus save his money and let Pantera blunder off the same way he came.

"What do you know of the *Bona Dea* festival?" she said.

His eyebrows shot up. "The Good Goddess?"

"Yes. Domitia insists I must go," Caerwin said.

"The name is not to be spoken by men. Did she not tell you that? What is that shrew about? You absolutely shouldn't."

"What? Why would Domitia insist?"

He lifted his wine up and drained it. "She must have some motive. Anyone could tell you it would be a mistake, especially for one such as yourself. Let the battle be waged by the noblewomen."

"I don't understand."

"Be cautious, little girl. Someone seeks to harm you."

Caerwin excused herself from Pantera, who had retrieved another cup of sour wine from the wine room attendant and now talked to himself as he walked along the edge of the garden. The midday flush of sunlight pouring through the roof opening reflected off his bald head.

She intercepted Antius as he hurried through the atrium with his lips pursed and forehead creased, talking to himself.

"I need your help," she said.

Antius stopped and looked at her with an annoyed expression. "What's the crisis today? Do you have a loose thread?"

"Aside from the fact that you're an ass and I'm forced to your company?" she said. "Hear this." She launched into a quick summary of the Domitia problem. "You hired her," she concluded. "Does she mean me harm?"

"She came highly recommended and seemed eager for the position."

"Who recommended her?"

He shook his head. "I don't remember. These petty intrigues consume my life," he muttered. "I'll find a replacement if you wish."

"Don't. Just send her away. I've already given Gethia to Varinia. Fimbria and Hermia are more than enough. I like doing things for myself," she said. "While you're here, what of Marcellus? He's always rushing about," she said. "I don't dare ask him anything."

"He extends too much time and money worrying about citizenship for you," he said with a sniff. "As for the legal matters, they grow as many heads as the Hydra."

"Please, Antius, I must know."

He studied her for a moment. "What you must or must not know couldn't concern me less. You're one of the reasons he's in such a state."

"That's not any fault of mine," she said. "He took me from my home and abused…"

"He's elevated you to expectations far above your station," he interrupted. "But never mind. His fortunes rest entirely in the hands of the *praetor* and his choice of a judge."

"Is that all?"

"No, of course that's not all," he said, starting to walk away. "I don't have time to satisfy your idle curiosity."

"What of the matter of his true mother?" she said, hurrying after him. "Did he know this man, this Melonius? Who knows about his relations with you or with Silverus?"

"Quiet, you fool!" His voice lowered to a whisper. "Think of what ears are about to hear these secrets! Do you wish to see him stripped of his wealth and exiled to a distant island?"

"No, of course…"

"Then stop asking questions. There is nothing for you to know. These matters require careful vetting and only in the most trusted circles."

"I thought no one could be trusted."

Antius stopped at the door to Marcellus' study. "No one can. I have documents to retrieve and an errand that presses me for time. Rest assured you'll be told whatever you need to know."

Rufus shoved the vestibule door open to admit Tatian, who hurried inside and adjusted his turquoise cloak. He wore a long tunic in darker blue and the curls of his light brown hair suffered their usual disarrangement. His casual survey of the room soon fastened on Caerwin and Antius, and he strode in their direction.

"The case draws attention in the emperor's inner circle," he said to Antius.

Antius rubbed his forehead. "Good or bad?"

"They say good. Calidius Vedius. They say there's no shortage of influence Vedius might wield if he could be convinced of Marcellus' innocence."

"Calidius Vedius," Antius said. He glanced at her briefly.

Caerwin's mind raced at the troubled expression on his face. Where had she heard that name before?

That Tatian had been immediately and thoroughly enlisted by Antius to assist in the legal matters swirling around Marcellus had not surprised Caerwin. The young man had fully applied himself in his study of legal matters and served as an important resource. He also knew his way around the important people in Rome. Had he advocated for this Vedius?

"He serves the emperor," Tatian said.

Antius paced. "What does he want?"

"If Marcellus knows Vedius, he should refresh his acquaintance and do everything in his power to gain his favor," Tatian said. "Assuming the relationship was not adversarial."

"Not exactly," Antius said, frowning.

~~~

Caerwin lingered near the throng of men waiting for audience with Marcellus. From what she could hear lurking near the office, the morning *salutatio* had become a boring repetition, always how wonderful Marcellus was, how important his esteem, how much they respected and admired him, and could he please appear in court to attest to their worthiness. Or could he please provide a *sestertius* or two for the well-being of his children. Some of the faces had become familiar but new ones appeared daily.

How must it be for Marcellus to face so much in his own struggle and yet hear these grievances while expected to reward their requests? She skirted the crowd to peek in and her heart wrenched at the sight. Dark shadows circled under his eyes. Why hadn't she noticed how gaunt he'd become? His hands…

He glanced up and for a moment, the men, the room, and everything else disappeared. She felt his touch on her skin. His breath warmed her cheek. The beat of his heart drummed against her chest. His dark eyes lingered on her, full of emotion.

Then his gaze returned to the man standing before him. As if a curtain closed.

She turned away from the door, rubbing her arms against a chill that had little to do with the weather. A man stepped into her path, well-dressed in heavy tunic, *braccae*, and dark cloak. He wore several rings and watched her with an expression of amusement.

"You're new in the Antistius house," he said, smiling. "What's your name?"

"Why do you ask?" she said.

"Why not? Are you a secret?"

"That's ridiculous," she said. "How could I stand here and be a secret?"

He tilted his head as if examining a peculiar object. "The flavor of your speech suggests a recent arrival in Rome. Let me see—Marcellus has just returned from Britannia. You must be of those lands." He rubbed his chin. "Copper hair, eyes the color of the Tyrrhenian Sea—yes, I'd say that's right. What do you say?"

"I say you're nosy and without sufficient work to occupy your attention," she said.

His bold laugh resounded through the long atrium and caused heads to turn. "Tell me, Briton wench, might a man find a hint of warmth in the kitchens of this house where perhaps he might also take a crust of bread?"

"Why do you think you should gain access to the private rooms of this house?" she said.

He stuck out his hand. "Sigilis," he said. "Even if you won't give your name, I'll give mine. I'm manager of the Antistius shipping fleet, here to give a long awaited report to Marcellus, assuming he ever gains a moment free of his impressive following."

She allowed him to clasp her hand, taken aback by his forceful approach and the humor in his smile. "You've been a guest here in the past?" she asked, withdrawing her hand.

"Many times. The matters that occupy my days revolve around the shipyard at Neopolis. Financial matters call me here from time to time but not often enough to justify the expense of my own *domus*. I hope there's a bedchamber I might occupy for my stay in Rome."

Her reserve softened. "Well then, I'm Caerwin of the vanquished tribe called Cornovii. Come this way."

She led him to the kitchen and, despite a frown from Gordianus, retrieved a half loaf of still-warm bread, a pot of soft cheese, and an apple. They retreated to the bench beside the oven where Sigilis tore into the bread like a starving man.

Halfway through the meal, he paused and sighed. "The ship only arrived this morning. It was a cold miserable journey. I apologize if I infringed on your privacy."

"You're the least of my concerns," she said. "I have no authority to allow you here, yet it seems to fall on me to decide what to do next."

"A slave new to the household?"

"Depends on who you ask." Caerwin dodged Gordianus at the chopping table and poured a cup of fresh milk for herself and Sigilis.

"Thanks. I'm asking you," Sigilis said.

"I could be a slave, but he says I'm not."

"'He' being Marcellus?"

She nodded. "I'm evidently a *peregrinus*, although I'm still uncertain exactly what dishonor or duty that places on me. My role in this household remains unclear, depending on legal actions currently underway. Or not, depending on the day and his mood. Or," she said, suddenly not wanting to be unfair to Marcellus, "the latest obstacle thrown in his path."

"Complicated situation." He drained the cup and brushed bread crumbs from his lap. He stood up and stretched. "I may live to see another day," he said.

Marcellus strode into the room. His gaze flickered, briefly acknowledging her presence before giving his full attention to Sigilis. "I thought I heard your voice. Antius said you'd arrived."

They clasped hands.

"I forced myself on your non-slave," Sigilis said with a laugh. "Are you yet free of your adoring throng?"

Marcellus frowned, glancing at Caerwin then Sigilis. "Forced yourself?"

"Just as I thought," Sigilis laughed. "Complicated." He patted Marcellus' shoulder. "Forced her to give her name and show me a bit of hospitality. I think she would have left me with old Rufus if I hadn't poured on the charm. Can we talk business now and might I enjoy your hospitality until my business in Rome concludes?"

"Of course. I'll have someone prepare a room. I apologize if my hospitality has been found lacking," Marcellus said stiffly, walking alongside Sigilis. "We've only arrived in the last few weeks and the staff is still not sorted out. Varinia should have met you."

"I joined the waiting crowd, so your staff wouldn't have known I required a welcome. It was only upon setting eyes on this clever woman that my hunger exceeded my restraint."

Caerwin followed the men, put on edge by the bantering manner of Sigilis. Did he intend to provoke Marcellus?

"Keep a firm grip on your restraint," Marcellus said. "I pay a high price for that clever woman."

"You bought her then? She said she didn't know if she was a slave."

Marcellus looked back at Caerwin. "I didn't buy her. She's not a slave. But each day I pay."

Another loud shout of laughter from Sigilis bounded through the atrium. "I catch your meaning. My most sincere condolences. Will we be graced by her presence in our meeting?"

"If she so chooses," Marcellus said. He turned and looked at her with an inquiring expression.

"Oh, please, might I?" she said, clasping her hands together in supplication.

Sigilis slapped Marcellus' back, snorting with glee. "So long overdue," he said.

Once seated, the men immediately launched into a discussion of all things ships.

"I brought the redesigned *liburna* up, if you want to see her," Sigilis said. "She's sleek, a real beauty."

"How fare the markets?"

"The Egyptians outpace us in warships, but what wars are on the horizon? The world is Rome's now and except for the pirates, we have no enemies. The money's in the big merchant ships, but there's some market for a few fast vessels for couriers and the sort," Sigilis said. "We near completion of our sixth ten-thousander. That puts us in a strong position for renewal of government contracts, now and well into the future. If Jove himself became emperor, he'd never dishonor the *Cura Annonae*—another grain shortage would bring riots in the streets. "

"That's the good news. What's the bad?"

"Shipbuilders and ship's crews both suffer the winter lull. I added a pittance to the builder's wage. Easier to train a man to row than to properly form a ship's hull."

"What of Neppius? Have you found a replacement?" Marcellus said.

"I hoped for your guidance on that. For now I've assigned each ship's captain the duty of issuing receipts for goods loaded and unloaded, but they aren't so well qualified for the task. The numbers never tally. The grain shipments alone could cause legal action if the curator finds discrepancies."

"Jove's stones!" Marcellus looked up and closed his eyes in an expression of despair that shocked Caerwin. "If I come out with anything, I'll have to sell interest in the business. I had hoped to avoid such action."

"We've had bad luck in the crops as well, if you didn't know. Drought and locusts plague northern Africa. For the third year." Sigilis said. "The Antistius farms aren't alone in the losses. I didn't want to tell you while you faced warfare, but now that you're here..."

"What do you think of using a few of our merchants on profitable cargo like silk?" Marcellus said. "We could make short work of olive oil, garum, wine—maybe marble or metal ingots. I haven't calculated exact margins, but I think we'd do well."

"I completely agree. It's the timing that's critical. In these winter months when there's no shipping, we need to secure contracts and plan our routes."

"I've had no time to meet with the curator." Marcellus glanced at Caerwin. "Each day my problems grow new problems."

"I can help with that. In fact, that's partly why I'm here. I'll solicit the curator's attention this very day." Sigilis dropped forward to rest his elbows on his knees as if taking careful consideration of his words. "Gossip precedes you. They say you may lose your fortunes."

"I could lose it all," Marcellus said heavily. "I could be exiled."

"The gods! I had no idea. What of the ships?"

Marcellus shook his head. "If things go badly…"

"I know you've been out of Rome, so perhaps you could use some referrals. There's a man, highly placed. He's done a favor for me before. For a price. Could I ask him?"

"Who is it?"

"Calidius Vedius—do you know him?"

Marcellus' face lost color. His stature changed. He stood up.

"Perhaps," he said quietly. "I have much to consider."

Chapter Seven

Leading his troop of clients, Marcellus strode down the avenue to see and be seen. Only a few days remained before the trial and the pace of his efforts to recruit support had reached a fever pitch. Junia with two of her attendants, Caerwin with Fimbria and Hermia, and a few of the household staff followed to the jam-packed Via Sacra to observe the sacrifice of a ram in honor of Agonalia. The festival marked an ancient propitiation to the highest gods, asking for the preservation of Rome's well-being.

Thousands of people packed the streets and tenements, a bizarre assortment of Latins, Egyptians, Greeks, Asians, Africans, Germans, Gauls—and many more. How many countries had Rome overrun? Surely the entire world resided in this city. Her ears buzzed with the hubbub of laughter and shouts in many languages. In the circle of soaring temples, splashing fountains, and flattering monuments to Rome's glorious past, her curious glances met equally curious return stares. People rushed past with bundles of goods or stood on the street corners eating one or another of the seemingly endless assortment of food from salted peas to fried fish, sausages, or pastries.

Caerwin lost sight of Marcellus and Junia after the blood-letting and songs, stopping with Fimbria, Cotta, and Falco for a lunch of chickpea cakes and honeyed fruit before going to the imperial *thermae*. Like the other three baths she'd visited so far in Rome, the extravagant building near the Forum far surpassed the bath house at Verulamium. Colorful murals of nude gods and goddesses covered the walls. Mosaics of sea creatures cavorting among waves passed underfoot. Making their way slowly through the crowded atrium and following lines of people past the exercise area, cold plunge, and then the steam rooms, they stopped at the wide arched entry to the *tepidarium*.

Nude bodies rimmed the long rectangular pool. A few swam. The sounds of quiet laughter, conversation and splashing water bounced down from the high ceiling. Adults of all ages and class crowded the warm room. Tables for massage and oiling lined the perimeter.

"Go on," she said to Fimbria. "I'll be along."

She wanted to believe what Marcellus told her about his situation with Junia. Her instinct said there was more to know, things that Marcellus didn't wish to tell her. Junia had stayed close to him today. Was this her normal behavior in public, insinuating that they belonged together?

Had he been infected by her charm?

Caerwin took her time carefully scanning the length of the pool, trying not to stand out in the busy multitude. Finally she spotted Junia at the far end. Her face in profile, the dark haired woman stood chest deep in the water. Laughing, she splashed water on her arms and gently bobbed up and down.

Caerwin could see the bounce of her breasts as she moved. She could also see the purpose of her movement, indeed the purpose of her entire play as she splashed water again, this time against the chest of a man standing nearby.

Marcellus.

Just as she thought.

Breathless, her pulse pounding a steady drumbeat in her ears, Caerwin hurried to the changing room to find Fimbria. Moments later with her nude body wrapped in her towel, she skirted the pool before discarding the towel to slip into the water near a group of women. With Fimbria following close behind, she slowly began easing her way toward Marcellus.

"Oh, I see what you're about. You're after Junia," Fimbria whispered.

"Yes," Caerwin said. "If she can do this, I can."

"Good!"

He stood with a cluster of men. Glorious in his nudity, he leaned back with his elbows resting against the pool rim. His dark hair curled at his nape and around his temples and scattered across his muscled chest. For a moment, Caerwin drank in the scene. He was the only person she saw. As her eyes feasted on his beauty and warm water lapped her body, she could not move or think.

Then her gaze shifted to Junia. Only a few steps away from Marcellus, she talked with other women, periodically turning in his direction to say something. Caerwin's blood pounded in her ears.

"Hold me," she said to Fimbria. "I might do something terrible."

"She deserves something terrible, doesn't she?" Fimbria said.

"I can't embarrass Marcellus," Caerwin said. "Tell me what to do!"

"Do what she does. If he complains, you can say you only imitated her."

"Excellent plan!"

Despite Fimbria's encouragement, Caerwin's courage faltered as she neared Marcellus. She had never been with him in the baths, strange as that seemed now. He'd given her no explicit directives about bathing, said only that she should partake freely of the women's baths. Well, women were here and this was a bath. Exhilaration and dread sent gooseflesh down her arms.

She came as close as she dared, about the same distance from him and his group of friends as Junia. She recognized Sigilis speaking with Marcellus. Antius, Tatian, the two lawyers…the gods!

"I can't do this," she whispered to Fimbria.

"Why not? Look around. What do you see?"

"People without clothes talking and laughing," Caerwin said.

"Exactly. Why can't you do that?"

Caerwin stared at Marcellus' perfect form as he turned toward Sigilis, the curve of his shoulder, the narrowing at his hips and the roundness of his buttocks. Sweat beaded on her forehead.

She wanted him. She could stand here all day just to see him like this. Her nipples puckered.

Minutes later, Junia saw her. With her mouth slightly parted in surprise, the woman stared at her with an expression of hate and fury. That made it all worthwhile. Caerwin lowered her eyelids slightly and smiled.

Then Sigilis saw her and his face changed as well. He motioned and said something. Marcellus turned as if expecting to see someone he didn't know. When his gaze fastened on her and recognition set in, his smile quickly changed. A furious expression spread over his face as started toward her.

"Dear Juno. Here," Fimbria said. "Let's play." She splashed water on Caerwin.

Stiff with anxiety, Caerwin forced herself to splash back. She also forced herself to laugh as she bounced up and down in duplication of Junia's act. In the corner of her eye, she could see Marcellus coming near.

She had no doubt of his anger. She could feel it searing her back like heat from a bonfire.

"What in the name of the almighty gods are you doing here like this?" he said from behind her. His voice, although lowered, resonated through her.

She turned, smiling and forcing a look of innocence. "Whatever do you mean? I'm having a bath, just like you and Junia." She laughed again, although her breath hardly sustained it. She felt dizzy.

Women standing nearby moved away as he grabbed her arm. "You are not having a bath, not here, not now. Get out and put something over your body."

His touch sent curling heat to her center. On impulse, she looked down to see that his *mentula* stood erect. "Is this for me or for Junia?" she said, reaching toward him.

His hand tightened on her arm. "Don't touch me. Do you wish to humiliate me in public?"

"Why is it humiliation if I do it but acceptable if Junia does it?" She wrenched her arm, trying to free herself. "You're spoiling my bath."

"You'll not have a bath. If you insist on this public display, I'll discipline you in front of the entire room."

"Discipline me?" Her eyes widened as she looked at him. "For what? For doing what all these other women are doing? Have you disciplined your precious Junia?"

"I'm warning you. You're not Junia. I don't care if she exposes herself."

"Because you enjoy looking at her," Caerwin said.

"I'm not having this conversation. You leave now or else."

"Or else what?"

Caerwin quickly found herself dripping face down over a massage table, her hands tightly held behind her waist. The slap of his big hand on her wet buttocks echoed off the high walls. A second and third slap met her ears before her body registered the sharp pain of his punishment.

"Marcellus!"

"You wanted this," he said, landing more blows.

Her skin heated. Her nipples hardened to points against the wet table. Her pulse pounded in her ears.

Slowly the sounds of the room penetrated her hearing. Except for a few titters and an undertone of continuing conversation, it seemed that many of the bathers focused their attention on the drama going on between her and Marcellus. She couldn't look. Shouts began, calls of "More!" and "Tame the wench!"

She couldn't see Junia from where she lay, but she knew without a doubt that the evil bitch watched in amusement. Tears scorched Caerwin's eyelids and slid over the bridge of her nose. She would never live this down. He meant to shame her, lower her to a slave's status.

Which was exactly what she was no matter what he said.

Blow after blow landed from his open hand, moving slightly each time so that every possible place from the top of her thighs to the upper curve of the mounded flesh felt the sting of his spanking. Her buttocks became the center of pain that radiated down her legs to the tips of her toes. The burn spread up her back. She thought her bottom must be bright red, and the thought of that only added to her complete mortification.

"Please," she sobbed.

Beyond the humiliation and the fury his act provoked, a flame of desire ignited so strongly she could think of nothing else. Joining the lingering moisture of the bath, silken wetness spread between her legs. She imagined his hand going there, prodding, provoking, forcing her response.

Abruptly, the spanking stopped. With a curse, he lifted her from the table and carried her over his shoulder through the changing room door to a small antechamber where he placed her on another table. His hand briefly soothed the fevered skin of her burning buttocks. His fingertips brushed between her legs. Her buttocks tightened as he pushed against her swollen vulva.

"Always a surprise, aren't you," he whispered, leaning over her as his hand worked between her thighs. "I can't resist you."

His finger penetrated. She groaned. A few hard strokes and he brought her to the precipice.

"Who will see us?" she whispered.

"You didn't fear being seen when you revealed yourself in the pool." He stroked a few more times, extending one of his fingers to brush her stiff bud. "Don't you wish to be seen? Don't you enjoy being punished?"

Voices from the adjacent rooms filled her ears, people laughing, talking. She'd never been exposed to this kind of intimacy in such a public place. Suddenly his seduction seemed part of the scene—the room full of people watching him dominate her, own her body, hold her down and slap her exposed buttocks.

Now he plied her sex in a room without a door. Anyone could walk in. Perhaps they watched even now!

Her excitement grew at the thought. The humiliation only added to the overpowering sensual experience. His husky voice whispered in her ear as her orgasm ignited. She didn't recognize her voice as the sounds of pleasure rolled out of her throat and resonated off the high walls. All she heard was his breath, his murmur of words.

With one last thrust, he stepped back. "Dress her," he ordered Fimbria. "See that she goes straight home."

Caerwin gazed up at him. Tears had dried on her cheeks. It hurt to sit on the bench. His erection tented his towel in front of him and all she could think was to touch him, to bring that taste into her mouth.

He lifted her chin to look down into her eyes. "Never challenge me in public, wild queen."

~~~

Caerwin took her place in the dining room at the corner nearest the head couch. From the moment she entered the room, she felt Marcellus' intense gaze following her as she moved. Her body hadn't recovered from the afternoon episode at the bath. She had refused his command for dinner, causing him to stand over her while Fimbria finished her hair.

With her hair set in tight curls from her forehead to her crown, Caerwin wore the turquoise *stola* with gold pins at the shoulders set with sparkling red stones and pearls. She glanced at him only a moment, long enough to see the heat in his eyes.

Let him feel whatever he must feel. Still flushed with rage over his treatment of her in public, she had vowed before the altar of Vesta upon returning from the bath. It was as if she spoke to Senna. She needed to silence the woman's voice whispering in her ear. She used her native tongue as she burned incense on the altar.

I will not come to him again.

She took her place on the side couch, keeping her attention on his mother and his sister Clivia as he introduced them to her. A man named Ursolus occupied the opposing couch, a person of such vast corpulence that he wheezed as he breathed and constantly tugged at his toga.

What possible good could come from meeting Tulla? The older woman's hair pulled back in a severe bun and her orange garments hung loosely over a gaunt body. Underneath the colored eye and face powders, shadows circled her small dark eyes, which settled on Caerwin periodically with a look so bitter that Caerwin cringed.

Clivia seemed a more amiable sort. At least she smiled when she spoke. Her small hands never rested, constantly flitting from her necklace to her elaborately curled hair to the folds of her bright yellow *stola*.

Servants quietly delivered platters of composed salad—a variety of greens, olives, sliced egg, and cheese. Caerwin lifted the ornate wine goblet, inhaling the aroma before rolling the delicious wine over her tongue. Peering past the rim of the silver cup, she studied Tulla.

"Does your compromised social standing allow no greater dinner company than this?" Tulla said.

Marcellus' jaw pulsed. "I've kept the company to family for tonight—there are sensitive matters to be discussed."

"I feared as much. Matina's husband thought it best she not attend," Tulla said, facing Marcellus. "He's of the Helvius house, as you may know. Not that you care about the reputations of me or your sisters. I may not visit again myself or receive you at my villa. Is it not enough disgrace brought by Petrus that you now openly consort with a provincial? And why is she here? She's not family."

Tulla's disapproving gaze briefly flickered toward Caerwin.

Marcellus set down his wine cup. "Were your ancestors not provincial *Paeligni*? I won't hear your disparagement of Caerwin." He cleared his throat and attempted a more conciliatory expression.

"As for the accusations, hundreds of men were ruined under Tiberius and Caligula. Who can claim to know the private acts of any man? Accusations fly in all directions."

"Indeed they do," Clivia said. "The gossip is rife. I assure my friends these are lies."

"What exactly are the accusations?" Marcellus said.

"It's hardly suitable for dinner conversation," Tulla huffed.

"Oh, mother, everyone has heard it," Clivia said. "You told me yourself that Father regularly submitted to men and engaged with freeborn boys."

"Yes, yes," Tulla said, waving her hand as if to ward off a venomous insect. "That doesn't mean it's an appropriate conversation with strangers." She looked pointedly at Caerwin.

"They use the term *cineadus*," Ursolus said. "But the problem is greater than that."

"Yes," Marcellus said. "The problem is greater because a man of high rank, this Clodius Galarius, has chosen to charge Father with *stuprum* for violating his brother Melonius. Allegedly, the boy was under the protection of his *bulla* when Petrus made him his *puer delicatus*. Upon reaching the wisdom of eighteen years, he recognized the degraded position Petrus had inflicted on him and committed suicide."

"Yes," Clivia said. "That's what I've heard."

"I think it's true," Tulla said. "Petrus had no morals."

"Or it's a convenient assumption," Marcellus said. "Nothing proves Petrus violated the boy. My men have uncovered no writings of Melonius stating the reason of his suicide. He could have willingly consorted with Petrus—Father had quite the flock of willing lovers, many of them freeborn. Then when gaining the greater perspective of age, Melonius might have felt his choices shamed his family. Young men become easily impassioned about honor, you know."

"There are rumors that Melonius caused Father's downfall by catching the attention of Tiberius," Clivia said in a lowered voice.

"They say the old goat took Melonius to Capri along with other abused children to practice all forms of vice."

"There's always gossip of such acts," Marcellus said. "Who would know if they involved Melonius? The mines seized by Tiberius upon Father's death were very likely the greater prize. Perhaps the emperor gained both his desires—the boy and the gold. Once Father had been driven to suicide, Tiberius had it all."

Red spots had appeared on Marcellus' cheeks. He drained his wine cup and motioned to the server. Caerwin cringed at the furious expression on his face.

"Whatever caused Melonius to take his life," he said, "they seek a million sestertii as settlement."

Tulla cleared her throat. "One million seems a lot. But I understand they are aggrieved. Still, it is a scandalous amount. It would bankrupt you."

"Hardly their concern," Marcellus said. "While I doubt it would empty my pockets, I might have to sell the villa at Herculaneum and perhaps divest either the shipping company or the farming operations in Tunesia."

"It's criminal that Tiberius seized the gold mines," Tulla said. "Petrus claimed they would bring fortunes."

"I've consulted a few jurists on the matter. They say there's little precedent for such a legal action nine years after the man's death," Ursolus said. "They can hardly find you or anyone else responsible."

"It's not unheard of," Marcellus said. "The sins of the father can be held against his estate."

"They should have filed their suit when Father died, then," Clivia said. "That's what Niger says—my husband. I've told him and my friends—this is so unfair. You served honorably at high rank against bloodthirsty warriors and deserve some peace when you come home."

Caerwin paused mid-bite to stare at Clivia. Blood thirsty warriors? She resisted the urge to speak on behalf of her countrymen. What good would it do? She squirmed in her seat to relieve flesh still tender from Marcellus' spanking, unwittingly stoking the flames of desire.

Marcellus glanced at her. For a long moment, unspoken words flew between them in chariots of air. His eyes glittered. Her breath caught.

"Thank you, dear sister," he said, dragging his gaze away from Caerwin. "I doubt those sentiments will sway Clodius."

Servants arrived with steaming dishes of the main course: roast chicken, sliced ham, and mullet stuffed with sausages. Much as she had learned to love fish prepared in this particular method, Caerwin had lost her appetite. The conversation had skated too close to the truth about the scandal that would swallow Marcellus if his participation became known.

Worse, her squirming only caused her clitoris to throb more insistently.

If Petrus would induct his own son into inappropriate sexual relations at such a young age, he would undoubtedly do the same with any other young man. Briefly, she wondered whether this fact rippled under the surface of Marcellus' anger. Perhaps he had known Melonius. Perhaps they had exchanged embraces. She sipped her wine as she studied the complex play of emotion across his face.

"Marcellus, let me say first I'm thankful for your safe return," Tulla interrupted. "I hope you approve of the care I've taken with the Antistius *domus* in your absence. It's been a hardship to oversee the property while living separately, but I could not live here. So I had to be in two places at once. And surely you recognize that my settlement under Petrus' will failed to provide me an adequate stipend. I had hoped…"

"Your mother has suffered greatly," Ursolus said. His fat fingers embraced another slice of ham. "As you can see, her health has been weakened. As her guardian, I hope to see that she gains your grant of a greater sum."

"None of which would benefit you, I'm sure," Marcellus said.

"Well, uh, I…" Ursolus started several sentences in a matter of seconds. The creases of his wide face extended into his neck as he tucked his head back. "Surely…"

"Never mind. What my dear mother does with her inheritance is none of my concern," Marcellus said. "In the circumstance, you would agree it's premature to make any promises."

"Yet you seem quite generous with your, uh, woman of Britannia. Isn't that also premature?" Tulla's lips pursed as she leveled her gaze on Caerwin. "It seems she doesn't lack any finery money can buy. What can you possibly expect to gain with this *peregrinus*?"

"I gain intelligent and entertaining companionship," Marcellus said. "Not that I have any obligation to satisfy your criticism. She's of a royal family and has quickly learned our customs and our language. Could you do the same?"

"Marcellus has shown me the wonders of the Roman world," Caerwin said, taking opportunity with the opening. "Thank you for raising such a wonderful son." She ignored the shocked look on Marcellus' face. "You see, before he and the Fourteenth Legion swept in to slaughter my kinsmen and enslave our women and children, I knew nothing of bathing or clothing. We ran around naked and ate slugs. We lived under the stars and cried out when rain and cold hurt us."

"Dear me," Tulla began.

"She's joking, mother," Clivia said, putting her hand on Tulla's arm. "Aren't you?"

"Yes, of course, she's making a joke," Marcellus said. He frowned at Caerwin and sighed. "Her people lived in well-built shelters and wove cloth just as we do. They herded sheep and cattle and grew fields of grain. She's telling the truth about our battle, though. Her brother and other men of her tribe died on our swords.

We lost few men compared to their losses, and the remaining people of the tribe were sold—including her mother. I saved her from the slavers, a decision made in a moment of either madness or inspiration—I haven't decided which."

"Oh my," Tulla said.

"He exaggerates," Caerwin said. "He took me as his slave, a term which he now denies. But, I assure you, I remain his possession."

"Surely there is something more pleasant to discuss," Tulla said, frowning as she dabbed her lips with her napkin.

"You brought it up, mother," Clivia said. She smiled at Caerwin. "I think she speaks our language quite well. She certainly is among the more beautiful women I've seen. For someone of such a pale complexion, at least. Is your hair bleached to this color?"

"Thank you," Caerwin said, returning the smile. "My hair is its natural shade. It's common among the Cornovii." Her smile faded. "I should say, it was common. I am the only surviving Cornovii."

"Not exactly," Marcellus said. "There are over two hundred Cornovii women and children living. But as mother says, to more pleasant things." Marcellus looked at Clivia. "During our journey, memories of my youth haunted me. We had some good times, did we not? Remember that servant we had, what was her name…Ken…Ken something? Did she teach you and Matina songs and stories like she did me?"

"Kensa!" Clivia laughed. "I do remember her. I don't remember her teaching me songs. But she had a gentle hand with you."

"Whatever happened to Kensa?" Marcellus said. "Did she die?"

Tulla motioned dismissively. "Too old to serve. I thought of selling her, but I would have been forced to pay someone to take her. I granted her freedom. Last I heard, she worked for her upkeep in one of the shops at the Forum."

"You turned her out?" he said. The emotion in his tone startled Caerwin. "Did you at least provide her an allowance?"

"Why should I?" Tulla said, shrugging. "She lived off our money and goodwill for years. I don't know what your father saw in her. She never worked hard enough to justify her position."

Marcellus set his cup heavily on the table. A tremor rattled his hand. "He grew up with her, did he not? Was she not Labeo's housekeeper? Is it not an honored tradition to care for those who spend their lives caring for us? The law forbids turning out an infirm slave."

"She wasn't infirm," Tulla said. "For a man of such appetites as Petrus evidently indulged, I'm surprised to hear you suggest that he had sentiment for anyone but himself."

"Perhaps the sentiment came first and his appetites came in answer," Marcellus said tersely. "As I've grown older, I've tried to understand him."

"So have I," Clivia said, pulling a sliver of chicken off a leg bone. "I remember him more from when I was little. I hardly saw him by the time I was ten."

"He grew worse with age," Tulla said. "I…"

"I don't wish to hear your criticism of him," Marcellus said. "But I would like to find Kensa, if you know of her whereabouts."

"Why on earth does it matter about that old woman?" Tulla said.

"I want to ensure that she's cared for. That's how I treat all my slaves."

"Even that one?" Tulla asked, motioning toward Caerwin.

"She's not a slave," Marcellus said. "As for your question of why is she here, I plan to make her my wife."

Caerwin's heart squeezed. After all this time, he chose this moment, this company, to say such a thing to her face. Blood drained from her head. Her lips felt numb.

Their three dinner companions stared at Marcellus as if he'd suddenly grown an extra head. Ursolus's wheezing became the only sound in the room. Lines formed around Tulla's pursed lips.

"Surely you make a joke at my expense," Tulla said after a long silence.

"Not at all," Marcellus said. "I had planned to petition the court for her citizenship, but my advisors say the time is not right to approach the emperor."

Clivia stifled a nervous giggle. "Well, that's…"

"I would have you wish me well. That's enough of the subject." Marcellus clapped his hands. At his summons, a musician hurried into the room and arranged himself in the corner where he began strumming a lyre and singing. Serving staff arrived with the last of the meal.

Caerwin tried to think of nothing more than the dessert course arriving at the table. Seeded cakes and an egg custard should have been a welcome end to a delicious meal, but her mood had shifted. Underneath her cold skin, her blood ran hot.

She didn't know what to think from one day to the next. He'd banished her from his bedchamber and regularly consorted with Junia. He'd embarrassed her before the entire city. Tatian had confirmed the fact that a citizen couldn't marry a non-citizen. Surely Marcellus taunted his mother as punishment for her years of neglect.

Her lips moved as she repeated her vow. *I will not come to him.*

Despite her vow, in the later darkness of her room, the bathhouse scene replayed in her mind. The bed tormented her sore buttocks. She felt his hand between her legs. Her clitoris throbbed. She clasped her hand there, taking up the memory as she touched herself.

~~~

Caerwin shrank back against the atrium column nearest her bedchamber, scarcely breathing. The voices of Marcellus and Junia rose and fell over the patter of rain through the *compluvium* and into the pool below. Several minutes passed as she strained to hear what they said. She could make nothing of it. She shook the skirt of her *stola* and walked toward them.

A tremor ran through her at the sight of Marcellus. His face changed as he saw her. His smile faded and a hard line settled in his jaw. She looked away, unwilling to acknowledge the distance in his gaze.

Instead, she looked at Junia. She wore a new *stola* in bright red with a gold pattern, colors that flattered her olive skin. As usual, her ebony hair had been fashioned in the latest style and glittering jewels embraced her neck and wrists.

"Good day," Caerwin said, walking briskly as if she planned to pass them by.

"Caerwin," Junia said. "Have you heard? Marcellus and I have reached a tentative agreement about the shipping business. I may become a partner."

Marcellus' lips thinned. "Thank you, Junia, but I had intended to tell her myself. At a more opportune moment." He shifted his attention to Caerwin. "We'll travel to the Bay of Neopolis in January, once the trial has been settled and assuming I'm not exiled."

Caerwin's breath became short and shallow as her pulse drummed in her ears. She thought for a moment she might pass out. Straightening, she couldn't stop herself from blurting out the first thing that came to her mind.

"Does this mean you'll be wed?" she said.

"What?" Marcellus said.

Junia tittered. "Poor thing, this must come as a shock."

"There is no marriage planned," he said flatly. His dark eyes burned into her. "I'm escorting her to the shipyard and then to her home. If we can negotiate agreeably with her managers and family members and if the gods allow me to retain the Antistius estate, I'll make her part owner of the fleet."

"Of course if she can manage a marriage as well, she will, isn't that right, Junia?" Caerwin said. Her brittle tone might belie her feelings but she didn't care. It took all her strength not to assault the *futatrix* with her fists. No wonder she flaunted herself before him at the baths. *Lupa!*

"Of course," Junia said with a broad smile. "What woman wouldn't be eager to wed such a fine man? He's proven himself in battle and now in these legal challenges that swirl around him like flies to honey. I'd be honored to serve as his wife, to keep his *domus* in order and relieve him of his worries at the end of the day." She placed her jeweled hand on his chest. "He knows *I* would be a faithful wife."

Marcellus placed his hand over hers. What did she mean with her insinuation? In the moment that their hands lingered together, Caerwin felt the blood drain from her face. What vicious intent lay behind that smile!

Not trusting herself to say another word, she ran. If he removed Junia's hand from his chest, she didn't see it. She didn't actually see anything but instead raced to the back garden in a state of blind panic.

Sobs heaved her chest as she stumbled through pouring rain. Pacing along the wet paths between shrubs and garden beds bare in winter cold, she tried to understand what he said. But all she could hear was Junia. Relieve him of worries—as if everyone knew that Caerwin served only as yet another problem for him to resolve. A faithful wife—did she know that Caerwin had let Hermia touch her? Did her exposure at the baths cause her to seem unfaithful? How could that matter when Junia herself had been in the same state of undress?

It was true she'd given her body to someone else, even if only for a few minutes and to her female slave. Worse, no matter what she did, the law would not change. She would be a *peregrinus* forever. She'd never be a suitable wife for Marcellus. If he managed to gain citizen status for her through whatever complicated process the courts might require, she would still not be one of them.

Junia knew how to put people at ease as much as she wielded the skill to prick them. Roman society knew her, remembered her family history and the accomplishments of her father and brother. Her family nestled firmly within the city's elite.

Marcellus would be well served with Junia as a wife. The realization of how close he might be to accepting that fate struck Caerwin with physical force. A spasm gripped her chest and she gasped for air.

"Dear girl, what on earth troubles you?" Tatian took her elbow, peering from under the hood on his cloak. "You're getting drenched."

"I'm f-f-fine," she stammered.

"You'll die of exposure if you stay out here one moment longer. Come along."

He steered her through the doorway and along the far side of the *peristylium* before hurrying her up the stairs and into a small room in the corner. A cabinet on the left wall held stacks of brightly colored garments and several pairs of shoes. To the right, a tightly made bed heaped with pillows. A small desk at the end faced a window that looked out over the hills to the north. He lit two lamps and closed the shutters.

"Here," he said, pressing a towel into her hands. "Do you need me to dry you?"

She took the towel, only in this moment realizing that water dripped from her hair. Her clothing clung to her skin. She dried her face and hands but then stood without knowing what else to do. After prodding the coals in his brazier, he looked at her with an expression of concern and sympathy.

"Don't look at me like that," she said. "I can't bear it."

He frowned. "I don't know how else to look at you. What can I do?"

"Keep me here. I can't go out there."

"What in the name of Jupiter has happened?"

"I can't talk about it."

He rummaged through his things and withdrew a long tunic in faded red. "You can wear this," he said, holding it toward her as if to size it against her body. "If you stay, you must change. I'll stand with my back to you." He crammed the tunic into her hands.

She hardly grasped what he was saying. She didn't care if he saw her naked. She didn't care that she might die of exposure. Marcellus would go with Junia, make her part of his life, and there was nothing she could do to stop him.

Tatian stood at the shuttered window while she fumbled with her clothing. The drenched *palla* fell to the floor, but her stiff fingers couldn't force the *stola* pin out of its clasp.

"Tatian, please," she said.

He turned then hurried to her. His fingers overtook hers as he pressed the pin open. Soon after the knot on her belt released and his warm hands eased down her cold arms as he swept the dripping garment off her body. She stood shivering in the wet tunic.

She wanted him to undress her. She wanted him to hold her in his arms and whisper comforting words. Tears rolled down her face.

"Dear girl," he said. "Lift your arms."

He peeled the wet linen off her and tossed it aside. Then he scrubbed her with the towel until feeling started to come back to her legs. He seemed immune to the sight of her bared female body, merely clucking in alarm at the icy touch of her skin and her chattering teeth.

"Come here," he said, leading her to the bed. "I must warm you."

She did as he asked, lying awkwardly on the bed until he nestled beside her and pulled her back against his chest. He wrapped his blanket around them both, holding her close. The sound of rain on the roof and the tick-tick of the brazier accompanied their breathing.

Gradually, her violent shivering eased. Lying against him, she realized how different he was from Marcellus. Not tall. Not nearly so heavily muscled. Still, he was taller than her and his body had a lithe musculature that from the first had reminded her of a young horse. His frame carried the same kind of promise—wide shoulders that could easily grow with time and effort into the strength of a warrior.

In one regard, his body did remind her of Marcellus, the *mentula* which she couldn't ignore in its rigid press against her back. She rolled away and sat up.

"I'm sorry if I've offended you," he said, swinging his legs off the bed. "Certain parts of men have minds of their own," he added, glancing at her over his shoulder with a grin. "Of course, you know that."

"I should know it," she said. Another shiver shook her body.

"Sit here," he said, dragging his desk chair to the side of the brazier. "You'll never feel warm with your hair so wet."

The touch of his nimble fingers soothed her as he stood behind her and one after another pin released. Her hair slowly fell past her shoulders. The wet tendrils began dripping. He muttered to himself as he finished releasing the last of the elaborate hairstyle. Water dripped from her nipples and rolled down to her thighs as he grabbed the towel and began scrubbing her hair dry.

"I've never seen a woman of such beauty as you," he said. "No wonder our master finds you irresistible."

"Tell me if you've slept with Marcellus."

"What?"

"You're his to take, are you not?"

"If he wished you to know, he would be the one to tell you."

"Meaning there's something to tell."

"Not at all." He knelt in front of her. "But I would never betray a confidence. If you wished to use me, no one would hear of it, unlike some of the slaves who occupy this dwelling."

She gripped the towel. Surely he couldn't mean...she watched his expression change. "Hermia?"

"I'm afraid so. She has let it be known that she pleasured you, and word has flown to Junia's staff, who in turn—I'm certain—have relayed the information to that eager witch. There's no doubt of how she'll use it. Anyone can see she has plans for Marcellus."

"She already used it, of that I'm certain." Caerwin's cold vanished as she leapt up from the chair. "I think she's already had him in her bed. When her journey with us had just begun, she made her intentions clear. Now I've given her a weapon. I didn't even care for Hermia, that thankless *lupa*."

"She's not quite a whore," he laughed. "Anyway, he doesn't want Junia. He only wants you, a choice easy to understand. If he takes me in a moment of need, it means nothing."

Her mouth opened then closed as she absorbed his information. That he knelt beside her to rub her legs again hardly entered her mind. Just as she thought, Marcellus had coupled with Tatian. He surely had taken Junia as well. She probably had him watched so she could arrive at the baths near him.

More than once, she'd seen Junia without clothes. No man would ignore a woman of such beauty. Junia had no shame in approaching him. She imagined him touching her, how Junia would reciprocate.

That dog! That liar! "He plans to travel with her to her homeland, this place called Neopolis," she said. "Do you know of it?"

"It's south of here. A journey of six days by carriage. But he'll probably brave the winter sea and arrive in one day." He paused, resting his hands on her knees. "Isn't that where she lives?"

"He says he takes her home, but Tatian, he plans to sell her a partnership in his shipping business. I know he must need money. At least, if he loses at court. Surely there's some other way."

Tatian's green-brown eyes watched her with a relaxed expression. Rain still damped his hair, increasing its natural curliness. She wondered about his ancestry. She wondered about his real intent. He seemed utterly innocent of any guile.

"I don't know who to trust," she added.

"I'm highly flattered that you confide in me," he said. "Spies are everywhere in Rome. I think we need to look closely at the allegiance of Hermia. I had the same suspicion for Domitia and I'm glad you sent her away. I think Junia pays them."

Caerwin leapt up, her fists clenched at her sides. "Of course she does! That would be her exact plan! I've been such a fool!"

He smiled broadly. "She has no weapon to compete with you." His gaze drifted from her breasts down the length of her nude body.

"By the gods! I'm embarrassing you," she said. "The warmth of the brazier…" She grabbed up his faded tunic and fumbled to bring the hem over her head.

Through the muffling of cloth over her ears, she heard the door open. A deathly silence ensured. Quickly, she tugged the rest of the garment down and opened her eyes.

Marcellus!

"By the gods of Olympus…" He stared at her with a look that chilled her blood.

"Sire, please understand," Tatian said. "I found her out in the garden, soaking wet and shaking with chill. I brought her here to dry her. Then we talked about Hermia's deceit. I was about to escort her to…"

"Silence!" Marcellus loomed over Tatian as if he would strike him with his fists.

"Marcellus—it's just as he said," Caerwin said. "Nothing has happened. Please don't be angry at Tatian."

He turned to her, his face stiff with rage. "Nothing has happened…did you sit here without clothing while you discussed

Hermia? What other lengthy topic did you address while revealing every inch of your body? Have you no shame?"

"My clothes were wet," she shouted. "Why does it matter to you? You spend your time with that woman. I find her in your bedchamber. You consort with her at the baths. You make plans to travel with her and sell her part of your business while I'm left in my room. What's it to you if I show my body to a hundred men?"

He grabbed her arm. "I won't have this conversation in front of Tatian." He turned to the white-faced tutor. "I'll deal with you later."

"Sir, please…"

Marcellus steered her out the door, down the stairs, and through the heart of the house without speaking. Her loose hair flew behind her. She couldn't bear to look up to see who might watch them, but she knew every single person in the household would hear of it even if they hadn't seen it. As he passed the alcove of ancestors, she caught a glimpse of Junia's shocked face.

She spat in her direction.

He didn't stop at her room. He yanked open the door to his bedchamber. Antius looked up in surprise from folding some of Marcellus' clothes.

"Out!" Marcellus shouted.

Antius dropped the clothing and hurried to the door.

"Gather all the staff to the far end of the house until I say otherwise," Marcellus ordered. "I'll have you whipped if any single person remains this side of the kitchen."

"Yes, yes sir," Antius said, bowing as he closed the door.

Caerwin tried to catch her breath as Marcellus paced. He looked at her then paced more. Finally, he rummaged through his trunk and pulled out a silk cord. She recognized it from his punishments at the fortress.

Her eyes caught his, questioning. Grim at the mouth, he came to her and ripped Tatian's tunic off her chest. "You'll wear no man's clothing," he said. "Not even a man who loves other men."

"Marcellus…"

"Don't talk. You only make it worse."

"But…"

He stood close to her, so close she saw the reddened rims of his dark eyes. A few silver hairs marked his temples. She closed her eyes.

"You have done nothing but make my life a living hell since the first day I saw you," he said, forcing her into a chair where he tied her wrists behind her.

"You're the one who took me," she blurted. "Don't tell me not to talk. I will talk."

Rigid, he took the other chair and perched on it as if restraining a wild animal. With his elbows on his knees, he gathered his hair in his fists and rocked back and forth.

"Why can't you trust me?" he said. "It's all I ever asked of you."

She twisted, trying to gain slack in the cord. "That's not true."

He went on as if he hadn't heard her. "You're the Siren who tempted Odysseus, calling me to the rocks. I'm wrecked on your shore."

"Marcellus, I don't know what you're talking about. I've done nothing wrong."

He looked up. Then his gaze traveled down her naked body. "Here on your sweet shore, all other things cease to matter." He leaned forward to caress between her legs, probing her crease. She flinched.

"Just as the first day," he murmured, lifting his hand to inhale her scent. "Only your song, sweet Siren."

Whirling away suddenly, he dragged a blanket from the bed to drape her body. He poured undiluted wine and drank the whole cup. Then he sat again in the chair, wiping his mouth with the back of his hand.

"I should have made sure Junia didn't have a chance to tell you about our arrangement before I did. Rest assured, I know full well how she seeks advantage over you. When she came to me with news of Hermia's act, I could see my reaction pleased her. You gave her a weapon and she used it."

Caerwin's mouth dropped open. "I gave? How was I to know Hermia couldn't be trusted? Or Domitia, for that matter? Domitia said I must attend the goddess festival with the forbidden name, but Fimbria and Pantera said I should not. I don't know who to believe."

"Antius will find replacements."

"I don't need replacements and if I did, can I not choose my own slave? You treat me like a child then say I should stop acting like one."

His jaw pulsed. "What have you done to deserve me treating you otherwise? I thought I could trust you, gave you privileges and in return, you risked death to escape the fortress. Do you know what torment I suffered when I found you were gone?"

"You suffered?" She forced a laugh. "My people are slaughtered, I'm held captive, molested, forced…"

"Stop—these are old complaints. Have I not cared for you? Do you not at this moment find yourself in one of Rome's best houses, well fed, attended, groomed, clothed?"

"I never asked to be in Rome or attended by your slaves. These are all things you value, not me."

For a moment, the solemn expression on his face pierced her heart. Despite her vow, she could not stop what lived inside her, this incessant crushing need to touch him, to see his smile.

Why couldn't she say what she felt, that she did care for him, that she only wanted to please him? She'd tried before to express those sentiments but the words simply would not form.

"Did you wish to be sold into slavery?" he said quietly. "Or be killed? Those were the choices."

She twisted against the cord. "I wished for none of it."

"*Those were the choices,*" he repeated.

"No one asked me. You made the choice for me."

"By the gods, yes, I did. Any amusement I hoped to gain has grown instead to be the trial of Sisyphus."

She remembered the Greek story and made noise of outrage. "I'm a trial? What can I possibly do? I have no authority over anything in this house even though you say you want me to behave as a woman of Rome. Don't the women of Rome see to the operation of the household—the meals, the staff, the daily operations? What of that do I affect?

"Unlike Junia, I hold no business matters by which to gain your attention," she continued, infuriated that she remained tied to the chair. "I take my lessons, but what does it serve me to know the steps of rhetorical argument when you're rushing off with her?"

"Are these matters of your concern?" he shouted. "No! I've explained why I must gain support among the prominent families of Rome. I've explained why Junia and her family matter. What else can I do for you? Have I not met your demand to know the name of each and every obstacle I face?"

"What else can I do for you?" she shouted back. "I appear as you would make me. I learn the ways of Rome. I attend your dinners—have I said or done anything that shamed you? Yet you rarely speak to me, you never touch me. You sent me away from your bed."

"Trust was all I asked. To believe in me. To think of what I intended, to remember my promises." He crouched beside her, brushing her unruly hair from her face. "You appear as a dream," he said softly. "There is nothing I can do to quench the fire that burns inside you, nor would I want to. I've explained and reassured, yet when you see me talking to Junia, you forget everything I've said and run off into the rain."

"She bribed my slaves to spy on me, to have me act in ways that would shame me. She flaunts her body before you yet you punish me for doing the same thing."

"You are not Junia." He pressed his fingertip against her lips. "Those slaves are gone, are they not? Why can't you find comfort in my promises? Have I ever failed to provide what I promised?"

Her eyes filled with tears. "I wake at night thinking you stand beside my bed."

He groaned and stood up. "I do."

"You could hold me. At least I would know you haven't forgotten me."

"Dear god, you are vexing." He closed his fist on her hair and pulled her face up for his kiss.

The soft pressure of his lips sent fire leaping through her veins. Her eyes closed as she lifted toward him. Her thoughts spun away.

Several moments passed as his kiss deepened and his hands caressed her hair and shoulders. The blanket slipped and his hands soon found her breasts. Her nipples had long since stiffened and their points leapt against his palms.

He jerked back, grabbed the blanket, and tucked it firmly over her shoulders. His hand shook as he poured more wine.

"This is why I can't hold you," he said. "I've experienced the worst men can do to each other. I've gutted them, watched their entrails spill out and the horror on their faces. I've beheaded them, mutilated their bodies, more than I could ever count." He sat heavily in his chair, facing her. "I've punished men, too, my own troops—cut off the hands of thieves and brought blood with the whip. These are things I learned to do in order to perform my duty, to protect the men in my charge. To serve Rome."

He laughed but his eyes were angry. "I knew nothing. None of that tested me as you do. I thought I was a man. I thought I knew control, possessed all the skills required of me. But in this?" He motioned toward her. "I'm defenseless. I'm a child wandering the wilderness."

"You punish me for your weakness," she said. The words came out without thought. She watched him flinch and she instantly regretted her words. What perversity drove her to say the worst thing? She longed to wrap her arms around him, to hold him against her breast and comfort him.

His eyes betrayed his hurt. "You think I want it this way? How did we fall so far from the kindness we once knew from each other? You tended my wounds. I confided the secrets of my life. I've asked for time, for a shred of understanding. Don't you understand the dangers I face? Soon these problems could be solved. Then I could have you in my bed and ravish you as I long to and not worry that you might be got with child. Can you not wait? Can you not remember my intentions from one day to the next?"

"I try, but how can I ignore what is before my face?"

He closed his eyes and let out his breath. His expression tore at her.

"Marcellus, please, I've tried to say things, but the words never come out. The night I came to your room, I wanted to tell you all the feelings I had. But when I came to your room, Junia was there. I do have…feelings. I see how you try." She licked her lips. Nothing she said expressed what she wanted to say. "I want to please you, give you the trust you ask. I truly do."

"What did you want to tell me?" he said.

She looked away. "That I…that you live in my heart," she said, spitting out the words before she lost her courage. "I wanted you to know that you matter—greatly—that I'm sorry I can't be all the things you expect. That I can't stop fighting…"

The fact of her dilemma confronted her in that moment, this war within herself. She loved him, but how could she?

How could she love a Roman?

"I would never ask you to betray yourself," he said stiffly. "If you can never love me, I will try to accept it."

"No, I…that's not what I meant."

"But it is, isn't it? You can never forgive me for what happened to your people."

"I don't know," she said. "I want to. I think the past will dim if I gain some standing in your eyes. I have nothing to feel proud of, nothing that I've done or can do, to make your days better. I'm still Cornovii."

"Your words speak of doing, not feeling."

"I have feelings—I said it, that you live in my heart. That I want to be with you."

"You did not speak of love."

"I want to speak of it, I do, Marcellus. My heart crushes in my chest. It hurts when I'm away from you. Is that love?"

Dampness glistened in his eyes. He looked shattered. "I want to say 'yes,' what you feel is love. But I'd be taking too much on myself. It's what I want to hear. I won't say it for you."

He stood up abruptly and went to throw open the doors to his garden. Cold air rushed in and he inhaled deeply. After a time, he spoke.

"You've given me more than I had and for that I'm grateful. I'll instruct Varinia to take you around with her to learn the household operations. Each manager will accept your presence whenever you're ready, whether you wish to learn the ways of the gardeners, or the cooks, or the cleaning. In business matters, you're free to sit in my office—if you're silent—and learn what occupies my thoughts. You're right—if you're to become the wife I long for, you must know these things. What else can I do to lighten your day?"

"You can tell me…Have you taken someone else as a lover?" She bit her lip as soon as the words spilled out. She didn't want to know his answer. "Tatian?"

He closed the doors and stood over her. "Did Tatian say something to make you believe that?"

"No, he refused to answer my question. He said it was your place to tell me if there was something to be told."

"Clever man," he muttered. "Yes, I've used him. He's my slave. There's nothing in it."

"Really?" Freshly enraged, she fought with her bonds. "Then why does it matter that Hermia touched me? Or for that matter, that Tatian saw me naked? Antius saw me without clothes the first day and even bathed me."

"That was entirely different."

"Untie me!" she shouted, wrenching her wrists against the cord. "You say I should trust you, but I can't. You wish me to live under your rules, but you have no rules for yourself."

He squatted in front of her chair and seized her arms. "This is what you must understand. Men and women do not live by the same rules. In Rome, women serve men. I would guess it was the same among the Cornovii."

"It wasn't but what does that matter to you? We're in Rome, so I must serve you no matter what you do. Junia shows you her body in the baths, stands in front of you and flaunts her bare breasts. If I do the same thing, you punish me, expose my most private needs to the world."

"I care nothing for Junia."

"Will you take many lovers this year?"

"Whoever I might take, they aren't lovers. I have room only for one person in my heart."

"Ha! You say such things and then show me the opposite. Untie me!"

He tore the blanket back and lodged his hand between her thighs. "This is mine. If you ever let another man see you much less touch you, I will kill you both. Do you understand?"

"No! I don't understand. How…"

He cupped his hand against her. "Your body knows its master," he said. "You may not love me, but you yield to your desire. Do you not?"

The pressure of his hand warmed her whole body. More than life, she wanted him to hold her. She could never deny her need. "Yes, but…"

He tore the knots loose and pulled her up as he wrapped the blanket around her. "Go. If you care for me at all, spare me your doubts and judgements. Trust me."

Chapter Eight

The next morning, Caerwin tucked herself back against the corner of Marcellus' office as the *salutatio* progressed. Finally the last client bowed and thanked Marcellus profusely for his generous gift of two *denarii*.

"That should be enough to carry your family until the spring, at least," Marcellus said.

"I'll enlist my kinsmen to appear in court on your behalf," the man said. "May the goddess Fortuna smile on you."

Antius closed the door behind him. Marcellus looked tired, even more tired than the day before. He hardly glanced in her direction.

"There's another person to see you," Antius said.

Marcellus stood up and came around his desk. "I told Manlius I would meet at his office," he said. "Who…"

The door burst open. With the help of a cane, a man stepped in. Tall and distinguished, he stood only moments staring at Marcellus before clasping him in his arms. Antius stood awkwardly at the door.

"My dear Marcellus," he said in a rough voice. "Since you won't come to me, I come to you."

"Vedius," Marcellus said.

Caerwin caught the tremor in his voice then watched in shock as Vedius kissed Marcellus. Their mouths met and lingered. After a long embrace, Marcellus pulled back.

"Dear Vedius," Marcellus said. His voice had become husky. "What tragedy has befallen you? Please, sit." He moved a chair forward for Vedius then another for himself so that they sat closely facing each other. Vedius took Marcellus' hand.

"I fell at the first battle," Vedius said. "Vespasian led us well but my horse took a Briton's lance. I couldn't jump free." He gestured toward his leg. "The bones set wrong in the journey back to Rome. Surgery followed, a torture worthy of the worst criminal.

Six years and it still hurts." He laughed and squeezed Marcellus' leg. "But you! Not a scratch?"

"A couple of scratches," Marcellus said. "Nothing to speak of." His gaze shifted toward Caerwin still sitting in the corner. He stood up and moved to the door. "My friend, meet Caerwin. I've brought Britannia home with me."

Vedius twisted in the chair to stare at her. "I…I thought you were alone."

He had a handsome face. His startled expression emphasized an aquiline nose and sensual lips. She forced a smile.

"She's learning our ways," Marcellus said. "Leave us," he said, motioning to her.

"So pleased to have time to get to know you," Caerwin said, gathering the skirt of her *stola* and stepping to the door.

"Don't," Marcellus said quietly, closing the door behind her.

Antius frowned as she lingered by the door hoping to overhear at least some fragment of their next words. She could hear their voices but not the softly spoken words. After a few moments under Antius' dark censure, she walked slowly toward her room.

She might be away from their company, but she had no doubt of their relationship. The familiar intimacy between them spoke without words. A man of high rank within the emperor's circles. A man whose messages Marcellus had ignored.

A man who still desired him.

~~~

The morning of the hearing, cold wind rushed through the Forum in advance of rain. Caerwin could smell it. She entered the basilica with her hair shrouded in the brown *palla*, Fimbria on her heels. Tatian took her hand and pulled her through the crowds already thronging the court. Aside from Antius, the rest of the slaves had stayed at the *domus* on Marcellus' orders.

She understood his reasoning. If his detractors meant to ruin him, the fewer of his inner circle to hear it, the better. So Tatian said.

She hardly slept the night before and if the sunken dark rings under Marcellus' eyes were any indication, he'd suffered much the same. In the days since Vedius had appeared at his office, Marcellus' behavior had been increasingly erratic. He sat through his morning *salutatio* as if he hardly heard his petitioners. He left home early and returned late.

People whispered as she moved through the crowd and she tugged the *palla* over her forehead. They made space on the benches near Marcellus. She had to stretch to see over the heads of his clients and supporters. Red spots marked his cheeks as he watched the judge Gavius Tiburs, appointed by the *praetor* because the opposing sides could not agree. Already angry cries from the crowd called out in favor of one side or the other.

A clerk serving Gavius pounded his staff on the floor and the crowd silenced.

"I've read the formula submitted by both parties," Gavius said. He motioned to Clodius Galarius and his speaker, Plinius Arrianus. "Present your *narratio*."

Plinius stood and flourished his hand, flashing his diamond ring and posturing. "Sire, learned colleagues, this is an old story often retold in the darker histories of our people. A man of wealth and influence takes for himself a freeborn boy still under the protection of his *bulla*. Our laws forbid such acts on penalty of death.

"My esteemed patron, Clodius Galarius, brings suit on behalf of his deceased brother Melonius whose young person suffered exactly such an assault at the hands of this man's father, Antistius Petrus." He pointed at Marcellus. "We agree that the circumstances are unusual in that both primary parties are no longer among the living. Let me assure the assembled jurists that we have no intention to attack this respected legate who has served nobly and bravely in our legions. We direct our suit to the Antistius estate. If Petrus still lived, we would accuse him to his face. If our beloved

Melonius still lived, he could say for himself what disgrace was put upon him.

"But we don't have these men. We only have this grieving family and the Antistius estate subsequently bequeathed to this man. Petrus profited from and expanded his wealth, and it belonged to him when he committed this crime. Our laws must be upheld and the fine must be paid. There can be no escape, even in death, from sins committed against our freeborn children."

Gavius turned to Marcellus. "What defense do you claim?"

Marius Praetextus stood, nodded to the judge, and met the angry stare of his opposing counsel before sweeping his arm to encompass the avid crowd. "Esteemed judge, jurists, we are eager to present our argument. These charges have lodged a heavy burden on my patron, but no greater than the weight left on him during his formative years in the daily knowledge of his father's extravagant ways. He hoped his offer of ten thousand sestertii to Clodius Galarius would provide suitable satisfaction. Keep in mind, his offer did not constitute an acceptance of guilt on behalf of his father. He simply hoped to keep such a sensitive matter from being aired in public. Clodius has refused the offer and pursues his demand for one million sestertii."

Angry shouts rose from Marcellus' supporters. Praetextus raised his hand to gain quiet.

"The point of our defense is that there should be no fine to pay," he said. "First, Plinius has not presented any evidence in support of the Clodius claim. Was Melonius violated? Who saw it? Who heard of it? Second, to force payment from a justly inherited estate at the expense of the innocent son violates every pretense of fairness embodied in our laws. Third, even if evidence were presented and even if we step outside our normal expectation of fairness, what proof can our opponents offer that Antistius Petrus committed such violation or that he alone held responsibility for such violation?"

The wailing voice of a woman penetrated the hubbub of the crowd. "Melonius was an innocent child," she cried. "I was his mother. I knew what he suffered."

A disturbance roiled in the benches behind Clodius and his supporters. An aging woman, disheveled in black garments, flailed as a group of women began escorting her out.

"She shouldn't be here," Tatian muttered. "There is much she'll not want to hear."

"What mother would not defend her son?" Caerwin replied.

"I agree with Tatian," Fimbria said. "She should have stayed home."

Several minutes passed before the woman's cries faded in the distance and the crowd's attention returned to the center of the court where Praetextus remained standing.

"Antistius Marcellus has served honorably. When the legate of the Fourteenth fell in battle, this tribune stepped into the role. He bore that responsibility for nearly two years before his term of service ended. He only now returns to begin his life as an upstanding and deserving citizen. He hopes to marry and raise children. He supports his aging mother. His shipping business serves the Goddess Annona in providing the grain we depend on for our daily lives. All of this depends on his ability to preserve his home and maintain the standards expected of his equestrian rank. One million sestertii would require him to sell his home and his ships, a staggering loss to him personally as well as to the Empire.

"I ask you, on behalf of this brave legate Antistius Marcellus, to look beyond whatever grievance—legitimate or not—the Clodius claim seeks to remedy. Consider instead Rome's long history of *aequitas* and *utilitas*. These traditions of fairness and practicality stand as the foundation of our greatness."

"Sir," Plinius said, standing to interrupt. "The noble argument made by our opponent might serve well in a simple case, but this is not a simple case. May we present witnesses to support our pleading?"

"Have you finished your *narratio*, counsel?" Gavius looked at Praetextus.

"Let him proceed," Praetextus said.

Plinius turned and motioned to one of the men standing behind Clodius.

The man gave his name and launched into a description of a scene in the public baths where he alleged to have seen Petrus with Melonius.

"What of this scene pertains to the case?" Praetextus asked. "If being seen in the baths with a young man were a crime, we'd all be criminals."

Surrounding listeners laughed. The man's face reddened.

"Did you witness any compromising acts between these two men?"

"I did. The boy protested."

"How did you know his name?"

"He wore an amulet. His appearance has been described to me."

Praetextus looked at the judge then back at the witness. "You never knew his name?"

"No, but…"

"Let me ask you—how many young men, or even older men, wear amulets? How far away were you—close enough to this encounter to see that what this young man wore was in fact a *bulla*?"

"As far as me to you, not far," the man said. In spite of the cool air wafting through the building, his florid face had become shiny with perspiration.

Praetextus pulled a thin gold chain up from under his toga's neck and held it forward, presenting a small circular amulet dangling there. "Can you tell me, sir, if this is a *bulla*?"

"Of course it's not—you're well past boyhood and this isn't a suitable occasion."

"You're right. I'm well past boyhood and this isn't a suitable location. But this is a *bulla*," Praetextus said, turning so that the crowd could see the gold talisman. "I wore it for one reason, to show that a well-intentioned person could assume they saw something they in fact did not see, in this case by the reverse. You saw it and did not know it. This unknown person you saw with Antistius Petrus could have been any boy wearing any kind of amulet."

Red faced, the man turned and dove into the crowd.

Praetextus ran his hands through his hair and waved his arms. "Haven't we all witnessed the scene described of Antistius Petrus at the baths? Countless young slaves have protested when their masters made use of them in this way, whether they disliked the act or not. Isn't protest part of that game? They say 'no no' when the master wishes to excite himself with the conquest. There is no crime in that."

The judge turned to Plinius. "Do you have any witness who actually witnessed anything, counsel?"

Plinius turned to another man who stood behind Clodius. "Acilia Glabrio, will you speak?"

Acilia came forward, straightening his shoulders and looking briefly at Marcellus. "I have direct knowledge of this man's participation in his father's calumny. As often as I saw Petrus, I saw Marcellus. He attended the sex clubs, he attended the baths, all the time willingly playing the role of the conquered as often as the conqueror." He motioned toward Marcellus.

A gasp rose through the long hall accompanied by words such as '*cinaedus*' and '*pathicus*.' Caerwin's heart slammed against her ribs. Exactly what Marcellus had feared, announced for the world to hear. He would be shamed.

The judge interrupted. "You make a strong accusation, sir, for which you will be liable if you have no proof. But the hearing isn't about Antistius Marcellus. It's about his father. Are you making a separate charge?"

The man waved his hand. "No, I was asserting my authority to speak. Very well. His father made a career of abusing young men. He used them in the baths, in his private rooms, at the clubs, and at his villa at Herculaneum. I know this because I was one of those so used."

Mutters rippled through the assembly. By now no one remained seated and several stood on the benches. The press of bodies forward shoved Fimbria against Caerwin and Caerwin against Tatian. Fimbria shoved back, retaking a bit of room for them.

"We've already established there is no crime in using young men unless they are of noble blood," the judge said.

"Yes. I accepted my place as a freed slave to receive such abuse, but Clodius Melonius did not. He appeared to be unaware of what Petrus expected and in the process of wooing the young man with wine, Petrus began to fondle him—shall I spell out exactly where he touched?"

"We all know such details," the judge said. "Did he protest?"

"No, he didn't protest. He seemed to enjoy it, as a matter of fact," Glabrio said.

"No!" Clodius Galarius shouted. He reached past Plinius and tried to grab Glabrio's shoulder. "You slur our family name with your lies!"

Plinius interrupted. "Whether or not he might have enjoyed it, as alleged here, the fact is that he was not of an age to freely decide."

Praetextus stood. "Might I point out that many young men reach the age of majority without a mature appearance," he said. "At sixteen years, many of us have only one or two whiskers. Even the most athletic may appear as youth. Am I wrong in this?"

He turned, lifting his hand to solicit commentary from the crowd. Shouts rose, mostly from the throngs backing Marcellus.

"Clever man," Tatian said. "Didn't I say?"

Caerwin tried again to see Marcellus, but the press of bodies kept him hidden.

"Did you know his age at that time?" Praetextus asked Glabrio.

Glabrio looked confused. "I did not," he said finally.

Praetextus turned to the judge. "Gavius Tiburs, I beg you to dismiss this case and turn to our countersuit. We have been harmed by these allegations and seek to recover some small settlement to ease our injury."

"We have not put forth all our witnesses," Plinius shouted.

Cries arose from the Clodius followers. "Justice for Melonius!"

"Very well," Gavius said. "Bring it."

"We call Helvius Sura," Plinius said.

"Jupiter and Mars, save us," Tatian whispered. "Tulla has betrayed us."

"What?" Caerwin rocked side to side on tiptoe, trying to see the witness. "Who is that?"

"Matina's husband," he said. "Marcellus' sister Matina." He closed his eyes and mumbled a prayer.

Helvius stood proudly in his white toga, staring briefly at Marcellus before turning to face the judge. "This man," he said, pointing at Marcellus, "is not the rightful heir of the Antistius estate. He can't defend what is not his."

Angry shouts and the pounding of feet rose to a deafening roar around Caerwin. "Slander!" "Lies!"

The judge's attendant slammed the floor with his staff. Finally the noise subsided.

"A weighty accusation, Helvius," the judge said. "You should present your proof and your oath or suffer the consequences."

"I swear on the Helvius house. I have proof in the word of my wife Matina, the sister of this man." He turned, addressing the crowd with his deliberate speech. "I should say, his *half*-sister.

Tulla, daughter of Fenius Clemens, mother of the daughters who are rightful heirs of her husband Antistius Petrus, has long ago informed her daughter Matina of the compromise her father made. In return for payment of both land and coin from the hand of Antistius Labeo, Tulla would be wed to Labeo's son Antistius Petrus and accept the bastard child he got upon a slave woman by the name of Rhian."

Caerwin covered her face with her hands. "No. No no no."

Fimbria wrapped her arm around her. "Shh."

Helvius waited until the uproar subsided. "We all know that a child gotten on a slave girl cannot inherit the father's estate. This man, Antistius Marcellus, is an illegal claimant."

"This claim is not part of the case," the judge said loudly. "Was there a trustee in charge of the estate?"

"Yes, the highly esteemed authority on family trusts, Nepius Fabianus," Praetextus replied. "I assure you and these desperate plaintiffs that the inheritance was entirely legal."

"Well, then," the judge said. "For the time, we set aside this point. The *clepsydra* moves swiftly toward the fifth hour. What further evidence do you have pertinent to the matter in question?"

"None," Helvius said, holding up his hands. He made his way back to the benches.

"Are there further witnesses to the alleged abuse?"

"Only the fact of the young man's suicide," Plinius said. "What but the degrading infamy put upon him by Antistius Petrus could cause such a promising life to end at his own hand?"

Praetextus made a gesture of impatience. "I am embarrassed for my colleague. His question begs a hundred answers. We all know the impetuous nature of youth. At the time of this tragedy— and make no mistake, we agree that this young man's death was a tragedy—evil reigned over Rome. We don't deny that Melonius may have willingly partnered with Petrus. He may have been one who preferred the role of *puer*. Perhaps it was the stigma of his preferences that drove him to his knife. But we must keep in mind the intrigues taking place in those dark years and the eager appetite of our disgraced leader for exactly such young men."

He surveyed the faces straining to hear his words. "Do we know that Melonius wasn't a victim of the Little God's sadistic games? We have heard only fragments of what occurred in the emperor's palace, but even that shocks us. What volumes do we not know? What degradations? What torments?

"We know that Petrus wasn't the only noble citizen of Rome to drink his cup of poison in those days. His sizeable share in the gold mines of Hispania were seized for the royal coffers upon his death—surely a familiar story. We can easily see that Melonius might have been part of the envied treasure. From what we've learned, his death came shortly after that of Petrus."

"We might even think that Melonius and Petrus had an affair of the heart and it was for love that the young man died."

With a curse, Clodius rushed to grapple with Praetextus. Shouts filled the basilica. Marcellus pushed between them. A roundhouse caught him in the jaw. He seized Clodius by the throat. Two attendants set their long staffs between the men, re-establishing the order of the court.

The judge stood up, holding up both hands until the crowd silenced. "There is much to be determined. I will consult with the jurists in attendance. I think the subject has become too tangled for easy or just conclusion. Perhaps the emperor himself will be the final word in this matter."

Caerwin stood shaking, gripping Fimbria's hands as the crowds began to file out of the basilica. Tatian made his way to Marcellus, joining the throng of supporters and legal advisors as they formed a thicket around him. She ignored the impatient urging of Cotta and Falco, fully aware that they wanted nothing more than to put the entire unsavory hearing behind them. Finally the admirers and advisors dwindled and Marcellus gathered the folds of his toga. He glanced up and caught her stare. The look on his face said it all.

That night Seisyll came to her in a dream. He walked along the road, only it wasn't the road they'd walked together before reaching the Ordovices camp. It was the road in Gaul where Senna lost her life. Bright yellow grain fields stretched to the distant blue hills. She stood on the stone paved road as he approached, his wild white hair flying in a stiff wind.

He walked with his staff, but he wasn't bent as he'd been in life. His eyes blazed at her as he neared and his mouth moved. She couldn't hear his words.

He stood before her. His words revealed in her mind.

Give him what he needs. You love him.

Caerwin had so many questions, so much she wanted to say, to beg forgiveness for his death, to thank him for being such a good friend, to ask what Marcellus needed. She tried to form words but her mouth didn't work.

Senna sent me. He smiled. Creases fanned out from the corners of his blue eyes. He looked almost young, robust.

These are her words, he said with his familiar grin. *You know I never said anything in so few words.*

Caerwin sat up in bed.

The dream haunted her morning. What did Marcellus need? Rufus turned away the stream of men at the gate. Except for a brief visit from Manlius, Marcellus kept his office door closed and she didn't dare interrupt. Antius and Tatian came in and out as she observed through her open bedroom door. Finally she could wait no longer. She intercepted Antius the next time he came out.

"What does he intend?" she said. "How is he?"

Antius looked skyward. "He thinks in circles. I have no idea where he'll stop."

"What does it mean, that the emperor must hear it?"

"That's anyone's guess. Praetextus and Manlius agree that it could go either way. For better or worse, Vedius may hold the key."

"He doesn't want to see Vedius," she said.

"He'll do what he must do. That's the nature of it."

"When?"

"For the sake of the gods, girl, is there no end?" he shouted. "No one knows! It's been one day and that not fully advanced to the sixth hour. Do you think that your knowledge of these things will help him in any way? If you want to help him, see to the house. Act as a wife would act."

Caerwin stepped back, shocked by the fury in Antius' eyes. "I…"

The door to Marcellus' office opened. He stood there with his fists on his hips. "What must I do to gain one moment's peace?"

"I only wanted to know…" she began.

Antius interrupted her. "She wants to know what you'll do and when you'll do it. I've told her you haven't said, and that if she wants to help, she should tend the duties of a wife."

Caerwin hardly heard what Antius said. Marcellus spoke to her with his eyes. She hurried across the atrium and tucked her arms around him, resting her head on his chest.

"I'm sorry," she said. "Sorry if you don't want me to touch you. Sorry that you suffer this terrible injustice. I only want to comfort you."

His hand came to her shoulder. She leaned back to look into his face. His lips met hers. For a long moment, the gentle contact between them conveyed a message that resonated to her core.

"Thank you," he said, brushing a tendril of hair from her forehead. "You've done that."

"Let me help you," she said.

He shook his head and stepped away. "There's nothing you can do. If the emperor won't hear the case, if the matter can't be resolved…"

"He'll hear it. Haven't you hired the best men to help you? What do they say?"

"They say I must persuade Vedius."

"I thought he was your friend," she said. "Why would he not help you?"

"He's known of my case since the beginning. He's the one who sent me the message as we came into Gaul, warning me and urging me to hurry. I thought I knew the man he was, but he's changed. He seems almost angry when he's around me."

"Does he want money?"

Antius sighed. "This isn't helping. We've been over this."

He took her arm as if to lead her away. She jerked away.

"If you've been over it and you don't have an answer," she said, "maybe you need another opinion."

Marcellus laughed. "Which you'll provide."

"Yes," she said, crossing her arms. "But with you alone."

Tatian stood up. "Whatever will help. Is that what you wish?" he asked Marcellus.

"I'll hear what she has to say."

She waited until Tatian and Antius with his scowl had closed the office door. With her legs crossed, she adjusted the folds of her blue silk *stola* across her knees. She had worn it because it emphasized her figure, because she wanted to distract Marcellus from his fears. She had no idea what she would say. Marcellus sat on the edge of his desk and waited.

"I, uh, well…" she said. "Vedius was one of your lovers? Like Silverus and Antius?"

He nodded. "He wasn't like them. He and I are of the equestrian class. What we had wasn't like what went on with other men my father brought into our circle, not like Silverus or Antius, or anyone else. He was clever and tender and we embraced each other for our feelings, not just our sex. We thought ourselves in love.

Caerwin's cold hands gripped in her lap. "He wants you back."

"He's married."

"But…"

"Yes, that wouldn't stop him from whatever liaison he might arrange on the side, but for either of us to participate, we'd risk disgrace. Neither of us could be the *puer*."

"What could he possibly expect of you?" she said.

"I don't know. I think he's hardened and bitter about his injury. He hasn't said what he wants. Like I said, he's changed."

"Yet he expects that what happened ten years ago…"

"Twenty. It began when we were fifteen. We risked exposure to continue but we couldn't stop ourselves."

"Years."

"Yes."

"I saw how you looked at each other. When you kissed…you still have feelings." She said.

He exhaled. "Yes."

She recoiled from the admission.

"Nothing of my feelings for him affect my feelings for you," he said.

How could it not? She closed her eyes and struggled to gain control over her panic. "Who knows about it?"

He shrugged and pulled up a chair. "I've told no one. Antius was there. Now Tatian knows some of it."

"What if Tatian is a spy for him?" she said.

"What would it gain him? Now that the trial has uncovered the secret of my mother, perhaps Vedius will lose interest."

"No. He'll see it as a way to force you to his will. He's in a position of power over you, isn't he?"

"Yes," Marcellus said. His voice softened and he leaned toward her. "You're right, clever little queen. He could see to my ruin and gain what he desires. Reduce me to slave and buy me to use. I care for him, but I don't want him."

She hardly trusted herself to speak. "I see. Thank you for your honesty."

"Caerwin, nothing of this changes my plans for you."

"What plans, Marcellus? You can't marry me. You may lose your inheritance—if not to the claims of Clodius then to your mother's status. The gods, you may lose your place as a citizen of Rome! What does that leave?"

"You. It leaves you. I'm not giving up." Tears reflected in his eyes. "I'm fighting."

~~~

Fimbria woke her when the sky had barely begun to lighten. She emptied the pail of hot coals into the cold ash of the brazier and lit the oil lamps.

"Oh, no," Caerwin mumbled, snuggling into the warm covers.

"You wanted an early start," Fimbria said. "Remember?"

"I was under a spell when I said it," Caerwin mumbled. "What possible good comes from walking about in the dark?"

Fimbria laughed, shaking out the dark green *stola* then holding the woolen tunic near the brazier to warm. Caerwin stood as the heated cloth slid over her head and body. With warm socks in her ankle boots and the *stola* belted around her waist, she fidgeted as Fimbria arranged her hair.

"Lucky for you," Fimbria said, fastening the last of the ringlets around the sides of Caerwin's head. "The natural curl in your hair gives you the fashionable style without much effort."

"I hardly care. I wake feeling tired. Couldn't I just lie abed all day?"

"That's not what you wanted," Fimbria said. "Have you changed your mind?"

Caerwin remembered Marcellus. "No," she said. "I can't."

The whole back of the house hummed with activity. Gordianus and his helpers returned early from the markets and she struggled to keep up with him as he rushed from the kitchen to the storeroom then out to the fire pit in the back garden. Saturnalia was upon them and days of feasting would tax even the most established kitchen. Junia's pastry chef Fimus, a thin dark haired man, occupied a worktable crowded with bowls, fruit, honey pots, and spice jars. Helpers streamed in and out.

Each time Gordianus turned and saw her standing there, a furious expression crossed his face.

"As if these rooms weren't crowded enough," he grumbled. "What possible good can come of this?"

"I could help," she said, stepping aside again as he carried a lamb carcass to his cutting table. He was a tall man with big bony hands and an ill-formed face. "Do you need onions chopped? I could gather herbs. Tend a fire, if needed."

His face flushed red. Redder than it had been a few minutes earlier. He seemed ready to ignite. "I have too many helpers already," he shouted, waving his arms toward the adjacent work table. "Look at them, the worthless fools—you'd think they'd never seen a knife before."

"Should I show them?" She swallowed, fearful that the next moment his patience would snap and she'd find herself on the other side of the *peristylium*. She watched three men cower at the nearby table and, hearing no comment from Gordianus, went to take the knife from one.

"Here," she said. "You can't attack an onion that way. See, you've made a mash of it. Slice one end off first, then the other. Clean." She made the cuts. "Then you slice it from head to toe, peel off the shell, set it sideways, and make your cuts one way, then the other."

The pungent odor of chopped onion brought happy tears to her eyes. She picked up another onion and handed it to the young man. "Try it."

The mound of chopped onions grew as each of the three men followed her instruction. Garlic came next. They gasped when she smashed the clove flat with the side of the knife but eagerly imitated her method once they saw the ease of the process. Baskets of celery, leeks, cabbage, and carrots presented the next task, all while Gordianus muttered and steamed around the small kitchen. Evidently he had never bothered to teach his apprentice cooks even the most basic skills.

She watched him work. An accomplished butcher, his sharp knife flew through two lamb carcasses. The scent of the raw meat transported her back to the Wrekin and her mother's smile. Two large pots of water had come up to boil to which he added the aromatic vegetables and the lamb.

"Stew, then," she said, looking at him.

He scowled but nodded.

"Rosemary? Thyme?"

He nodded again.

Signaling the helpers to accompany her, she took a small knife and hurried outside. "That's thyme," she said, pointing to the low creeping plant with its tiny dark green leaves. She grabbed a handful, cut the bunch loose, and held it close to the young men's faces. "Isn't that a lovely scent?"

The rosemary bush yielded pungent, luxuriant spires, and they also cut some sprigs of mint and a handful of parsley. The cold air sharpened her senses. She felt close to her homeland here with fragrant herbs in her hands and high gray clouds obscuring the sun. A silent prayer flew to the sky in remembrance of her mother.

She paused to remember her dream and smiled. Whatever she could do to comfort Marcellus, she would. Senna had heard her earlier vow not to go to him. Even from the land of the dead, the faithful woman had sent her message to remind Caerwin of the man she truly loved.

Two men arrived carrying a heavy wheel of aged cheese. Other helpers soon returned from the markets with baskets of apples and pears as well as a smaller quantity of figs along with some fruits she didn't recognize. Still other helpers scurried about in the back garden, some tending the fire pit where a spit turned with its heavy burden of two pig carcasses while others squatted amid a flurry of feathers from the chickens and ducks they were plucking.

Caerwin stood in the warm kitchen and inhaled the aroma of lamb stew. Gordianus had said little since she returned with the herbs. She'd caught him watching her from the corner of his eye as she helped stuff the poultry with onion, celery, and sausages. Maybe she flattered herself, but it seemed he yelled less this afternoon.

She washed down the tables and cleaned the knives. Nearby, Fimus beat eggs to froth.

"A custard?" she said.

He nodded stiffly, as if to speak to her would violate some edict etched deep in his soul. Or perhaps Gordianus had cut out his tongue. "Lemon," he said finally. "Have you tasted them?"

He motioned toward the lemons being sliced by a helper. She bit into the flesh and gasped.

"Sour," she said, her mouth puckered into a grimace.

His pallid face broke into an enormous smile. She'd never seen so many teeth.

"Sour," he nodded, highly pleased with himself. "With enough honey, the taste is perfect."

Two helpers gripped the lemons to squeeze out their juices. She lingered long enough to watch him add cream to the eggs and honey to the juice before beating it all together. At dinner, she eagerly awaited the reaction of Marcellus and the guests as they tasted the sweet-sour custard. Fimus had topped the soft confection with sweet brown syrup. She scraped her dish and wanted more.

Despite the success of Junia's pastry cook, the dessert failed to sweeten her opinion of Junia. The next day, as on most days, Junia's messengers beat a steady traffic past Rufus and a convoy of summoned merchants arrived with their samples only to suffer her withering criticism and be sent on their way without even one sale. Perfumes, wigs, jewelry—in short, goods to suit whatever whimsy passed Junia's mind. The merchants arrived smiling and left muttering.

Junia's four chair porters stood stiffly at the entry as she fluttered out the door to take her seat in the chair. At the flick of her crop, they lifted the ornate chair and stepped forward. Her retinue of slaves hurried after her—a footman, secretary, personal assistant, two armed guards.

"I can't keep up," Caerwin said to Varinia. "What can she possibly find for all of them to do?"

"Their presence demonstrates her wealth and importance," Varinia said, making a face. "It doesn't matter if they do nothing." She lowered her voice. "I dare say she has one to sponge her behind."

The two women stood by the emptied atrium pool watching as workers scrubbed the tiles sparkling clean. All morning she had accompanied Varinia as they toured the width and length of the *domus* with a crew of workers who wiped the walls, dusted statuary and works of art, and cleaned the floors. Men arrived carrying buckets of fresh water to refill the reservoir.

Varinia sat beside her on one of the *peristylium* benches to take the noon meal. The scent of pig fat burning on the coals filled the air.

"How often do they drain the pools?" Caerwin asked.

"In warm months, every moon," Varinia said, pushing her hair back from her face. "Unless Jupiter is angry and holds back the rain."

"How much of this is the woman of the house expected to know?" Caerwin asked. "Are these duties under her command?"

"Depends on the household," Varinia said. Her speculative gaze lingered on Caerwin before turning back to her piece of cold chicken. "Some women leave it all to the slaves, especially among the very rich. But the more virtuous wives poke into every corner and keep lists of tasks so that if she sees someone idling, she can set him to work immediately. She also spins wool and weaves cloth, oversees the care and education of the children, tends to any business or estate she owns, and keeps up the husband's interests if he's away."

"A daunting list," Caerwin mused. "What would it take to list all the tasks? It seems the list would be never ending."

Varinia smiled. "It would. Each task leads to another."

"I've seen no spindle or loom—did Tulla not weave?"

"If she did, she took the tools with her. Rufus said she moved away shortly after his master died. He's had a long quiet time in this house."

"Less work, I suppose, but lonely. Do you despair of finishing your work?"

"Not at my point in life." Varinia lifted her shoulders in a gesture of acceptance. "Thankfully I've learned enough to gain higher position. But for them..." She pointed to the covey of slaves knotted together near the back entry. "I was like them once. All I knew was work. You learn to perform your duties at a certain pace. You find peace in that—and rest, if you know how to do it. The master has no reason to whip you if you always seem busy. At least, some masters. Others whip for any reason or no reason at all. The work must stretch to fill the hours sometimes. Other days—like today—there is too much."

She motioned again. "These slaves are new to this *domus*, none of them used to this household, this master. Those owned by Junia think themselves better and stand apart from those hired by Antius even though she treats them with abuse. You don't see any of them helping clean today, do you?"

Caerwin shook her head. "She abuses everyone."

"On the other hand," Varinia said, "Antius spends too little time enforcing discipline. It's left to me to make threats, and I can't watch them all. He should hire a manager to help him, but he says

Marcellus wishes to keep the staff at the least possible number. Surely there are idlers and miscreants among them, but they're clever in finding ways to avoid my watch. They'd rob us blind if they had a chance."

"Can you blame them?" Caerwin said. "Do they only have bread and cheap wine or that miserable porridge?"

"They—we—have it better in this household than many others. If there's a clever bone in their bodies, they'll quickly learn the truth of that. Although," she said quietly, "I don't see why the household must pay for Junia's slaves' food. Junia obviously doesn't lack wealth."

"Does Marcellus know?"

Varinia shrugged. "I won't be the one to tell him. She's had her man whip some of our slaves because they offended her. I doubt he knows that either. Even at that, our staff knows this is a generous household. Here we have regular supply of beans, apples and raisins, sometimes eggs and olives, treats from the pastry shops if we have a spare coin. We're far better served than many freedmen—some dig through garbage to find a scrap."

"I thought the government parceled out grain to the poor."

Varinia licked the last of her soft cheese from her fingers. "Only grain. No meat, no cheese, no olives. It's a miserable life. Some sell themselves into slavery to avoid such deprivation."

Caerwin gasped at Varinia's expression. "Did you?"

"My mother had no choice," the older woman said, shrugging. "My father fell in battle and she had no heart for another man. There were three children. I wasn't as fortunate as you."

"I'm not..." Caerwin frowned and lapsed into silence as Varinia hurried off to her duties. Caerwin's position in the household troubled her. Even without the authority of a wife, she now attempted to serve the wife's role as Antius suggested. She walked through the atrium and stopped at the altar of Vesta to burn incense and pray.

"Senna, I know you hear me. I beg you, speak to the gods on my behalf. If I'm to serve Marcellus, I must learn many things for which I have little patience. Grant me patience."

Chapter Nine

Caerwin lingered near the office door as one after another client made their morning plea for Marcellus' favor. Every few moments, she paced in the atrium, unable to ignore her growing annoyance with the demands placed on Marcellus. She wanted to tell him of Junia's abuses. The more she thought about what Varinia told her, the more outraged she became.

Sigilis strode through the doorway, his cloak flaring. As soon as she saw him, her cheeks flamed.

"Behold the beauty of the baths," he said, laughing.

"Please," she said. "Don't speak of it."

"Why not? You've become a celebrated figure."

"Celebrated in the worst way," she said.

"But what a figure!" He laughed again. "Don't worry. Your infamy will fade. Tomorrow or the next day, especially with Saturnalia on the horizon, others will take your place at the center of gossip." He smiled reassuringly. "I have to admit, if you held the reins of my heart, I might have done the same. He's without reason on your account."

"I never asked…"

"That's part of it. Don't you see? Men want the challenge. Unlike Junia who throws herself at him, you hide seductively behind your furious dignity. You have little in common with her."

"Yet she's a citizen and I'm not. He can marry her but not me," she said. "He won't…He doesn't want to get a child born a bastard."

"That's exactly why I'm here. I think he'll be quite happy with my news."

Ill at ease, Caerwin sat in her corner of Marcellus' office as Sigilis forced his information past Marcellus' preliminary dismissal.

"The language reads thus," Sigilis said, opening a scroll. "'Those who would finance, build, and operate merchant ships will be paid large bounties. Ship owners servicing the *Annona* will be exempted from harbor taxes in all Roman ports. Further, ship owners are exempted from performing civic duties required of all wealthy citizens.'"

He glanced at Marcellus who sat unmoving then continued reading.

"'If the ship owner is a Roman citizen, he shall be exempted from the *lex Papia Poppaea*. If the ship owner possesses less than Roman citizenship, he shall be able to gain full Roman citizenship. If a woman, the ship owner shall be granted the privileges normally reserved for mothers of four children."

He set the scroll on his lap. "These changes are already written," Sigilis said. "They fear another shortage. Claudius has only to make public announcement."

"It's too much to believe," Marcellus said. "The tax concessions, yes, I can see that. But citizenship? I was told on good authority that he was sensitive to issues of citizenship."

"This is why," Sigilis said, brandishing the scroll. "Why give away citizenship unless it serves the interests of the empire? This explains Junia's insistence on buying part of the fleet."

"By the gods! I've made a verbal commitment to her," Marcellus said. "My finances require it."

"You're thinking like a cornered man," Sigilis said. "Since when does the Antistius I know think that way?"

Marcellus huffed. "Since I became cornered."

"Think of this. These reforms have been in the works for months. You know how these things work. It comes down to your connections. Somehow Junia must have heard of it. She wants control of the Norbanus silk business and freedom from her old uncle Magnus."

He pounded Marcellus' desk with his fist. "Don't you see? Married to you, as she tells me she must, she gains it all. Beware of that! Only days will pass before you fail to wake from your night's sleep and then she owns it all. Would it be the first time a scheming woman wielded a dose of poison for power and wealth?"

Marcellus sighed and shook his head. "I hardly think…"

"That's just it," Sigilis said. "You haven't been able to think. You've been surrounded by every possible distraction while she smiles and waits. I've heard you plan to take her to Neapolis."

"I do, but only after the legal matters are settled. I may have nothing left to sell."

"Why wait? I return there when Saturnalia ends. I could take her."

"Oh!" Caerwin leapt up from her chair. "Could you? That would be wonderful." She looked at Marcellus. "Unless you want her here."

He glared at her and she sat down.

"Her uncle has spoken in court. What other reason does she remain?" Sigilis said.

"Her money," Marcellus said flatly. "I've spent much of my reserve in courting support for the trial. Little good that did me. The lawyers extract my lifeblood as well, and the household requires a steady flow of *denarii*."

Caerwin put her hands on her hips. "You would staunch some of that flow by sending her away. Does she pay anything toward her costs? She and her slaves eat our food and none of them help around this place."

"I can make you a loan," Sigilis said.

"The gods! My own manager offers me money. Is there no end to my embarrassment?"

"I'm rich," Sigilis said. "You pay well and I've recently come into the estate of my father."

"Oh, forgive me," Marcellus said. "I didn't know."

"He suffered an undignified illness. I was glad he found a peaceful end."

"So tell me again," Marcellus said. "The point of a ship owner gaining citizenship. From what status?"

Sigilis grinned at Caerwin. "Make her a ship owner," he said, pointing at her. "She becomes a citizen."

Marcellus slammed his chair back and tore open the garden door. The room had become warm on the unusually mild day. Sunlight poured through the opening. He stood there staring out.

"Can it possibly be that simple?" Marcellus said.

"Not simple, but possible," Sigilis said. "Claudius hasn't announced the new rules. The Senate has yet to give its approval. They will and soon."

"You forget one thing. My fate is not decided," Marcellus said. "I can't give or sell property that I may not rightfully possess."

"You only have to convince Vedius to assist your case with the emperor," Sigilis said.

"And if he stands to gain if I lose everything, then what?" Marcellus said. He closed the door and dropped into his chair.

"What does he want?" Sigilis said. "He has more wealth and power than almost anyone except the emperor."

Marcellus looked at him without speaking.

Caerwin stood up, unable to bear one more minute of Marcellus' torment. She knew what Vedius wanted. He would never say it to Sigilis, but Marcellus faced a terrible dilemma.

Sigilis looked at her and then at Marcellus. "He wants her?" he said.

"*Alea iacta est*," Marcellus said, rubbing his forehead. "The die is cast."

~~~

The next morning, the household prepared to attend the opening Saturnalia celebration at the Temple of Saturn. Caerwin accepted Fimbria's choice of clothing, her purple *stola* with the red silk *palla*. The talented woman wove ribbons through Caerwin's hair and left the ends to dangle with a few curls along her neck. Caerwin loaned Fimbria and Varinia some of her garments in keeping with the tradition that servants should wear their master's clothing.

The procession of their household as well as those of neighboring houses filled the avenues as they advanced toward the city center. She finally spotted Marcellus some distance ahead surrounded by Antius, Tatian, and some of the regular clients. They stopped at the fringe of the crowd gathering near the temple.

Marcellus caught her eye and beckoned. He wore a long-sleeved tunic in bright red and belted with a gold sash. A dark red cloak held by gold pins swooped from his broad shoulders. Despite the wear etched in his face, her heart skipped a beat as it always did when she saw him. Smiling, she waved back and turned to Fimbria.

"I'm going to my mother's house," Fimbria said. "Will you need me?"

"Go, enjoy the day," Caerwin said. "I'll be fine."

She hurried to catch up with Marcellus, Falco and Cotta close behind her.

"Stay with me," Marcellus shouted over the noise.

With her hand tight in his grasp, he pulled her through the crowd toward the high steps of the Temple of Saturn. The temple columns, set within terminals elaborately carved with fruiting vines, leaves, and the tools of agriculture, soared toward the sky. Once inside, she viewed the enormous veiled statue of Saturn at the heart of the temple. The only visible parts of the god were his lower legs and feet and one hand which held a golden scythe.

"Bonds of wool surround his legs at all times but today," Marcellus said. He pointed to the heaped mounds of woolen fabric near the feet. "He's the god of wealth, of agriculture. We bind him to the earth so he doesn't abandon us."

"So very Roman," Caerwin said. "You make even the god your slave."

He laughed and pulled her next to him. "I can always trust you will see the other side of it. I'm never unamused in your company."

"You didn't seem amused when you disgraced me in front of everyone at the imperial *thermae*," she said.

His face became stern. "You belong to me."

She started to speak but he put his finger on her lips. "No. Today we forget our troubles and celebrate the Golden Age, a time before cities and armies and laws."

"Before slaves?"

"Before slaves." He leaned close as priests entered from a rear door and began lighting candles. "Ovid wrote of it."

"'*First was the Golden Age. Then rectitude spontaneous in the heart prevailed, and faith. Avengers were not seen, for laws unframed were all unknown and needless. Punishment and fear of penalties existed not.*' Have you not read it?"

She shook her head.

"Ask Tatian, he'll supply the book. A terrible loss for which we all suffer," he said, wincing as drums and brass horns began to play.

"What happened to the Golden Age?"

A shadow crossed his face. "Another age began. Prometheus gave us fire and the civilizing arts. His brother Epimetheus gave Pandora a jar holding all the evils and she opened it. We learned too much and used it badly."

Sonorous tones wailed from the *hydraulis* as the songs began. She didn't know the words but she hummed along, thrilled at the rich vibration of Marcellus' voice and the warmth of his hand over hers. Whatever the legends of these Roman gods, she only cared that for one moment in this one day, she and Marcellus stood together in peace. As songs and chants rose and fell, she couldn't keep the smile off her face.

Once the priests had offered prayers and the sacrifices had been made, the crowd moved slowly outside. With his arm firmly wrapped around her waist, Marcellus stopped on the temple steps looking over the brightly garbed crowds still thronging the plaza. Surrounding the Forum, the great temples, statues, and official buildings of the Roman Empire stood like sentinels. Fountains splashed in brilliant sunlight. In the distance, the hills of Rome gleamed with their buildings, streets, and greenery.

Nothing in her life had been this overpowering. The city, the empire, all of it seemed summed up in this man standing beside her with his strength and beauty, his internal conflicts and passions. His easy use of violence. His knowledge of all things. His absolute power to conquer and hold her.

They descended the steps and walked a short distance. His head turned sharply and he looked down on her as if to speak. His face, which had become thinner in the last weeks, lightened with a tender expression. For a breathless moment, Caerwin thought he would kiss her or speak words of love.

She would say what she longed to say. "Marcellus, I…"

His gaze shifted to someone approaching and his face hardened. "Vedius," he said, raising his voice over the clamor. "Yo Saturnalia!"

As Marcellus moved away from her, Cearwin turned to see Vedius in a bright blue cloak. The color accented the blue of his eyes. She hadn't realized in their brief previous meeting that he had blue eyes. The contrast in his tan face accented his beauty. He clasped Marcellus shoulder to shoulder, gripping his hand before stepping back.

"Yo Saturnalia, Marcellus! The gods smile on us today." He motioned to the sky. "No rain. For the last three years, the festival suffered cold and rain. You've brought us good fortune with your return."

"Or the weather simply changed," Marcellus said, laughing.

"Come to my house later," Vedius said. "I have the best Pompeian wines and more food than we'll eat in a full cycle of the moon. I've hired a troupe of Syrian dancers."

"I can't promise about tonight. I have my own household to attend. Come sample my banquet and enjoy our acrobats and musicians."

"Would that we celebrated at Herculaneum," Vedius said. "Do you remember our times there?" Vedius glanced around and lowered his voice. "We must talk."

"Yes, we must," Marcellus said, clasping Vedius on the shoulder and walking several steps away.

Caerwin struggled to hear the rest of the information so lightly bandied between the two men. Vedius was the same type of man as Marcellus, his compelling magnetism apparent even without any act or word. Despite their casual tone, she could see the strain in Marcellus' body. At the speaker's platform at the head of the Forum, musicians beat brazen pans and rattled sistra and tambourines to accompany singing. People snapped their fingers in time and sang, making it impossible to hear what else the two men said.

She didn't need words to see the tension in Marcellus or the equally energetic desire in Vedius. Even if she hadn't witnessed their embrace in Marcellus' office, she could have derived the truth of their intimate past. Looking for escape, she stepped back and planted her foot directly on the boot of Falco.

He grinned, happily munching his way through a fistful of bacon. Smoke plumed from open grills. Nearby tables groaned under food supplied for public feasting—sausages, bacon, ham, fishcakes and fried fish, oysters and smoked meats spread over the wide planks alongside roasted vegetables, bread, cakes, and other foods easily taken by hand. The sight of his greasy lips and her conjured image of Marcellus coupling with Vedius turned her stomach. She broke into a sweat.

"There's more feasting at the Senate," Marcellus said, returning to her side and guiding her across the Forum plaza. "Do you want to go there?"

She swallowed, trying to contain her nausea. "I want whatever you want."

His eyes warmed as he looked on her. "You're more beautiful today than I've ever seen you." He leaned close to whisper in her ear. "What I want? To lock you in my bedchamber and make love for the rest of the day."

"Could we? I need time with you."

"You know I can't," he said. "Much as I wish for it. Instead, I will drink until I don't know how much I suffer. You should go home before the crowds become rowdy."

"I want you to be free of all this torment," she said.

He shook his head and looked over the crowd. "Another moon at least, if the gods will."

Morning sun beat down from a high blue sky. Shouts of "Yo Saturnalia!" flared up from the crowd every few minutes. Already wine flowed freely. Young men in bright clothes walked through the crowd dispensing figs, nuts, dates, and other dainties from baskets. She and Marcellus arrived at a table where noblemen in gaudy garments shouted and beckoned with the cheap pottery cups they offered filled with wine.

"Caldus!" Marcellus approached one of the men. "You give service!"

"Take a cup from me, old friend. You need it, don't you?" Caldus shouted. Red-faced and wearing a conical felt hat, he grinned broadly as he topped the cup to brimming.

"I need it," Marcellus agreed, taking the cup and gulping down the contents. "The best of your vineyards?" he said, grimacing.

Caldus laughed. "You'll come for a visit at my *domus* and we'll drink the good wine." He thrust his fist into the air. "Yo Saturnalia!"

"Yo Saturnalia!" Marcellus shouted. He held his cup for more and Caldus filled it. Marcellus started to turn away.

"Take care," Caldus called after him. "I'll make an offering to Fortuna on your behalf."

Marcellus lifted the cup and smiled. But as soon as they melted into the crowd, Marcellus' smile vanished. "He pities me," he said stiffly. "'Oh, Fortuna,' he said, 'goddess who admits by her unsteady wheel her own fickleness, always holding its apex beneath her swaying foot.'"

~~~

Caerwin allowed Marcellus to hire a chair to take her home. She felt miserable. The intense sun or the press of the crowd or the smell of so many people and foods might have been the cause for her distress, but underneath simmered the conversation of Vedius and Marcellus that lingered in the base of her throat. A powerful man like Vedius would suffer no limits in his appetites. How much favor could he exert from Marcellus? He honed some edge, that much was clear, and even if Marcellus didn't need his help, their behavior signaled affection. She'd known of Marcellus' appetites since her early days at the fortress when his relationship with Antius and Silverus had been revealed. How had she let herself drift into the belief that he would love only her?

His words from those times came back in full force.

I have never been close to a woman.

Confused and disoriented, once home she traded the silk clothing for her utilitarian linen *stola* and hurried to the kitchen where Gordianus shouted commands to his frazzled assistants. Barricaded behind his pastry table with flour to his elbows, Fimus raised his hands in supplication.

"What can I do to help?" she said.

Gordianus surveyed her with rolling eyes as if climbing down from a height. "There's nothing for you to do," he said, untying his apron to reveal his yellow tunic. "I've labored for days to prepare this feast." His loud laugh echoed through the *peristylium*. "It's a day free of labor, isn't it? A day when slaves and laborers throw off their work and expect to be treated as the master? A meal awaits us, served by the master and his household as if they were the slaves. Except, it isn't the master in here butchering lamb or roasting fowl or baking honey cakes. It isn't the master sharpening the knives or scouring the pots. It isn't the master…"

He stopped abruptly and scowled down at her. "You look sick."

"I think I stood too long in the sun," she said, pressing the back of her hand against her cheek. "I feel hot."

He hustled her out of the smoky kitchen and motioned toward a bench on the shaded side of the garden pool. "Sit here. I have just the remedy."

She accepted his command, uncertain at the moment whether her legs would hold her. He returned a short time later with a cup of steaming liquid.

"Liquorice tea," he said. "Let it cool first. Now, what have you eaten today?"

"Some bread, I think."

"Cheese? Fruit?"

She shook her head. "There was no time."

"Surely with all the feasting, you ate something at the Forum."

Her stomach lurched at the memory of Falco with his fistful of bacon. "No," she said emphatically.

"Fruit then," he said, folding his arms.

He returned with sliced pear, sliced apple, and pine nuts. She sipped the tea and admitted she felt better. The fruit went down easily and as she munched through the mound of small sweet nuts, she tried not to think of Marcellus' past or the power of a well-placed man like Vedius. Her effort proved useless. All she could think of was the precarious position Marcellus now found himself in and the advice from others to recruit Vedius' help and the fact that Marcellus didn't want to see Vedius while Vedius obviously wanted to see Marcellus.

The next time Gordianus bustled past, she blurted her question. "Do you know anything of a man named Calidius Vedius?"

His forehead furrowed. "I can't think of it," he said finally. "Do you feel better?"

"Yes, thank you for taking good care of me," she said. "I think I'll ask Rufus."

Outfitted in his aging red tunic and yellow cloak, Rufus lounged on his seat by the entry gate. She crouched by the bench, which caused him to spring up and take her elbow in a way that made clear she was to sit.

"I didn't mean to interrupt," she said.

"Interrupt…you mean, provide some small diversion to my otherwise miserably empty midday? What can I do for you?"

"You'll need your rest, won't you, for when the crowds arrive?"

"You speak the truth," he said. "I will. I've learned to wish Saturnalia lasted only one day. Or not at all."

"What's left of it after today? The Forum swarms with people."

"All of them drunk and gluttonous, I'm sure," he said. "There are two more days of feasting and drink with gift giving on the third day. For some it runs the week. In my younger days, I could find pleasure in it. Sadly, wine holds no interest now," he added, making a face.

"What's left?" He squinted up at her. "The same thing only more of it. Here and in most private houses instead of the Forum. I warn you, things easily get out of hand. I've seen the most sober matron, Tulla herself, disrobe amid the revelers. Although she was younger then and still hopeful of Petrus' attention. I shudder to think of it now."

"Rufus—you cheer me," Caerwin said, laughing. "Tell me—do you know of a man named Calidius Vedius?"

He rubbed his chin mouthing the name. "How would I know him?"

"I think he and Marcellus were close when they were younger."

"The master was a popular young man," he said. "He enjoyed many friends, always doing things. They played hard—wrestling, boxing, swimming. He frequented the drill grounds—ball games, racing horses. I don't know what he did when they went to Herculaneum or the other villas—there were rumors." He frowned. "Now, what did you ask me? Oh, yes, this man Clodius, er, Calidius. I can't say I remember the name."

Caerwin thanked the old man and wandered back through the atrium. A steady traffic of workers and shouted curses emanated from the back of the house, but she had no strength for engaging further with Gordianus. With a glance around the long room, she slipped into Marcellus' bedchamber and made her way to his bed.

He wanted her trust. But he'd never been close to a woman. And he was a Roman. How could she trust him? Curled into his blankets, she held his pillow close to her face and inhaled his scent.

~~~

The sound of a door slamming brought her awake. At first she didn't know where she was. Marcellus' voice caught her off guard. The gods! She'd fallen asleep in Marcellus' bed.

What could she say? Maybe she'd say nothing, simply get out of the bed and go to her room. Anywhere but his bed.

Another man's voice interrupted her thoughts.

"Let me touch you," the voice said. Clothes rustled. "I've waited all day. I've waited years."

"You've touched me," Marcellus said with a half laugh. "My affections…"

"Don't say it again. How can you care more about a *Brittunculi* than me? We made promises."

"Yet you married and sleep with your wife," Marcellus said.

"You're not jealous."

"We've changed."

"Your words hit like fists," Vedius said. A groan, the rustle of clothing. "Would that I had the body of my youth. I'd throw you to the floor and we'd grapple for position like we did on the field."

Caerwin's eyes flew open. Shadows cast by a lamp crossed the ceiling. She couldn't look. She couldn't move. Whatever they did, she didn't want to see it. Without doubt, the other man was Vedius. She squeezed her eyes shut.

The gods! What if they came to the bed?!

Marcellus laughed. "You often got the better of me. In every sport. Your vigor is not diminished even if your leg suffers. I can see it in your face."

"My dearest friend—you flatter me. Unlike me, you still carry the beauty of your youth," Vedius said. "Added to that are these limbs, this body beaten to perfection by the rigors of war. What man could resist you?"

"Time moves on," Marcellus said. "You have children and a brilliant career. I envy your skill in the ways of empire. Holy Jupiter, you've earned the emperor's trust! I only know the edge of a sword."

"Would that I knew the edge of your sword," Vedius said, chuckling. "Fires of Vulcan! I've had too much wine. Forgive me."

"It's Saturnalia, is it not?"

"Sometimes I dream of you," Vedius said. "You're over me. I'm in ecstasy. Have you thought of me at all?"

"You were my first love. How could I forget?"

"Is it this deformity that repels you, this miserable misshapen leg?"

"Do you think so little of me? I'm not so changed. We're no longer boys. Surely you recognize the risk. Where would it lead? Any meeting would of necessity be tawdry and furtive."

"If you wanted me as I want you, none of that would matter."

"Do you not love your wife?" Marcellus said.

"The question insults me. She's part of my life as much as any woman can hold my heart. I can help you. Come stand by me. Let me touch you."

"You know I want to please you," Marcellus said.

Vedius laughed. "For what I mean to you or for what I can do for you? Is my touch familiar?"

"Yes, yes. Where does this lead us?" Marcellus said.

"Why not have both? There, oh," Vedius said.

"Such a mouth on you," Marcellus said. "Oh, Jove's stones."

"I never forgot your taste. There's elder and musk. The gods, is any man more perfect? Look at that *mentula*. Mars himself sports a lesser beast than this."

"Oh!" Marcellus drew a sharp breath. "I can't do this."

"Mm, don't think of that now. Let me favor you."

"Vedius."

Caerwin held her breath at the sounds of struggle. Incoherent words followed. A slap. Something hit the floor and shattered. Furniture scooted.

"Was it too much to ask? A simple moment for me to express my affection, and you reject me?"

"I can't be your *puer*," Marcellus said. "Do you wish to be mine?"

"Now insults? You'll regret this," Vedius said, breathing heavily.

The door opened and closed. Caerwin waited. Did they both leave? Did she truly wake? She moved her hand then her foot. Then she sat up, threw the covers back, and looked around the darkened room. A broken pitcher scattered over the tiles and wine spread in a long red stain. Furniture sat askew.

Dread grew in her like a sickness. She opened the garden door and inhaled the cold air. Night had fallen. Sounds of revelry curled over the compound walls—distant horns, shouts, singing. She closed the garden door and walked across the room.

She listened at the door briefly then slipped along the shadows toward her room. A mob of people milled around in the atrium. The front entry stood open and Rufus was nowhere in sight. Two men, arm in arm, sang loudly as they walked the perimeter of the pool. One misstep and they both fell into the pool, splashing everyone nearby and triggering a wave of raucous laughter.

A group of men squatted to throw dice, shouting over their bets. Wine, broken cups, and bits of food littered the tiled floor. In the dim shadowed area by the ancestors' death masks, a man held a woman by the waist, barely visible as he bent her forward. Shouts erupted from the back of the house followed by a chant of '*futuo futuo.*'

If Marcellus… Her temper flared. These people had no respect for this house or for the man who owned it. Vedius had taken advantage. Everyone took advantage. She hesitated only a moment before striding through the crowd. She had to find him before he put himself further at risk.

At the dining room, a lonely musician strummed his lute to mostly empty dishes and a few people passed out on the couches. The kitchen had been abandoned to the revelers. Bared ribs of roast pig and few roast chicken carcasses remained with shreds of meat still hanging. Vegetables. Bread. Spilled wine. She shook her head.

"*Futuo futuo!*" The shouts grew louder as she neared the back of the *peristylium*. More naked people splashed in the pool despite the cold air. The shouting mob circled a hidden activity, evidently someone engaged in intercourse in public view. She walked close enough to assure herself that Marcellus wasn't among them. She didn't want to know who they were. The scene reminded her of her humiliation at the imperial baths.

She knew few of these household slaves and even fewer of the guests that reeled from place to place. Who looked after the house?

Fire leapt in the pits. People surrounded the flames, laughing, eating, and drinking. Groups of men played dice or knucklebones and shouted at each throw. She stepped over vomit and followed the paths through the fruit trees, along the garden beds, at each place examining the faces of the men. Her stomach heaved. Marcellus was nowhere to be found.

Caerwin stood in the passageway near the kitchen, trying to decide what to do. The words exchanged between Vedius and Marcellus repeated in her ears. Vedius made threats. Everything around her had turned upside down.

Hurrying back inside, she ran up the stairs to Tatian's room and knocked. A long silence then the door opened. Tatian held a towel around his waist. A younger man sat in the bed.

"Sorry, I...I'm looking for Marcellus," she said.

"I haven't seen him since this afternoon," Tatian said. "Do you need me to look for him?"

"No, no, sorry," she said, backing away and closing the door.

She stood on the walkway looking down on the melee underway in the *peristylium*. How could Marcellus let things get so out of control? Did Romans completely lose their senses at Saturnalia?

Sigilis stood in the kitchen.

"Yo," he said. "There's nothing left."

"A few morsels of meat and fowl," she said.

He rummaged through the lower shelves to retrieve a plate of pastries. "Want one?"

"How did you know to find that?"

"Gordianus shared his secret." He consumed half a pie in one bite. "I'm too old for this."

"The house is wrecked," she said, retrieving one of the pies and putting it on a small platter. Suddenly experiencing intense hunger, she picked at the meat bones, pulling off a few remaining shreds. The roasted chicken melted against her tongue. "Should I make everyone leave?"

He shrugged. "What can you do with drunks? The party I just left was worse."

"Have you seen Marcellus?"

"I saw him late at the baths, but not since. Why?"

"He was here early in the evening but then he left. I thought he should be here—it's his house."

"His problem. He's a big boy, don't worry about it. Can I do anything for you before I fall into bed?"

"Thanks, no."

She made her way back across the open space into the atrium. No one was in the pool and it seemed the crowd had thinned slightly. Junia's bedchamber door stood open. Voices wafted from the dark room, but Caerwin refused to look inside. Why did she care if Junia coupled with an army of men—or women? If Marcellus had fallen into that pit, she couldn't bear to know it.

She went to her room, uneasy with the situation. Where was Marcellus? Should she try to exert some control, tell people to leave?

On what authority? She had none.

She pushed the door open with her hip and set her plate on the table before turning to light the oil lamp. Loud snores issued from her bed. With the lamp held high, she peered at the intruder.

Marcellus.

~~~

Caerwin spent the night in Marcellus' bedchamber with the door locked. A knock sounded early and she sprang from the bed fully dressed. A bedraggled Marcellus stood there with Antius at his side.

"Why are you here?" he said in a hoarse voice.

"You were in my bed," she said.

"The gods."

Antius escorted him to the bed. "I found him in the kitchen as the first cock crowed."

"No man should drink that much wine," Marcellus said. "I'm ruined."

He looked ruined. A bruise marked his left cheek. His eyes were puffy and bloodshot. Caerwin didn't trust herself to speak and backed out of the room.

Traces of dreams flickered in her mind, scenes of Marcellus and Vedius, both without clothing, kissing, making love. There had been something about the road in Gaul, her horse galloping at breakneck speed as brigands chased close behind. Then the brigands became Vedius. His horse came beside hers. He smiled at her. Then he was Marcellus. The last thing she remembered was Marcellus on his white horse, his mouth moving with words she couldn't hear. She shook her head as she arrived at the kitchen.

The back of the house suffered the same damage she'd seen the night before. Only in daylight, it looked even worse. Gordianus glanced at her then nudged the bread toward her, a cold loaf from the previous day. She managed to eat a small portion before her stomach rebelled. Several of the house staff slowly swept and mopped the floors. Matters didn't improve through the day. Marcellus walked through the house and reviewed the grounds before returning to his bedchamber where he remained.

The third day of Saturnalia brought a mild revival. A hearty lamb stew sent aromatic tendrils through the house reminding Caerwin she'd hardly eaten. Slaves who had visited relatives returned. Caerwin pulled her chair beside her trunk and retrieved the candles and other small items she had obtained for the gift giving. As she spread them out on her bed, she remembered the last Saturnalia. Although only a year had passed, her life had changed so much. The fortress, Senna—all of it came flooding back.

She dug to the bottom on her trunk to retrieve the small round amulet. The wheel of Taranis whose thunder warded off evil. Senna's gift. The circular piece had been rubbed so smooth the dark red wood shone. The carving showed the careful detail of a dragon's head and tail amid interlocking swirls.

Scapula! She flinched thinking of his fists. Even now, her body remembered the impact of his blows, the searing slice of his knife. She should have worn the amulet that night instead of setting it aside. But she doubted even Taranis himself could have saved her from the evil living in that man. Her most intimate flesh still bore the scars of his depravity. No matter how well she might come to understand the degeneracy of Rome and the ironclad military hierarchy that rendered Marcellus powerless to protect her, she could never forget the beating she suffered at Scapula's hands.

She lifted the leather strand over her head and pressed the amulet against her chest. Some innocence lingered here, a thread still connected to her place among the Cornovii. Senna had told her of the woman who sold the amulet and her story that it had been found lying on the ground near the river. Surely of her tribe, then. She had known the power of Taranis all her life.

It had been too precious to wear. Now it was too precious to leave in the trunk.

When the rest of the gifts spread before her, she recounted their destined recipients. Each of the many household staff would receive a traditional pottery figurine and a candle whose light would coax the sun to its return. To Fimbria, Tatian, Gordianus, Rufus, and Varinia, she would distribute writing tablet and stylus, combs, perfumes, pipes, cups, and spoons. For Marcellus...

Caerwin picked up the tunic made of white *ralla* and held it up to the light. She could see her hand through it. Did she dare follow through with her plan to give it—and herself in it—to Marcellus? Would he want her after his encounter with Vedius?

Fimbria knocked and came into the room.

"Yo Saturnalia," she said. "I've heard the house descended into debauchery while I was gone."

"More than I care to remember," Caerwin said. "Here—I thought you'd enjoy this tablet. I think none of the others know how to write."

"Thank you," Fimbria said, smoothing her hand over the fancy wax tablet frame. She held the ornate stylus. "How beautiful! Thank you. Here's yours." She retrieved a book from her satchel. "My grandmother's prized possession."

"With pictures? Oh!" Caerwin stared at the drawings. "What...?"

"The erotic works of the Greek physician Elephantis. She shows positions for intercourse, spells to gain affection, practices of childbirth and abortives, a complete manual suited to a young bride. Keep it well hidden. It's scandalous."

Caerwin hugged Fimbria. "This is an expensive gift," Caerwin said. "Thank you. I must repay your expense."

"It cost me nothing," Fimbria said. "I've studied it. If the day ever comes when I need to see it, I know where to find it."

"I may never need use of it," Caerwin said, holding the bound group of parchment sheets on her lap. "The days pass but time stands still. I want Marcellus' troubles to end."

Fimbria laughed. "That will never be. He's a powerful citizen with important duties both political and financial. Men like that are always targets."

"There's more to it," Caerwin said darkly. "More than I can say anything about."

"You mean the rumors that plague him? Surely you know that rumors follow all prominent men of Rome. It's what the lesser people do for sport, that and the arena." She stood up. "Come now, it's Sigarillia. The sun renews itself."

Afterward at dinner, Caerwin, Junia, Sigilis, and Marcellus carried platters of food to the dining room where the managers reclined on the opulent couches. Antius lifted his wine cup, grinning as Marcellus poured him more wine.

"This work suits you," Tatian said, holding his cup and adding his impudence to the role reversal.

"It's a stupid tradition," Junia said. "Whoever thought of it?"

"Don't challenge the gods," Marcellus said. "Remember that once we all were equals."

"Not in my lifetime," Junia said tartly. "I've forbidden my slaves to participate. It's a tiresome game."

"I'd like more of the stuffed fish," Fimbria said, lifting her eyebrows at Junia. "Could you fetch it?"

Junia's nostrils flared. Under Marcellus warning gaze, she spun around and stalked out of the dining room.

Sigilis grinned at Fimbria. "Well done."

"Go easy, or you'll suffer tomorrow," Gordianus warned. "She's the worst."

"Does she abuse you?" Marcellus said.

"Who doesn't she abuse?" Varinia said. "Even her attendants act as though she's the emperor. She had two of Gordianus' staff flogged for failing to provide the exact fruit she wanted, and that's the least of it."

"That's not her right," Marcellus said. "Why haven't I heard of this?"

"No one wanted to add to your troubles. This is all the more reason to accept my suggestion," Sigilis said. "I depart in two days."

Junia whirled back into the room. Those seated at the table exchanged glances.

"Be glad we weren't the cooks," Caerwin said, standing at the end of the couch as Junia let the platter thump to the table. "I for one am glad to serve Gordianus. His efforts toward this holiday feast can never be fully rewarded."

"Hear hear!" Tatian said, raising his cup along with the others.

"Thanks to all of you," Marcellus said, taking a corner of the couch to sit. "I'm giving each of you a *denarius*, and to each of your workers I bestow five *sestertii*. It's not as much as I would like, but the next few weeks may see my financial destruction."

"Think on pleasant things tonight," Antius said. "Have some wine."

Caerwin watched the old Greek's eyes twinkle and suppressed a giggle.

"No wine," Marcellus said quickly. "The very thought…"

"Yo Saturnalia," Tatian said. "I think we're all ready for life to get back to normal."

Caerwin carried empty platters to the kitchen and began cleaning the utensils. Marcellus came up behind her.

"The kitchen becomes you," he said, leaning to kiss her on the neck. "It pleases me that you take more of a role in the household."

"You noticed?"

"Sorry I haven't been my best lately. There's much I feel sorry for..."

"Don't," she said. She wasn't ready to hear him talk about Vedius. "Can I meet with you in private?"

"The gods? More trouble?"

"After dessert?" she said, stifling a grin.

"Give me wisdom, Minerva," he said.

An hour later, Caerwin stood in her bedchamber taking down her hair. She wore only the *ralla* tunic. Even in the low light of the lamp's flame, the fabric revealed the shadow of her nipples and the lines of her cleft. She bit her lip. Maybe she shouldn't do this. Maybe the sight would only spark his anger.

Her urgent need to distract him could go horribly wrong. So much about him remained a mystery. Yet living with him since their arrival in Rome had opened her to so much greater understanding. She could see what Senna meant. He did care for her. He suffered.

She had never known someone the way she knew Marcellus. She wanted him always beside her. She wanted his child. The troubles that plagued him burdened her as well.

With her long cloak pulled close around her, she hurried down the atrium to his room.

"Come," he said to her brief knock.

He sat at his table in his sleeping tunic with his bare feet nestled in a fur rug, his masculine form set in stark relief by the glow of his oil lamps and gleaming brazier coals. Again she felt afraid for what she planned. Whatever happened with Vedius, surely Marcellus would accept her. She needed to show him what she felt even if the words never quite made it out of her mouth.

At the same time, she risked stirring his rage by presenting herself in a sexual pose when he had made it so clear he would not take her. Would he send her away?

She stepped closer, enough to see his hands had formed fists. He looked up at her. She let the cloak fall to the floor.

His gaze traveled down her body. Red spots appeared on his cheeks. His nostrils flared. With a groan, he bent forward to rest his head in his hands.

"What tender agony you bestow on me," he said.

"It's my gift to you," she said. "Make of me what you will."

"Why do you do this?" he said, sitting up abruptly and glaring at her. "I've told you…"

"Yes, Marcellus, you've told me," she snapped. "Now I'm going to tell you. I can't get a child if your seed flows down my throat. Is that not true?"

"The gods! Can I give your mouth my seed and do nothing else?" He shook his head. "I don't trust myself."

"You've trusted yourself with the lives of ten thousand men. You've trusted yourself with a fleet of ships, men and cargo, with matters before you at court. Why do you think you can't trust yourself with me?"

"I've tried to tell you." He stood up and put his hand to her cheek. He towered over her. She could hear his harsh breath. "You are an entirely different matter. I've said before—you are mightier than any wind at sea, any enemy's sword. Do you not understand? I'm powerless before you."

"No," she said, grasping his hand and lowering it to her breast. "I have control. You're not alone."

He groaned as his hand cupped her breast. Then he stepped away and took her hand, holding her at arms' length to look at her.

"Almighty Jupiter, give me strength. Never has a woman been so perfect," he said.

She turned slowly, luxuriating in his attention. Her breasts strained against the thin fabric. Moisture gathered between her thighs. Her very skin prickled with the sensation of his stare.

"I'm lost," he said. "Tell me what to do."

"Touch me. Touch everywhere, as much as you want. When you think you'll lose control, let me take you in my mouth for your release."

He shook his head. "I'm already out of control." He motioned to the erection prodding the front of his tunic.

"Do you want to touch me before I take you in my mouth?"

"The gods! Yes, yes," he said, grasping her breasts. "Take this off," he said, tugging at the tunic.

She shook her head. "No. Do what you can with it on me."

"Sorcery!" He laughed. "This, then," he said, sliding his hands under the hem of her tunic to massage her buttocks.

He nestled his face against her shoulder and inhaled the scent of her hair. She rubbed her cheek against his short dark curls. This man. Tears filmed her eyes. How could she love someone this much?

Love. How could she have ever denied it? Yes, he was Roman. But more than that, he was a man. Half of him descended from a native tribe, did he not? Why could she not say she loved him?

He pulled her against him. Flares of heat spread through her core as her breasts flattened against his chest.

"Take my mouth, please," she said.

"Caerwin."

His lips crushed hers. He softened, brushing side to side and plying the crease of her lips with the tip of his tongue. She met him with her tongue, opening to his demand.

Her knees failed. She clung to him as he drove his tongue into her mouth. Curling and plunging, their tongues tangled in a sensual dance.

He pressed the thin cloth against her vulva, teasing the fabric along her swollen folds and grazing the tip of her clitoris.

"Is this a game you can play?" he said. "I'm struggling for restraint."

"Oh, will this never end?" She swiveled her hips to gain more force from his hand.

He stepped back. "You said you could control me." His dark eyes shone in the dim light. "Do you already announce defeat?"

"You would enjoy that, wouldn't you?" she said. "Winning even when you don't want to win?"

"Oh, before the gods, I want to win."

"You've won, don't you see that? I come to you asking. When have I ever done that?"

He scrutinized her with a twisted smile. "You have, yes. I'd rather have the whip than this punishment, the torment that you offer yourself and I can't have you."

"Lie on your bed," she said. "You'll have my mouth."

He shook his head as he walked to the bed. "Dangerous. I can easily overwhelm you."

"But you won't." She knelt beside him on the bed then pushed his tunic to his waist. "Look at you," she said. "You're eager for me."

"Yes, by the gods, I'm eager. I'm desperate."

She cupped his taut sac in her hand, lifting the weight gently. "I see you are," she said, smiling at him.

She bit her tongue to stop the words that hung there. *What of Vedius?* she wanted to ask. *Did his touch make you desperate? Did you accept his demands? What do you risk in his displeasure?* She closed her eyes and tried to forget her fears about Vedius.

Marcellus threw his head back against the pillows as she trailed her fingertips between his thighs and up the length of his organ. The big shaft bucked upward, beckoning. She circled the tip with her lightest touch.

He gripped the trailing ends of her hair. "Please."

She held him with both hands, directing him toward her mouth as she teased with her tongue. His pungent aroma filled her nose. She closed her mouth over the head of his cock and sucked.

In all the times he had told her what power she held over him, she hadn't understood the full truth of it until now. His loins lifted as she pulled him deeper. The rasp of her tongue scraped the silken flesh. Down then back up, with each downward stroke she brought him closer to the choking point of her throat.

She wanted to choke, suffer whatever small punishment came with this giddy pleasure. Gooseflesh pebbled her arms as the broad head of his *mentula* jammed to the back of her tongue. Quickly adjusting her position to straddle his chest, she laughed at his exclamation in having her buttocks looming at his face.

"What am I supposed to do with this?" he said.

"Nothing."

"Impossible."

"I'll stop if you touch me," she said.

"Slavering hounds of Hades," he said. His fist pounded the bed.

She took him swiftly to the depths of her throat, triggering her gag reflex but satisfying her need to quiet him. She held his stones more tightly, eliciting another groan. With half of his length spreading her mouth, she freed her other hand to tease along the insides of his thighs up to the tight ridge behind his sac.

As she touched him, inspiration grew. Pressing back along the ridge, she circled his anus with her fingertip. Surely men who coupled gained pleasure here. The opening winked as she touched it.

The response sent a surge of excitement to her clitoris. Her saliva drooled down his stones and she made use of it, dragging it in little strokes until she lubricated his anus enough for her fingertip to push inside.

"No!" he said, trying to move her hand away.

She lifted her mouth off him. "Yes. Don't complain. Didn't I say 'no' and you ignored me?"

"This is different."

"No, it's not." She sucked on the head of his cock. It had darkened to angry red. Veins bulged on the shaft. "If you want me to finish, you'll do as I say."

"*Merde!*"

She grinned and bent down to engulf as much of his length as she could manage. At the same time, she pressed her fingertip against his sensitive opening. With the next wink of his sphincter, the first inch of her index finger invaded the hole.

"No, no! I'm going!" he said.

Her throat opened more as she bobbed up and down. His shaft exuded heat. She could smell his need, felt the grasp of his tight ring on her finger as she stroked the small opening.

He gripped her hair, forcing her down on his cock as his hips thrust up in sudden hard jerks. She swallowed in a frantic rush, drinking him down. Her finger wriggled and prodded in rhythm with her mouth and the agitation added frenzy to his release. His seed filled her throat.

When his *mentula* relaxed in her mouth, she knelt back, shaking. He sat up and wrapped her in his arms, holding her so tight she could hardly breathe.

"I love you, brave little queen," he whispered into her hair. "More than words can say."

Chapter Ten

"You made a commitment!" Junia's shrill voice roiled through the atrium. "I have plans."

Caerwin stood outside Marcellus' office with Antius. Marcellus had excused the last of his clients for the morning and summoned Junia. Caerwin thrilled at the certain knowledge of what Marcellus would say. Sigilis had told her the night before.

"She'll throw things next," Antius whispered.

"I'm sorry if you've made plans," Marcellus said. "I've told you from the beginning that these matters were uncertain. I know less now than I did when we left Britannia. I've made you wait long enough, and Sigilis has offered to take you home. I think it's time."

"Are you not a man of your word?" she yelled.

"I can't keep you here indefinitely. I can't predict what the court will say next. It would be unfair to expect you to stay. If I can sell ships to you, we can negotiate through Sigilis."

"No! You don't understand. What about us?" Junia said.

"There was never an 'us,'" Marcellus said quietly. "I've never given you cause…"

"What about my injury? I suffered…"

"As did we all. You've been well recompensed," Marcellus said.

"You've seen me without clothes. I've slept in your house. What will people say?"

"Half of Rome has seen you without clothes. Sigilis has slept in my house as well, along with slaves in such numbers I've lost count."

Caerwin bit her lip but she couldn't suppress her grin. Her face ached with it.

Something hit the wall and broke.

"Didn't I say?" Antius whispered.

"My uncle spoke for you," Junia said. "This is the gratitude?"

"I'm very grateful," Marcellus said.

"I'm going to tell him you're not a man of your word. He'll make it known."

"It's easy to see why your husband left you," Marcellus said. "The more I'm around you, the greater my sympathy for him. Who would want a woman like you, someone who knows of the emperor's planned concessions to ship owners and keeps it a secret from a proposed business partner? Who could trust you?"

"Concessions," she huffed. "Well, that would have come out. If you paid attention to your business instead of that savage who drags you around by your stones, you would have known."

A chair scraped. "Get out of my house," he said.

"I'll ruin you."

"Try," he said.

The door to Marcellus' office flew open and Junia tore past the assembled group of eavesdroppers. Her eyes glassy in rage, she hardly paused to look at them before marching off to her room. Her bedchamber attendant glanced at them and then followed Junia inside the room where a series of crashes and thuds marked the progress of her temper.

Sigilis walked up and stood beside Caerwin. "People in the next *domus* are surely entertained," he said quietly.

Caerwin smiled at him. "I can't thank you enough."

"She's a winter storm, fast to rise and ugly to see. I've weathered plenty."

Marcellus came to the door, looked at them, and grinned. "I enjoyed that," he said.

"Good you take what pleasure you can," Sigilis said. "What progress with the legal matters?"

"There is no progress. Vedius holds all the power. I'm not favored."

"I thought you had words with him," Sigilis said. "I saw you together in the baths at Saturnalia, did I not?"

Marcellus nodded. "We both drank too much. I think he resents his injury. I'm made to suffer for it."

Sigilis nodded. "He's overproud of his position, then?"

"That's the core of it," Marcellus said.

"I've sent my messenger to Ostia to alert the crew. If the winds are kind, we'll be home in one day."

"I can't thank you enough," Marcellus said.

"Remember my offer—if you need money, let me know."

"I'm humbled."

Caerwin watched Antius walk away with Sigilis, deep in discussion on logistics of Junia's luggage and the availability of carts.

"Can I have a moment?" she said.

Marcellus motioned toward his office.

"I need to know—what does Vedius hold over you?" she said as she sat down. "Will he cause your ruin?"

Marcellus paused by his desk and turned. "He could. He asks the impossible."

"I need to tell you…that night, when he came here."

Marcellus' eyes narrowed. "Saturnalia?"

"I was in your bed."

His forehead knotted. "How can that be?"

"I came home after the celebration and went there. I wanted to feel close to you. When I woke, it was to the sound of your voice. Then I heard him speak. I dared not move."

He sank into his chair and rested his head in his hands. "He loves me."

"Does he love you? Or does he love what he used to have with you? Maybe he loves who he once was, a strong young man who could wrestle you to the ground, a man that he's not anymore."

"Much as we've changed, we've also remained the same," Marcellus said, speaking as if to himself. His dark eyes fixed on her with an expression of despair. "I can't deny what we meant to each other. Those memories tug at me."

"If you didn't love me, you could give him what he wants. You'd secure your future."

"I do love you and I would never wish otherwise. My future is with you."

Caerwin shook her head. "What future? If you lose your estate, if you're no longer a citizen, what do you have? You won't be able to marry me."

"Yes, yes, the gods! Must you remind me? I can't sleep, I can't eat."

"What would it harm you to have him, give him what he wants?" Caerwin said.

Marcellus sat unmoving, watching her with an expression of disbelief.

"You said you cared for him," she said.

"I do. But I don't desire him as I once did. We were young and reckless. We hardly considered infamy or how it might affect our lives. He doesn't want me for one night. He wants to rekindle our love affair. Even if he sometimes took the submissive role, I would lose all standing to receive him. I can't understand why he wants to lower me."

"Because you're beautiful and strong and not crippled," she said. "He said as much."

"I had too much wine. I hardly remember what we said," Marcellus said harshly. "Mostly I remember him touching me, taking me in his mouth." He exhaled. "The gods. We fought."

"Only Vedius knows what is truly in his heart. Does he wish to punish you for being whole? Or does he need your love to salve his deep wound? You have to find out before you can know what to do."

"Where does this wisdom come from, little queen? I'm in awe of you," he said.

"It doesn't seem like wisdom," she said, flushing in the warmth of his smile. Had she lost her senses? Did she mean what she said? These words had come without much thought.

Mere weeks had passed since her anger and jealousy toward Marcellus overwhelmed any tender feelings. She'd never been able to say she loved him even though in private moments she acknowledged the truth. Could she truly endure the certain knowledge that Marcellus coupled with Vedius, that she had urged him to do so? Could he carry on a relationship with Vedius without withdrawing from her? Was that the only remaining path?

Her dreams foresaw it.

"I only speak for myself," she admitted. "I want you. I want our future, our children, the life you promised. If sharing you with him means we can have that future, then I must share you."

~~~

Cunning as always, Junia waited until Marcellus left before she inflicted her rage upon her slaves. Caerwin stood in the atrium with clenched fists listening to the whack of a cane. Porcia came out of the bedchamber with her tunic clutched in her hands. Tears streaked her face.

"Who does she beat now?"

"The next in line," Porcia said, gulping down sobs.

Caerwin pulled Porcia away from the wall to look at the damage. Angry red welts marched in vivid rows down her thin back. Evidence of previous beatings appeared in faded bruises and pink scars.

Caerwin's blood pounded in her ears. As she threw back the door to Junia's room and marched inside, she saw nothing, thought of nothing—except beating Junia. Her slaves lined the bedchamber wall, stripped of their clothes as they waited for the cane. Her manager Zeno held down the head of a young man bent to the cane as Junia inflicted the blows.

Junia hardly had time to react as Caerwin yanked the cane from her fist. She rapped two hard blows on Zeno's head. He backed away holding up his hands to protect his face. Then she turned to Junia and let the cane fly.

Whack, whack! Stiff blows landed on Junia's shoulders, arms, and head as she shrieked.

"Zeno, get the cane!" she cried, twisting to escape another strike.

"You insufferable bitch," Caerwin shouted, hitting Junia's back. Let Zeno or any of these miserable slaves try to stop her. She felt like she had the strength of ten men. "How do you like this?"

Caerwin grabbed the neck of Junia's stola and ripped it loose from the shoulder pins, then tore at the tunic until the fabric yielded to her rage. Junia fought back, screaming and grabbing for the cane. With the flesh of her upper torso fully exposed and Caerwin's blows landing everywhere, Junia's outrage descended into terror.

"Zeno! You bastard. Matho! Gaurus! Help me," Junia cried.

"Why should they help you?" Caerwin shouted. "Haven't you done the same to them?"

Caerwin grabbed the cluster of curls on Junia's head and pulled her down so that she could apply the cane forcefully to her backside. Whack whack—the cane slapped against Junia's well-fed flesh. Ugly red lines began to rise.

Someone grabbed the cane from behind. Caerwin fought until she turned and saw Sigilis. With a grim smile, he pried her fingers from the pliant rod.

"I think you've made your point," he said quietly. "Let go of her hair."

Caerwin blinked and released the hair as she shoved Junia back against the wall.

"I want her whipped!" Junia yelled, sniffling between her sobs. "I'll bring charges! I'll have her killed."

"You deserved every inch of it." Sigilis said. "You have no legal grounds to harm her. You, however, might be brought before the courts for abuse of your slaves."

"I have witnesses. She attacked me!"

"What witnesses?" Sigilis said, motioning around the room as Junia clutched her clothing.

The remaining slaves hurried out of the room. Shaking all over, Caerwin staggered to the door and looked out. An audience of household slaves—Varinia, Gordianus, Fibria and more smiled as her confused gaze moved from one to the next.

Zeno paused in the doorway, his scarred face wrinkled in a grin. "We saw nothing," he said. "You said you were selling us today. We're ready."

"I'll handle the transaction," Sigilis said to Junia. "Find the bills of sale. I'll take them to the Graecostadium and look for a decent slave seller, if there is such a man. You need to pack. The cart will come for your things at the tenth hour."

"Get out!" she screamed. The door slammed.

~~~

Caerwin had eaten nothing for breakfast and now her head ached. Still shaking, she hurried to the kitchen behind Gordianus.

"Can she bring charges?" she asked.

"She's leaving," Gordianus said. "She won't want it known that she was beaten, much less by a Briton. She'll go without much fanfare."

"What if she causes more trouble for Marcellus?"

"He would thank you," he said. "Think no more of it. Now tell me, is your appetite still playing tricks?"

She shook her head. "I wake hungry but as soon as I smell food, I feel sick. So many events have upset me—and I have strange dreams. So much hangs in the balance with Marcellus…" She shook her head.

Gordianus grunted as he lifted a bowl of bread dough to the table and began punching it down. Fimus and a helper had their heads together over the chopping table as their knives worked through a pile of apples.

"What can I have for lunch?" she said, stealing a slice of freshly pared fruit.

"There's leftover fishcakes," Gordianus said. "Is the master eating here?"

Her stomach flopped at the mention of fishcakes. "He's gone. What besides fish?"

With a small platter of apple, pear, and cheese, Caerwin settled in the *peristylium*. Something nagged at the back of her mind, something Senna had said. It must have something to do with Marcellus, but she couldn't put her finger on it.

Surely it had to do with her shocking admission of her vision of a future with Marcellus. Her proclamation astounded her as much as it surprised Marcellus. Senna had known the truth all along. She would offer a prayer to her as soon as she finished lunch.

Household slaves rushed back and forth, still laboring to bring the house out of the Saturnalia mess. Varinia passed with a brief smile in her direction. Moments later Fimbria sat beside her.

"You're the new hero of this *domus*," Fimbria said.

"I don't know what happened," Caerwin said. "I couldn't stop myself."

"It was a noble act but I fear you exhausted yourself. You look pale," Fimbria said. "Do you feel well?"

"I think the holiday unbalanced me. My taste for food is off."

"You've been tired for weeks. Are you ill?"

Caerwin shook her head. "I don't feel ill except in the morning. The last time I felt this way…" She stopped and thought of her desperate condition upon returning to the fortress. Senna had sat with her holding a cold cloth to her forehead.

If I didn't know better, I'd think you were with child. Senna's expression had been bemused, concerned.

Caerwin's back stiffened as her mind raced. She crammed the platter into Fimbria's hands. "No. It can't be."

"What?" Fimbria said.

"My courses. I've had no courses since I arrived here."

Fimbria's eyes grew large. "November."

"The first of November."

"It's the end of December." Fimbria smiled knowingly. "Two months. Sick in the morning. Tired. You're with child."

"No, no, I can't be. He hasn't touched me." Caerwin scrubbed her face with her hands then remembered. Of course—the first night here. A swift calculation brought her to the unavoidable truth.

"Once," she whispered.

"Juno protect you," Fimbria said. "Once is all it takes. We must offer prayers and sacrifice to the goddess."

"No. It must be a sickness," Caerwin said. She refused to believe it. "I forbid you to speak of this. My courses could start tomorrow."

Her face flushed hot while her body felt cold. Clammy. If Marcellus heard one word of this—she couldn't think it. She grabbed Fimbria's hands. "Please, promise me."

"I promise," Fimbria said. "But what the gods will…"

"Don't say it."

Caerwin rushed to her room and locked the door. With the shutters spread wide, she peered up at the sky. A few thin clouds veiled the blue expanse.

Did his child grow in her belly? Her hands cradled the area. She could feel nothing. Her breasts had been sore, but she'd given that no thought. She remembered her mother's teachings, the certain signs, how the child would grow, how she would feel. At each point, her symptoms met the prediction. No matter what she said to Fimbria, in her heart Caerwin knew it was true.

"Oh, nooo," she wailed. She curled up on her bed as hot tears rolled down her cheeks. "No, no, no."

~~~

Situated at the south end of the Forum behind the *Basilica Julia*, the slave market occupied a large open arena surrounded by shops and smaller structures. As the litter bearers set her down, Caerwin realized she'd passed the stadium many times without recognizing its purpose. Wooden pens lined both sides of walkways that branched off from the center track. Trailing Sigilis and Junia's slave band and with Fimbria, Cotta, and Falco close behind her, Caerwin walked along stunned as she saw the pens held humans.

She had insisted on coming. Now she wished she'd stayed at home. Groups of citizens in their finery browsed the shops and stopped to gawk at the pen occupants while munching their sausages and bread. Drawn by morbid curiosity, Caerwin approached one of the pens.

Two women and four young children stared back at her. Any grass had long since worn away from the ground under their feet. A closed gate at the back of the pen led into a ramshackle wooden building. Other pens joined on either side.

"There's nothing you want to see here," Zeno said as she began walking between the pens.

Sigilis doubled back and took her arm. "Don't complicate this," he said.

"My people might be here," she said, pulling away to rush from pen to pen.

Slaves stared back with blank eyes, unkempt in ragged dirty tunics.

"It's been too long for your people to be here, if they ever were," Sigilis said, forcibly steering her back to the center thoroughfare. "Slaves don't stay here that many months."

"They might be here," she said, jerking her arm from his grasp.

"My sympathies to Marcellus," he said, rolling his eyes. "Come now, I can't leave you here."

"I have Fimbria, Cotta, and Falco," she said, venturing through another section of pens as Sigilis strode along behind her. "And the litter bearers."

"Who themselves must be sold," he reminded her.

"I'll buy them," she said impulsively. "What price?"

He shook his head. "Will you please stop? My time is short. Let me find a reliable seller."

"He's done you a favor," Fimbria said. "Don't anger him."

Caerwin grudgingly retreated from the pens and followed Sigilis toward a wide central platform. A young boy with a placard hanging from his neck stood naked as the seller began his pitch.

He is fair and handsome from the top of his head to the bottom of his feet. And he will be yours for 8,000 sestertii. This home-born slave is prepared to serve at his master's nod. He knows a little Greek; he is suitable for whatever task you want. With this wet clay, you can make whatever you please. He even can sing something untrained but sweet when you are drinking.

The seller walked the boy across the platform, lifting his arms and making him turn. He pointed to a man in the audience.

You know, sir, any promises lessen the buyer's trust, when someone who wants to get rid of his goods praises a slave on sale more lavishly than is right. Nothing forces me to sell. I am not rich but I am not in debt. None of the slave dealers would do this for you, and I would not do this for everybody.

Several men cast bids. Finally the bidding stopped and after an exchange of money and documents, the winner led the boy away.

"I can't bear it," Caerwin said. "What will he do with him?"

"Don't think of it," Fimbria said. "This is the way of things. There's nothing to change it. Perhaps his cook needs an attendant. The boy might be well fed and educated. You don't know."

"Oh, no, look," Caerwin said. The next sale began, this time a young girl. Two other people stood on the platform, waiting their turn under the auctioneer's cry. One of them was unlike any person she had ever seen.

"What is that man?" she said. "The small one on the right."

"The dwarf? Oddities are in great demand. Wealthy households prize them for entertainment. He'll go at a good price."

"What's entertaining about someone suffering such a deformity?"

"Some have talents in singing or juggling," Fimbria said. "The main attraction is the body. People are entertained by the shortness of their limbs and the peculiar way they walk. See," she said, motioning toward the platform where the dwarf had come up for sale. "Some think they carry magic."

"His genitals seem overlarge for his size," Caerwin said.

"That's part of the interest," Fimbria said. "They're all different. Wealthy patrons vie with each other to procure the most bizarre entertainers. Dwarves are especially favored in the arena."

The auctioneer shouted out the attributes, turning the dwarf, making him bend and extend his arms and legs, and otherwise contort into all position positions to fully demonstrate the odd proportions of his nude body. What he might have felt or thought as the auctioneer prodded him, Caerwin could not imagine.

A man in expensive clothing came to Sigilis. She didn't try to hear what they said. The simple movement of their hands told her everything she needed to know. The sale was quickly negotiated and Junia's slaves led away. The sight of Porcia melting into the shadows of the pens wrenched her heart.

The weight of Rome's excess settled on Caerwin's shoulders. The very air thickened in her lungs. She felt as if she might drown.

"Take me out," she said, climbing back into the chair.

"Is it the smell?" Cotta said. He stood to one side as the litter bearers lifted the conveyance.

She shook her head. "Everything. The expressions on their faces, the desperation—I could have been there," she said.

"Thank the gods you were not," Fimbria said. "Thank Marcellus."

Caerwin turned to face Fimbria where she walked beside her. "Were you here?"

"I was," Fimbria said. "Those who command higher prices are kept in nicer pens in the back or in private shops elsewhere.

Those in the front—these are the ones who can't read, who can't speak our language, or who have scars of many beatings or a bad reputation for impudence or laziness."

Sigilis caught up with them. "I've learned a fair price for the litter bearers. Strong men are expensive, especially if they can be trusted not to run off. If you want these, they'll cost you eighteen-hundred sestertii each and that's a good price. Do you have the money?"

The question took Caerwin off guard. She had said she'd pay, but how could she? Marcellus provided a few sestertii each week for her to spend in the marketplace but nothing like this. If he wanted to have them, wouldn't he have bought them already, if not these, then others? These were more mouths to feed. He had made it clear he wanted to save money. What if he didn't have the funds?

"Set me down," she said. "Take them. I'm sorry, Zeno—I can't speak for Marcellus and his money is contested."

She turned away from the expression on the men's faces. It was more than she could bear. With a quick apology to Sigilis and with her attendants close behind, she hurried away from the plaza and its incessant flux of people in all their pursuits. Messengers dodged this way and that as they ran past while merchants' slaves trotted along carrying oversized bundles of goods. Shoppers clustered at storefronts. The shouts of vendors pierced the air, beckoning customers to their pastries or fine cloth or leather goods. People called from high windows as they dumped their pots and she dodged a beggar as she passed the entry to the imperial bath house.

Her pace slowed as she came to the grassy exercise yard beside the huge bathhouse. Encircled by a low wall of the same pale gold stone as the imposing *thermae*, men in loin cloths or in the nude grappled in wrestling matches, lifted weights, climbed suspended ropes, or punched heavy bags. She stopped, drawn to a particular figure with his back to her. She couldn't look away.

Entangled with another man, both of them glistening in sweat as they strained for advantage—it was Marcellus.

Oh, dear Sabrina! Every muscle bulged in his rigid body. Only the narrow strip of cloth covering his loins obscured his full splendor.

Their position shifted as she drank in his beauty. Calculated, methodical, his movements reminded her of their sex. The sheer power he exerted in the struggle penetrated her stomach. She'd known his strength, assumed his prowess in battle. But she'd never seen him like this with the full evidence of his dominance on display. The two well-matched men strained against each other, their arms and legs intertwined. Marcellus ducked his head to the side then levered his shoulder. The man's stance shifted and Marcellus landed him on the ground.

His chest heaving, Marcellus stood as Antius hurried over with a towel. He quickly wiped his face and neck, took a drink. Another man approached. They spoke several moments then began circling, seeking advantage, sizing up.

Her skin prickled as if someone watched her. She shifted her gaze. It took her a moment to discover what triggered her instinct. There, in the shadow of the building, his weight resting on his cane, Vedius watched Marcellus with rapt attention. His toga had slipped slightly from his shoulder. It wasn't hard to see the sense of ownership in his stance.

As if she had spoken his name, his head turned and he stared directly at her. For a long searing moment, questions passed through their locked gaze that neither of them could answer. What he might feel, she couldn't define.

His gaze finally shifted back to Marcellus, dismissing her from their world. It was a world she could never be part of. With one fleeting glance back at the two men wrestling, Caerwin resumed her quick pace along the street.

~~~

Caerwin and Fimbria walked slowly through the streets with Cotta and Falco grunting under the burden of the chair. Junia would sell it, or Marcellus might keep it, she didn't care. Vedius' dark stare still burned her, caused her neck hair to stand. Only hours earlier she had felt so confident, spoken so bravely as she encouraged Marcellus to please the man. She'd been impulsive, drawn by emotions she didn't understand. What grievous mistake had she made?

"Shall we stop for lunch?" Fimbria asked. "I could use some refreshment."

"So could I," Caerwin said.

They sat together at a table in a corner tavern, sipping watered wine, nibbling pastries, and watching people of all kinds flow through the intersection. As had become her habit in each shop she visited, she asked about an older woman named Kensa. She had become accustomed to the shrugs and blank looks. The same happened here. No one knew of Kensa.

The two men had fish cakes. The smell turned Caerwin's stomach. Only halfway through her cup of watered wine, foreboding overtook her and she stood up.

"We could browse the shops," Fimbria said, standing beside her at the street corner. A cool wind shifted their clothes. "There's a remarkable jeweler two streets over. He sells the most exquisite engraved gemstones, truly a wonder to behold."

"I'm sorry—I would find no pleasure in it," Caerwin said. "My day is spoiled with Junia's slaves and the worry facing Marcellus."

Fimbria took her arm. "You need to rest, if…"

"Don't say it," Caerwin warned.

A grunt and scuffle caused them to turn.

"Stop," Cotta said.

Caerwin shifted the hood of her heavy cloak to see more fully behind her. With a face reddened in his exertion of carrying the chair, Cotta stood with his arm braced against the chest of an older woman dressed in a toga. Bright red paint colored her lips and dark blue rimmed her tired eyes. She smiled at Caerwin.

"Please, mistress, I must speak with you," the woman said.

Falco frowned as he stood ready to move the woman away. "She's a *meretrix*," he said. "The master would be angry."

"*Lupa*," Cotta growled. "Go about your dirty business."

"It's unseemly to be seen with such a woman," Fimbria said. "You should leave her."

"No," Caerwin said. "I'll hear what she has to say. Speak up," she said to the woman.

"My name is Natalia," the woman said. "It's a delicate matter meant only for your ears."

Caerwin glanced at the two men and then at Fimbria, who shook her head. "Very well—we can talk over here."

Her attendants frowned as she walked a few paces to a shuttered store front next to a butcher shop. Her nose wrinkled at the smell of old meat. Natalia followed her, glancing around as if someone watched her.

"I saw you in the court," Natalia said. "You're with Antistius Marcellus, are you not?"

Caerwin nodded, suddenly apprehensive for what the woman might say.

"I knew his father, Petrus," Natalia said. "I want his son to know—Petrus spoke to me at length during our times together. I was sworn to silence, but since he's dead… His was a miserable life. Does his son know this?"

"He knows his father had his torments."

The woman's eyes narrowed and she leaned so close Caerwin could smell wine on her breath. "Torment hardly describes it. He suffered worse than the great beasts that die in the arena. Worse than criminals crucified along the road. He couldn't bear to see that boy, so much did he remind him of a woman. Does he know about his real mother, this girl Rhian?"

Caerwin stiffened. "He spoke of her?"

"He did. He paid me to beat him and once he exhausted his tolerance for pain, he lay weeping as he talked. He loved that girl." She nodded vigorously. "Yes, he did. He got her with child more than once and each time she and her mother used potions to end it. But the last time, the one that became your man Marcellus, she refused. She hid her condition. It was not until the child was born that she shared the truth with Petrus."

Natalia looked around to where Fimbria, Cotta, and Falco waited impatiently several paces away. "Petrus' father, I can't remember his name—he was a powerful man. Petrus was still a boy. He had nothing to use against his father. His father…"

"Labeo," Caerwin said. "His father was Labeo."

"Yes. Labeo. He wanted to dispose of the girl and the baby. Petrus pleaded for their lives. The concession was that the girl would be sent away if the baby could be made legitimate."

Natalia twisted her hands together. "Oh, how that poor man suffered. Each time he repeated his story, he sobbed over how his father's men tore the baby away from her, deaf to Petrus' pleas for mercy. Petrus tried to follow, but his father—this Labeo—had him locked in a room. He said he still heard her cries in his dreams.

"He couldn't bear to touch a woman after that. He only wanted me to hurt him. I knew he had a wife. He got two children on her under threat of disinheritance. When his boy Marcellus got older, Petrus spent most of his days with drink. That's when he'd come to me, when he had to talk to someone about these old memories. None of his men knew of it—no one knew. His wife treated him badly. She was forced to raise a child who wasn't hers."

Natalia fingered the folds of the dingy toga. Caerwin thought she must have once been beautiful, but her hair had thinned with bleaching and the cosmetics had toughened her skin. A fake beauty mark on her cheek added to her bizarre appearance. Caerwin wondered if such a status would be her fate if Marcellus lost his case.

"What do you want?" Caerwin said.

"That man treated me well. All those years—he always came back and was generous with his money. Finally he stopped talking about her. I want his son to know how much he loved him. Tell him—once this Labeo died and Petrus controlled his own fate, he bribed the men who took Rhian away. It had only been four years and the memory was fresh. He tracked her to Herculaneum. Evidently the family had a villa there."

"Yes, there's a villa."

Natalia's dark eyes widened. She put her hand on Caerwin's arm. "No one should suffer what she did. That monster put her in one of the houses there, a place where men…" Tears glazed her eyes. "Petrus agonized over that. Some houses—they attract a certain kind of man. He said she'd been beautiful. Labeo had her cheek branded so she could never escape her degraded status. Men defiled her in the worst possible ways. The master of the house told Petrus these things."

"She wasn't there?"

"She had taken her own life only weeks before he got there. Her remains had been disposed in a common pit."

"The gods! How can I tell Marcellus such horrors?"

"He needs to know,' Natalia said. "When I saw him at court and heard the charges, I knew I had to tell him. But a woman like me—if I came to him, I would only bring more shame."

"Did Petrus know Rhian was his sister?"

"His sister? Dear Juno, protect us all." Natalia stared at Caerwin. "The monster did that to his own child?"

Caerwin bit her lip. "I've said too much. Can I trust you to keep this secret?"

"I've told no one these things for many years. I will take it to my grave."

Caerwin rummaged in the purse fastened to her belt and pulled out a *denarius*. "Here," she said, pressing it into Natalia's hand. "Thank you. If Marcellus wants to question you further, will you allow it?"

"It would be my honor. These are the corners I frequent," she said, motioning around them.

~~~

Exhausted and overwrought, Caerwin tried but failed to nap. She wanted to walk and never stop, take a road anywhere and go to its end. Gordianus had brought a platter of fruit, cheese, and olives to her room, pleasing enough to her appetite when she stopped pacing long enough to take another bite to her mouth.

"Oh, Senna, where are you now? I need your guidance more than ever. Shall I tell him what I've learned? Already he suffers too much."

Deserting her quiet bedchamber, she stood at Juno's altar gazing up at the smooth marble face and trying to discern if the goddess could help her. This was the supreme deity who guarded women. Would she extend her wisdom to Caerwin?

"Give me a sign, great goddess. Should Marcellus learn of his mother's fate? Will he be harmed if I tell him?"

She placed a block of incense in the basin and set it aflame. Gradually the aromatic smoke wound up along Juno's cloak and encircled her mute head before drifting toward the *compluvium* and out into the late afternoon sky. Had she asked the wrong question? Did the goddess answer those who weren't of Rome?

Rufus swung the door open allowing Marcellus and Antius to enter. Was this the sign? She stood with her hands gripped together as he approached.

"Much has happened since you departed this morning," she said.

He frowned. "To what end?"

"Junia is gone," she said.

"So quickly?"

"I hastened her departure." She grabbed his hands, suddenly afraid of how he would react. "After you left, she began beating her slaves. Forced them to undress and used a cane." Her anger roared back to life as she remembered. "I couldn't bear it. I went into her room and seized the cane from her hands and began beating her with it. I wouldn't have stopped, but Sigilis came in and took the cane from my fist."

Marcellus' forehead had gathered in a frown and he stared at her with such an intense look that she began to tremble. Had she added to his burden? What might come of this?

"You beat her?"

She nodded. "I tore down her dress just as she'd done to Porcia and beat her bared backside. Her skin bore the welts. She threatened to have me arrested, whipped, or put to death."

He scrubbed his cheek and closed his eyes briefly. "How did you overpower her so completely?"

Caerwin peeked up at him as if any moment he might begin to shout. Or tie her wrists to the wall and use the lash. "I was seized by my anger. I could only think of Porcia's back, the angry red welts and scars of earlier beatings. I think nothing could have stopped me," she said. "Was it wrong of me?"

A slow smile crept across his face. "I want to be provoked. I should react in a way that makes certain you will not indulge in such acts without considering the possible consequences. But none of that overtakes my pleasure in hearing what you did. If ever a person deserved beating, it is Junia. You did what a man could not do."

He clasped his arms around her and held her tight. "Thank you, my Cornovii tyrant."

She closed her eyes and savored the comfort of his embrace. He smelled of wind and scented oil. His heart beat resolutely against her cheek. If only she could always be here, safe in his arms.

"Oh," she said, startling back from his grasp. "I, there is…Marcellus, there is something else."

"Did another person suffer your wrath as well?" His eyes twinkled in amusement.

"No, but if I could have…Sigilis took Junia's slaves to the market. I went with him…"

He stepped back and frowned. "That's an unsavory place. I didn't give my permission."

"Don't blame Sigilis. He didn't want to take me, but I insisted. I rode the chair. What a horror," she said. "People caged like animals, exposed to passing view like meat in the marketplace. To think of my mother, my kinsmen in such a place… I wanted to free them all and burn the place to the ground."

"Thank the gods you refrained," he said. "You'd be tried on capital charges and there would be nothing I could do to save you."

"I wanted to buy Zeno and the other men who bore Junia's litter, but I had no money. And I thought if you wanted a chair and litter bearers, you would own them already."

"I await the outcome of my legal challenges," he said, walking with her toward his bedchamber. "Is it so difficult for you to walk where you want to go?"

Briefly, she hesitated. "No, not at all," she said. "It was the situation. And," she added impulsively, "it got worse."

Marcellus poured wine and gestured for her to sit. As evenly as she could manage, the story told by Natalia spilled out. With each fact revealed, Marcellus' expression grew more stricken. He drained his cup and poured more. The ewer rattled against the rim of his goblet.

"He told her that Rhian's remains had been placed in a common pit." She put her hand on his arm. "Marcellus, I'm sorry to give such news. I worried whether to tell you. It only adds grief to the burdens you already bear."

He shook his head, looking at her with tear-glazed eyes. "My poor mother," he said in a broken voice. "What suffering."

She sat with him not speaking. His shoulders shook in his weeping. When he wiped his eyes dry, he stood up abruptly and stalked out of the room. She heard a loud shattering noise and rushed out to find him in the ancestor alcove standing over Labeo's broken death mask.

"Let the ancestors curse me," he said. "It could not be worse than I am already cursed. He is doubly my grandfather. Would that I could tear him from my flesh."

He threw himself to his knees in front of the *lararium* and looked up at the shrine. "Was there ever a good man among my forefathers?"

He stood, jostling aside the containers for salt and milk to set a piece of incense to flame at the sacred lamp. As the smoke curled upward, he lifted his face to the painting that ornamented the altar: snakes and plants showing the fertility of the fields, people surrounding a sacrificial fire, images of bread, meat, and eggs, all of it framed by colorful garlands and flowers.

"Why has this evil blood come to me? Will I burden the future of any child with this inheritance? Why should I expect anything but ruin when I come from such corruption?"

A chill ran through Caerwin. She had felt it before in this place but now it seemed a live presence. She had thought it the spirit of Petrus. When she looked at Petrus now, his face straining forward as if to escape the bonds of death, she saw that he had never been the evil presence she had imagined. The scourge emanated from his father. As she surveyed the broken mask of Labeo, she wondered if his foul spirit had been released and would now roam the house.

Her hand went to her belly.

~~~

An unnatural silence spread through the house as evening settled. Marcellus didn't leave his room and Caerwin told Gordianus to prepare a plate for him. Marcellus didn't look up as she set the platter on his table.

"Should I have said nothing?" she said.

"My search for my mother has ended," he said quietly. "Leave me."

She stood in her room with a cup of wine, sipping as she stared out the open window. Rain fell steadily in the dusk and her lamp flame flickered. In the grim chill, it was hard to believe that the sun made its return toward summer.

She poked the charcoal and added another scoop to the brazier. She couldn't get that woman out of her mind. Even more overwhelming was the image of Marcellus with his shoulders bent in grief over the horror of his mother's end. He'd never had a real home or known the warmth of family. Was there so little of the world to be enjoyed, such a slim supply of good? Every thought that came to her mind spoke of suffering.

Could she bring a child to this? Senna had spoken of ending life in her womb to spare the child a life as a slave. Marcellus had sent her away from his bed for the same reason. Now with the curse of his ancestor on his shoulders, would Marcellus want this child?

She dug through her trunk to find the book Fimbria had given her. As she pored over the lines of script, herbal recipes, and advice, one thing became clear. If the life she carried, this child of Marcellus, were to be stopped, her time had nearly run. Three moons, she murmured, counting on her fingers the moons since her arrival in Rome.

Any later attempt would risk her life.

Chapter Eleven

Days passed in torturous slowness as the ides of *Januarius* approached and with it, Marcellus' trial. He left early and returned late, increasingly isolated and anxious. When he allowed it, Caerwin held him, kissed his hand or cheek, but the affection set his jaw and he would hurry away.

Matters worsened with a visit from Tulla. She arrived late in the afternoon, Ursolus in tow. Varinia brought her to the dining room where Caerwin and Marcellus shared an early course of boiled egg and salad.

"You could have prevented this," Tulla said. Her voice quivered with anger as she shook her finger at Marcellus. "Have you no spies? You could have had someone killed. Bribed the right people. You know nothing of how these things are done."

"Sit down," Marcellus said. "At least pretend to good manners." He motioned to the attending helpers. "Bring her some salad."

"I won't eat," she said, standing at the corner of one of the dining couches. "The food would congeal in my stomach."

"Say what you must and leave, then," Marcellus said. "I have no patience for your hysterics today."

"She fears she may be brought before the court," Ursolus said. "She helped perpetuate a fraud upon the empire."

"The least of her sins." Marcellus laughed. "Should I feel sorry? Why are you here?"

"She wants to complain," Caerwin said. She turned to Tulla, biting down her seething anger. "It's your mouth that caused these troubles, not Marcellus. You felt sorry for yourself and set your resentments off on Matina. Now her greedy husband hopes to gain more of the Antistius estate."

"You don't exist," Tulla said furiously. She turned to Marcellus. "The estate should be mine. I earned it in all the years of neglect with a man who never cared for me. It was never rightfully yours."

"How dare you come here, uninvited, unannounced?" Caerwin stood up and walked toward Tulla. She wanted to hit her. Her fists clenched as she stood over the frail woman. "Do you have anything else to say? Anything worth hearing?"

Tulla shrank away from her. "Has this savage struck you dumb? Does she speak for you?" She gestured toward Marcellus. "At least your father knew how to handle such things."

"He killed himself," Marcellus said.

"Exactly," she said, backing up to the door.

Caerwin stepped toward her. "Get out," she said. "Don't come back."

Marcellus came behind her and together they escorted Tulla and Ursolus to the door. By the time they reached Rufus, Ursolus' breath wheezed and his cheeks had reddened.

"Look here," Ursolus began, stopping at the threshold. "She has a right to be concerned."

"Late in the game to think of that," Marcellus said. "Let her hire counsel."

~~~

Caerwin attended festivals, took the baths, and wandered the marketplace. The house suffered Marcellus' absence. She attended his morning *salutatio* only because she needed to see him and hear his voice. He rarely arrived home for dinner. Whether he catered to Vedius' demands or pursued the regard of wealthy patrons, she didn't want to know.

Despite her growing despair, she continued to ask about Kensa in the various places she stopped. If she could but give him one word of good news, one hint of Kensa's fate, Marcellus would be encouraged. It would be a propitious sign of the gods' favor. But no one knew of her.

On the few warm days, she sat in the garden or dug in the earth to remove weeds or encourage new growth. She suspected

Fimbria must have said something to Gordianus because he tempted her with bowls of fruit and small savory loaves of hot bread made more delicious with fresh soft cheese. She made offerings to Juno, to Minerva, and at her own small shrine built around the pot of her home earth. Clutching the amulet of Taranis, she prayed to her mother and Senna for guidance.

No guidance came. She remembered none of her dreams. She could not bring herself to buy rue or any of the other herbs required to still the life inside her.

In one of their increasingly rare morning sessions, she questioned Tatian. "The mask of Labeo still lies broken on the floor," she said. "Why does no one clear it away?"

"Marcellus ordered it left where it is. I think he considers restoring it, but Antius claims the man's *lemure* haunts the house," Tatian said.

"*Lemure*?"

"Just as we are protected by the friendly *lares* of dead kinsmen," Tatian said, "we also can be harmed by the malignant dead. Those are the *lemures*, restless spirits who do evil."

"My people knew of this," she murmured. She remembered the leaping bonfires, two of them built so that purification from any evil could be gained by walking between them. It was the time when herds were brought down from the hills for the winter and the veil between the living and dead grew thin. She shuddered.

A day later, Marcellus and Antius returned late with a large parcel wrapped in goatskin and an old woman dressed in black. Marcellus took her aside.

"Antius and this sorceress Merulia have convinced me," he said. "The *lemure* of Labeo has been fed by two generations. We need to send it away."

This was the most animated Caerwin had seen him since the breaking of the mask. She didn't know whether to be encouraged or afraid. She felt both.

At midnight, they assembled in the atrium. Shadows leapt from the oil lamps as Merulia poured libations of spring water over the broken mask and spat black beans onto the floor. Gordianus and Fimus joined her in clashing bronze pots together to drive the spirit away. Bent and uttering strange words, the old woman walked barefoot around the mask three times.

"At every *Lemuria*, these acts must be repeated," she said finally, looking sternly at Marcellus. "He wants to come here. He wants a tie to the earth."

Antius brought the parcel to the atrium and unwrapped it to reveal a mask of such horrific features that everyone gasped. Green colored and larger than life, the face shrieked from its gaping mouth. Round holes fit in the eye sockets on either side of a long pointed nose. Antius hung it on the wall across from the *lararium*.

"Whatever evil tries to descend here will be driven away by the mask," the sorceress Merulia said. "What of the amulets?"

Marcellus opened a pouch and withdrew a handful of small silver amulets strung on leather cord. Each formed the shape of an erect phallus. With a finger crooked by age, the old woman took one and examined it in the dim light.

"These are well crafted," she said. "Silver, just as I said. Well done."

Merulia put the amulet back with the rest and motioned to Marcellus. "You must pay special attention to *Februalia*. Attend the ritual purifications. Also *Lupercalia*—follow the tradition and you will thrive. Take extra care with any woman who might be with child." She glanced around and her rheumy gaze settled on Caerwin.

"You," the old woman said. She snatched one of the amulets from Marcellus' hand. "Wear this now."

Caerwin shivered as the sorceress' fingers grazed her neck in bringing the amulet over her head. Did the woman somehow know that a babe nested in her womb? The old woman patted the amulet as it rested against Caerwin's breastbone. Her milky eyes gazed into Caerwin's.

"You and what you care for are safe," she said quietly. Caerwin wondered if she spoke directly into her mind. "I'll say no more." She waved her hand around her. "Where's my bed? I'm an old woman in need of sleep."

~~~

Whether the result of cleansing by the sorceress or the haunted effects of a dream she couldn't fully remember, Caerwin faced the next day with renewed energy. Unexpectedly, she consumed a hearty breakfast and hungered for lunch by the fifth hour. Patting the phallus amulet where it nestled on her chest beside the wheel of Taranis, she hurried down the avenue toward the Forum and the shop where Fimbria had found the remarkable jewelry.

When she awoke that morning, emotion from her dream filled her with hope. But the more she tried to remember it, the more the dream scattered from her memory like clouds before wind. The only thing she remembered was a man's hand and on it, a gold ring. Whatever the dream tried to tell her, she couldn't determine. But if she could in some way work the gods' will on behalf of Marcellus, she would.

"Take me to the place of rings," she urged Fimbria.

"If you mean the carved stones I mentioned, he holds more than rings," Fimbria said.

"I need to see the rings."

Like most of the shops in the marketplace, the tiny enterprise tucked into the street level front of a four-story insula. People leaned from upper story windows and balconies, carrying on conversations. For the first time in weeks, the smell of bacon roasting at a nearby eatery didn't turn her stomach. Fimbria led her inside.

A stout man with graying hair watched from a curtained doorway as the two women surveyed items placed on display on two narrow tables. Bracelets, necklaces, earrings, pendants, amulets, and rings gleamed against a dark table covering, colorful stones set in bronze, silver, or gold. She saw nothing that spoke to her.

"The finer pieces are at the back," Fimbria said, gesturing toward the man. "Do you know what you want?"

Caerwin shook her head. She had no specific plan for her purchase. Whatever pleased the gods would make itself known to her. She fingered first one gold ring then another then spent some time sorting among the fibula. Maybe she grasped at straws. Maybe the dream meant nothing.

"Do you have more?" she asked the man.

"What do you seek?"

"A ring for a man. Something that will give cheer and good luck."

"With a stone? Gold?"

Had there been a stone in the dream? She couldn't remember. She nodded. He briefly vanished behind the curtain then returned holding a tray. Several rings lined up on a padded cloth, all of them with careful workmanship in gold. The stones ranged in color from green to blue to red.

"What about the carved stones?" Fimbria said.

The man turned without speaking and brought out another tray of rings. The stones were larger, brighter, and worked with intricate images. One particular stone captured Caerwin's attention, a large red oval set in a wide gold band. An eagle with wings half spread and its head in profile had been carved into the stone.

"That one," she said firmly. "How much?"

"One hundred *denarii*," he said without hesitation. He handed her the ring. "My finest piece."

The burnished gold glinted dully in the light. On closer inspection, she could see that details of feathers and even the eagle's eye had been wrought with consummate skill. The blood red stone reflected light deep inside so that the eagle seemed to breathe.

"It's a fine piece," Caerwin agreed, handing the ring back to the dealer. "But much too expensive."

"She'll pay only forty," Fimbria said.

Caerwin had saved most of the allowances given each week for her shopping, but she had only sixty *denarii*. Even at forty, the ring cost more than she thought she should spend. Much as she had struggled to learn more about the costs of household operations and the flow of money under Marcellus' close watch, she really had no perspective. Her idea of surprising him with a token of her affection now struck her as irresponsible.

"Forty?" The man's voice rose. He motioned helplessly around him. "Do you think I am here for my pleasure? Each day I struggle with my painful leg and family responsibilities for only the few *sestertii* I gain in this trade. There are many mouths to feed in my care. I am expected to support my aging aunt and she can do nothing to earn her way. I cannot stand here and listen to such a miserable offer. Ninety, that's as low as I can go."

Caerwin took Fimbria's arm. "Come, I can't do this. Too much hangs in the balance for me to spend so much."

Fimbria pointed again at the ring. "Let it go for fifty, then," she said to the man.

The man's voice keened in high pitch as he ripped his hair. "Seventy, not a sestertius less."

"Come," Caerwin repeated to Fimbria. "I don't have that much."

"Fifty-five," Fimbria said. "Take it or we leave."

"Sixty-five."

Fimbria took Caerwin's arm as they walked toward the door.

"Oh cruel Fortuna that my one chance to eat today drives such a hard bargain," the man lamented loudly. "I have no choice if my family is to be fed. Fifty-five then, but you practice robbery."

Caerwin counted out the *denarii*. As she handed the coins to the man, she repeated her familiar request. "If you wish to gain more coin from me, listen to this. I seek an old woman named Kensa. If you hear of her, find me on the *Quirinalis* at the Antistius *domus*."

His glance flickered up and he stopped in the middle of lifting each coin to his belt pouch. "Kensa, eh? How would I know her?"

"She's an aging freedwoman who spent most of her life in the Antistius household—I don't know her looks."

"Antistius—the same house as the man made famous in court?" He eyed her shrewdly as if calculating what he might gain.

"The same," Caerwin said. "But if you bring me the wrong woman, I will know and you will suffer for it."

He struck his chest and rolled his eyes. "The gods have spoken. I know this woman. Wait," he said.

He disappeared behind the curtain. Caerwin could hear his footsteps dying away.

"Do you think he really knows of her?" Fimbria said.

"I think he would do anything for money," Caerwin said. "Finding her in this way is far too convenient."

Several minutes passed before a shuffling sound approached. Moments later the curtain drew back and the merchant appeared with an old woman at his side. Her shoulders stooped and her clothing hung in tatters. She stared vacantly about her.

Yet there was something—Caerwin drew a sharp breath as she noted the woman's cheekbones, so similar to Marcellus. It could not possibly…

"This is Kensa," the man said. "She sees only shapes and shadows."

"Kensa." Caerwin stepped toward the thin woman. "Can I ask you a question?"

"I know little," the old woman said. She turned her face toward Caerwin. "But you may ask."

"What was the name of the young boy you tended?"

"I have tended many young boys in my life. There was one..."

"Yes, one you held in your arms and taught another language."

The woman tilted her head and an expression of sadness crossed her features. "Marcellus," she whispered. "My little Marcellus."

"Oh," Caerwin said. Her throat choked on emotion. "You must come with me."

"I have nothing for you," Kensa said.

"I seek nothing from you," Caerwin said, gripping the woman's hands. "I come for Marcellus. He needs you."

"You are not Tulla or one of her girls. Who are you?"

"If the gods will it, I am to be the wife of Marcellus," Caerwin said. "Caerwin of the Cornovii, of Britannia."

Under her breath, Kensa repeated the words as if saying them herself would make her understand their meaning. Her face strained toward Caerwin as if by some magic her eyes could suddenly see. "Caerwin," she repeated. "Woman of Marcellus. Is this a dream?"

"Not a dream," Caerwin said firmly. "Fimbria, tell Cotta, hire a chair and bring it here." She turned to the merchant. "Does she have possessions? I wish to take her to our home."

"Does she wish to be taken?" he said. "Where would you take her?"

"To our home, the Antistius *domus*. She knows it."

"Yes, I know it," Kensa said quickly. "I may see the world in blurry shapes, but my mind and heart are not impaired. I pray each night that I find him again. The gods have heard me."

~~~

Caerwin could think of nothing but finding Marcellus. Kensa. She couldn't believe it. She glanced up every few moments to see the old woman gripping the arms of the chair carried by Cotta and

Falco. She wanted to shout or weep, stand on the highest building and lift her voice to the gods.

They stopped at the imperial *thermae*, but Marcellus wasn't in the exercise yard. She had the men wait with Kensa as she and Fimbria hurried inside. The atrium echoed with the sounds of a hundred voices as she strode past the food vendors. He wasn't in the sweat room or the cold plunge. Finally she spotted him at the warm pool, standing as Antius scraped him with the curved blade of the strigil. As she watched, Vedius emerged from the changing room with a towel wrapped at his waist and stood beside Marcellus.

Suddenly hesitant, Caerwin stopped at the entry.

"Do you want me to go beckon him?" Fimbria said.

"No, I…need to catch my breath," Caerwin said. "What if this is wrong? What if she's not truly Kensa?"

"She knew him," Fimbria reminded her. "She knew Tulla as well."

A sour taste collected in Caerwin's mouth as she watched the two men. There was no denial that Vedius matched Marcellus in beauty. He had a handsome face and confident carriage. He might have suffered terrible injury in his leg, but he had maintained the rest of his body's strength. Aside from his limp and the deformity of his lower left leg, he was just as robust as Marcellus. It was easy to see how they would have been well matched.

Most compelling in the scene before her eyes was the affinity between the two men. Had Marcellus spent more time with Vedius? Did the two men meet daily? Had Marcellus heeded her advice to yield to Vedius' desires? A pang of regret lodged in her stomach. Had Marcellus found his old affections rekindled?

Would he set her aside? Would she end up like Tulla, left alone as the man she loved took his pleasure with other men? She chewed her lip.

With the assistance of his personal attendant, Vedius maneuvered down the steps into the water. Her curiosity won over her modesty as she surveyed his genitalia. Even flaccid, his *mentula* nearly matched that of Marcellus. A vision of their coupling sprang fully formed to her mind and sent a hot flush to her cheeks.

If Marcellus only pretended to enjoy Vedius' company, Caerwin couldn't detect it. Her breath caught as he left his towel with Antius and joined Vedius in the water. Such magnificence! He was greater than the splendid marbles of Rome's greatest heroes and gods that stood larger than life in the Forum. Here was a god in living flesh. Her entire body longed to be with him. She felt as if a cord connected her heart to Marcellus so that with his each move and gesture, she tugged after him.

His laughter and animated demeanor matched that of Vedius. The two men stood close together at the pool's rim. Intense emotion etched Vedius' face as he attended every word and motion Marcellus made.

"I can't go to him," she said to Fimbria.

"Let me," Fimbria said. "What do you want me to say?"

She turned to leave. "He'd be angry for me to come here."

Fimbria stood watching Marcellus. "He does what he must."

"What do you know of it?"

"That he must court Vedius? Tatian said Vedius can help him. The ides are tomorrow."

Caerwin glanced at Fimbria and clamped her mouth shut. It was true the time had finally run. Whatever would happen to Marcellus and his future would be determined the next day. She had urged him to protect his future even if it meant yielding to Vedius' demands. If he did…

Let Fimbria and Tatian believe this was a simple political maneuver, a promise of monetary or social favors. Neither Marcellus nor Vedius would risk any demonstration of affection that would impact their public reputation. The fewer who knew the true nature of the two men's relationship, the better.

"Let them go," she said, turning on her heel to rush out of the bathhouse. "I have time to converse with Marcellus when he comes home. You're right. With court tomorrow, this matter of Kensa must wait."

"Don't think it more than it is," Fimbria said. "Marcellus loves you. It's easy to see that."

"If that were the only thing…" Caerwin looked up at the sky, filled with emotions so strong and so conflicted she only wanted to cry. "I can't make sense of it," she said. "Rome is a beast with many heads."

Fimbria laughed. "Exactly that, and you're not the first to see it. Have faith. Trust him. He's a strong man. He'll find his way."

~~~

Marcellus stayed away late attending an important dinner, or at least that was the message he sent to her. That he bothered to keep her informed of his whereabouts pleased her, but she couldn't dismiss the growing certainty that he fulfilled Vedius' desires. She had urged him to consider it, and why would he not? What was a discrete coupling compared to the risk of losing everything?

Caerwin and Fimbria settled the old woman in a comfortable bedchamber where they summoned Gethia and two other women of the house to bathe, groom, and cloth her in fresh garments. The brazier glowed with hot coals, and Kensa embraced the warmth flowing from it. It wasn't Caerwin's imagination that Kensa stood straighter and her face shone brighter with the dignity of a new white tunic and heavy cloak, her graying hair fastened in a neat bun. Caerwin sat with her to eat dinner.

"You know this house, do you not?" Caerwin said.

"I do." Kensa sipped her wine. "These were the walls that saw the best and the worst of my life."

"I'm sorry for what you've suffered. Had you lost your sight before Tulla sent you away?"

"Tulla." Kensa huffed and groped for her bread. "I retained sight until the last few years. I thought I could enjoy life as a freedwoman. I actually thanked her for freeing me. Only after working at the ovens did I start to understand that freedom held its own burden. If not for my sister's son Donatus—the jewelry merchant—I would have died in the gutter."

"The news of your manumission infuriated Marcellus," Caerwin said. "He said a family should protect and honor slaves who have given their lives in service."

"Tulla hated me," Kensa said. "This was a house divided."

Caerwin tempted Kensa with sweet treats after the main courses had been sampled. The old woman's eyelids began to sag soon after and Caerwin walked her to her bedchamber and pulled the warm blankets over her. Her tears fell silently as she left the room. This could be her mother in a few years' time. If she lived. She knelt at her pot of earth and sent her prayers to the gods on behalf of old women.

~~~

The next morning, the crush of men talked loudly and urgently at *salutatio*. The ides of *Januarius* had arrived and court convened at the third hour. Caerwin hovered near Marcellus' office until he rose to leave.

She clung to him. "I give you strength," she whispered against his chest. Her words shook with the pounding of his heart. "Take this to always remember me." She pressed the ring on his finger.

"What have you done?" he said, examining the glinting red stone against the light. "An eagle?"

"It speaks of you," she said. "I hope you like it."

"You inspire me with your beauty and spirit, little queen," he said, kissing her cheek. "I will wear it always."

He leaned back to survey her appearance. She wore the russet *stola* with its matching *palla* fastened by a simple gold pin. Fimbria had carefully styled her hair in a modest fashion so that her natural waves formed both sides of a center part and the length twisted to a bun at her crown. Only the gold and silver wire bracelets he had first given her at the fortress ornamented her wrist.

"I have reason to hope." He brushed a kiss on her cheek. "Stay always with your attendants," he said. "I depend on your safety."

With that, he set her away from him and with one last dark glance, strode out of the *domus*. So much in his face spoke of his resolve. But she saw his fear, his vulnerability. She wanted to walk before him with a sword in her hand, striking away his obstacles.

His flock of clients clustered behind and around him, a long knot of men in their best clothes. Their cloaks whipped in a stiff wind.

"I wish I could be there," Rufus said. "The houses of Rome will stand empty this morning with everyone at the basilica."

"The weather portends against us," Antius said, frowning up at the clouds scudding across the early morning sky. He'd cut himself shaving and the age lines on his face etched deep.

"Or with us," Fimbria said cheerfully. "Perhaps Jupiter's anger gathers against Clodius."

Caerwin couldn't wait another minute to follow, eager to gain a seat close to Marcellus. Her stomach churned, empty save for the bit of fruit she had coaxed down. "Let's make haste, then," she said abruptly.

Antius continued to watch the sky as they began walking down the avenue. Cotta and Falco wore their new clothes proudly, both of them dressed in white wool tunics and dark gray cloaks. Gordianus joined them as well, the cleanest she remembered seeing him.

Crowds packed the Forum in far greater numbers than a usual day of markets and courts. Cotta and Falco pressed close around Caerwin as they crossed the Via Sacra and approached the basilica. Stationed up the steps and along the interior corridor, the Praetorian Guard stood stiffly on watch. Armored under swirling red cloaks and short swords prominent on their hips, their stern demeanor signaled the emperor's expected presence at the proceedings.

Caerwin trembled at the sight of them. Excruciating memories rose to confront her—her first glimpse from the heights of the Wrekin as the Roman army marched toward them, men in numbers greater than she ever imagined. The melee of fighting, shouts, clash of swords and death cries swept over her. Virico with his life's blood draining between her fingers. The heartbreaking line of captives, her mother, her kinsmen, bound in chains as they walked out of her life and into the world of slavery. In the flash of memory, she watched Silverus fall on Seisyll's dagger and a Roman sword slice away Seisyll's life. She took a deep shaky breath as Antius hurried her past rows of fancy litter chairs, their wealthy passengers already seated inside.

A friend of Tatian waved at them from the packed benches behind Marcellus, and they made their way toward him. Marcellus huddled in intense discussion with Praetextus and Manlius and other jurists brought to his cause. Across from them, Clodius and his team watched and talked among themselves. Facing them both from the aisle's end, the praetor Flavius Maximus and another man stood near a red-draped table on the high platform as they awaited the emperor.

The basilica grew ever more crowded. They had been seated some time when Antius nudged her and pointed. They watched Tatian plow his way through the throng to reach Praetextus. After handing him a scroll, Tatian looked up, waved, and climbed the rows to reach them. He wedged himself between Antius and Caerwin.

"Did you find anything?" Antius said.

"I think it's what he needs," Tatian said, still out of breath. "I hope."

"What is it?" Caerwin said.

He shook his head. "I won't tempt Fortuna by speaking of it. Send your prayers." He looked around and pointed. "Look at the jurists. I knew this would attract a strong following. There must be twenty or more."

Caerwin looked where he pointed. Rows of men sat behind the high table. A few wore tunics with the broad red stripes of senators, more the narrow stripes of equites. Several elite plebians sat among them, their status marked by their lack of a toga.

"That's Crispus Opilio with Flavius," Tatian said. "He's one of two special jurists the emperor appointed three years ago to handle cases of inheritance. I don't know how he'll judge this."

"Won't it rest on the emperor's decision?" Caerwin said.

"He won't decide against their advice," Tatian said. "Unless he's angry. Which I fear. He has a reputation for temper on subjects for which he's passionate. Citizenship is foremost among them."

She wiped her clammy palms against her garment. Would this truly go against Marcellus? Her lips moved in a silent prayer to Almighty Jupiter. His will ruled Rome. Surely he knew the good in Marcellus' heart.

A ripple went through the rowdy gathering as the praetorians stamped their feet and shouted, announcing the emperor. Caerwin had never seen him and watched in surprise as he advanced down the center corridor. Garbed in a dazzling white toga with a wide purple band along its edges, his tall, thin appearance belied the power inherent in his position. His determined gaze cast over those in attendance with curiosity as much as authority. Shouts of acclamation and greeting rose along his passage and as he took his seat at the high table, a general cry of respect and praise filled the air.

Flavius Maximus stood to lead the proceedings, speaking loudly as he acknowledged both parties to the complaint and then briefly outlined the matter before the court. No other proceedings were held this morning, so they enjoyed unusual stillness in which to hear clearly.

"For the moment," Maximus said, "we set aside the original complaint of Clodius against Antistius on the charge of *stuprum* as it pertained to the deceased Clodius brother Melonius and his alleged violation by the deceased Antistius Petrus. Parties to the complaint are the brother of Melonius, Clodius Galarius, plaintiff, and the son and heir of the accused, Antistius Marcellus."

Maximus motioned toward the men at the mention of their names. He cleared his throat. "The complainant argues that even though Petrus has died, his estate should be required to pay the demanded damages in the amount of one million *sestertii*. Our laws may be said to support such a claim. The defendant argues that there is no proof that Petrus committed the alleged offenses, that there is no evidence that the alleged offenses caused Melonius to take his own life, and that there is evidence that Melonius suffered personal insult in the excesses of our former emperors Tiberius and Caligula whose crimes of such manner are well known.

"Those matters remain to be resolved. What confronts us now is the following. In the process of presenting testimony in support of the Clodius claim, a witness—one Helvius Sura—stated that his wife Antistius Matina had learned from her mother Fenius Tulla, wife of Antistius Petrus, that Marcellus was not the legitimate child of Petrus but rather the child of a slave woman named Rhian. At the time of this child's birth, seeking to wrap the boy in a legitimate name, Petrus' father Labeo contrived a marriage between Petrus and Tulla and made it appear that the child was born of that union.

"Before the court now is the question of the rightful citizenship of Antistius Marcellus."

Murmurs erupted among observers as Maximus sat briefly to engage in a quiet discussion with Claudius and Opilio. Caerwin shifted nervously in her seat. Whatever these men decided would determine Marcellus' entire future. He had done nothing wrong yet he risked losing everything, even his standing as a Roman citizen. She shifted side to side to peer past the heads of several men sitting between her and Marcellus to see his clenched jaw and rigid posture. How many times had he prepared for battle with the same resignation, the same self-possessed resolution to do whatever must be done? Her heart wrenched for what he must be feeling.

Maximus stood and the crowd quieted.

"By the long-honored laws of Rome, a citizen would have to free a slave before the slave could be adopted or married. In the case of the slave Rhian in the household of Antistius Labeo, her child by Petrus was born a slave. Since this slave known to us as Antistius Marcellus was never freed by law, he could not be adopted by Petrus to be his legitimate son. Therefore, he could not inherit.

"Moreover, even if he had wished," Maximus said, "Petrus could not have freed him because of rules put forth by Augustus Caesar that a slave must reach thirty years of age before manumission. Petrus would have had to free the mother Rhian to affect the status of her son. But according to information discovered recently by Antistius Marcellus, at the time Labeo died and left his son Petrus as the head of the family, Rhian had died. Make no mistake—Petrus wasted no time or resources in his effort to find her. At that time, the child was only four years.

He sighed. "I must say, the circumstances of her death are among the most regrettable I've ever heard. The acts of Antistius Labeo in this matter bring shame on his memory. We can never know why he chose this path."

"That said, let us return to this tangled matter before us. In finding Rhian dead, Petrus could never marry her as a freedwoman and could not legitimize his son Marcellus after the fact in that manner, if even that were legal. I'd be interested in the opinion of my learned colleagues on that point—we haven't explored the law as it pertains to that question.

"On the bare bones of legal fact," Maximus said, "Antistius Marcellus is a slave."

Shouts erupted from the stunned crowd. Caerwin couldn't move. Fimbria's tight grip squeezed Caerwin's hands but she hardly noticed.

"They can't do this to him," Antius said angrily. "He's done nothing wrong."

"Surely that's not the end of it," Tatian said. "We found documents. What's wrong with Praetextus?"

Claudius held up his hand and the attendants on either side of the podium rapped their staffs on the floor. Silence soon fell despite lingering murmurs.

An angry flush marked the emperor's cheeks as he faced Marcellus. "C-c-citizenship is a sacred trust of Rome," he began. His voice quavered slightly and his head trembled. "We punish false claims of citizenship as a capital offense. We have put back into slavery any freedman who claimed equestrian status. Why should we accept a slave as citizen in this case?"

"What's wrong with him?" Caerwin whispered to Tatian. "Is he ill?"

"The gods have seen that the infirmities plaguing his body pay for the strengths of his mind," Tatian whispered back. "He's been a lifelong cripple."

Marcellus stood and faced the emperor. "May I speak?"

Claudius motioned with his hand to show his permission then sat down.

"Thank you for hearing me, sire," Marcellus said in a forceful voice. "Throughout my life, I knew nothing of these matters. I have not purposefully set out to deceive as does someone falsely claiming citizenship. My parents treated me as their legitimate child, even Tulla who knew of the deception from the start. It was my grandfather Labeo who began the falsehoods that now threaten my destruction.

"The path he chose caused ruin and heartbreak for my father, for my mother Rhian, and for my stepmother Tulla. I can't answer for him or explain what he did. That my mother's newborn child was torn from her arms as she was sent to serve the most sordid brothel of Herculaneum is a torment that I can hardly bear. That my father was locked away to prevent his interference in that criminal act also tears at my conscience. Learning these circumstances has allowed me to understand the hostility always present between Petrus and Tulla and the disregard she exhibited in her treatment of me.

"I am not speaking on behalf of the suffering I knew as a child in ignorance of these truths. I will say that only an aging slave woman showed me affection, a woman I now know was my grandmother. None of this kept me from serving Rome to the best of my ability. I excelled at my lessons. I won competitions at the exercise field. By the time of my majority, my father had begun to show interest and took me to our wheat farms in Tunesia and our ship yards at Neapolis so that I might learn the skills needed to take over those duties."

Caerwin's attention shifted to a man only now taking a seat among the jurists. Vedius. What did he play at here? His gaze riveted on Marcellus. She could gather nothing from his expression.

"For ten years first in Germania and then in Britannia," Marcellus said, "I have honored the insignia of Legio Fourteen Gemina, watched Rome's eagle fly triumphant over our fields of battle, all while knowing in my heart that I was only one among many countrymen serving your will. You, sir, in your most excellent leadership of our triumph over the Britons, understand the rigors in that theater of war. When our legate fell in battle at the far western frontier, I stepped into the role and performed admirably under the governorship of Ostorius Scapula. I return from Britannia ready to take up my family's business in building ships and shipping grain in service to *Cura Annonae*.

"I can't undo what my father has done." He hesitated as if he had more to say. "I beg you to find a rightful place for me, for my future, in your considerations."

Praetextus stood up as Marcellus sat down. "Your honorable eminence, if I may, I'd like to provide some additional information on the matter of this man's citizenship."

"Are we to replow old ground?" Claudius said. "I am sympathetic to the innocence of your patron in that he didn't initiate the deception himself. However, the laws of citizenship are clear."

"I assure you, this is new and relevant information," Praetextus insisted.

"Very well, then proceed," Claudius said.

He looked tired. Maybe his decision had already been made. Everything he said led away from a judgment favorable to Marcellus.

"Late yesterday we discovered documents filed by the jurist Cipius Fabianus, surely known to you and our esteemed colleagues as a man of notable expertise in the matter of *fideicommissum*. He was the *fiduciarus* hired by Antistius Petrus to formalize his last wishes. I've only this morning obtained a copy and submit it for your review."

He handed the scroll to the emperor.

"What's the subject?" Claudius asked.

"Our question of citizenship, sire. Cipius sought to bridge a delicate gap between the rights of the living and the wishes of the dead. At the time he contemplated his death, Petrus didn't want to create problems for his son by advertising he'd been born a slave. Cipius fulfilled his patron's wish to provide an orderly manumission for Marcellus and to clear a path for his rightful place as a citizen.

Praetextus pointed. "I believe you'll see the document shows that after extensive consultation with Cipius, Petrus willed that if information came out about Marcellus' slave status, then Fabianus would publically file the information for the record to free Marcellus and bequeath him the estate as a citizen."

"Counsel, did Cipius file these papers appropriately?" Claudius asked. "If so, why was there no public announcement?"

"They were filed appropriately but not easy to find. He paid seven witnesses to execute the documents, a procedure recognized by our laws. Then he swore them to secrecy. We recovered them in old records at the Tabularium. Cipius must have believed he would live long enough to reveal their existence, so he tucked them in with unrelated contracts."

"Odd that you found them," Claudius said with a frown.

"Our clerks searched every document filed by Fabianus, admittedly a lengthy process."

Claudius waved his hand. "No matter what the records say, the inheritance came before his legal status and therefore is technically void."

Murmurs spread through the assembly.

"The emperor won't be swayed," Tatian said tersely. "He's made up his mind."

"Is this the great justice of Rome?" Caerwin said. "Decide before hearing the facts?"

"There is a provision," Praetextus said loudly, sending his voice over the disturbance in the room. "Our laws allow for a man to administer a trust without actually receiving the inheritance held within it. I tell you now, the skill with which Cipius executed the wishes of Antistius Petrus is nothing short of genius. As executor of the trust himself, Cipius had the right to bestow full power of oversight to Marcellus, which he has done. Upon his father's death, Marcellus took control of the estate as if it were his inheritance. Only Cipius knew that he stood as the silent link between Marcellus and the legal machinery of his circumstance. I remind you—until this matter came before the court, Marcellus himself knew nothing of his true mother."

"Not exactly true," Caerwin muttered.

"*Shh*," Antius said. "Say nothing."

"This is highly irregular," Claudius said. "How did these details come to your attention? Cipius has been dead three years."

"We could call it the turn of Fortuna's wheel, but in truth, its discovery came only by a stroke of luck. The scrolls setting forth this matter were within the records of Cipius' personal estate. Until we saw it for ourselves, we dared not trust its reliability. During our admittedly brief review, we have found nothing in the process or language of the document that causes us to question its legitimacy."

"Convenient, wouldn't you say?" Claudius said.

"Yes, we agree it's convenient," Praetextus said. "These matters often turn on the unexpected interference of the gods, do they not?"

"What proof do you have that this is not simply a skilled forgery?"

"The scroll bears Cipius' seal."

"I would see his seal on other documents to compare," Claudius said. "Send a runner to the Tabularium. Bring me five documents under Cipius."

The emperor turned to private discussion with Maximus and Opilio as several of the jurists came to their huddle. Including Vedius. He crouched behind the emperor's chair, all of them intensely engaged. After a time, Vedius and the other jurists stood to return to their seats. She watched him as his gaze settled on Marcellus.

Was it an expression of pleasure? Anger? Desire? Frustration? His forehead creased and his eyes narrowed as he lingered, staring at Marcellus. Then he turned and took his seat.

Caerwin's mouth had gone dry. A cold wind ran through the basilica, heavy with scent of rain, and she felt the low rumble of distant thunder in her throat. She wished to be huddled in her bed with the blankets tucked over her. No, she corrected herself. She wished to be huddled in Marcellus' bed, his arms wrapped around her and his quiet breath in her hair.

So many months had passed in her acquaintance with Marcellus. She regretted so much of that time had been wasted in her childish rebellion. Senna had cautioned her so many times. Even now she could hardly grasp the risk she had taken in her escape, but she understood his anger about it.

More than once, he had saved her from terrible harm. She had been too naïve to understand the threats that faced her, but Marcellus had understood from the start. That he had seen her, desired her enough to take her, still shocked her. From that first moment, she had known him in ways she didn't understand.

As if he spoke to her in some forgotten language.

She knew the language now. It was the language of a man and woman destined to join.

How had she changed so much? She had softened, longed for him more than she hated him, accepted a future that centered on him. Did the child teach her this? Was this the inevitable course of love?

She was seized with an urgent need to tell him she loved him. Again she shifted in her seat to gain a vantage point where she could see Marcellus. He sat with his head in his hands as Praetextus and Manlius talked with two other men. The very air shimmered with tension.

A runner arrived, bowed to the emperor, and handed him the bundle of scrolls. Agonizing minutes passed as the emperor and his two companions pored over the documents. She could make nothing of their expressions.

"I die a thousand deaths," Tatian muttered.

"What further proof do they need?" Caerwin said. "Surely the seals are the same."

"I saw many of them in our search," Tatian said. "They all bear the same mark. It's because the emperor doesn't change his mind easily."

Caerwin's heart lodged in her throat as Maximus stood, holding his hand up for silence.

"The seals match," he announced. "We agree that Cipius wrote the documents."

A brilliant flash and immediate loud crack of thunder ripped the air. Dead silence shrouded the basilica then shouts erupted.

"Jupiter speaks!"

"The will of the gods!"

Antius muttered words Caerwin didn't understand. "*Oblativa ex caelo.*"

She looked at Tatian. He gripped her hands. "A spontaneous sign from Jupiter himself," he said. "Powerful augury."

"Does it favor Marcellus?" Caerwin asked.

"Only if the emperor says it does," Tatian said.

Claudius stood as the excitement died down. In the silence, the roar of torrential rain filled the air. He lifted his voice to a shout.

"Jupiter is among us!" he said. Assenting cries echoed through the long hall. He cleared his throat. "The matter requires more thorough deliberation than we can engage in this location. Jurists will join me in council at the palace. We will reconvene in one hour of the water clock."

～～～

The hour passed in unparalleled agitation. People stood in place, unwilling to relinquish their seats. Caerwin's stomach rumbled as food vendors made their way along the central aisle, their rain-soaked cloaks dripping onto the marble floor. Much as the aroma of sausages and pastries caused her mouth to water, she resisted the temptation. If she ate, she'd throw up.

She couldn't keep her eyes off Marcellus. He paced near his seat, oblivious to the flux of things around him. His eyes were cast down. He repeatedly rubbed his forehead. Now and then, Manlius or Praetextus walked beside him, clamping a hand on his shoulder and bending close to speak quietly. More than once Marcellus shook his head as if denying what they said. She could make nothing of it, what outcome they predicted, what tragedy they warded against.

She knew. If the emperor held his angry stance against the citizenship infringement, Marcellus would be stripped of his citizenship and his wealth. Slavery would not become him. She'd heard of rebellious slaves provoked by pride to resist beatings and verbal abuse. He would be sent to the mines where men died. Or killed outright.

Or he would end up in the arena.

The thought froze the blood in her veins.

Antius surely shared her anguish. He leaned forward with his head hung down in a posture of hopelessness. What would happen to him?

What would happen to her?

To the child?

If the ruling went against Marcellus, she would not tell him of the child. She would find the herbs and make the potion, end its life to save it from slavery.

No. She could not take the life of this child. It was the child of Marcellus, as precious to her as anything life could offer. She would find a way to escape, make her way to some other nation, some place where Rome could not find her.

Exhaustion swept over her. There was no place Rome could not find her. Rome ruled the world.

A new thought struck her. She felt as if the lightning had hit her head. If Marcellus was to be a slave, what if Vedius bought him?

She closed her eyes. It was useless to think of these things. Surely the omen of thunder would go in Marcellus' favor. The god had spoken just at the moment to confirm Cipius' documents. How could it be interpreted any other way than to confirm that Cipius had carried out Jupiter's will?

Her back ached. Her head throbbed. Her mouth was dry and she happily accepted a cup of watered wine from Tatian who returned to the seats with two cups and a wrapper of fish cakes. She had to look away from the cakes but fortunately the cold humid wind blew past her, taking the smell with it.

Fimbria returned from her journey to the latrines and now, belatedly, Caerwin realized she should have gone with her. But the blast of a horn signaled the water clock's arrival at the designated hour and with it, the jurists filed into their seats followed by Maximus and Opilio. Claudius did not appear.

"The emperor doesn't attend?" Caerwin whispered to Tatian. "What does that mean?"

"I don't know," he said. "Either way, he's satisfied with the decision."

Before a hushed audience, Maximus stood and motioned with his arm.

"Antistius Marcellus, stand."

Marcellus stood stiffly, his arms, his legs, even the folds of his white toga unyielding as the very granite of the earth. She thought he trembled, but it could have been an effect of her own shaking. Her heart drummed against her ribs.

"On the matter of your birthright, we find that the procedures and document wrought by Cipius Fabianus are within the boundaries of our laws. Therefore, you are declared a ranking citizen of Rome with all the rights and privileges enjoyed by your equestrian class as passed down through all previous generations of the Antistius gens."

Shouts swallowed the last of his words. Her gaze riveted on Marcellus, Caerwin saw him stagger back slightly as the court's decision sank in. Praetextus sprang up, slapping him on the back and helping him regain his legs.

Fimbria hugged her close. Tatian and Antius shook hands, laughing. All around them, supporters of Marcellus exchanged embraces or laughed or shouted—the basilica echoed with jubilation.

Not everyone celebrated. Clodius sat stone faced through the uproar and even more so, Helvius Sura who sat nearby. Caerwin looked away from him. She would not let her anger for him, for Tulla and the rest of those people spoil her moment of intense happiness.

Praetextus held up his hand again and the audience again silenced.

"To the original matter, then, of the Clodius claim against the Antistius estate, the matter will come before us tomorrow at the third hour. Whatever witnesses are needed should be on time. Have your arguments tightly prepared. The emperor tires of the matter."

With that, the judges stood. Slowly, the jurists and everyone else made their way toward the entries while knots of people stood talking. Caerwin suddenly needed to pee so badly she didn't know if she could walk to the latrines. But she paused in her rush to the aisle, torn by her need to embrace Marcellus.

It would be impossible. She could only catch glimpses of his dark head. Surrounded by well-wishers, he would need time to collect himself. He would want to prepare for the argument against Clodius. Much awaited him. She could see him at home. With a last hopeful glance, she hurried away with Fimbria.

~~~

Caerwin rushed from place to place in the house, instructing Gordianus to prepare a special dinner. She set incense to flame at the altars of Jupiter, Juno, and Minerva and propitiated Vesta with a sacrifice of salt and milk. With Kensa's frail hand wrapped in the crook of her arm, she led her to the kitchen for lunch.

"I have good news," she said. "The matter of inheritance I mentioned to you? The emperor found in Marcellus favor. He is to retain his citizenship."

A big smile wreathed Kensa's face. "He deserves it," she said. "He always tried to be the best at everything he did."

"One matter remains," Caerwin said. "The complaint of Clodius."

"What is that? Do I know that name?"

Caerwin explained.

"Petrus took too many risks, but I understood why," Kensa said. "He never recovered from losing Rhian. It changed him."

"Do you think he would have taken a freeborn boy?"

Kensa shook her head. "I don't know. He kept many secrets about his personal affairs. I know he cared nothing for Tulla and she hated him for it. He would reveal nothing to her. She would have used it against him."

"She spoke of his perversity."

Kensa laughed. "She lived for each new rumor and the city was full of them. Like a rabbit in a snare, she darted this way and that. She had no courage to escape. I wondered if she killed him herself."

"What? Did he die here?"

"He died of poison at the villa at Herculaneum." Kensa waved her hand. "That doesn't matter. She could have hired someone. They say poison is a woman's tool. Such things are done all the time, especially in those days when Caligula held us all by the throat. Anything could be bought."

"But...he prepared for it, swore out legal documents, as if he planned to die."

"Perhaps he did. I don't know what happened. I always thought she would find a way to kill him, that's all."

Long after the meal ended and Caerwin lay in her bed trying to nap, one thought then another chased through her mind. If Tulla killed Petrus, did she also kill Melonius? If she had found an assassin clever enough, both could have seemed like suicide.

Could anyone be so determined, so full of hatred, that she would claim two lives? How would she have known of Melonius?

The idea of Tulla having a hand in it contradicted the legal preparations Petrus had made. Unless she had threatened. Unless she had tried and failed and he prepared.

Did she plan all of this, thinking to gain the full estate?

If so, why wait until Marcellus returned from ten years at war? Why not make her claim as soon as Petrus died?

Maybe she hoped for Marcellus' death in a faraway land. The chances were good that he would die on the front lines of battle. Then she would be spared any messy legal action that would bring disgrace on her and the family name.

Caerwin sat up. If Petrus knew of this, surely he would have made some statement in his legal papers. Had they looked at every possible scrap in Cipius' documents? Was there not some scroll with Tulla's name on it?

~~~

Rufus closed the door firmly and she heard the sound of Marcellus' voice. She yanked open her bedchamber door and flew across the atrium to wrap her arms around him.

"I'm so happy for you," she said.

"Come with me," he said sternly.

He led her to his bedchamber. One worry then another raced through her mind. What caused this anger? Had something happened? As soon as he closed the door, his serious expression vanished and he pulled her against his chest to kiss her.

"It's a great day," he said. "Words cannot describe the relief I feel. I want nothing but you."

"The worry lasted too long," she said, laughing as she nestled against the folds of his toga. So warm, so comforting.

He stroked her hair. "Would that all the problems had been solved. I would ravish you for the rest of the day. I remain fearful of the Clodius matter."

Her suspicions about Tulla rose afresh. "I hope the court finds against Clodius and his ridiculous claim. I think Tulla is behind this. She provoked her daughter and in turn Helvius, and he prodded the matter with Clodius."

"Is that what you think?" he said gently.

"I'm sure of it," she said bitterly, looking up at him. "It makes perfect sense."

"I love your temper," he said, brushing her cheek with his fingertips. "I love how your skin turns pink and your eyes spark blue fire. Nothing arouses me faster."

"You have a peculiar appetite," she said. "It's a serious subject."

"I'm reminded of my greatest appetite," he said. His hands cupped her buttocks and pulled her against him so that his stiff cock pressed against her. "I hunger for you in ways I never knew possible. What sorcery is this?"

"A woman's body?"

"This particular woman is more than her body." His lips grazed hers then trailed down her jaw to her neck. Gooseflesh pebbled her arms. "She's a perplexing package of tart and sweet, hot and cold, clever and stubborn. I'm completely enchanted, as much now—no more—as the first day I saw you."

His hands came to her breasts. Desire laced through her belly. "I long for you," she said. "I fear you'll never treat me as you did before. I dream of the baths with your hand slapping my buttocks, you forcing my pleasure. I dream of being tied while you lash me. Oh!"

His hand came between her legs. Through the garments, the heat of his palm sent pulses through her vulva. "You dream of it?" he whispered. He massaged her, causing her flesh to swell. "I lie awake with it. I see your bared breasts trembling with your nipples pinched tight. I see your *cunnus* exposed, dripping with sweet nectar."

He grabbed up her skirts and cupped her bared flesh. "Wet," he whispered, stroking the seam while she squirmed. "For me."

"What of my thought that Tulla planned all this?" she said.

He walked her to the bed, pulling at her clothes until only the tunic remained. "Who is Tulla? I can think of nothing but my need to taste you. Can you help me stop before I give you a child?"

"I...I don't know," she said. Words hovered on her lips, words telling him she already had his child, that she was nearly three months gone. His hands stilled. "Yes, yes, I will. Just…touch me."

He laid her gently against the bed then tore at his clothes until he stood only in his tunic. With a groan, he spread her legs and knelt between them, bending as he ran his hands from her ankles to her buttocks. He shoved her tunic above her waist then used his thumbs to spread her open.

"Oh, I can't stand it," she said.

"You pleasured me," he said. "I was thoughtless and selfish not to return the favor." His words whispered against her skin. He kissed along her thighs, her belly, and down to the mound that quivered in anticipation. "I'm so tired of the troubles that come between us. This is all I want."

"Ohh."

"Shh, let me taste you."

His tongue flicked against her fevered skin, up one side of her vulva and then the other. She shuddered as he toyed with her, as he teased every inch except the part that screamed for attention. Finally he licked up the seam and settled his mouth over her clitoris.

"It wants me," he said, touching the tip of it with the tip of his tongue.

"The gods! Marcellus!"

He laughed. "This is my field of flowers, the ocean wilds, the mountaintop."

"Stop talking."

A low chuckle rumbled in his throat. "Do you want me?"

"Yes, yes, I want you. Do you plan only to torture me?"

"I thought you enjoyed your punishments."

"Use the lash!" she said. "This is too much."

He spread her more widely and licked again, then again, until the pulsing of her clitoris beat against his tongue each time he touched her. The lightness of his touch sent her to frenzy.

"Please," she said, gripping his hair. "Anything."

"What do you mean?" he said, laughing. "This?"

He sucked the delicate tip against his teeth, suddenly savage in his manner. It was as if he would eat her alive. His lips, tongue, even his chin joined the service of his hands until she didn't know what he did or where he touched her. He chewed her labia, drove his tongue up her vagina, bit and sucked on her clitoris, plunged his fingers inside her.

Her fist came up to mute her cry of pleasure. His onslaught took up a rhythm. Tension on her clitoris rose to fiery pitch. Her muscles clenched as the cascade of orgasm overtook her.

He rode her as wild spasms erupted, still sucking her clitoris and stroking inside her until the last of her shaking groaning tumult faded. He buried his face against her wet center, lapping at the fluids that mingled with his saliva.

"Sweeter than honey," he groaned, sitting up to his knees. He pulled up the front of his tunic to wipe his face. "Are you harmed?"

"Yes, I'm harmed," she murmured. Words came slowly to her mind and slower still to her lips. As if she'd forgotten how to speak. As if words didn't matter. "You've made me speechless. You made my thoughts disappear."

He laughed. "You don't need thoughts or words. I'm all you need."

Savoring the languid feel of her body, she rolled over and sat up to face him on the bed. "You are all I need. If anyone is harmed, it is you. All these months I haven't been able to say what I needed to say. What I felt. What I've known for a long time."

He held her hand and kissed her fingertips. "I don't need anything but you."

"No." She shook her head. "You need to hear me say it. I love you, Marcellus. That's all that matters. I love you so much my heart aches with it. My days pass full of love for you. I only hope to someday be the woman you need me to be."

"My queen," he whispered. His eyes shone with tears. "You have always been that woman."

The news of Kensa hit him with visible force. She watched him as he approached the old woman, the reverence in his step, the brief hesitation before he swept her into his arms. They both wept as he sat close to her side in the dining room, coaxing her to speak of whatever subject she wanted to discuss as they made their way through a long relaxing meal.

Gordianus delivered a dinner of sumptuous simplicity. The first course included aged olives steeped in brine, a stew of shellfish fresh from the sea, beets cooked in a cream sauce, and a salad of sliced boiled egg over lettuce, arugula, mint, and mallow leaves. For the main course, as Caerwin basked in the afterglow and feasted on the simple sight of this man she loved, Gordianus served roasted chicken coated with herbs and pepper and lentils stewed with celery and onion. Heated water diluted the delicious wine from Pompeii, sending warmth down to her toes.

Not that she needed the heat. Residual tremors cascaded over her body. Her swollen labia remembered his tongue and with each tremor still pulsing there, a smile burst to her face that she could not restrain. The conversation between Kensa and Marcellus hardly required her attention and her thoughts drifted. Fimus arrived with his toothy smile, a tart lemon custard, and pastries of crisp crusts layered with honey, cinnamon, and nuts to fill the last possible opening in her stomach.

"A feast," Kensa said with a sigh. "Am I dreaming?"

"Many more to come," Marcellus said. "I can never give you enough to make up for what you've suffered."

"Doesn't that remain to be seen?" the old woman said. Her clouded eyes settled on him. "What of the morning? Aren't you still at risk?"

He turned to Caerwin with a questioning look.

"I told her," Caerwin said. "About Clodius and his claim against you."

"Don't be troubled by this," Marcellus said. "There's nothing you can do."

"Think of it," Kensa said, frowning. "Tulla held enough hate in her heart to arrange your father's death. She's a bitter scheming woman. If she knew of Melonius, she would have arranged to have him killed as well and make it seem like suicide. You weren't here like I was to watch her pace and mutter."

Marcellus sat without speaking several minutes. "We thought... That is, with Caligula at his worst, many men were driven to take their own lives."

"Caligula never turned on the shipping trade. He was at least smart enough to fear the masses if they didn't have grain." She shrugged. "I have no proof, only my suspicions. But she was always greedy—she wanted the money. She thought Petrus owed her for a lifetime trapped in a loveless marriage. What more clever way could she devise than this?"

"It was Labeo who ruined her life, not Petrus," Marcellus said. "I'm descended from a monster."

"Don't think of him, Marcellus," Caerwin urged. "Is there any chance that Petrus knew of her plans and instructed Cipius to preserve some evidence? Did Tatian find anything about Tulla?"

"We haven't looked for it," he said quietly. "Is she capable of such a complicated plan? How would she know of Melonius?"

"Didn't she scold you for not knowing how such things are done?" Caerwin said. "About having spies? About hiring someone killed? Maybe she criticized you in guilt over what she'd done."

"Ha!" Kensa laughed. "She isn't capable of guilt."

"If she spied on Petrus, she could have known about Melonius," Marcellus said. "Petrus was made vulnerable by the amount of wine he consumed. The only times I saw him composed, even authoritative, were our travels to Tunesia and Neapolis. In those places, he knew what he must do, who he must praise, who he must punish. It was as if a different man had taken his place.

"Once he felt satisfied that he had done what he could to assure my future, he couldn't drink fast enough. I had my own interests in those last years before I joined the legions, but I do remember Melonius. They loved each other, as much as a jaded old man and a hopeful young boy could know love. What Petrus had lost, Melonius gave him. While Petrus lived in a shell of bitterness, Melonius exuded vibrant interest in theater, music, poetry—all the beauties of life. If Tulla had even a hint of how Petrus favored the boy and provided him with expensive gifts, that might have been more than she could stand."

"Then she would make it a scandal enough that his family would seek damages and ruin you in the process," Caerwin said.

"She hated you," Kensa said. "Many times I heard her say you were lower than the dirt beneath her feet. Even more, she hated that she must pretend to be your mother. Her family traces its heritage back to the early Republic. Mixed race offended her."

"What was the circumstance of my father's death?" he said. "I found no information when I returned to settle the estate and couldn't stay long enough to ask questions. Do you know?"

"A messenger arrived from Herculaneum with news he'd been found dead in the villa. As I remember it, Tulla reacted strangely. Not surprised. She assigned the arrangements to others, never helped clean or dress the body. She hired professional mourners for the procession."

"Did the death report describe the manner of his death? Was it truly poison?"

"If it did, I didn't hear of it. Sorry," Kensa said, smiling as she reached for his hand. "I'm not much use."

"You're worth your weight in gold twice over," he said. "And that's only for the love you gave me in our many years together. I'm sorry that I caused Rhian's death."

Her face turned sharply toward him. The clarity in her expression startled Caerwin. She could see the beauty of her youth, the strength that carried her through decades of grief and suffering, first as a slave to Labeo and then under the abuse of Tulla.

"You did not cause her death," Kensa said in a strong voice. "Labeo's hands alone bathe in her blood. Always remember—he is not your only ancestor. The lineage of my kinsmen also runs in your veins." She sighed and her shoulders sagged. "All this has tired me. Would you mind if I found my way to bed?"

Marcellus jumped up from the couch and helped her to the bedchamber, summoning Gethia to attend her. Then he strode toward the back of the house. Caerwin followed. Her neck prickled, a reaction she'd come to expect when outrage stirred him.

"Tatian!" he called.

Tatian's door opened.

"Come down, I need to talk with you."

Tatian hurried down the stairs. In tersely spoken words, Marcellus questioned him about Cipius' documents.

"I'm sorry," Tatian said. "I remember seeing nothing about Tulla. But understand, I looked only for the words that had to do with Petrus and you, sir. If her name appeared, I might not have seen it."

"Mars Ultor!" Marcellus paced the length of the garden pool, back and forth. "This day grows overlong. Are my senses up to this task? Something must be decided. Antius!"

Antius emerged from his nearby bedchamber. "Sir?"

"Take a message to Manlius. Tell him I must see him at the first hour. Ask him to bring any legal advisor who might be useful. Here, write my message. I can hardly think."

Antius hurried to fetch a square of parchment, his ink and stylus then sat at the table to write. Marcellus outlined the points, pausing only when Antius gestured to slow down while he wrote. As he spoke each new detail of his suspicions, Antius and Tatian became more agitated. At the finish, Antius stood and placed the message before Marcellus with the hot wax for his seal, which he imprinted with his inherited signet ring.

Marcellus walked as far as the front door with Caerwin at his side, then stood in the opening as he sent Antius, Tatian, Cotta, and Falco off into the night.

"Mercury, speed his path," he muttered. "The streets aren't safe in the dark. I'm hopeful no ill befalls them. At least Manlius lives this side of the worst parts of the city."

His arms wrapped around her. "You must be ready for sleep."

"I admit it," she said tiredly. "I can't wait to pass the night in your arms. Can you bear it?"

He frowned, confronted with the struggle that still faced him. "I dare not," he said. "Venus comes to me the strongest at night. I wouldn't sleep well for wanting you."

"Sleep well, then," she said, rising on tiptoe to kiss his cheek.

Chapter Twelve

The eager crowds had thinned slightly from the day before. Caerwin looked around the basilica, focusing on the seating behind Clodius and his counsel to see if she could spot Tulla. She'd never noticed her in attendance at the previous hearings, but now with her suspicions aroused, she felt certain Tulla must have been at every one.

Several women wore their *pallas* so far forward over their foreheads that she couldn't easily distinguish their faces. She shifted her attention to seek out Helvius Sura. Finally she spotted him, sitting three rows back from Clodius. Two women sat behind him. She'd never seen Matina but when she recognized the thin face of Tulla, she knew the woman next to her must be Sura's wife.

Had they attended each time, waiting to see if their nefarious plan produced the results they desired? Did Tulla play her daughter and son-in-law with the same insidious skill she had manipulated everyone else? The more Caerwin thought about it, the more she was convinced that Kensa was right.

But what proof? Marcellus had been sequestered with Manlius by the time she finished her morning ablutions. She had taken extra time at her little shrine, an arrangement of the pot of earth beside a lamp, a candle, and incense. Her dream had wakened her in the middle of the night, Senna's hand brushing her forehead. Then it wasn't Senna but her mother. Both their faces were indistinct but bathed in misty light. They had whispered words of comfort but she couldn't remember anything they said.

The Praetorian Guard slammed their boots to the floor and shouted. The crowd stood and cried out acclamation as the emperor strode down the center aisle. She studied his face, anxious to see what clue she might derive from his expression. But his composed countenance gave nothing away.

Maximus stood and quickly summed up the nature and status of the Clodius claim. She watched as Clodius turned to his counsel,

Lampronius Abito and Granius Arrianus. She could tell by their confident demeanor they felt little concern about the strength of their case.

She whispered a quick prayer to Minerva as Arrianus stood to begin his remarks.

"No matter what my esteemed colleagues might say on behalf of their client Antistius Marcellus, the facts do not change. Clodius Melonius died at his own hand. He suffered the shame that no freeborn child should ever suffer, that is, he lost his innocence to a man who wanted to use him. This man could have taken any slave boy to satisfy his lust. Instead, he stalked Melonius, courted him with gifts. Who knows what promises were made, what lies were told, to sway this innocent boy.

"Did he yield out of desire as the defendant charges? If he did, he yielded without understanding the consequences. He was never in a position to be the provocateur, never in charge of his decisions. It was Antistius Petrus and his perverse appetites that controlled this affair. From the first day of their meeting, it was Petrus who cajoled, manipulated, and arranged for this injustice.

"We call Clodius Galarius to speak."

Clodius stood in the aisle facing the emperor and judges.

"Tell us," Arrianus said. "Tell us what you knew of your younger brother's fall into corruption."

"Sires," Galarius said, bowing to the emperor. "My younger brother was a tender youth. With great affection, he tended our dogs and his parakeet. He helped our mother with small tasks, not because our servants couldn't manage but because he enjoyed the duties and his time with her. He was sensitive and clever. His tutors remarked on his *ingenium*, his natural skill for learning. His *grammaticus* praised his skill at poetry and his quick grasp of Greek. By all expectations, Melonius would have been an important and talented citizen of Rome.

"We had no reason to think that his extended visits to Neapolis had to do with more than his desire to follow the teachings of Virgil who, as you know, made that city his home. Yet it was there that he fell prey to Antistius Petrus. We know from his visits home that his speech became more, er, florid and his manner more affected. We attributed this to his natural tendency to absorb whatever surrounded him, and we knew that Neapolis suffered a strong Greek influence. We urged him to return to Rome, but he wouldn't hear of it.

"His residence with our cousin and benefactor, Acilius Pictor, offered him the finest of houses and a watchful eye. We say nothing to besmirch the name of Ancilius Pictor. He is of strong moral character and upholds the respect for tradition and a firm comprehension of *pietas* that we expect of all Roman men. Just as our father taught Melonius from the earliest age, Acilius continued the righteous upbringing suited to young men of our standing.

"We didn't know until after Melonius' death that he had convinced Acilius that he had been invited to stay at the house of a noted rhetor, one Piscius Curio, who lived at Herculaneum. We later learned this was a deception, that the house where he took residence in that city was none other than the villa of Antistius Petrus. It was within the shelter of that home that this sordid matter reached its culmination and became the shame that caused him to take his life."

The crowd rippled with whispers. It seemed to Caerwin that sizeable gaps existed in this narrative. She was relieved to see that as Clodius turned to retake his seat, Praetextus stood.

"Sire," he said, bowing to the emperor, "I have questions for this witness."

"Proceed."

Praetextus faced Clodius across the wide aisle. "Clodius, you failed to give any specific dates for the actions of your brother once he traveled to Neapolis. Can you tell us his age at that time?"

"He had gained fourteen years."

"And I understand that at the time of his death, he was eighteen. Is that right?"

"Yes."

"So for four years, he lived outside the observation of you or anyone in your immediate family."

"Except for visits home."

"During those visits, did you notice any hint of unhappiness or distress?"

"No, but..."

"For all you and the rest of your family could determine, he lived well."

"Yes."

"At what time did he leave the residence of your cousin to live in Herculaneum?"

Clodius' cheeks took on a red flush. "I don't know exactly. It's been many years."

"Can you not remember if it was soon after he moved to Neapolis or closer to the time of his death?"

"It was some time after he moved there, perhaps a year or so."

"I'm surprised that you don't have a more specific date in mind. You've alleged that his suicide resulted from the shame he suffered at the hands of Antistius Petrus while he was still under the protection of his *bulla*. Yet you are uncertain when this abuse occurred. Do you agree that at some point during those years, a boy takes on the *toga virilis* as a sign of his coming of age? Was this not a ceremony you attended?

"It was," Clodius said. "The summer of Caligula's first year. It was a time of celebration."

"Do you agree that when a boy takes on the status of manhood, he is responsible for making his own decisions about his sexual activity? And if so, do you agree that even if a young man chooses a path that leads to infamy, he has the legal right to do so?"

"No, I don't agree, not when he's led to that choice by influence that began while he was still a boy."

"You assert that Antistius Petrus influenced Melonius while he was still under the *bulla*. Yet the evidence presented in support of this allegation fails entirely. You don't know what age he was when he first met Petrus or what influence Petrus had on him at that time. Isn't it possible that like many clever young men, Melonius embraced the Greek tradition before he ever met Petrus? Isn't it possible that he took a liking to Petrus and enticed him to a sexual relationship that suited them both?"

Clodius' face became even redder as Praetextus pressed his point. "No!" he shouted. "He wouldn't have shamed our family. He was coerced."

"That's what you want to believe, but you have no evidence." Praetextus faced the judges and emperor. "In our previous hearings, I ventured the guess that Melonius might have become an object of interest to our previous emperor Caligula or before that, Tiberius. We argued that the palaces of both these former rulers were rumored to be places of sexual excess. The confiscation of Antistius Petrus' gold mines by Caligula seemed to support the notion that Caligula desired Melonius and used the infamy of his relationship with Petrus to justify his seizure of this wealth and to force Petrus' suicide. Subsequently, as a result of the emperor's abuse, Melonius took his own life.

"This was a theory. We admit we had no evidence in support of these ideas. Our objective was to show that without a direct line of evidence, the claim of Clodius holds no merit. We still abide by that point. But, if you please, with new information, we pursue a different theory, one that has come to our attention in these last few days."

Praetextus cleared his throat. "Let me ask you, Clodius, in what context did you first decide to press your cause against the Antistius estate?"

"The matter disturbed our whole family. Why would we not seek recourse?"

"Yes, of course, but you took up the cause six years after the death. Why wait?"

"Well, we, uh, we discussed it at length," Clodius said. "We still grieved."

"Do you remember what first caused you to think of such a thing?"

"Not exactly?"

"Might I prod your memory, sir? I take it that you and Helvius Sura are friends."

"We are."

"Might I ask if he suggested such an action to you?"

"He has supported our decision, if that's what you mean," Clodius said.

"That's not what I asked," Praetextus said. "Did he suggest that seeking damages from the Antistius estate might compensate for your loss of Melonius?"

"I can't say," Clodius said.

"Can't or won't?" Praetextus said. He turned to the judge's table. "Might you instruct this witness that he must answer the question to the best of his ability?"

Maximus frowned. "Need I remind you of your oath, Clodius Galarius?"

"No, sir. Yes, he encouraged me. He saw how grieved we were. He tried to help."

"When did his 'help' occur—shortly after the death?"

"Some time after, a year or more, I think."

The emperor raised his hand. "Counsel, I weary of this. What point do you make?"

"The point is that we have reason to believe that neither Melonius nor Petrus took their own lives but instead were the victims of a clever plan conceived and executed under a scheme of Petrus' wife Tulla."

A buzz ran through the crowd at his statement.

"We believe that she further pursued her vengeance against her husband Petrus by planting a seed in her daughter's mind and through her in Helvius Sura that would grow into their belief that Antistius Marcellus should be forced to suffer the consequences of his father's relationship with Melonius."

Praetextus pivoted and took a document from Manlius, which he waved in the air. "What I have here is a very interesting statement by Antistius Petrus, written in his hand and attested by Cipius as his legal counsel. It states, in part—let me read here,

My suspicions have increased that my wife Fenius Tulla attempts to bring about my death. After an extreme illness, I have begun using tasters to sample my food when I eat in her company, which I avoid whenever possible. I can't say in what manner she will make further attempts, but I want it known that if I die in mysterious circumstance, she is the cause.

Caerwin gasped, her reaction joining that of most observers as a hubbub erupted. She quickly sought to view Tulla, but the woman no longer remained where she had last seen her. Helvius Sura sat with a stony expression on his face.

"What are you saying, counsel?" Claudius said. "Get on with it."

"What I'm saying is that Petrus and Melonius suffered this woman's jealousy in their admittedly scandalous relationship. She had cause and means to hire spies and assassins to carry out her wishes. When she had achieved her primary goal of their murder, she then hatched her next plan which was to disenfranchise Marcellus from the Antistius estate so that she and her daughters would be the sole heirs. It was an easy task to plant anger and greed in the heart of her son-in-law, Helvius Sura, and to propel him to his careful advice to his close friend Clodius Galarius."

The emperor shook his head. "If all this could be true and she conceived such an immoral plan to enrich herself, why would she embark on a route that would deprive the estate of a million *sestertii*?"

Praetextus shrugged then gestured eloquently. "I can only say that for a woman spurned, vengeance is a mightier reward than wealth. She held no affection for Marcellus, whom we've learned was not her child but instead foisted upon her in a loveless marriage. She had reason to harbor deep and abiding anger."

"Indeed," Claudius said. He turned to Clodius. "Can you say when or what was said by Helvius Sura in this matter?"

"I cannot sir," Clodius said.

"I want to hear from Helvius," Claudius said. "Is he present?"

"I am." Helvius stood and made his way to the aisle as Praetextus and Clodius took their seats.

"Tell me what you heard, if anything, from your mother-in-law on the matter before the court," Claudius said.

"Sir, I assure you that I know nothing of any murderous plan by Tulla. I know what my wife Matina has told me, that Marcellus was born of a slave woman named Rhian and that Tulla had been sold into marriage by her father in an arrangement by Antistius Labeo. Tulla made it clear to Matina that she had no role in this deception, and that she thought it a crime against the state. I share that opinion no matter what legal maneuvers Petrus and Cipius engineered."

"Spare me," Claudius said. "That matter is settled. Did you have any agreement with Clodius that if he won his suit, that any amount of the settlement would come back to you or your wife or Tulla?"

Helvius cleared his throat. "He offered a modest sum in exchange for my trouble," he said.

"How modest?"

The room became so still that Caerwin could almost hear Helvius' heart beating. He looked as if he wished to drop through the floor. She grinned. How clever of the emperor.

"A hundred thousand *sestertii*," Helvius said quietly.

"A tenth of the claim. Modest in relative terms, then," Claudius said. "What of this would be shared with Tulla?"

"Half, sir," Helvius said.

"Half. And what of the rest of the estate? Once deprived of its guardianship by Antistius Marcellus, would not the shipping concerns and the wheat farms and the various rural estates and homes all fall under our rules of inheritance, with division among the two daughters and Tulla?"

Helvius shifted uncomfortably. Caerwin twisted side to side to see what expression marked the face of Marcellus, but she couldn't see him. Her heart was leaping out of her chest.

"I-I don't know, yes, I suppose it would."

"Are you telling me, standing here in our court of justice, that you never once considered that a full one-third of this sizeable wealth might fall into your hands?"

"I might have…"

"I'm staggered by your arrogance," the emperor snapped. "Take your seat, Helvius Sura."

Claudius consulted with Opilio and Maximus. Vedius and a few other jurists stepped forward to participate in the hasty conference. Caerwin's hands clenched so tightly her nails cut her palms.

Finally the emperor stood and settled his gaze on Clodius and his counsel. "The waters of this matter have become too muddy for further deliberation. As the defendant's able *causidici* has pointed out, there are multiple reasons to question whether Antistius Petrus served any role in Melonius' death. Our courts are busy with matters far more pressing than this. We cannot discount the voice of Jupiter who finds favor in Antistius Marcellus. Evidence is thin to prosecute Tulla, wife of Petrus, for conspiring to have him and his alleged lover murdered, but I personally will ask a jurist to explore charges that may be developed. As to the matter brought before this court, that the Antistius estate should pay damages for the death of Clodius Melonius, it is dismissed."

Shouts erupted across the packed chamber at the emperor's words. Excitement thrilled through Caerwin. Everyone around her exchanged jubilant comments and shook hands. She lingered as the crowd dispersed, watching as one after another man came to Marcellus to express congratulations. Finally she waited on the basilica steps for him to emerge.

Blinking in the midday sun, Marcellus cast his gaze around until he spotted her. In a few quick strides, he caught her around the waist and embraced her.

"You have saved me," he said. "You and Kensa. Without Kensa's advice, I wouldn't have known. Without you finding her, where would I be?"

"The gods sent me a dream. I only acted on it," she said. "How did you find the letter so quickly?"

"Manlius' clerks found it—he didn't mention who found it, but I expect he will. I join him and the others at the baths."

"Vedius, too?"

"Vedius—yes. He and I—there is much to say, but now isn't the time. I can hardly contain myself."

She had never seen his smile so glorious. In the bright sunlight, the sharp features of his face and the curve of his lips drew her touch. She leaned up and kissed his cheek then traced the curve of his jaw with her finger.

"Would that I could be there," she said.

He frowned. "No."

She laughed. "I obey your order, sir. I'll take the baths nearer home, one just for women, and then rest until you return home. Perhaps I'll lie naked on my bed and touch myself while thinking of you."

His face darkened and his nostril flared. "Sorceress! Shall I bathe in the company of all these men with my *mentula* stiff?"

"I'll think of that as I lie on my bed," she said, grinning and turning away.

She didn't look back to see whether Vedius joined Marcellus as soon as her back was turned. Her instinct said he did. Her lunch and bath only made her more agitated. By the time she returned to the *domus*, a headache pounded her temples. After Fimbria took down her hair, Caerwin threw herself back onto her pillows already knowing that sleep would not come. She flopped from side to side and rubbed her throbbing head until her hair tangled.

She threw open the shutters to the warm afternoon and paced the length of her room. What about Vedius? Since the court's decisions came down in favor of Marcellus, she could only assume that Vedius had not done what he threatened. Did that mean Marcellus and Vedius... She couldn't form the thought.

Yes, she had urged him to please Vedius, to do what he must to secure his future. Now she wondered how she could have been so foolish. Did she not realize how much it would affect her?

But then, why did it matter if they touched each other or even coupled as men do? Hadn't he taken Tatian? Antius? Silverus? He had told her clearly that she was the first woman he ever cared for.

He had no choice. How would she feel at this moment if she hadn't urged Marcellus to appease Vedius and Marcellus had lost his cause? There would be no future for her.

Do I trust him as he asked? Do I believe he loves me? If he loves me, can he not also love another?

She poured a cup of wine and drank it halfway. Madness threatened if she stayed in this room another moment. Pulling on an old faded *stola* and her sandals, she rushed through the *peristylium* to the gardens outside.

The cool air lifted her hair and comforted her forehead as she walked along the paths. The gardeners left nothing undone, not even a spare blade of grass that needed pulling or a dead leaf to remove. At the far corner, a small fountain splashed under the watchful eye of Priapus, a small bronze likeness of the erotic god with his oversized *mentula*. His face spread in a lusty grin as he held up his ewer from which the water poured forth.

She sat on the nearby bench with her head in her hands. Her worries needed a speedy resolution. There was no one she could talk to about this matter without risking harm to Marcellus. If he and Vedius had become lovers, if after all these years their affections had rekindled… But in reality, those affections had never died. Marcellus admitted he still cared for Vedius. She groaned and tugged on her hair as if she could pull her jealousy and worry from her head.

She had no choice. If he loved Vedius, if they resumed their early passion, she could only accept it. The thought of Marcellus in an embrace with Vedius—the imagined scene burned her cheeks with jealousy.

Yet…dared she admit that the idea also provoked her? If she watched them, if she joined them…

"No!" She stood up abruptly and gasped when she turned to see Marcellus standing there, an amused and lustful expression on his face.

"Do you say 'no' to me when I have not yet touched you?" he said. "What phantoms beset you, set your hair awry, torture your mind?"

He said it gently, joking, as he closed his hand over her unruly mane and pulled her close. His lips drank from hers as if a man dying of thirst and she the only drink. Her knees softened and she sagged against him.

"I hoped to find you in your bed as you promised, naked and wet," he said, muttering close to her ear.

"I couldn't rest," she said. "I must ask. What of Vedius?"

He wrapped his arm around her waist and began walking back to the house. "Not even one day to celebrate before new worries arise?"

"Not new," she said. "Vedius has haunted our footsteps since the messenger, has he not?"

"Indeed," he said. "So why today of all days?"

"How could I not question his role in your success? He made threats. Sigilis and everyone said that to win, you should gain Vedius' favor."

"Wait until we gain my bedchamber," he said quietly. "The house has many ears."

He stopped by the kitchen to retrieve a meat pie from Gordianus' secret cupboard.

"Not such a good hiding place with you and Sigilis both knowing of it," she said. "What will be left?"

"Nothing," he said, smiling as he consumed the crusty snack. "No food shall be wasted. Besides, I'm starving."

"Did you not eat lunch?"

"I did, but that was hours ago." He closed the door to his bedchamber and poured wine for them both then opened the garden doors. Light filled the room and he shifted their chairs to face the outdoors.

"In a few months, the air will be too hot in Rome. By then, we should be happily settled at Monte Rosa, my villa near Neapolis."

"Not at Herculaneum?"

"No. I'm placing that villa on the market. Too much has happened there."

She leaned back and sipped her wine. "Vedius had good memories of it."

"My father died there. Whether by his own hand or the paid henchmen of Tulla, his life ended on those floors."

"Yes, sorry, I didn't mean…"

"Before we arrived here, I had always envisioned a life at Monte Rosa." He waved his hand at the mural covering the wall with its peaceful herds on green slopes and rows of vines. "Much as my father loved it, he spent little time there. Tulla resented any time away from Rome. But for us children, it was a paradise of cooler air and a slower pace. Kensa and other servants brought us there. We were free of our parents and their constant strife. Flocks of chickens roamed the grounds. We had hunting dogs to follow around and the caretaker was a friendly man. I don't know if he's still there. Maybe the place has fallen into disrepair. These are matters I must attend now that my greatest threat is past."

"About Vedius," she began.

"I don't wish to think of Vedius. I wish to think of you." He stood and grabbed her up against him. "Each morning I wake from dreams of making love. Dreams aren't enough. The Senate has deliberated on the emperor's new orders for concessions to ship owners. It's been approved. That means we only must accomplish a few tasks to make you a citizen. Do you know how I long for that day?"

"Likely no more than I long for it," she said.

"Each day you grow more beautiful. There's a glow about you. I didn't think it was possible to love you more. Just earlier in the garden, when I saw you sitting there with the sun setting your hair on fire, I could not move. I'm shaking even now, my need is so great."

"Then let me taste you," she said. "The day has been your triumph, two days of triumph and little celebration."

He groaned as her hand slid down his abdomen. "Tie me if you must taste me. I can't restrain myself."

She laughed. "You tied instead of me?"

"Yes, please, take me in your mouth. But don't let me loose or I'll surely overwhelm your every defense and take you where you stand."

"Shall I leave you tied, then?" She stroked him through his clothing, unable to refrain from making him suffer. "As soon as your bonds are loosened, won't you still overwhelm me?"

"Oh, you play the tyrant well. Tie me," he said, turning away to dig out the rope from a nearby cabinet. He held it toward her and backed up to the bedpost. "Quickly before I regret my restraint."

She stood on the bed to gain enough height to tie his hands above his head. With his toga unwrapped, she tugged his tunic above his waist, exposing his eager cock. Veins already stood along its length, testament to his hopeless condition.

"I wake like this," he muttered. "I must take the cold plunge at the baths before I'm fit to join the others. It's a torture only you can address."

She pulled the last knot on the rope and tested her work. "Can you free yourself?"

He jerked against the ropes as she watched. The gods, what a spectacular sight. More than the sea or the Alps, this man was the supreme marvel of the gods' handiwork. The tendons of his arms strained and his chest muscles bulged as he pulled. He succeeded only in tightening the knots.

"No," he said. Flushed, his face seemed to swell as she toyed with him through his tunic. She pulled it higher to expose his chest and tucked its length into the neckline.

"Mm," she said, licking the tips of his nipples. "I shall enjoy this."

"By the almighty gods, don't drag this out. I'm in pain."

"Yes, yes," she said, sucking one nipple past her teeth and chewing lightly. "You're in pain. I too suffer, if you remember." She stepped back and raised her tunic to press her fingers between her legs. "I too wake each morning in need of your touch. The need only grows as the hours pass."

She glanced up with a smile to see the dark fury gathering in his eyes. "You see?" she said, holding her fingers to his nose. "Is that what you think of?"

In a quick move, his lips fastened over her fingers and sucked. A spire of need laced down her stomach and caught between her thighs. The rough texture of his tongue could have been there, so acutely did she feel his caress. She backed away, determined to stay in control of her appetites.

"Temptress," he whispered. "I beg you…"

She put her fingertip to the tip of his cock. The heat burned her skin. "This? Is this where it hurts?"

"You know it is," he said.

She whisked her tunic over her head and ran her hands over her breasts and down her sides. Her nipples had long since come to hard points. She pulled a chair nearby and placed one foot on it so she could expose herself to his view. Temptation and desire mingled as she stroked her clitoris. The little hooded bud grew in size as she played until it poked outside the lips of her labia. As she teased herself with a finger, her juices flowed, lubricating her motions.

"Ohh, I think I might die," she said. "Why isn't your mouth here?"

"I promise you, you will suffer of this," he said hoarsely. "If you care for me at all…"

"I do care," she said, stepping close so that her nipples grazed his chest. "I want your attention fully concentrated. No other thoughts but me."

"I couldn't be more concentrated," he said. "For the sake of the gods…"

"You mean for the sake of Marcellus."

She pulled the chair closer and sat, leaning forward to touch the tip of his cock with her tongue. Hot, smooth, the foreskin tasted like him. She licked lightly around the rim and grinned at his sharp intake of breath.

More light licking and little nibbles took her up and down the length of his shaft, over the knotted flesh of his sac, even to the quivering muscle of his thighs and abdomen.

"Caerwin," he said. It was a plea, a demand.

She glanced up and smiled. "I love you."

He'd begun moving involuntarily by the time she finally took him in her mouth. She seized the base of the organ and brought as much of the length into her mouth as she could manage. Chills ran down her arms as the massive prick coursed over her tongue.

That faint moaning sounds issued from his throat, that his body shivered, none of that penetrated her intense pleasure as the tumescent column surged to the back of her throat. Her eyes rolled back as she sucked and licked, plunging back and forth as his breath grew harsher.

He was close. She sat back. "What do I win for pleasing you?" she said.

He swore. "Don't play with me," he warned. "I will make you suffer."

She laughed. "I didn't know I would enjoy this so much, the mighty Roman warrior tied and defenseless against a feeble *Brittunculi*."

"I swear to you…"

"I want to make it last."

"It's lasted long enough."

The edge in his deep voice almost scared her. What would he do to her? She couldn't think of it. All she could think of was the sight of him with his muscled thighs straining under the condition of his cock. His chest heaved as he tugged on the rope.

"I feel almost guilty," she said, leaning forward again to suck him into her mouth. For a few moments, she took only the enlarged head within her lips. The flesh had turned dark purple and droplets leaked from the tip.

"It does look a bit painful," she said, licking the tip. "Is this better?"

She took him swiftly to the back of her throat. His hips lunged forward. She grabbed his buttocks and buried him to the greatest depth she could manage, working her tongue against him.

With his groan, his seed began to spurt down her throat. She rode him to the last tremor. Shaking, with a last gentle suck, she let him free of her mouth.

Relieved of its dark color, the organ remained stiff as she backed away.

"Untie me," he said in a shaky voice.

"Is it safe?"

"What would I do?" he said. "I'm relieved. I'm in your debt."

"I don't trust you," she said, wrapping herself against him and leaning up for a kiss. "Do you taste yourself on my lips?"

"Yes, vixen." He managed a half-hearted smile. "Come now, my hands are asleep."

She climbed up on the bed and tugged at the knots. "If your hands sleep, they're the only part of you so doing. The rest of you has been fully awake."

The rope fell away and he gripped his hands together. "Awake and tormented by a wicked temptress."

"Did you not enjoy it?"

"Yes, yes, I enjoyed it, hated it, suffered. Is that what you wanted?"

"I wanted to give you something you wouldn't forget. Something no one else can give you."

He pulled her into his arms. "You made a success, I assure you of that."

"Mm, I love your temper."

"You do?"

"Marcellus, what…"

He lifted her onto the bed and before she could react, he turned her face down and fastened her wrists to the bedposts. She kicked as he grabbed first one ankle and then the other. He tied them as well.

"You said…"

"I warned you," he said.

"But…"

"You've wanted this."

"I'll scream."

"I don't care who hears. Let them burn in the flames of Tartarus."

"Wait…" The thought of his discipline sent fire streaking through her. Her clitoris throbbed. Damp gathered between her thighs.

"Not waiting. Hopefully you'll enjoy this as much as I will."

He wrapped a scarf over her mouth then retrieved the familiar lash. He held it for her to see and she eyed the leather strands with sudden apprehension. He looked angry. Had she tormented him too much?

She bit her lip. The pain always came first, the slow burn that at some point switched over to pleasure. It had been so long. Could she endure the punishment?

He began lightly, dropping and dragging the lash over her shoulders and arms. She twisted and moaned into the gag, eager for him to bring her to complete submersion. Too many thoughts crowded her mind, distracting her from this man who held her in his thrall.

Slowly the lash began to heat her back. Soon the skin on her buttocks took fire as if coals had been laid there. From her ankles to her neck, he wielded the wicked lash until her breath gasped and her moans rolled continuously. Her nipples stood at stiff knots against the bedclothes and her clitoris thrummed with each beat of her heart.

She laughed uncontrollably as he released her bonds, turned her, and fastened her face up. Sweat glistened on his forehead as he bent over her. "My savage queen," he whispered, kissing her cheeks and forehead as he fastened a gag over her mouth.

She lay spread open before him whimpering in anticipation. He loomed over her like a stallion in rut, his cock darkly magnificent despite his release only a short time before. His hands soothed her from face to feet, luxurious long warm strokes that only drove her fever higher. Light feathery touches circled her vulva but didn't appease the spots that longed for embrace. His tongue licked at the very tips of her nipples, causing her chest to rise up toward him in desperation.

He didn't speak. The intensity of his attention alternately frightened and thrilled her. The lash became a being in its own right, finding her most secret places and bestowing its fiery rain. He spared nothing, not the tender flesh of her swollen breasts, not her delicate exposed center leaking with need. She writhed. Tears streamed from her eyes. Her screams died in the twisted cloth over her mouth and still he flicked the leather strands.

In a sudden cry of need, he tossed the lash aside and bent to lick her tortured flesh. First teasing her nipples, his kisses made their way across her stomach and thighs before finally landing on her agonized vulva. As his lips clamped over her distended clitoris, her orgasm exploded in wave after wave of tremors that shook her whole body.

"I want to take you," he said.

"Yes, yes," she said, but her words didn't escape the gag.

The tip of his cock nestled between her thighs, prodding here and there, each contact setting off another shattering orgasm. He loosed the gag then tucked his elbows on either side of her shoulders and held her in his arms as he leaned forward to kiss her. As his tongue plunged into her mouth, he drove his cock past the sensitized lips and all the way to the depths of her womb.

Her muted scream scorched her throat. Her hips rose up to meet him. It had been so long. He was so big. Each stroke set off a dazzling spark of intense pleasure.

Her eyes flickered open to see his face, this man she loved with all her heart. He smiled down at her.

"Mine," he said hoarsely.

He fucked her a long time. She ceased to think. This was all that mattered.

She felt him growing larger, hotter, and then suddenly he withdrew. Kneeling between her legs, he seized himself and jerked until his seed started to fly. Long white streams landed across her belly and breasts. With a grunt, he thrust forward as he delivered the last of his gift.

She swallowed and licked her lips. "I need my hands," she said, tugging on the rope.

He quickly untied her. All she could think of was the creamy liquid anointing her body. She rubbed his seed across her breasts, over the tender flesh between her legs.

"Everything you do incites me," he whispered, leaning down to kiss her.

"Why haven't you done this before?"

"Seed knows its way," he said. "One drop early and a child is made. Today I didn't care. I had to feel you around me."

He wet a towel and bathed her, then coated her front and back with soothing lotion. Her eyelids drooped as his big hands massaged her body. Marcellus. His bed.

"Are you harmed?" he said, nestling beside her.

"I'm perfect," she said, unable to stay awake one instant longer.

Chapter Thirteen

Marcellus paced in the Tabularium hallway outside the clerk's office. Caerwin sat watching him, twisting her fingers together. Sunlight beamed past tall arches, lighting the long hallway framed in carefully hewn gray stone. If she wanted to stand at one of the arches to look out, below she would see the full length of the Forum and its busy traffic.

Clerks and administrators emerged from office doorways, bustled down the hall, or passed by in groups of two or three quietly discussing their business. Caerwin hardly understood this industry of men who wrote things on scrolls or wax tablets. This seemed to be the heart of the Roman Empire, this recording of words and ideas, agreements, birth records, laws, tax records, contracts. Marcellus had rattled off a long list as they journeyed here this morning.

If the clerks didn't write them, they read them or copied them or put them away in some specific order, or searched for them. The enormous three story building perched just below the Temple of Jupiter on the hillside that dropped down to the Forum, imposing its inscrutable timeless mission over the entire population. She had peered up at it many times as she passed by shops or, nearly a month ago, on their last sojourn at the basilica for the court's judgment on the Clodius matter. But inside these towering walls, she felt small and foreign.

What would it mean to be a citizen of Rome? Much as she wished for an end to the enforced chastity between her and Marcellus... well, they had become increasingly inventive in ways to circumvent precise abstinence. But his agitation only grew each time he touched her, and she wanted nothing more than his worries behind him. His promise of an idyllic country life had taken ever stronger appeal as her belly became more rounded.

How much longer would it be before he noticed? Her breasts had become heavier. The bones of her hips no longer protruded as clearly—she had gained weight. She alternately felt languid and sleepy or driven and energetic. At every turn, she wanted something to eat.

She chewed her lip, aware of how angry he would be when he learned the secret she'd been keeping. If only this task before them could be ended. She glanced up at the sound of his voice. Sigilis had arrived.

"Neptune smiled on us," Sigilis said. He smiled at her as she joined them. "The winds brought us north without heavy weather. It will take more good fortune to find favorable wind on our return."

"How does she ride?"

"Like a queen." Sigilis winked at Caerwin. "Like her namesake."

"I haven't told her," Marcellus said. "Already she takes airs. Exerts herself against me. I am rethinking my plan."

"Are you talking about me?" Caerwin said hotly.

The men laughed.

"Who else?" Sigilis said. "There is only one woman in Marcellus' world. Surely you know that by now."

She crossed her arms. "What I think I know and what remains to be known are as far apart as Britannia and Rome."

Marcellus pulled her against his side. "We are naming our newest *liburna* in your honor. It shall be 'Regina.'" He smiled at her frown. "The word means 'Queen' in your language. Your carved likeness will lead us at the ship's prow. The goddess Salacia will watch over us from the stern."

She thought he teased her but then she saw the serious expression on Sigilis' face and knew it was true. "My likeness?"

"Your head and chest," Sigilis said. "I would have preferred the craftsman model his work from you directly. It would have been the most favored figurehead in all the merchant fleets. But as the figurehead is often spared of clothing, I feared Marcellus would have the man's stones in his hand before the first hour of work commenced."

"Your position goes to your head," Marcellus said sourly to Sigilis. "I may change my mind about this sale."

"Sale?" Caerwin looked at Marcellus then Sigilis. "Why is everything you speak of so mystifying? I've never seen a figurehead. Who is Salacia? What sale?" She stamped her foot. "Why am I involved in something I know nothing about?"

"He's a man obsessed," Sigilis said.

"Salacia is Neptune's queen, goddess of the sea," Marcellus said. "A beautiful nymph who eluded his advances until he made her his. She's crowned with seaweed and wears fishermen's nets in her hair."

Caerwin suppressed her flattered smile and huffed. "This is what you think of me, that my hair smells of fisherman's nets?"

Sigilis' shouted laugh echoed off the high ceiling. "Well played. She matches you at every turn."

The growl deep in Marcellus' chest promised Caerwin she would suffer for her frivolity. She grinned up at him, eager for his punishment. His mouth twitched.

"What sale?" she repeated.

"I'm selling Sigilis a ship," Marcellus said. "Unless he provokes me further. Nothing is yet carved in stone, old friend. Don't press your luck."

"Hardly luck at the price I'll pay," Sigilis said. "But better that than the price she'll pay." He nodded at her with a knowing look.

"What price? Marcellus—what is going on?"

"Sigilis can't rest unless he stirs up trouble. It's a wonder *Antistius Naviportans* still functions." He took her shoulders in a firm grip. "There is no price. Today I sign over a ship to your ownership, just as I sign over one to Sigilis. He pays a token price, nothing near to its true value, a concession I make in the dubious assumption that he's worth more than his wages. You pay nothing."

"He says 'nothing,'" Sigilis said. "This is but one more tie with which he binds you to him."

"I know nothing about owning a ship," she said.

"Which is why Sigilis earns a discount on his price. He will do whatever needs to be done on behalf of your ship."

"What ship is it?"

"The new ten-thousander," Sigilis said, his face suddenly serious. "She's a beauty, well-designed and carefully crafted. She'll make you proud."

She grasped Marcellus' arm. "You would give me this ship?"

"I would," he said, beaming at her. "She's a match for you, strong, capable of whatever challenges face her. I've already given her a name. It's not a traditional name, not the name of a woman, but I think it will please you."

"Not traditional, not suitable," Sigilis grumbled. "I can't change his mind."

"Must you constantly prick me?" she exclaimed. "Tell me now."

"Cornovii," Marcellus said, his face instantly sober. "I name it Cornovii."

Tears filled Caerwin's eyes. "Cornovii," she repeated. An enormous lump formed in her throat. She could say nothing else.

"May she fight through the sea as valiantly as her namesake defended her homeland. You have become all things Cornovii to me," Marcellus said. "I could name the ship nothing else. She's yours."

"I…I'm unequal to your gift. I have much to learn," she said, snuffling. "Who can teach me what I desire to know? What are my duties as the owner of a ship? How do you track the loading and offloading, the formation of a crew? Who will be the *trierarchus*?" A thousand questions crowded her thoughts. "I must know how it looks inside and out."

"None of this is your concern," Marcellus said. "You own it in name only. Leave the rest to me and to Sigilis."

"But I want to know," she said.

"Her hair threatens to ignite," Sigilis said, slapping Marcellus on the shoulder. "You'll have no rest on this until she stands on the foredeck with wind in her hair and the *trierarchus* under her command. I can see it now."

"Can we simply make it through the morning?" Marcellus said.

"What are we waiting for?" Sigilis said.

"Another man. Vedius," Marcellus said, nodding in the direction behind her.

"Vedius?" Caerwin looked around to see Vedius approaching.

"Sorry I'm late," Vedius said. "The emperor claims my days and I live to please him. I have only a short time before he expects my return."

Marcellus introduced him to Sigilis. "And you've met Caerwin."

Vedius looked at her. She lifted her chin and met his stare. As before, unspoken volumes weighted the exchange. He seemed less hostile than previous times, but under such close scrutiny from Marcellus, perhaps he disguised his true feelings. In such a position as his, Vedius no doubt had become highly skilled in keeping his inner thoughts and feelings to himself. She had yet to extract any explanation from Marcellus about whatever arrangement he and Vedius had reached. Her inquisitive stare uncovered no hint.

"Have you discussed my request with Claudius?" Marcellus said.

"I could not press him," Vedius said, shifting his gaze back to Marcellus. "I had to wait until the opportune moment."

"Meaning?" Marcellus' jaw twitched.

"Meaning—he waved his hand as if of all matters, this concerned him least. I secured his signature without further discussion."

"The gods, man, you had me twisting in the wind," Marcellus said. "What now?"

Vedius grinned. "You fare well in the wind, it seems. At full sail, you travel where few else go. But come, I've no more time to enjoy watching you dangle. The papers are in the hands of your men Antius and Tatian."

Vedius escorted the group to a nearby door. Inside, the room stretched along the length of the building to tall windows covered in glass. Ample sunlight illuminated rows of men working diligently at long tables. The scrape of pens and the murmur of voices filled the room. Caerwin surveyed the room in wonder.

Tatian hurried up one aisle to greet them. Caerwin spotted Antius still at a table.

"I've copied the sample you gave me," Tatian said to Vedius. He pressed the parchment sheet flat on a nearby table, quickly reading the bill of sale. "Two of them. One bill of sale is granted to Abito Comes Sigilis for the *liburna* under the name of *Aquila*. The other is granted to Caerwin, a ten-thousander under the name *Cornovii*." He glanced up at Marcellus. "Is that right?"

He nodded.

"A ten thousander?" Vedius said. His eyebrows rose. "Cornovii? Do they sail under your colors?"

"Of course," Marcellus said. "We are one fleet." He turned again to Tatian. "Where are the documents stating our partnership?"

Tatian shuffled the pages and extracted another sheet. "Here. The terms you stated."

Antius arrived with still more parchment. Marcellus read the document specifying the details of the partnership then handed it to Sigilis, who pulled up a chair to read through it.

Caerwin studied the bill of sale, unfamiliar with some of the words. Why would she question it? She trusted him.

"Does this say that in exchange for your ship, I must bow to your every command?" she said. "Because if those are your terms…"

"Those are my terms," he said sternly.

"Where do I sign?" she said, grinning.

Antius provided an ink pot and reed pen. Marcellus signed first then Caerwin crafted her name in Roman letters. All the watchful eyes made her nervous and ink leaked to the page in a round blob.

"Don't fuss over that," Tatian whispered. "Just relax and remember what I've shown you."

Relieved by his encouragement, she finished the last letter with a flourish.

Sigilis returned with the partnership papers. "I have no complaint," he said. He handed it to Caerwin.

"Should I read it?" she asked.

"Always read before you sign," Vedius said. "It's a fundamental rule of business."

His comment set her off-balance. Did he ridicule her? "Tatian. Can you help me?"

It took several minutes as she struggled through the dense language of the contract. Tatian explained words and concepts. Her head throbbed in her effort to understand the meaning, not just what the words said, but what commitments she made in agreeing to the terms.

The contract required that she make her ship available at all times to the operations of *Antistius Naviportans*, that its upkeep, crew, and activities would fall under the management of *Antistius Naviportans*, and that she would make no arrangements regarding the ship that deviated from whatever arrangements the company made. It further stipulated that at whatever time she might wish to sell or otherwise dispose of the ship even in a will, she would grant it back to the former owner at no cost.

She seized the reed pen and signed the contract. "Nothing this says will keep me from wanting to know more about the ship," she said, handing the pen to Antius.

"You'll be welcome to board her when you visit Neapolis," Sigilis said. "I'll personally show you around."

"When that time comes, *I* will show her around," Marcellus said. "You'll have work to do."

Vedius chuckled and placed yet another parchment on the table. "Can we get this concluded?"

Marcellus picked up the page and read. His face became very serious. Without saying a word, he handed the page to her. At the top, she recognized the name *Claudius Caesar Augustus Germanicus*. Other words required Tatian's assistance. It was an imperial warrant authorizing the registration of her enfranchisement. The emperor's signature was marked by his seal.

Her citizenship.

"What do I do?" she said.

"Sign your name to it," Vedius said. "I'll give it the seal."

Again she took up the pen and this time her letters formed more smoothly. Vedius waited while Antius brought the sealing wax and melted a dollop at the end of her name. Vedius then pressed his gold ring to the wax, leaving the emperor's head in profile as it appeared on the *denarius*.

She didn't know what to say. She looked up at Vedius, trying to understand his thoughts. Her gaze shifted to Marcellus. "Is that all? After all this time and worry, is that all?"

"That's all," Marcellus said. He turned and briefly clasped Vedius to his chest. "Thank you."

Vedius gave a curt bow and turned on his heel to stride away. The rest of them walked slowly down the long corridor and out into the midday sun.

"The weather turns to spring," Antius said, straightening his back. He looked at Marcellus and grinned. "Sap rises."

~~~

Fimbria fussed with Caerwin's hair. Everything about the morning had set Caerwin's nerves humming and the tight curls forming under Fimbria's fingers only added to her irritation. Marcellus refused to consider her argument, but she knew she was right. Their union had long since been consummated.

"This is an absurdity," she complained, popping another grape in her mouth.

"It's what he wishes," Fimbria said. "Now sit still."

"Why? That's what I don't understand."

"You said he had tried to make you as a Roman lady from the first, did you not? The clothing, the hair, the grooming?" Fimbria patted another curl in place.

"Yes, even more absurd. He gave Senna an impossible task. And in a legion fortress!" She laughed. "It's even more ridiculous now that I look back on it."

"Yet here you are about to become his bride. In Rome. In the tradition of Roman citizens. He has worked a miracle."

"He's a stubborn arrogant man," Caerwin said. "He bends the world to his suiting."

A sharp knock at the door sounded then Clivia stuck her head in. "All is prepared," she said. She stepped inside and closed the door behind her. "The sacrifice has been made and the *auspex* arrives with good omens. Marcellus wears holes in the floor with his pacing. Are you ready?"

"It's kind of you to host us this way," Caerwin said.

"I wanted to do it," Clivia said. "I'm ashamed of my mother. I don't quite believe she could have murdered my father, but she hasn't denied it to me. All of it makes me sad." Her hands fluttered from her hair to her *stola*. "Oh dear, I'm sorry to even mention that. At least I can give Marcellus a bit of the family he deserves."

"There," Fimbria said. "Last curl in place." She picked up the red-orange veil of silk and fastened it at the crown under a woven ring of greenery. The sheer cloth extended past Caerwin's shoulders in the back and just past her nose in front.

She wore a white tunic under her white woolen *stola*, gathered at the waist under a woolen girdle tied in the special knot of Hercules required of all proper Roman brides. Only the groom was allowed to open it. Caerwin's complaint that she was not a proper Roman bride fell on deaf ears. On her feet were slippers of the same red-orange color as the veil.

"You look beautiful," Clivia said. "The veil is the exact color of your hair. I'm so jealous."

"What will your friends say?" Caerwin said. "Do they know I'm not Roman?"

"Niger and I have said as much as needs to be said. They're happy to celebrate with us because they're our friends. Come now, are you ready?"

Caerwin nodded and Clivia opened the door. Caerwin swallowed down an unexpected rush of excitement as she walked toward the gathering at the far end of the atrium. All her life she had looked forward to her wedding day. She had spent hours spinning colorful thread from washed fleece she had dyed with her own hands, even more hours at the loom weaving the bright plaid cloth of her marriage dress, all the time imagining as young girls do how her husband would look, how marriage would be. After the death of her father, her brother Virico had comforted her that he would serve in their father's place to provide her bride gift. Their family's wealth of sheep and cattle offered a rich bequeath to her wedding partner, and in return, the groom's gift in equal value would benefit their future.

Now she married a Roman in a foreign land without kinsmen or herds.

Nothing was as it had been. Nothing that she had expected could ever come to pass. Not only had she come to love a Roman, she had become one, even if in name only.

She would never be real Roman. She was Cornovii. She would live by Rome's rules and face life as a Roman wife, but her pot of Wrekin earth would remain her most treasured possession. Her mother's face might have become a misty memory, but she would always be her mother. The traditions she had learned all the years of her life guided her as she approached the crowd of well-wishers.

A flush heated her cheeks as her gaze settled on Marcellus where he stood at the front of the gathering. He wore a white tunic under his dazzling white toga. His dark eyes glittered as he watched her approach.

In absence of her own mother or female relative, Caerwin was led to Marcellus by Clivia. As her hands slipped into his warm grasp, he smiled at her. Her heart slammed against her ribs.

Could this be real?

The *auspex* stepped forward in his ornamented robes, raised his hands, and uttered a short prayer before delivering the favorable reading of the entrails from a sheep sacrificed in advance of the wedding. He lit the fire on the nearby altar of the *lararium* before speaking loudly with his face raised to the sky.

"Most holy Mother Ceres, Nuptial Juno, and the heavenly gods, with wedding-torches set ablaze we call High Heaven to witness this marriage. Janus, god of thresholds, openings and closings, bless this union. Keep the hearts and minds of Marcellus and Caerwin always open to each other. Juno Pronuba, goddess of matrimony, make the marriage fruitful. Jupiter, father god, keep this couple in your watchful protection."

Marcellus cleared his throat as he released her hands and placed an offering of flowers at the altar before lighting incense. She trembled as his gaze settled on her.

"By Jupiter and Juno," he said, "and all the gods and goddesses, I swear. I declare that I do willingly consent to take this woman to be my wife." His rich voice resonated through the room and sent gooseflesh down her arms. "Caerwin, I promise to love and keep you, to protect you from all harm, to enrich you as I am enriched. I swear myself as your partner in all things, never to neglect or forget the pledges we make this day, never to set you aside."

As his vows concluded, he placed a gold ring on her third finger, left hand.

As Caerwin had shown her, Fimbria stepped forward with red ribbons. Caerwin took Marcellus' hands in hers and watched as Fimbria wrapped their hands together. This was Cornovii tradition, this handfasting that would tie them forever as one.

She spoke in her native tongue. "*A Grá, thabharfainn fuil mo chroí duit. Gealltanas Síoraí.*"

Her voice quavered as memories flooded back from all the ceremonies she'd witnessed as a child. She cleared her throat and spoke more clearly as she related the rest of her vows in the language of Marcellus.

Ye are Blood of my Blood, and Bone of my Bone.
I give ye my Body, that we Two might be One.
I give ye my Spirit, 'til our Life shall be Done.

You cannot possess me for I belong to myself.
But while we both wish it, I give you that which is mine to give.
You cannot command me, for I am a free person.
But I shall serve you in those ways you require
and the honeycomb will taste sweeter coming from my hand.

Fimbria lifted the veil. Marcellus leaned toward her. Tears brimmed his eyes as he kissed her, a touch so gentle she felt only the warmth of his lips.

Shouts rose from those in attendance as the red ribbons were unwrapped from their wrists. Dazed, Caerwin smiled and accepted enthusiastic congratulations. The entourage quickly took to the street on a hasty journey to the Antistius *domus*, accompanied by musicians and boys carrying limbs of white thorn. Wedding guests told bawdy jokes to keep ill omens at bay and shouted '*talassio*', an age-old wedding cry whose meaning no one could remember. Nuts were thrown to ensure fertility.

Happiness swelled in Caerwin's chest as they hurried through the late afternoon. As the jubilant band passed shops and houses along the street, others joined with shouts and well wishes. At the entrance of the Antistius *domus*, with Rufus grinning from ear to ear, she followed Tatian's earlier instruction to anoint the doorway with olive oil. She then tied strips of woolen cloth about the door to bring good luck. Marcellus swung her up into his arms to ensure she did not trip as she entered the *domus*.

Once inside, she and Marcellus walked to the *lararium* where they touched fire and water to purify themselves and wash away any strangeness carried from outside. Others waited in the familiar atrium, among them Praetextus, Manlius, Vedius and women she thought must be their wives. Even Vedius' presence did not quench her joy. The room had been decorated with colorful ribbons and laurel branches.

Gordianus and Fimus had outdone themselves in preparing the wedding banquet. Pompeiian wine flowed like water. A first course of fresh oysters had been laid out on a long cloth-draped table that sparkled with silver goblets and polished ewers. They served winter lettuce, olives prepared in several fashions, steamed asparagus, boiled eggs, and leeks and gourds prepared with special sauces. The guests fell on the offering like ravenous beasts.

After her first cup of wine and a serving of oysters and eggs, Caerwin took a seat in the dining room and tried to relax. Clivia joined her for a time, using the opportunity to introduce first one then another of her friends. Like Clivia, these women had a lively sense of humor and casual outlook on their lives. She found herself laughing at their comments and thinking she might enjoy their company at the baths.

Soon roast pig, roast duck, tender cuts of lamb, and stuffed mullet crowded the groaning table alongside favored sausages, bread, white beans stewed with garlic and onion, three kinds of cheese, and mushrooms sautéed with garlic and butter. More singing erupted as musicians plied their flutes, lutes, and drums, and Marcellus took her hand to dance.

"I don't know how to dance by your tradition," she whispered.

"Just let me lead you, wife" he said close to her ear. His cheeks were rosy with wine and exuberance. "It's not hard."

Not difficult by his experience, perhaps. She stumbled as he moved in a sideways direction. He lifted her against him and spun around, an exercise intended as much to show her his state of arousal as to ease her worry about the dance steps.

"Oh, it seems it is hard," she said, laughing as she twisted slightly to abuse his eager cock.

"Temptress! This day is never-ending," he said. "Would it be rude to take you to my bedchamber now?"

She laughed. "You've done this to yourself. We could have joined the day I became a citizen. It is you who changed horses midstream to decide we must wait until we married."

"Never did days pass so slowly," he said. "I wanted the gods to be pleased. Everything had to be put in place. And no one can marry in February. It's bad luck."

"Thank the gods that March has arrived," she said. "Fimbria tells me June is the best month for weddings. Why didn't we wait?"

He started to say something but she leaned up to kiss him. He growled. She had begun to get the idea of his dance and matched his steps. Around them, the atrium echoed with music and laughter.

Several other couples danced as well. Even Rufus had joined, swinging Varinia from side to side.

"What other duties demand us before the night is ours?" she said.

"Only to be good hosts to our guests."

"I've seen you with Vedius. Is that his wife?"

"It is. I should introduce you," he said abruptly, taking her hand.

They found Vedius in the dining room.

"My wife, Caerwin," Marcellus said, bowing to the woman at Vedius' side. "Caerwin, this is Bettia."

Caerwin smiled in acknowledgement of the dark-haired woman. Taller than many of the Roman women she had met, Bettia had a friendly smile and a pale complexion. She wore a rose-colored stola in fabric shot through with gold thread and her hair was arranged with similar gold threads woven into the curls. An elaborate necklace featured red stones set in gold and matching earrings dangled from her ear lobes.

Despite the extravagance of her dress, Bettia greeted Cearwin with what seemed to be sincere interest. "You're of Britannia, I understand. Are many of your kind so lovely?"

"Thank you, that's very generous. I never considered it at the time and now that I wonder, I can't look to see. Many observances seem to suffer a similar obstacle, don't you think?"

"How clever of you to notice," Bettia said. "It's true that much slips through our fingers. The attention of our husbands, for example." She patted Vedius' arm. "I'm proud of what Vedius has accomplished but it seems he's become married to the emperor, so little do I see him. Before that, I became spoiled by his ready companionship during his long convalescence."

"Did he complain overmuch, as men do?" Caerwin said. "Marcellus lay abed at the fortress without waking for weeks before finally coming to his senses. Upon awakening, he immediately complained about the food the doctor ordered and grumbled that he couldn't swing a sword."

Bettia laughed. "Men are all the same. They glory in battle of any kind and suffer with inaction."

"Even battles of the mind," Vedius said. "Which I engage on a daily basis. How else do we please the gods?"

"I plan to battle the vines of my farm and the herds that roam our hillsides there. Perhaps," Marcellus said, grinning at Caerwin, "I will also battle my wife. She rarely backs down from a challenge."

"She matches you in that," Vedius said. "You seem well fitted." He lifted his cup. "A toast then, to the newly married."

They lifted their goblets together.

"Juno's blessings on you both," Vedius said. "You are my dearest friend. How can I say how much happiness I wish for you?"

Caerwin sipped her wine. Marcellus had never answered her questions about Vedius, about whether he had conceded to his demands, whether they had revived their old intimacy. Now seeing the clear emotion in Vedius' eyes, her questions all rose to the surface. She held her thought through the rest of the endless festivities, the goodbyes, the congratulations, the last servings of honeyed cakes.

Finally the night quieted. She stood in Marcellus' bedchamber drinking in his beauty as he shed his toga and stood before her in his tunic to unfasten the pins of her hair.

"What of Vedius?" she said. "No more evasion, please. I need to know."

"Not tonight," he said.

"Yes, tonight. Right now."

He sighed. "It's our marriage night."

"Marcellus."

He said nothing as he removed the last of her hair pins. His strong hands buried in her hair, pulling it loose from the confining arrangement and massaging her tormented scalp. Did he plan how to tell her things she didn't want to hear? What words to say?

"I met him often," Marcellus said, bringing her to stand before him as he wrestled with the complex knot in her belt. "The gods, I love you. Even after the wear this day has put on you, you are still the most beautiful woman the gods ever gave breath."

"You won't distract me with your flattery," she said. With the knot undone, she backed away and sat across the small table from him. "You met him often. At the baths?"

He sighed. "Yes, at the baths. And at the exercise yard, where he watched me compete against other men. That was one of our greatest pleasures, competing that way."

"Where else?"

A long silence. "We met at a room in an *insulae* he owns. We needed a private place."

"A private place," she repeated stupidly. This was worse than what she had feared. "How many times?"

"We met there three times," he said quietly.

"What did you do there?"

"Caerwin, I wish you wouldn't ask me. I want you to enjoy this night."

"I won't enjoy anything until I know about you and Vedius. I deserve to know."

"These are not things women should know. Men have their own lives."

She stared at him in the lamp light. "I urged you to please him, did I not? Didn't I say you should do what you must to ensure your future? Your future is entwined in mine. If you lost everything, so would I. Now that your troubles have seen a favorable outcome, do you not see that I would think you followed my advice, that you gave Vedius what he desired? I only need to know the terms of it, what he expects in the future."

He scrubbed his face with his hands. "The first time, we only talked. I told him how much I had changed, that I had never loved anyone like I love you. He didn't want to hear it. He suffered in hearing it. He said I would have to prove I had changed. He believed that if we touched each other like we had in the past, I would remember my feelings for him."

"And?"

"We met the second time. We drank wine, remembered our past times. I warmed to him as he thought I would. He spoke words of love as he touched me. I tried to give the response he expected. I let him take me in his mouth."

Marcellus poured wine and drank then offered her a cup. She refused. Her mouth had gone dry but not of thirst. What would he say next?

"He was always a careful lover. His talents are enriched in his relationships with a young slave and perhaps many more. I didn't press him on that point. He made me erect. He begged me to reciprocate. I couldn't turn him down."

His careful glance assessed her reaction. Caerwin hoped not to show anger or jealousy or grief. This was an unfinished story. She would wait for its end.

If only it ended.

"You made love," she said.

"We had sex," he said. "We used our mouths and our hands, we kissed, we took each other in the way men do."

Breath left her body. She could hear her blood rushing through her veins as she sat numbly waiting.

"I agreed to meet him again. That was the third time. We met in the same place. He greeted me warmly then sat holding my hands while he told me it would be wrong for us to meet again. He said we had both changed, that time changed us, our lives changed us, and it would only tarnish the love we'd known before if we tried to relive it."

"I was surprised," he said. "He was right. The whole time we had pleasured each other, the passion we'd known in the past wasn't there. It felt contrived. I knew it then but didn't realize he knew it, too. I had hoped he would know. We held each other a long time, sad that we'd moved on. We grieved for our youth and its innocence, its simple pleasures."

His voice broke. "We can't go back. He knows that now. He's determined to be a good friend and has shown that he can. It was Vedius who sent clerks to dig through the records in hopes of finding some scrap of evidence of my father's innocence. He asked me to send Tatian and Antius at the last when nothing had yet been found. I might not be here today if not for the efforts of Vedius."

He reached up and used his thumb to wipe a tear that had fallen down her cheek.

"It's true we can't go back," she whispered. "I finally knew that for myself when I realized how much I loved you. I can't go back to the Wrekin. You and Vedius can't go back to those years. Thank you for telling me."

"I never wished to hurt you," he said.

"Hold me," she said.

"I am the happiest man alive."

In the warmth of his arms, as he removed her wedding dress and kissed her, something inside her loosened. This night, there was no need of the foreplay that had marked their previous lovemaking. With their bodies relieved of clothing, he took her to his bed. He touched her gently, reverently, as he brought himself over her. When he joined their bodies, she saw a vision of two figures set against a dark sky. They moved toward each other and became one.

~~~

Kensa sat across from them, basking in the morning sun that poured down through the *compluvium* above the back pool. Caerwin made her third trip to the kitchen for more bread and soft cheese, nabbing a fresh pear on her way. Marcellus' eyebrows rose when he saw her plate.

"Still hungry?" he said. "Did our marriage celebration wear on you so greatly?"

She grinned. Ever since she woke, she had tried to imagine how she would manage this moment. She had devised first one speech then another. None of it stayed in her mind.

"I need to eat more," she said. "But it's not the celebration that causes my appetite."

"Then what," he said, reaching over to grasp her hand. "Do you think that our first night has already given you a child?"

"No," she said, wagging her head side to side. "Not last night. But our first night here. Do you remember that night?"

His forehead furrowed. "You speak riddles. Our first night here? I took you to bed, I remember that. We had been traveling for so long. We only wanted rest."

"But we didn't rest, did we? Not at first."

His frown deepened. "What are you saying?"

"We made love. You planted your seed in me." She couldn't keep the smile off her face. "It grew."

"What? What do you mean? That was...November?"

She nodded. "November. I didn't know, of course. I didn't know until Saturnalia, when Fimbria put the pieces together. I was always tired, sleepy. I was sick in the morning. These are signs women know."

"You're with child," Kensa said.

"I'm with child," Caerwin said.

"Since November?" Marcellus stood up. He loomed over her as his voice rose to a higher pitch. "Since November?"

"An August child, July if it's early," Caerwin said, smiling as Antius joined them.

"Wait. This can't be. I didn't touch you," Marcellus said, pacing now alongside the long pool and garden.

"You did touch me that first night," Caerwin said. "Just as you said, it only took once. The seed knew its path."

Antius stared at her then Marcellus before a smile spread over his face. He laughed and slapped Marcellus on the shoulder.

Marcellus tugged his hair, stopping to stare at her. "Is this a joke?"

She shook her head. "I couldn't tell you until you had accomplished all the things you needed to accomplish. To make it safe to have a child. I'm a citizen. I'm your wife."

"Oh, the gods. Jupiter, Mars, Minerva and Juno, have mercy on me," he said.

"I thought you'd be happy," Caerwin said. All her hearty breakfast gathered at the base of her throat. "Are you displeased?"

"What kind of future can our child expect with the Antistius linage? I'm terrified," he said.

She saw that he was. He sat beside her with a face as white as his tunic. His dark eyes bulged as if he had seen a ghost.

"Marcellus, my boy," Kensa said. She scooted over to him and reached for his hand. "Each child has its own future no matter its ancestry. I remember when Rhian found she was with child again. You were the child she carried. We had worried together the previous times, knowing the nature of Labeo. I knew him better than anyone. He had raped me when I was thirteen. His seed gave me Rhian, the most beautiful child I ever knew. She made me happy from the first day I felt her quicken in my belly.

Caerwin watched her smile fade. "He raped me many times. I was a receptacle for his anger, his greed, his lust. I wasn't the only one. I hated him and made sure not to carry another child for him to abuse. I feared what he would do to the child Rhian carried, but I never expected him to send her away. What he did…"

Her voice broke and Caerwin's heart overflowed with sadness for the old woman. She glanced up at Antius as she put her arm around Kensa and pulled her close.

"That's all in the past. Here you have a new start," Kensa said, wiping tears from her cheeks. "I'm still young enough to look forward to your child. I was only fourteen years when Rhian was born and nearing thirty when you came into our lives." Her face tilted toward Marcellus. "Now another thirty-five years have passed. Perhaps the gods will grant me a few more years to live in peace with my great grandchild."

"But I'm doubly Labeo," Marcellus said. "What curse of this lineage will haunt the child?"

"Marcellus! I thought you wanted a child," Caerwin said. Her pulse echoed in her ears. "I thought you would be happy. It's too late. I can't end it in my womb. I wouldn't even if you wished it. I already love it."

"No," Antius said sharply. "I'll make sacrifices. The gods will care for you. A child, Marcellus. Think of it!"

Caerwin looked at Antius, surprised to see the emotion in his face. This would be like a child of his own, she realized.

"It's all a shock," Marcellus said. "I didn't know how much I feared the inheritance of Labeo."

"Always remember my ancestors are also yours," Kensa said. "On his third invasion of Britannia, your own great emperor Julius Caesar befriended my father Mandubracius, son of Imanuentius, king of the Trinovantes tribe of Britannia. They were a powerful tribe holding lands along the eastern shores of that place, centered around the great river Tamesis. I wish I could have seen that world. These ancestors struck their own coins and traded with the Romans as free people.

"My father was an old man when I was born. I only knew him a few years but I remember clearly how strong he was even in his advanced years. His eyes brightened when he talked of his native lands. He and Caesar became friends. When Imanuentius died in battle with a neighboring tribe, Mandubracius fled to Gaul under Caesar's protection. Later the great Caesar helped conquer the warring tribe and put my father on the throne."

Kensa sighed and renewed her grip on Marcellus' hand. "The peace did not last. When he saw the way of things or perhaps because he had learned to enjoy Roman ways, **Mandubracius** left Britain with Julius Caesar and never returned. Caesar went on to fight Pompey and left my father at a villa in the hills. He had children by several concubines, women who would have been his wives in his own land. I never knew my sisters or brothers, but I know there were many. Once he died, my mother became a slave in the household of a high ranking Roman who had been close friends with the emperor. By then the emperor had been assassinated."

"Your mother," Caerwin said. "Was she Roman?"

"No," Kensa said. "She was Trinovanti, one of several who traveled with him through Gaul. I am Trinovanti," she added proudly, pointing to Marcellus. "You are Trinovanti."

"No wonder you fit me so well," Caerwin said, smiling up at him. "Marcellus, don't you see? We are both of Britannia. You're the grandson of a king."

Color had returned to Marcellus' face. "What you tell me—is it known to be true?" he asked Kensa. "You say you were but a child with this man who claimed to be your father. How old were you when he died?"

"I was ten," Kensa said. "He wasn't the only one who told me of my ancestry. I remember him clearly. He was my father. I saw him in your features the day you were born."

"I'm—beyond words," he said.

"There is much more I can tell you as our days go by," Kensa said. "I want you to know it all, the stories he told of their hunting and weapons, their joy in feasting and drink, the long traditions celebrated in song. These are your stories. You will tell them to your children."

"Thank you for this," Caerwin said. She had wept and dried her tears more times than she could count as Kensa told her story. "This is the peace he needed."

Marcellus turned to her. "My bride, my beautiful queen—I would have nothing without you. Surely the gods spoke to me the first day I saw you."

His big hand reached to her belly. "This is my new life," he said, gently pressing. "Can he hear me?"

"Or she," Caerwin laughed. "Probably. I don't know if he hears you, but perhaps he does."

"Or she," Marcellus said.

"The child will quicken soon," Kensa said. "You'll feel a flutter in your belly. It will be the child moving about."

"Oh, the gods." Marcellus stood up to renew his pacing. "Do we harm it when we…"

"No," Kensa said, laughing. "Enjoy your wife. The child will take enough of your time once it's born."

~~~

Caerwin stood looking across the vista below. Fertile countryside bloomed green as far as she could see. Behind her, dinner in the Monte Rosa villa awaited her as the long day drifted toward evening. The villa surpassed her wildest expectations. Built in the same plan as all Roman houses, this place had ripened with age. Red-orange roof tiles, gray stone walls with climbing vines, even the worn mosaic floors spoke of generations. Separate structures housed the caretaker and still other workers and their families, those buildings too softened by time.

The aging caretaker and his wife treated her warmly. Marcellus praised them for their diligence in caring for the place. A contented band of workers tended the vineyards and crops. Sheep grazed the hillsides, pigs foraged in the adjacent woods. She inhaled the clean air. High above a bird of prey circled.

She knew without looking it was an eagle.

She carried the small pot of earth in her hands. In the few weeks since their arrival, she had come to know this as her home. Unlike the *domus* in Rome, this place had much in common with her homeland—not only its fields and nearby forest, but the buzz of bees and birdsong, the affectionate dogs that followed her everywhere, even the smell of the air.

This would be her home and the home of her children.

She knelt and removed the lid on the pot. The dark brown earth of her homeland waited. Here was the spirit of her mother, of

Senna, of Virico and Seisyll. They had come with her here, to this place she would live for the rest of her days. Her children would not be Cornovii. They would be Cornovii and Trinovanti and Roman. These were the ways of the world.

She heard footsteps, knew without looking that Marcellus stood nearby. She turned the pot over and shook until the last crumb of dirt fell to the ground. She spread it with her hand, settling it through the grass.

"What is that?" Marcellus said.

"Dirt from the Wrekin." She stood up and brushed her hands together. "I no longer carry my home in a jar."

He pulled her back against him and nestled her belly in his hands. His chest rose and fell. His heart beat against her ribs.

"You're my home," he said gruffly, nuzzling his face in her neck. "Come, my queen, dinner waits."

Author's Notes

Dear Reader,

We come to the end of our story of Caerwin and Marcellus. They'll live on in our hearts, making their way through the glorious years of Rome at its peak. I've lived with these people for over two years, hearing their fears and dreams, watching them struggle and learn. I'll miss them.

Can we leave them at that? No. Let me share my thoughts of their futures. Ever ambitious among the city's jurists, Tatian remains at the Antistius *domus* house along with Rufus and Varinia. It's a place Marcellus and Caerwin will stay on their infrequent visits to the city. Grandmother Kensa along with Marcellus' aging companion Antius as well as Fimbria, Gordianus, and even Fimus live at the Monte Rosa villa with the caretaker and other slaves and freedmen who have long called the sprawling farm their home. There'll be joyful harvest celebrations and cozy winter feasts with neighbors from nearby villas. Vedius and Bettia might even journey south for a visit, or Clivia and Niger and their children who are, after all, Marcellus' nieces and nephews.

Never one to ignore a challenge, Caerwin insists on learning more about the shipping industry. She and Marcellus make regular visits to the docks at Neapolis where they join Sigilis in the daily work of operating a huge shipping enterprise. Caerwin even learns to love sailing and takes a strong hand in the company's operation. Do she and Marcellus exchange heated words about all this? Of course. Might they steal a few moments for covert sex in a cargo hold among amphorae of wine or olives? What do you think?

I picture the happy couple with at least three children who grow up well loved, as rowdy as their mom and tender hearted as their dad.

The first two children are born before Kensa succumbs to old age, bringing great joy to their great grandmother. At least one son carries forth the intensity and stature of his father and fulfills his duties to the Empire by joining Legio XIV Gemina, the same legion Marcellus led. Stationed in an area of Gaul now known as Provence, the son serves proudly in equestrian rank like his father for a period of six years, fortunately not a time the legion saw battle. At least one daughter enjoys her mother's beauty and brains and marries well to settle in nearby Naples. All their children produce housefuls of their own children, enriching Caerwin and Marcellus' later years with a flock of grandchildren.

I've made every effort to create a story as historically accurate as possible. While all characters (except the emperor and certain others) are fictional, the social patterns, beliefs, clothing, food, settings, customs, and laws are as the Romans experienced them. Although a rich historical record of these times survives, there are gaps which affected some parts of this story. In those cases, I extrapolated probable scenarios from what history tells us. For example, I found nothing that described the groom's attire at a wedding and went with the toga because, well, I like seeing Marcellus in a toga.

The reign of Claudius Caesar was one of the most progressive and enlightened periods of the Julio-Claudio era. From the time our story ends in early summer of the year 49, Claudius will rule only another five years before his fourth wife Agrippina murders him with poisonous mushrooms, driven by her ambition to put her son Nero on the throne. This infamous last emperor of the dynasty would oversee the disastrous fire of 64 that destroyed a large part of Rome, allegedly 'fiddling' while the city burned. Flimsy insula jammed side by side fueled the fire, which burned five days.

In 79, when Caerwin celebrates her 49th birthday and Marcellus becomes 64, Mount Vesuvius erupts and destroys Pompeii, Herculaneum, and many other towns lying south of the conflagration. Fortunately for our aging couple and their beloved home, Monte Rosa lies north of Neapolis and avoids the fallout of ash and poisonous gases that kills thousands and buries entire cities.

Is this the end of this story? Yes. Might there be offshoots, maybe short stories or novellas that delve into the secret lives of Tatian, Sigilis, or other minor characters? Might we at some point watch Vedius and Marcellus struggle with their attraction? I simply don't know. Obviously, there are still vignettes rolling around in my head.

As for greater Rome, I have to say that I've been repeatedly amazed with the details of Roman civilization. I had studied all this in college, read more over the years, but until I dug up details of daily life for the Caerwin novels, I really hadn't appreciated the many ways in which Rome set the pattern for everything that would come after. After two thousand years, our laws, our religion, even our weddings still follow Rome's model. From the perhaps mythical beginnings of Romulus and Remus establishing Rome on the Palatine hill in 753 BC to the sack of Rome by invading Goths in 410 AD, over a thousand years passed.

Please note that many of the features we associate with Rome in modern times had not yet been built at the time of our story. The Colosseum was begun under Emperor Vespasian in 72. Also still standing are Emperor Trajan's Column built in 113. The Forum remained in its original location under the shadow of the Temple of Jupiter, but a few later emperors erected their own forums and monuments in that area. Even built of stone, Rome's temples, basilicas and other important buildings decayed or burned and successive building projects renewed them. The ruins of Rome today reveal a conglomeration of these generations.

As for the Celtic tribes of Britain, the Cornovii, Ordivices, and Trinovantes were real. Kensa may be fictional but the Trinovantes were led by the man named as Kensa's father, Mandubracius. His relationship with Julius Caesar is attested in Caesar's *De Bello Gallico*. (See https://en.wikipedia.org/wiki/Trinovantes.)

A Glossary of Foreign Terms
Terms explained in context are not included here.

Advocati	Men knowledgeable of the laws summoned to one's side in legal cases
A Grá, thab...	Gaellic. "My love, I give my heart to you. Eternal promise."
Alea iacta est	Literally, "The die is cast." A statement attributed to Julius Caesar on January 10, 49 BC as he led his army across the Rubicon River in Northern Italy. With this step, he entered Italy at the head of his army in defiance of the Senate and began his long civil war against Pompey and the Optimates. This act triggered the end of the Roman Republic and its rule by elected senators and the beginning of the Empire and its rule by emperors.
Ande-Dubnow	Celtic afterlife, world of delights and eternal youth where disease was absent and food was ever-abundant (See https://en.wikipedia.org/wiki/Annwn
As	Lowest value Roman coin. Struck of bronze or copper, during the first century AD an 'as' could buy a pound of bread or a litre of cheap wine, or, according to Pompeiian graffiti, the services of a cheap prostitute. 1 gold aureus = 25 silver denarii = 100 bronze sestertii =

	400 copper asses (See https://en.wikipedia.org/wiki/Roman_currency)
Aurascio	Modern Orange, France
Braccae	Men's trousers usually knee length
Brittunculi	An insult meaning "Little Briton"
Bulla	An amulet given to male children nine days after birth and worn around the neck as a locket to protect against evil spirits. A boy wore a *bulla* until he became a Roman citizen at the age of 16. For freeborn boys, the *bulla* served as a visible warning that the boy was sexually off-limits
Cabilonnum	Saône-et-Loire, France
Causidici	Men experienced in legal matters who spoke in legal cases
Cinaedus	Effeminate man
Collis Quirinalis	The Quirinal Hill is one of the Seven Hills of Rome at the north-east of city center.
Comfluvium	A space left unroofed over the courtyard of a dwelling in Ancient Rome through which the rain fell into the impluvium or cistern.
Cunnus	Basic Latin word for vulva
Cura Annonae	The Romans used the term *Cura Annonae* ("care for the grain supply") in

	honor of their goddess Annona. See https://en.wikipedia.org/wiki/Cura_Annonae
Denarius	A silver coin equal to four sesterii, roughly $3.50 in today's money. Average day's wage for lowest rank Roman soldier and common laborer. See '*As*'
Domus	The type of house occupied by the Roman upper classes and some wealthy freedmen during the Republican and Imperial eras. These structures often included elaborate marble decorations, inlaid marble paneling, doorjambs and columns as well as expensive paintings and frescoes. Along with a *domus* in the city, many of the richest families also owned at least one separate country house known as a villa.
Durocortorum	Modern Reims, France
Fideicommissum	One of the most popular legal institutions in Roman law for several centuries. It translates from the Latin words *fides* (trust) and *committere* (to commit), meaning that something is committed to one's trust.
Fiduciarus	One who holds a thing in trust for another; a trustee.
Fullones	A Roman cloth-launderer. Few Roman households cleaned their own laundry.

	For a description of the cleaning process, see *https://en.wikipedia.org/wiki/Fullo*
Futatrix	Latin profanity. This seen in Roman graffiti: CAESARI SERVILIA FUTATRIX, "Servilia is Caesar's bitch."
Futuo	Fuck
Garum	Fermented fish sauce
Gaul	More or less the same area as modern France
Gesoriacum	Modern Boulogne, France
Gwyn ap Nudd	Celtic, Welsh term; ruler of the Otherworld
Hydraulis	A type of pipe organ blown by air, where the power source pushing the air is derived by water from a natural source.
Insulae	Many poor and lower-middle-class Romans lived in crowded, dirty and mostly rundown rental apartments, known as *insulae*. These multi-level apartment blocks were built as high and tightly together as possible and held far less status and convenience than the private homes of the prosperous.
Lararium	Lares were ancient Roman guardian deities. Roman household shrines of any kind were known generically as *lararia* (s. *lararium*) because they typically contained a Lares figure or two. Painted lararia from Pompeii show two Lares

flanking a genius or ancestor-figure, who wears his toga in the priestly manner prescribed for sacrificers. Underneath this trio a serpent, representing the fertility of fields or the principle of generative power, winds towards an altar. The essentials of sacrifice are depicted around and about: bowl and knife, incense box, libation vessels and parts of sacrificial animals.

Lex Papia Poppaea A Roman law introduced in 9 AD to encourage and strengthen marriage; included provisions against adultery and celibacy.

Liburna A small sailing ship used for raiding and patrols. It was 109 ft (33 m) long and 5 m (16 ft) wide with a 1 m (3 ft 3 in) draft. Two rows of oarsmen pulled 18 oars per side. The ship could make up to 14 knots under sail and more than 7 under oars.

Loculus Latin word literally meaning *little place* and was used in a number of senses including to indicate a satchel. Satchels were carried by Roman soldiers as a part of their luggage.

Lupa Latin slang word for prostitute

Magiovinium Modern Fenny Stratford, England

Manduessedum Modern Mancetter, England

Medicus	Physician
Mentula	Penis
Merde	Shit
Meretrix	Registered prostitute of Ancient Rome
Mistral	A strong, cold, northwesterly wind that blows along the Rhone valley through southern France into the Gulf of Lion in the northern Mediterranean with sustained winds often exceeding forty kilometers per hour, sometimes reaching one hundred kilometers per hour. It is most common in the winter and spring, and strongest in the transition between the two seasons.
Neapolis	Modern Naples, Italy
Paeligni	An early Italic tribe from the central area now known as Abruzzo. They came into alliance with Rome in 305-302 BC.
Palla	Traditional Roman mantle worn by women, fastened by brooches. Rectangular.
Paterfamilias	The *paterfamilias* was the oldest living male in a Roman household. He had complete control of all family members including his wife and children, certain other relatives through blood or adoption, clients, freedmen and slaves. He had a duty to father and raise healthy children as future citizens of Rome, to

	maintain the moral propriety and well-being of his household, to honor his clan and ancestral gods and to dutifully participate—and if possible, serve—in Rome's political, religious and social life.
Pathicus	A male submitting to anal sex
Peregrinus	Term used during the early Roman empire from 30 BC to 212 AD, to denote a free provincial subject of the Empire who was not a Roman citizen. *Peregrini* constituted the vast majority of the Empire's inhabitants in the 1st and 2nd centuries AD. In 212 AD, all free inhabitants of the Empire were granted citizenship by the *constitutio Antoniniana*, abolishing the status of *peregrinus*.
Peristylium	The *peristylium* was an open courtyard within the house; the columns or square pillars surrounding the garden supported a shady roofed portico. The courtyard might contain flowers and shrubs, fountains, benches, sculptures and even fish ponds. Romans devoted as large a space to the peristyle as site constraints permitted.
Praetor	A title granted by the government of Ancient Rome to men acting in one of two official capacities: the commander of an army or an elected magistrate, assigned various duties which varied at different periods in Rome's history.

	Praetorium denoted the location from which the *praetor* exercised his authority, either the headquarters of his army, the courthouse of his judiciary, or the city hall of his provincial governorship.
Puer	Boy; *Puer delicatus*—an "exquisite" or "dainty" child-slave chosen by his master for his beauty as a "boy toy." The boy was sometimes castrated in an effort to preserve his youthful qualities. The emperor Nero had a *puer delicatus* named Sporus whom he castrated and married.
Salutatio	The *salutatio* took place every morning in the Roman Republic and Empire. It was considered to be one of the central aspects of the start of the day, a fundamental part of Roman interactions between citizens of varying status. It was used as a sign of respect from the patrons to the client. The *salutatio* only went one way, as the clients greeted the patron but the patron would not greet the clients back in return.
Sestertius	See 'As'
Stola	Traditional outer garment of Roman women, a long tunic often with long sleeves, belted at the waist

Stuprum	In Latin legal and moral discourse, this term describes illicit sexual intercourse, a sex crime, or criminal debauchery.
Subligaculum	Kind of undergarment worn by ancient Romans. It could come either in the form of a pair of shorts, or in the form of a simple loincloth wrapped around the lower body. It could be worn both by men and women.
Tepidarium	The tepidarium was the warm (*tepidus*) bathroom of the Roman baths heated by an underfloor heating system. The word also refers to the heated pool in the room.
Trierarchus	Ship's captain, separate from whatever military commander might be aboard
Trinovantes	One of the Celtic tribes of pre-Roman Britain. See https://en.wikipedia.org/wiki/Trinovantes
Tunica interior	First layer of clothing for both sexes, usually worn under an exterior tunic
Tunica intima	Woman's undergarment, equivalent to a slip
Verulamium	Modern St. Albans, England

Quotes

By all the heavenly gods that rule the world,
And command the human race,
What does this hubbub mean, and all these savage
Faces, turned towards me alone?   Horace, Epode V

"I curse ___, And her life and mind and memory and liver and lungs mixed up together, and her words, thoughts and memory; thus may she be unable to speak what things are concealed, nor be able to laugh."
    From an actual Roman curse tablet excavated near London. See original at http://www.britishmuseum.org/research/collection_online/collection_object_details.aspx?objectId=1362950&partId=1

"Gaia, Hermes, Gods of the Underworld, receive Junia, sister of Quartus."
    From an actual curse tablet circa 100 BC. See original at http://blogs.getty.edu/iris/an-ancient-curse-revealed/

"First was the Golden Age. Then rectitude spontaneous in the heart prevailed, and faith. Avengers were not seen, for laws unframed were all unknown and needless. Punishment and fear of penalties existed not."
    Ovid's *Metamorphoses* 1:89 Full text at http://perseus.uchicago.edu/perseus-cgi/citequery3.pl?dbname=PerseusLatinTexts&query=Ov.%20Met.%201.89&getid=1

"Oh, Fortuna, goddess who admits by her unsteady wheel her own fickleness, always holding its apex beneath her swaying foot."
    Ovid *Ex Ponto*, iv, epistle 3.

"He is fair and handsome from the top of his head to the bottom of his feet. And he will be yours for 8,000 sestertii. This home-born slave..." etc.
    Actual sales pitch by a slave seller as cited by Horace in his *Letters*, 2.2.1-19

Terms of concessions granted to ship owners are copied from the actual terms established during the reign of Claudius.
    See "The Roman Empire and the Grain Fleets: Contracting Out Public Services in Antiquity," by Michael Charles and Neal Ryan, Queensland University of Technology. https://apebhconference.files.wordpress.com/2009/09/charles_ryan1.pdf

Most holy Mother Ceres, Nuptial Juno, and the heavenly gods...
    Roman wedding vows. See http://www.ancienthistoryarchaeology.com/romanweddingsandmarriage.htm

Ye are Blood of my Blood, and Bone of my Bone.
I give ye my Body, that we Two might be One.
I give ye my Spirit, 'til our Life shall be Done...
    Celtic wedding vow. See https://www.documentsanddesigns.com/vows-and-verses/celtic-wedding-vows-and-celtic-blessings/

Printed in Great Britain
by Amazon